Dedication

Maleia. Michelle. Nils. My three beleaguered beta readers,
who were forced to read the same scene at least thirty times
before I cut it entirely, and of course my sis, who brought all my
scattered words to life. I needed all of you to make this happen.
Thank you so much for your love and support.

CAT

For Cat, beloved little sister, my constant companion on this
long and winding journey, and the colleagues, friends, and
students who encouraged me to keep moving forward.

KIT

BOOK 1:
THE BLACK BULL OF NORROWAY

Words by Cat Seaton

Pictures by Kit Seaton

IMAGE COMICS, INC. · Robert Kirkman: Chief Operating Officer · Erik Larsen: Chief Financial Officer · Todd McFarlane: President · Marc Silvestri: Chief Executive Officer · Jim Valentino: Vice President · Eric Stephenson: Publisher / Chief Creative Officer · Corey Hart: Director of Sales · Jeff Boison: Director of Publishing Planning & Book Trade Sales · Chris Ross: Director of Digital Sales · Jeff Stang: Director of Specialty Sales · Kat Salazar: Director of PR & Marketing · Drew Gill: Art Director · Heather Doornink: Production Director · Nicole Lapalme: Controller · **IMAGECOMICS.COM**

[redacted]

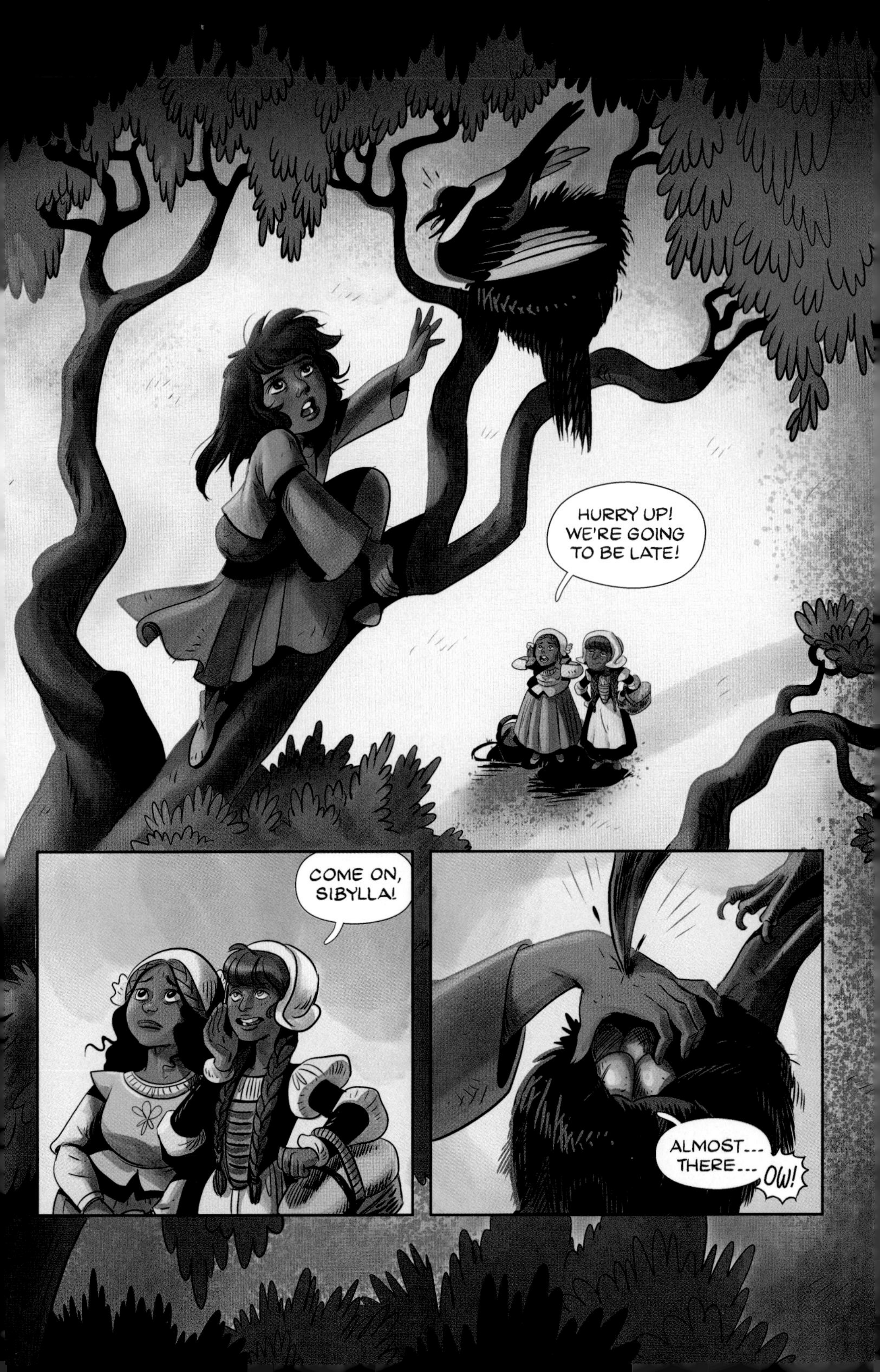
HURRY UP! WE'RE GOING TO BE LATE!
COME ON, SIBYLLA!
ALMOST... THERE...
OW!

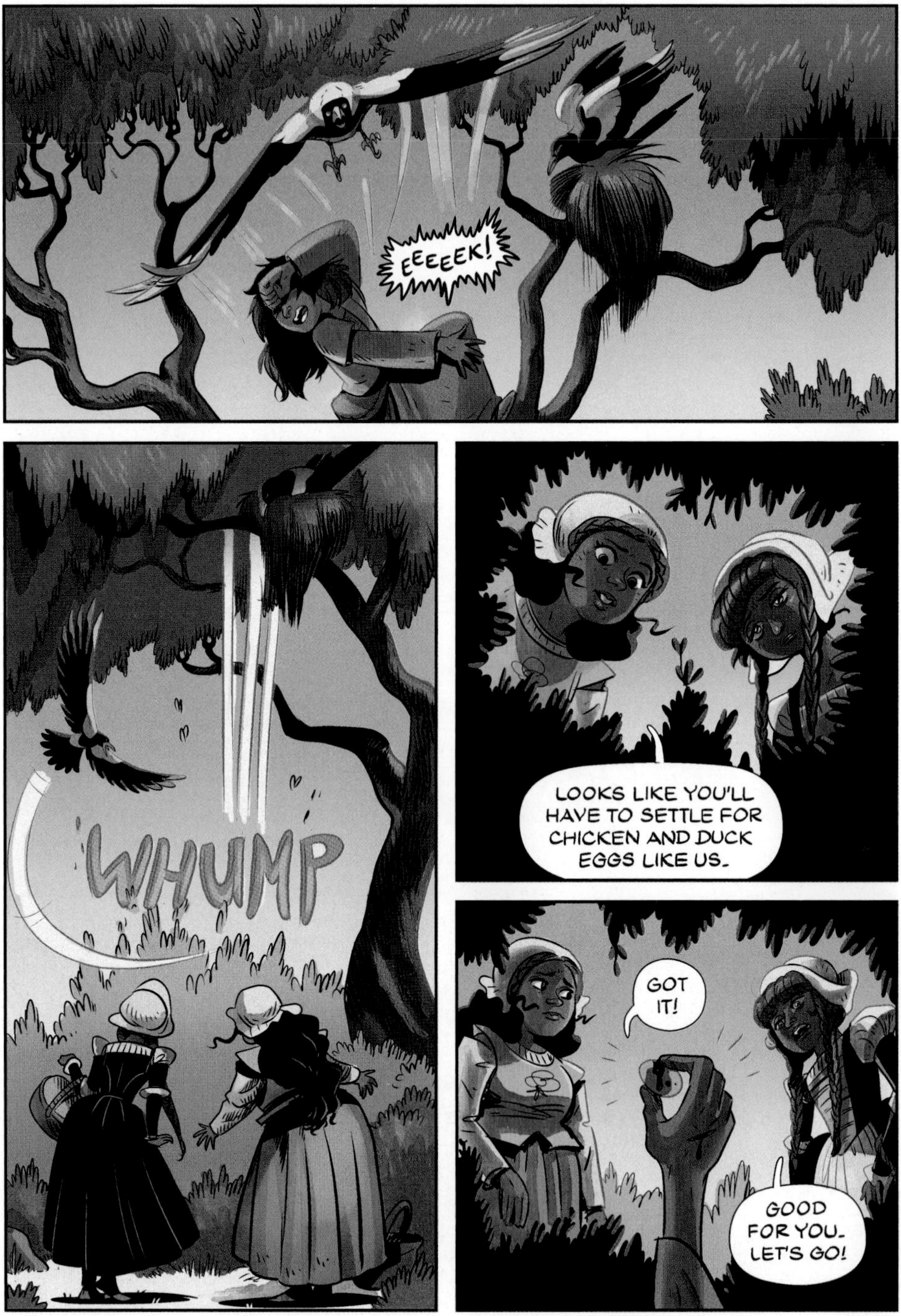
EEEEEK!
WHUMP
LOOKS LIKE YOU'LL HAVE TO SETTLE FOR CHICKEN AND DUCK EGGS LIKE US.
GOT IT!
GOOD FOR YOU. LET'S GO!

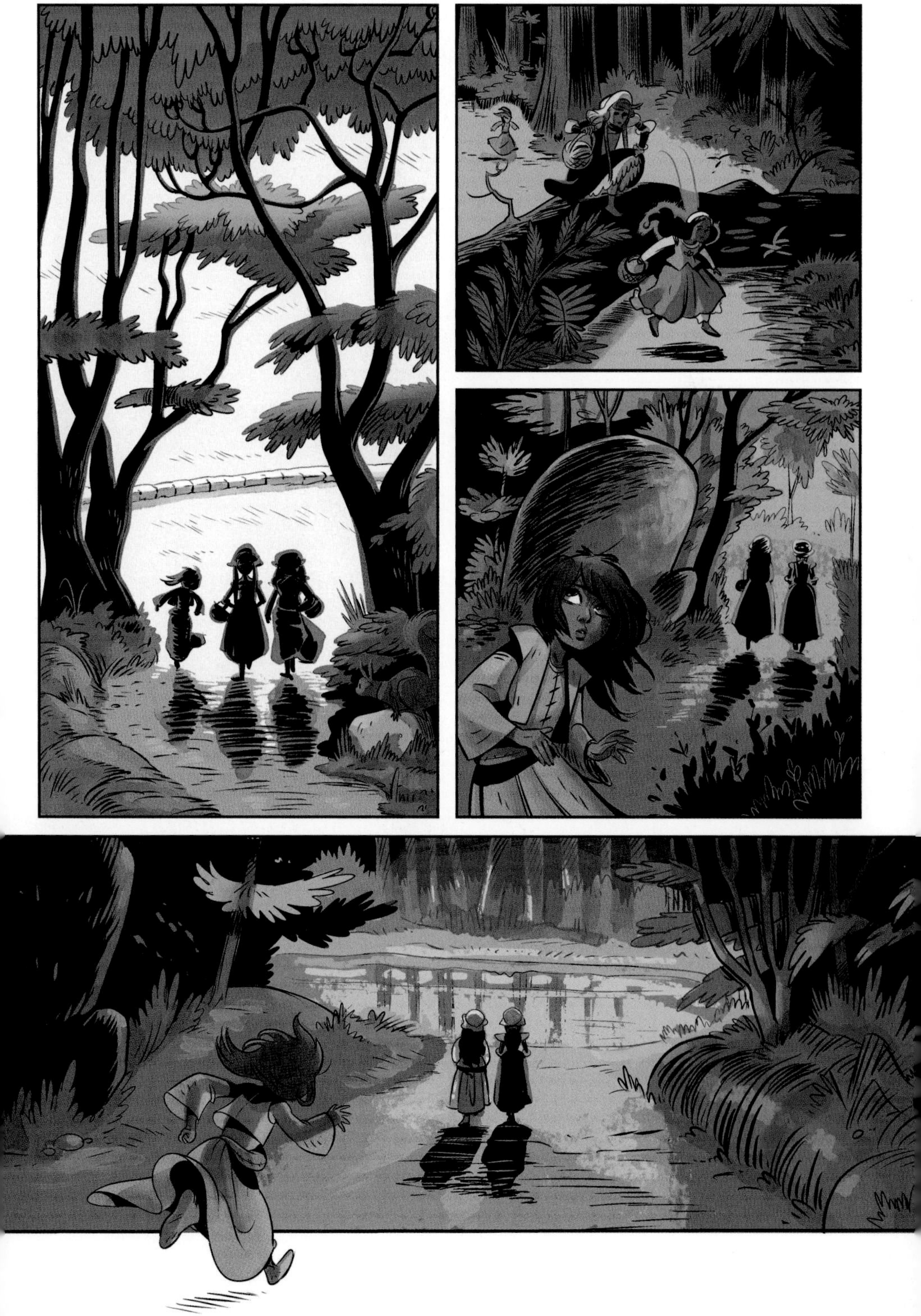

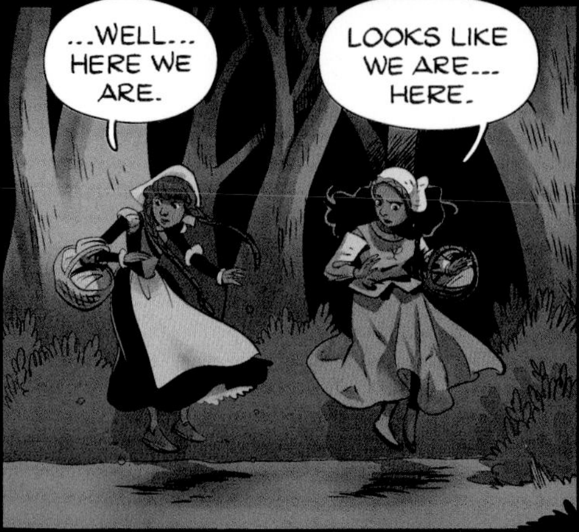
...WELL...
HERE WE
ARE.
LOOKS LIKE
WE ARE...
HERE.

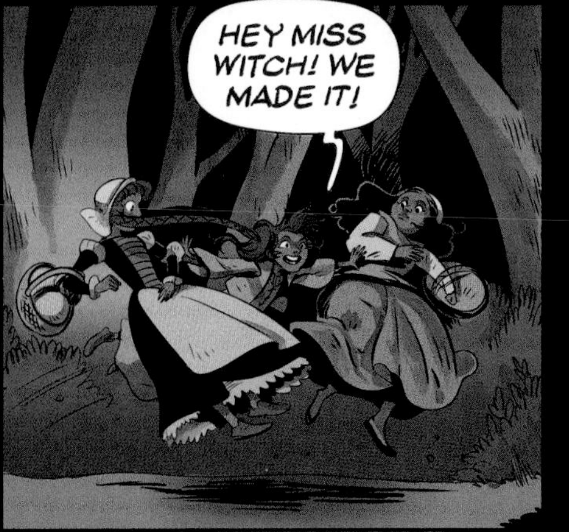
HEY MISS
WITCH! WE
MADE IT!

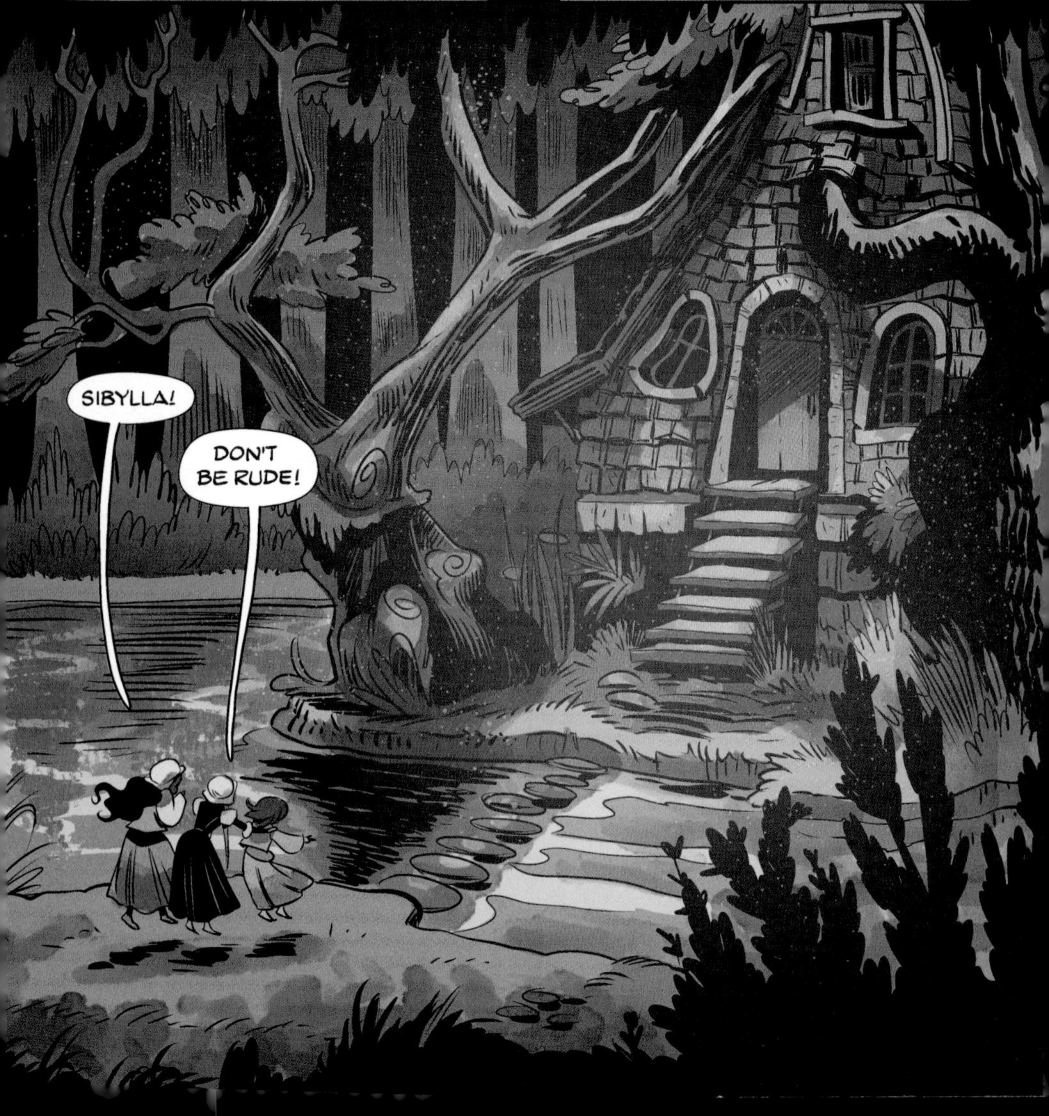
SIBYLLA!
DON'T
BE RUDE!

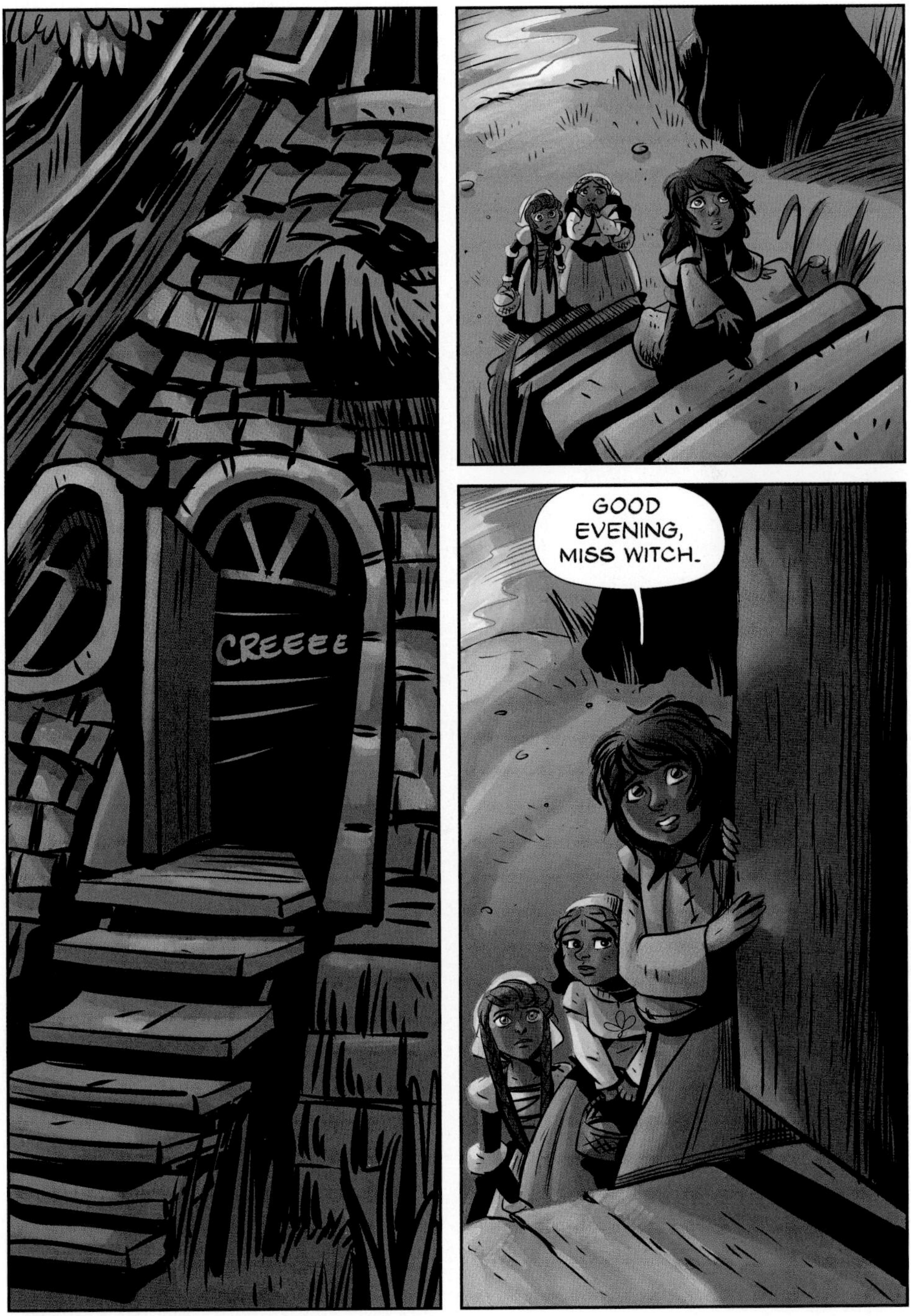
CREEEE
GOOD EVENING, MISS WITCH.

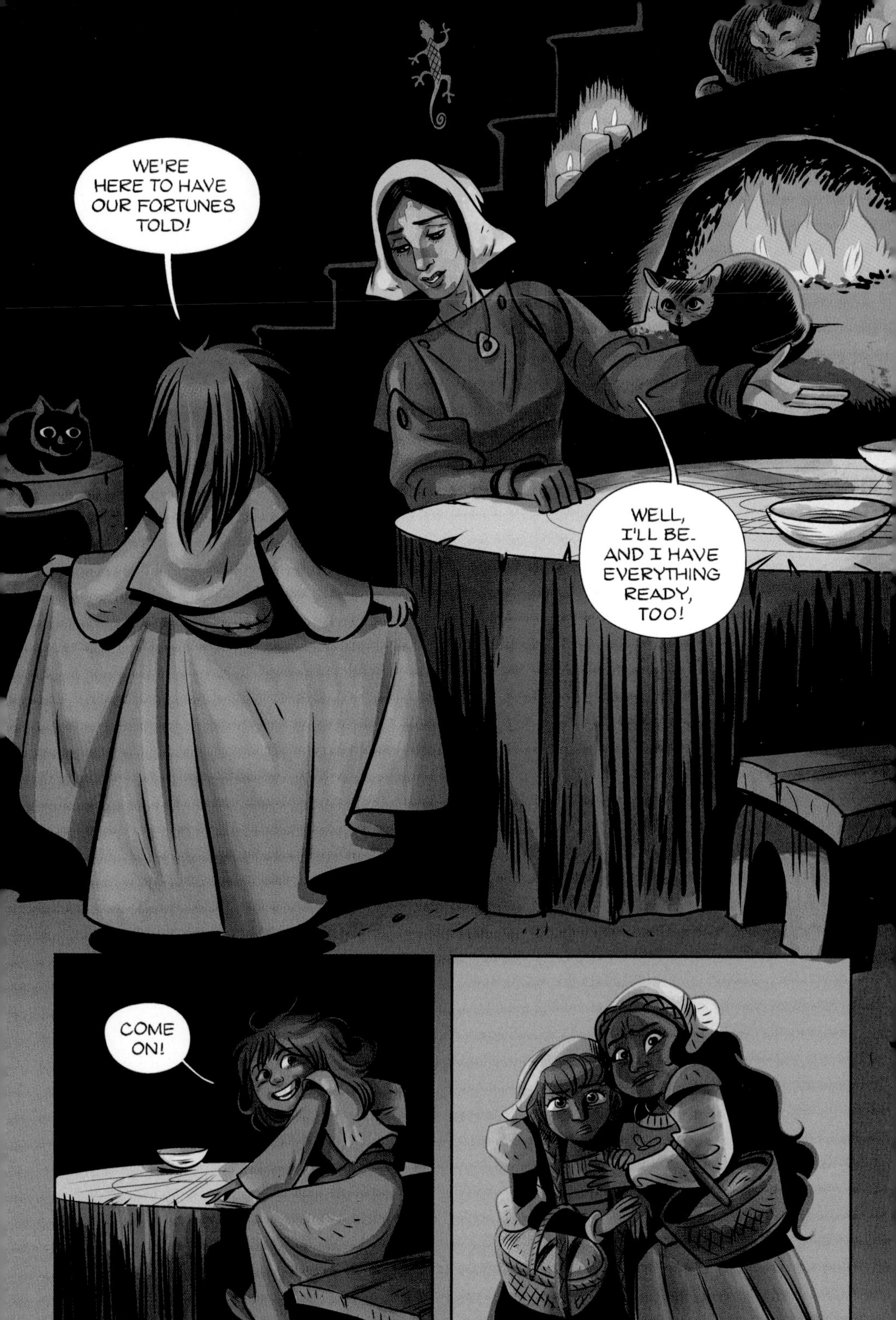
WE'RE HERE TO HAVE OUR FORTUNES TOLD!
WELL, I'LL BE. AND I HAVE EVERYTHING READY, TOO!
COME ON!

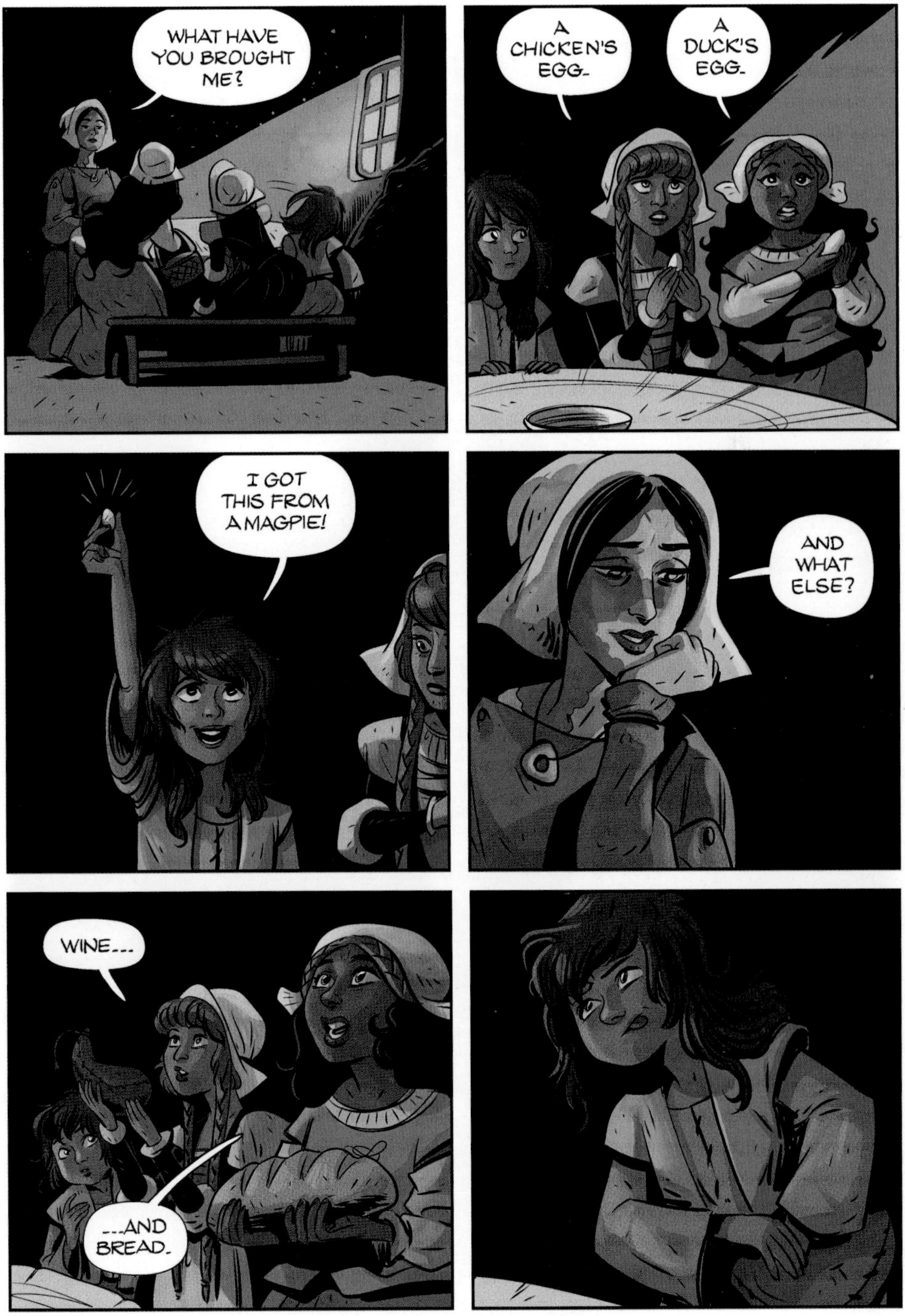
WHAT HAVE YOU BROUGHT ME?
A CHICKEN'S EGG.
A DUCK'S EGG.
I GOT THIS FROM A MAGPIE!
AND WHAT ELSE?
WINE...
...AND BREAD.

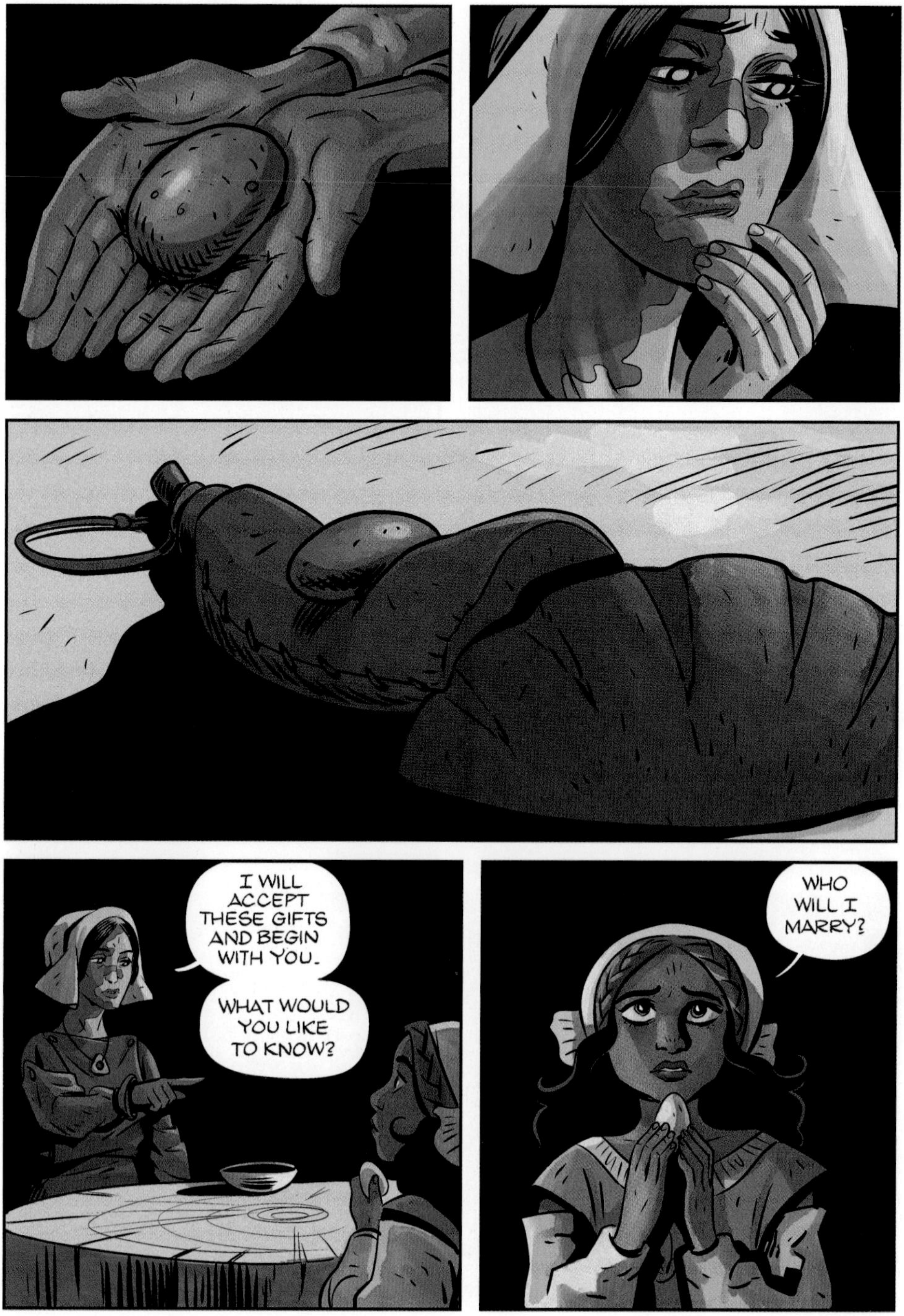
I WILL ACCEPT THESE GIFTS AND BEGIN WITH YOU.
WHAT WOULD YOU LIKE TO KNOW?
WHO WILL I MARRY?

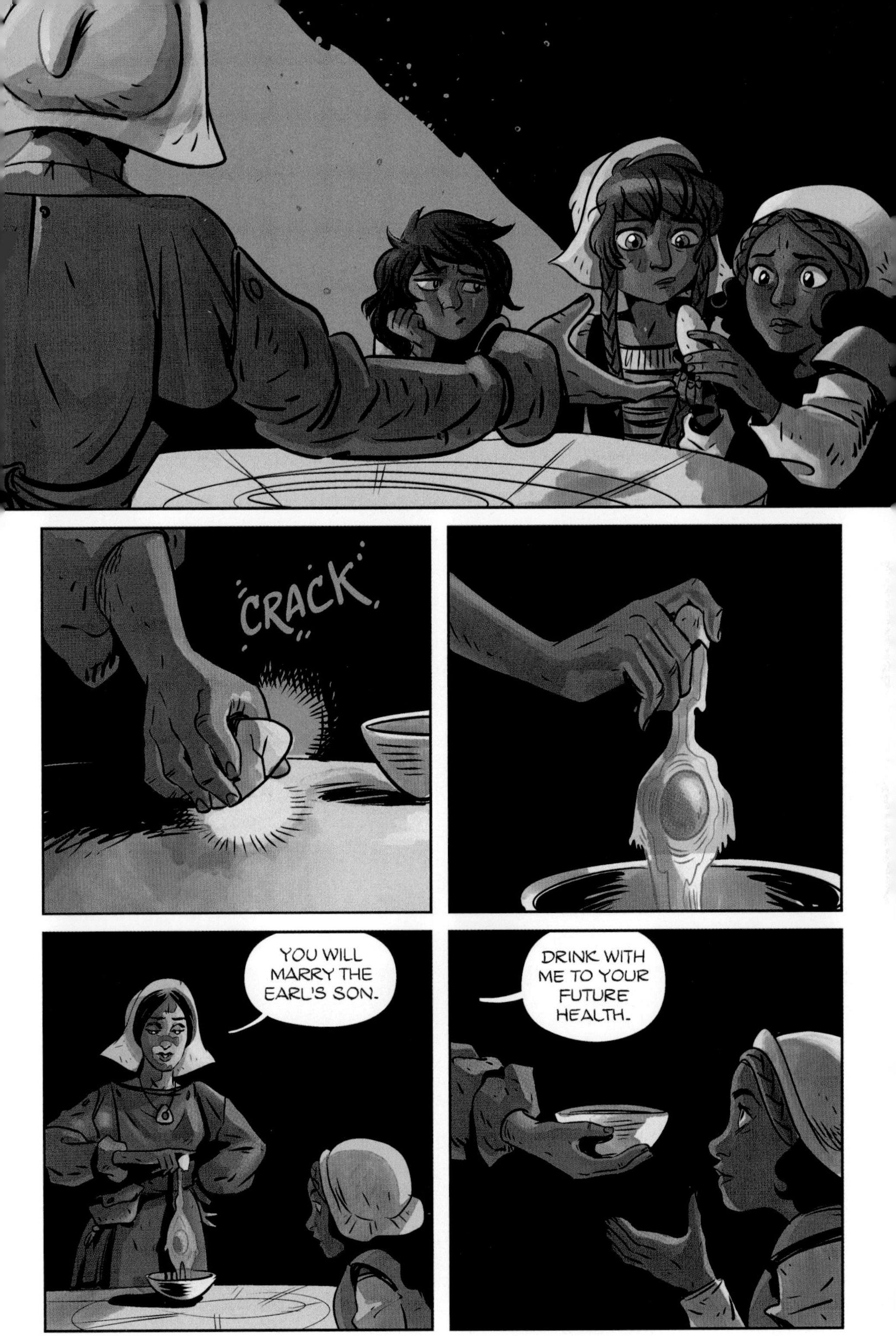
CRACK
YOU WILL MARRY THE EARL'S SON.
DRINK WITH ME TO YOUR FUTURE HEALTH.

gulp.

AND WHAT DO YOU WISH TO KNOW?

I TOO WISH TO KNOW WHO I MIGHT MARRY.

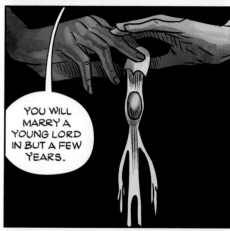

YOU WILL MARRY A YOUNG LORD IN BUT A FEW YEARS.

DRINK WITH ME TO YOUR FUTURE HEALTH.

ulp.

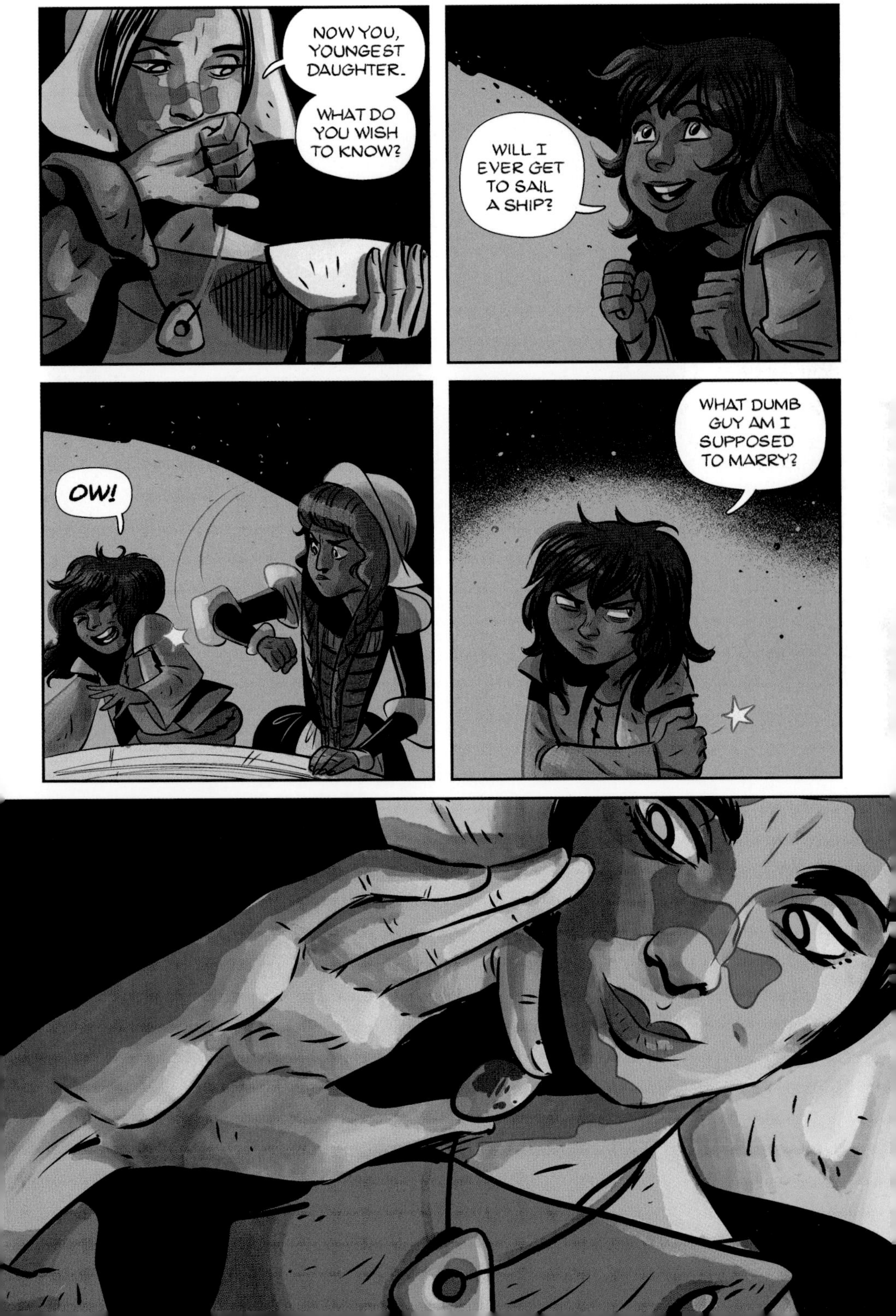
NOW YOU, YOUNGEST DAUGHTER.
WHAT DO YOU WISH TO KNOW?
WILL I EVER GET TO SAIL A SHIP?
OW!
WHAT DUMB GUY AM I SUPPOSED TO MARRY?

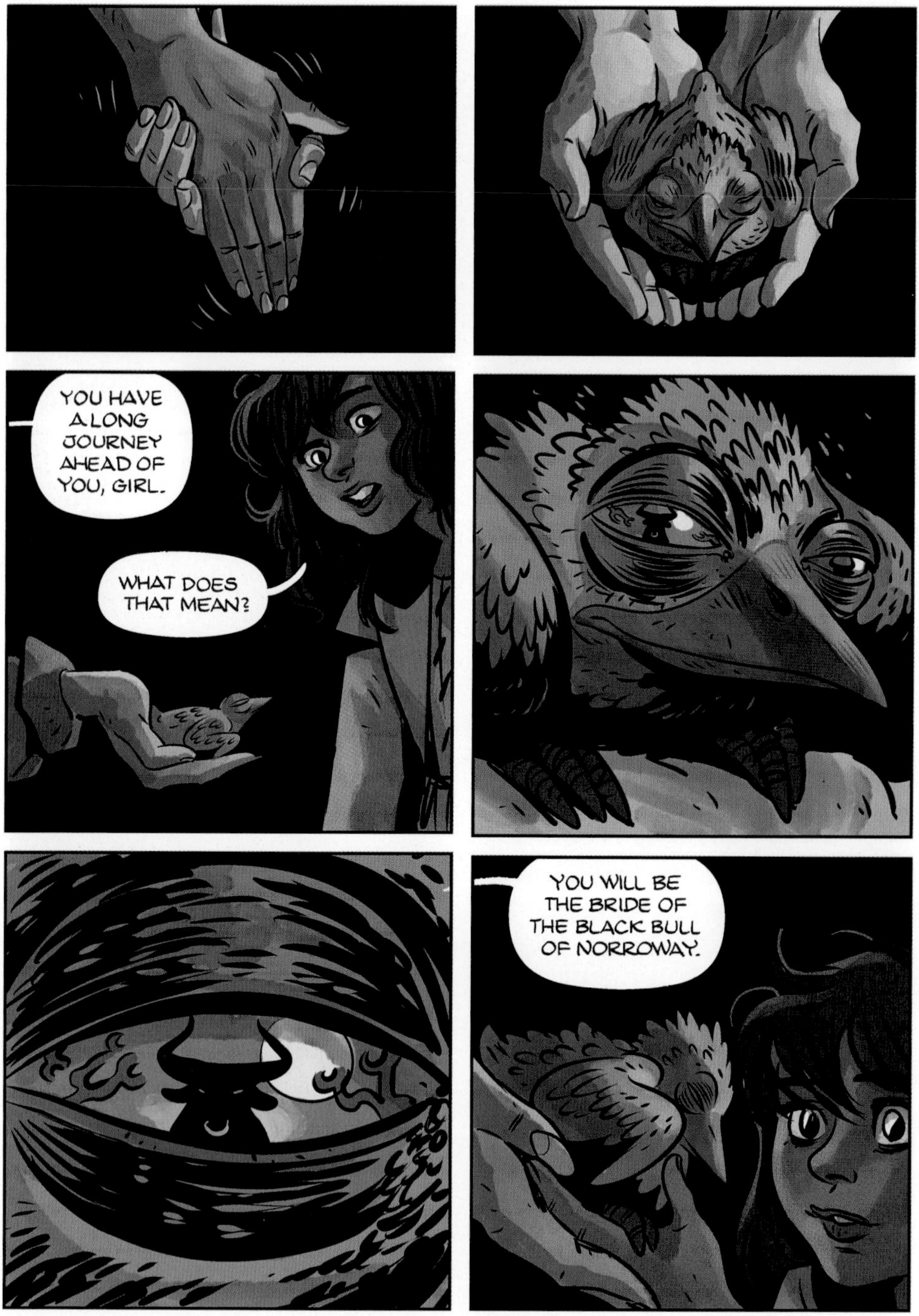
YOU HAVE A LONG JOURNEY AHEAD OF YOU, GIRL.
WHAT DOES THAT MEAN?
YOU WILL BE THE BRIDE OF THE BLACK BULL OF NORROWAY.

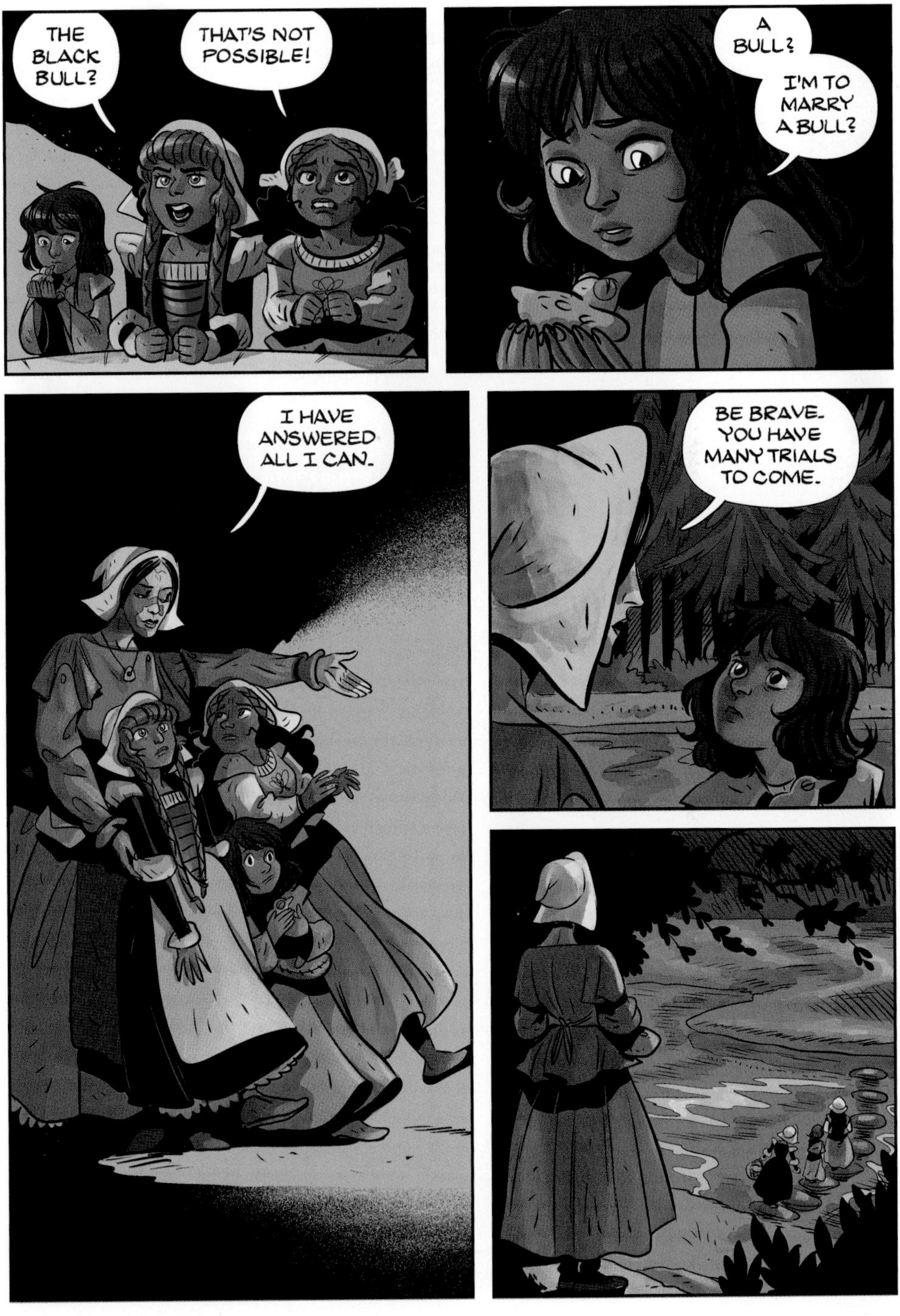
THE BLACK BULL?
THAT'S NOT POSSIBLE!
A BULL?
I'M TO MARRY A BULL?
I HAVE ANSWERED ALL I CAN.
BE BRAVE. YOU HAVE MANY TRIALS TO COME.

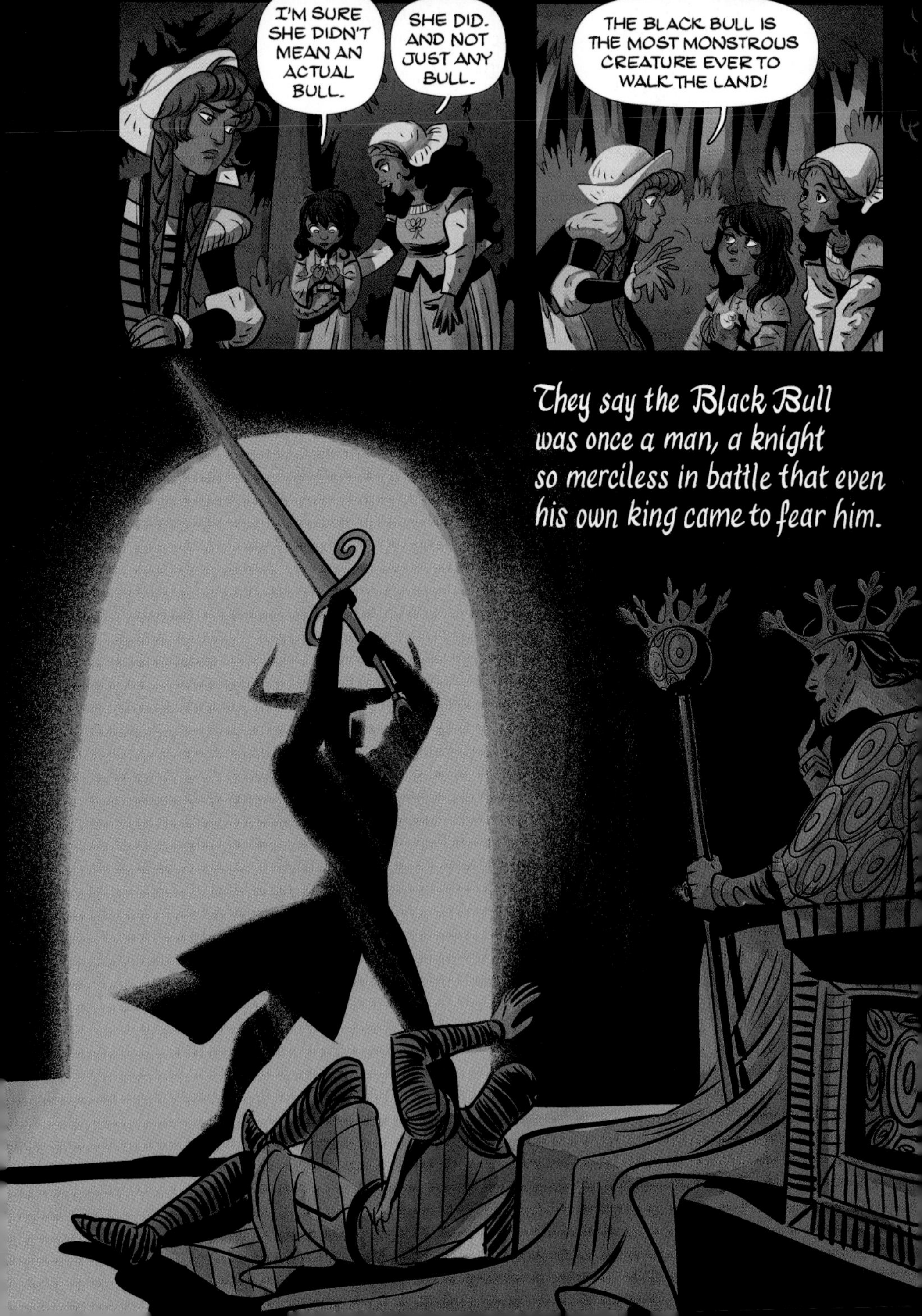
I'M SURE SHE DIDN'T MEAN AN ACTUAL BULL.
SHE DID. AND NOT JUST ANY BULL.
THE BLACK BULL IS THE MOST MONSTROUS CREATURE EVER TO WALK THE LAND!
They say the Black Bull was once a man, a knight so merciless in battle that even his own king came to fear him.

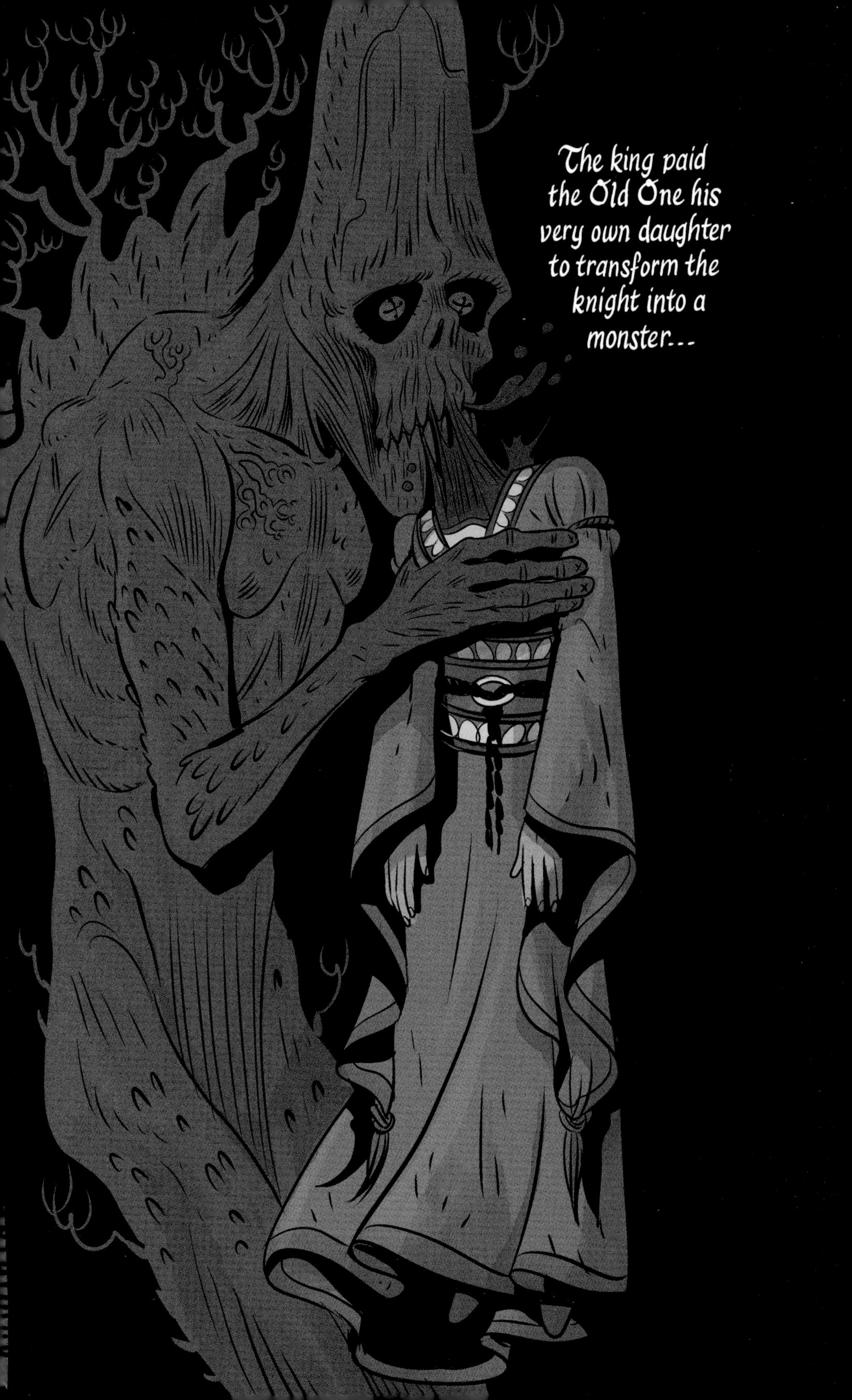
The king paid the Old One his very own daughter to transform the knight into a monster...

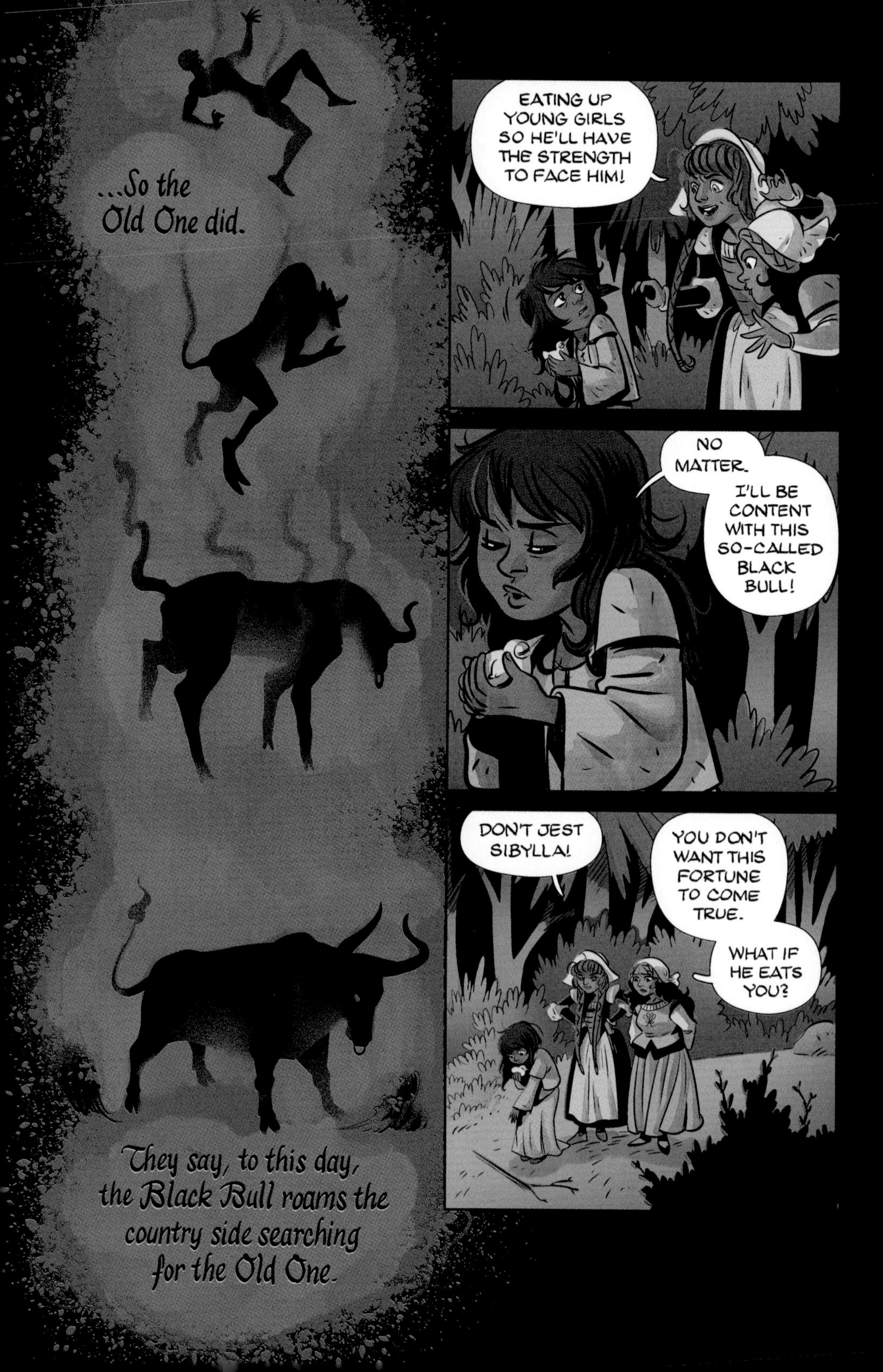
...So the Old One did.
EATING UP YOUNG GIRLS SO HE'LL HAVE THE STRENGTH TO FACE HIM!
NO MATTER.
I'LL BE CONTENT WITH THIS SO-CALLED BLACK BULL!
DON'T JEST SIBYLLA!
YOU DON'T WANT THIS FORTUNE TO COME TRUE.
WHAT IF HE EATS YOU?
They say, to this day, the Black Bull roams the country side searching for the Old One.

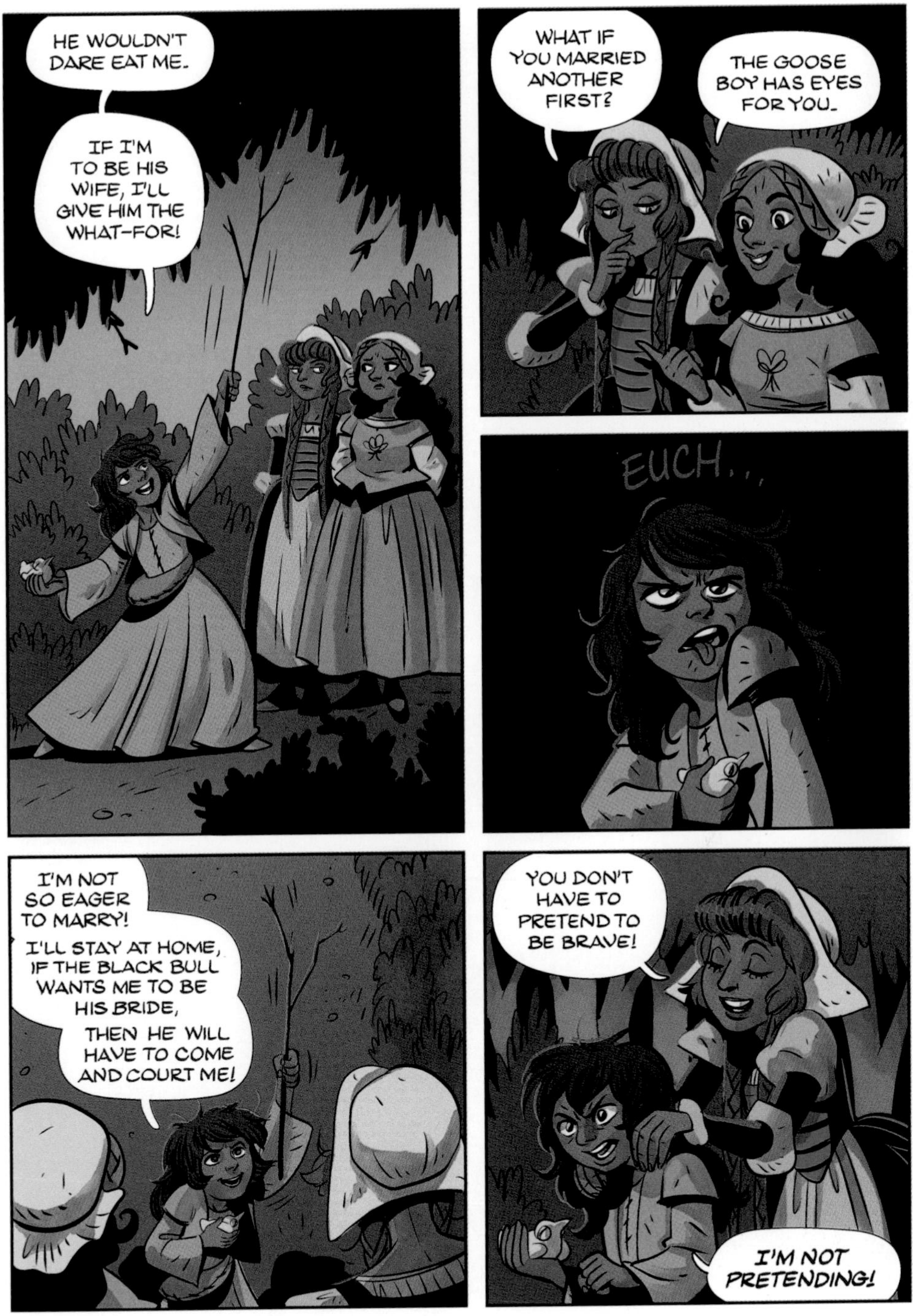
HE WOULDN'T DARE EAT ME.
IF I'M TO BE HIS WIFE, I'LL GIVE HIM THE WHAT-FOR!
WHAT IF YOU MARRIED ANOTHER FIRST?
THE GOOSE BOY HAS EYES FOR YOU.
EUCH...
I'M NOT SO EAGER TO MARRY!
I'LL STAY AT HOME, IF THE BLACK BULL WANTS ME TO BE HIS BRIDE,
THEN HE WILL HAVE TO COME AND COURT ME!
YOU DON'T HAVE TO PRETEND TO BE BRAVE!
I'M NOT PRETENDING!

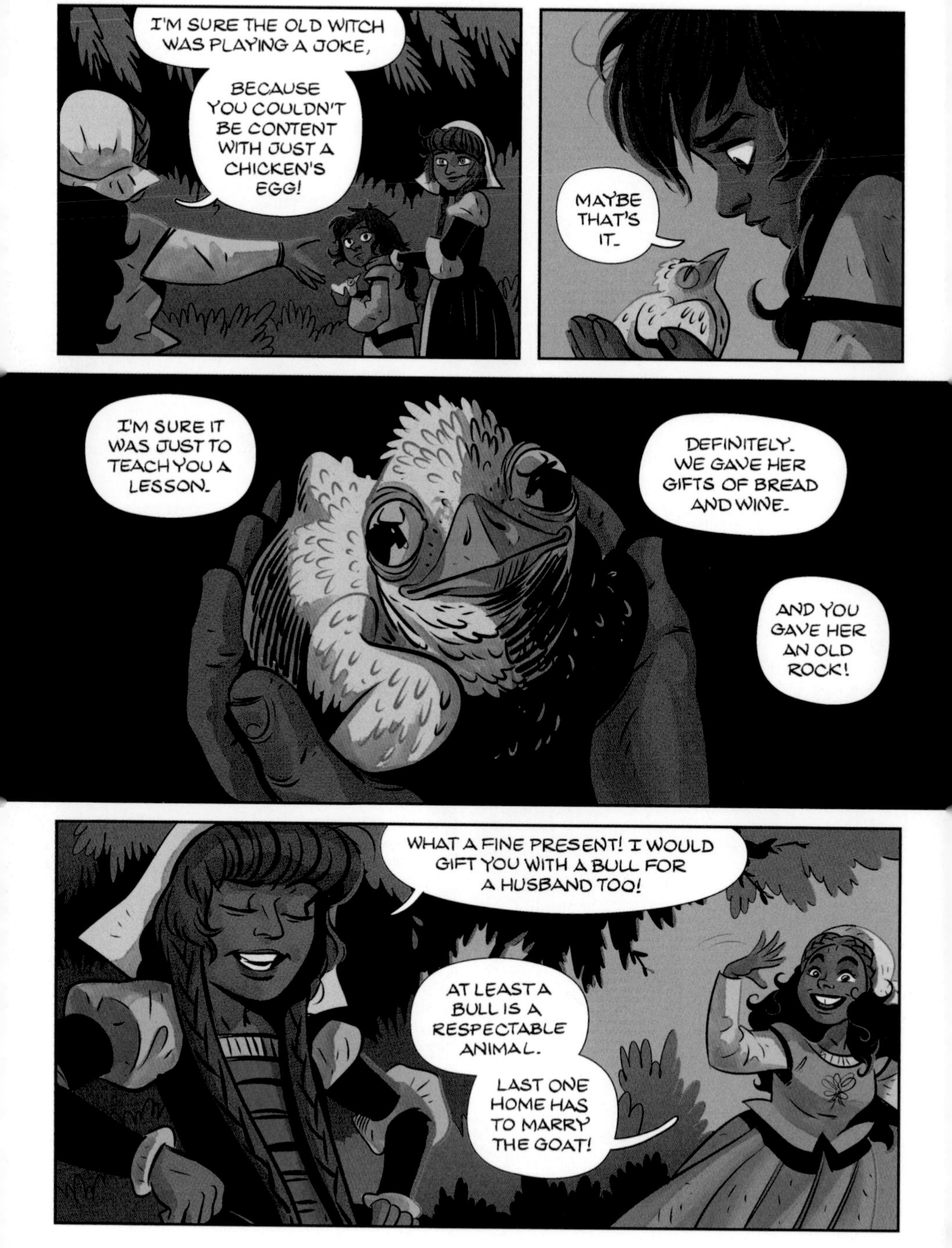
I'M SURE THE OLD WITCH WAS PLAYING A JOKE,
BECAUSE YOU COULDN'T BE CONTENT WITH JUST A CHICKEN'S EGG!
MAYBE THAT'S IT...
I'M SURE IT WAS JUST TO TEACH YOU A LESSON.
DEFINITELY. WE GAVE HER GIFTS OF BREAD AND WINE.
AND YOU GAVE HER AN OLD ROCK!
WHAT A FINE PRESENT! I WOULD GIFT YOU WITH A BULL FOR A HUSBAND TOO!
AT LEAST A BULL IS A RESPECTABLE ANIMAL.
LAST ONE HOME HAS TO MARRY THE GOAT!

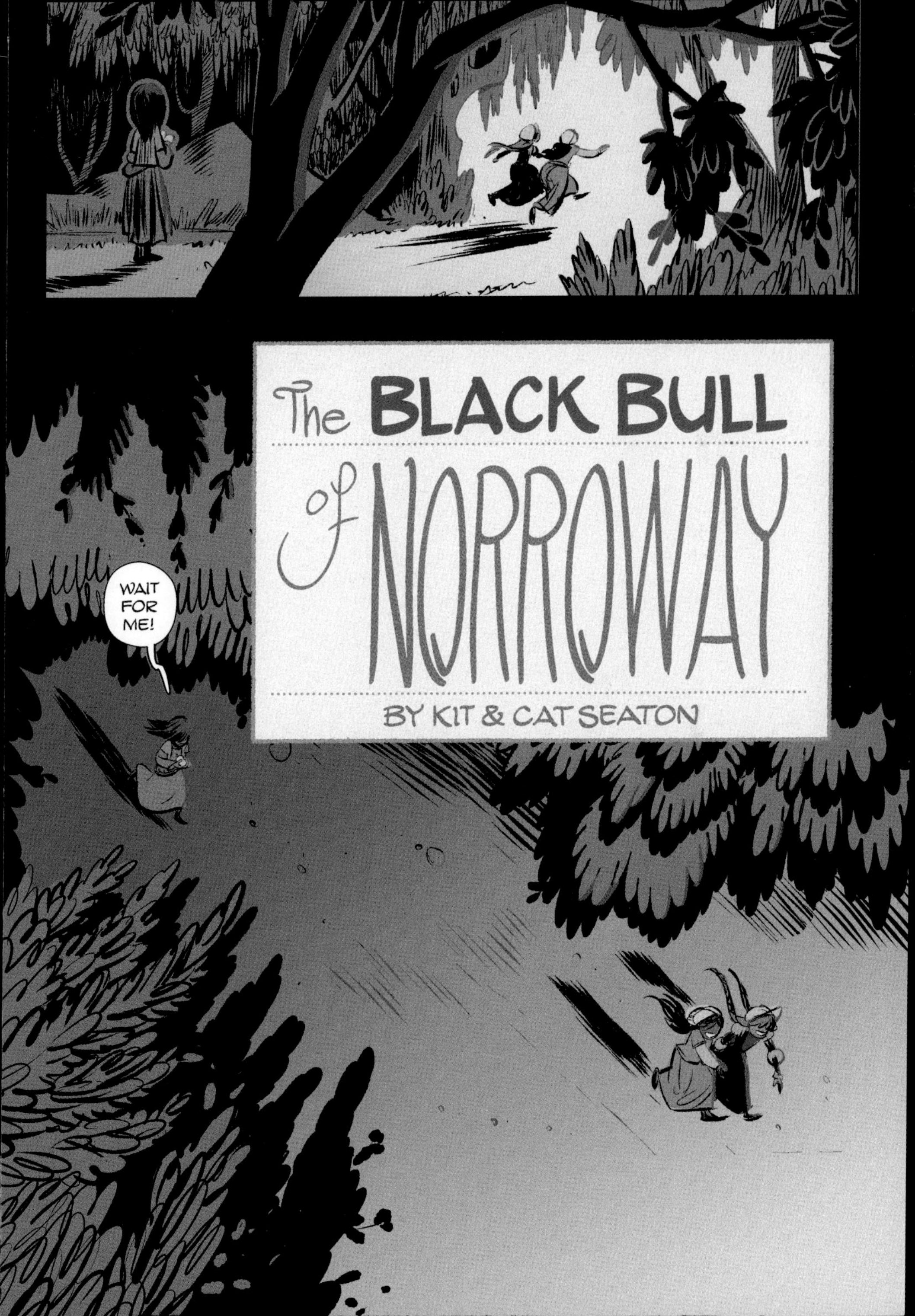
The BLACK BULL
of NORROWAY
BY KIT & CAT SEATON
WAIT FOR ME!

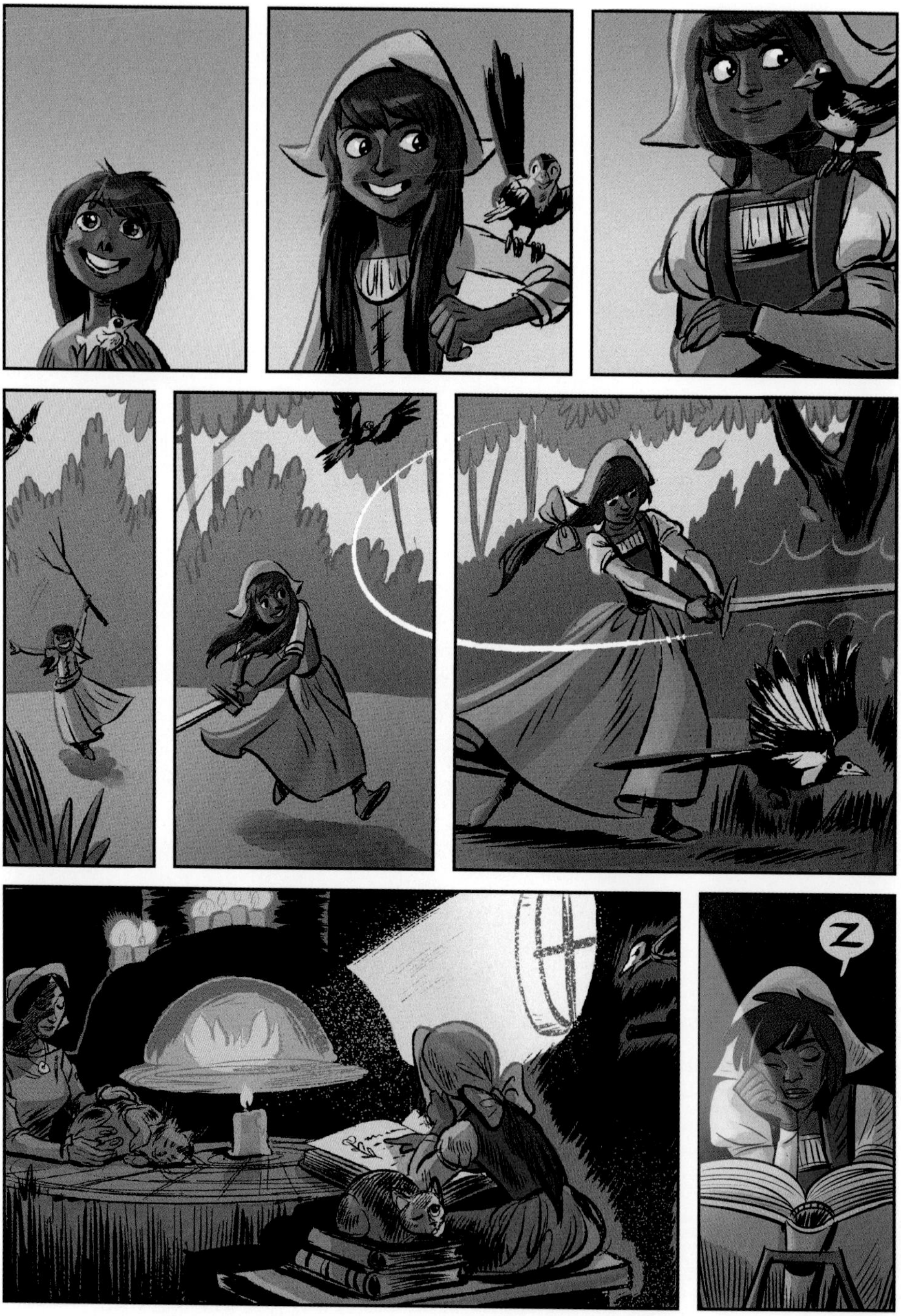
Z

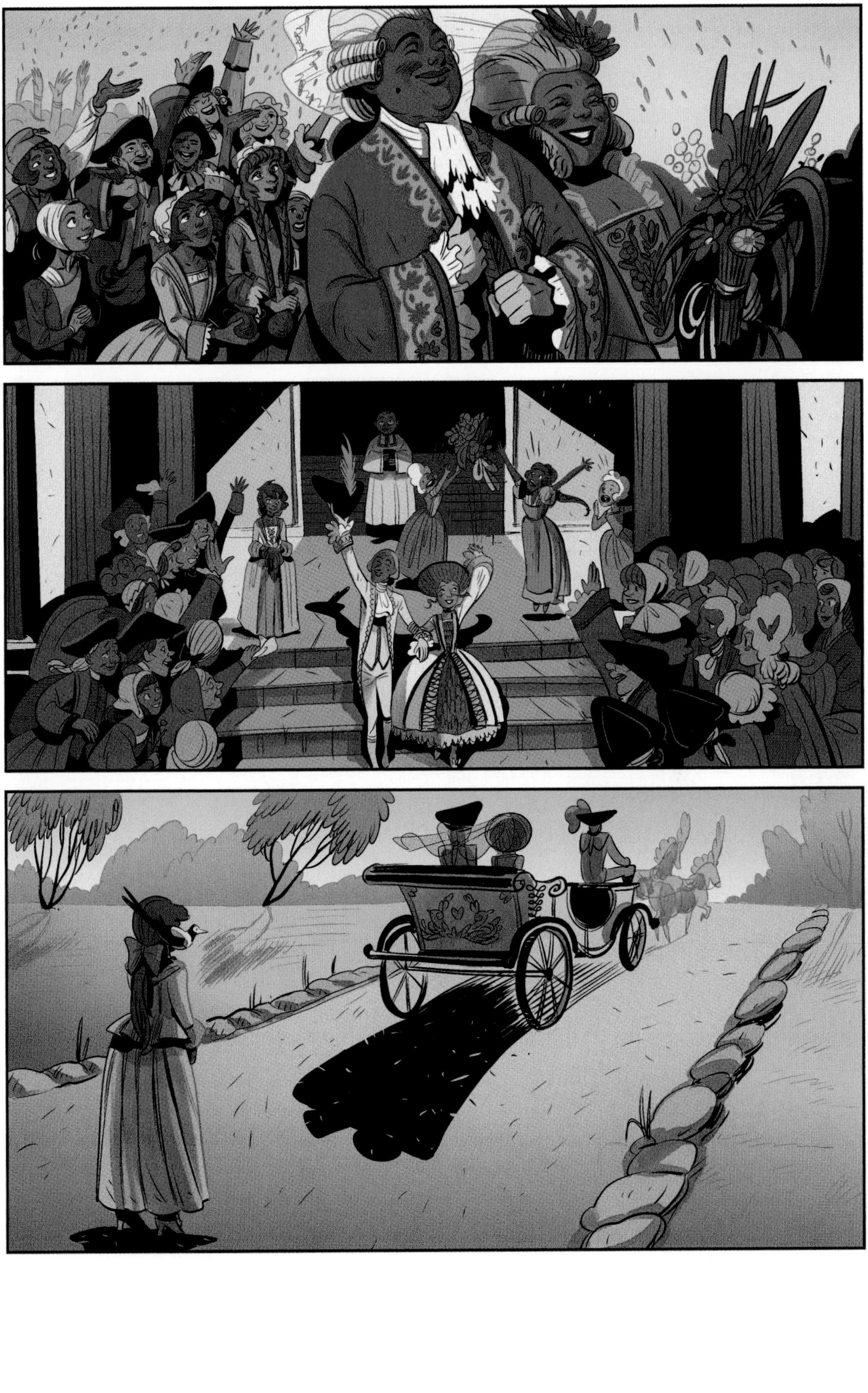

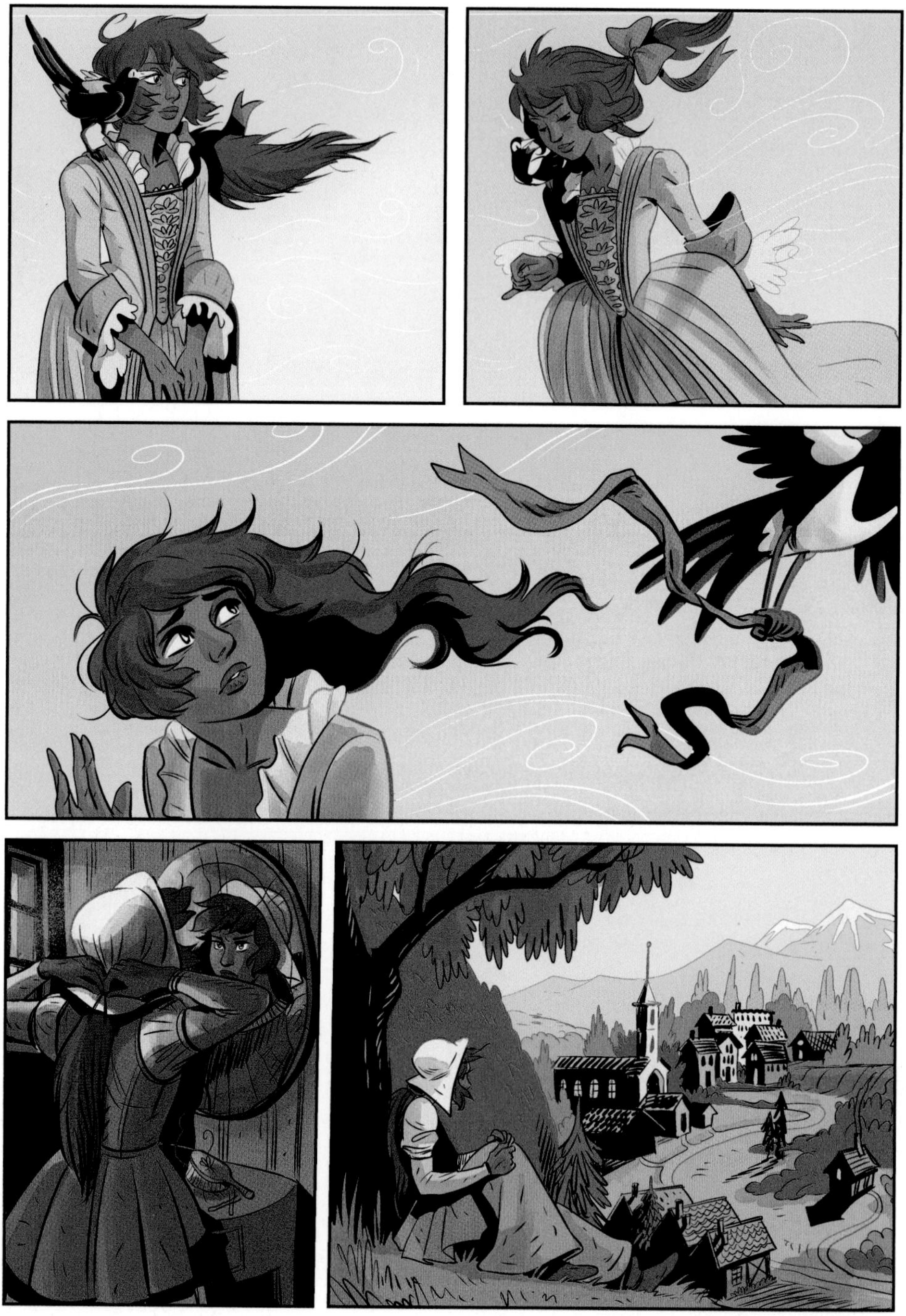

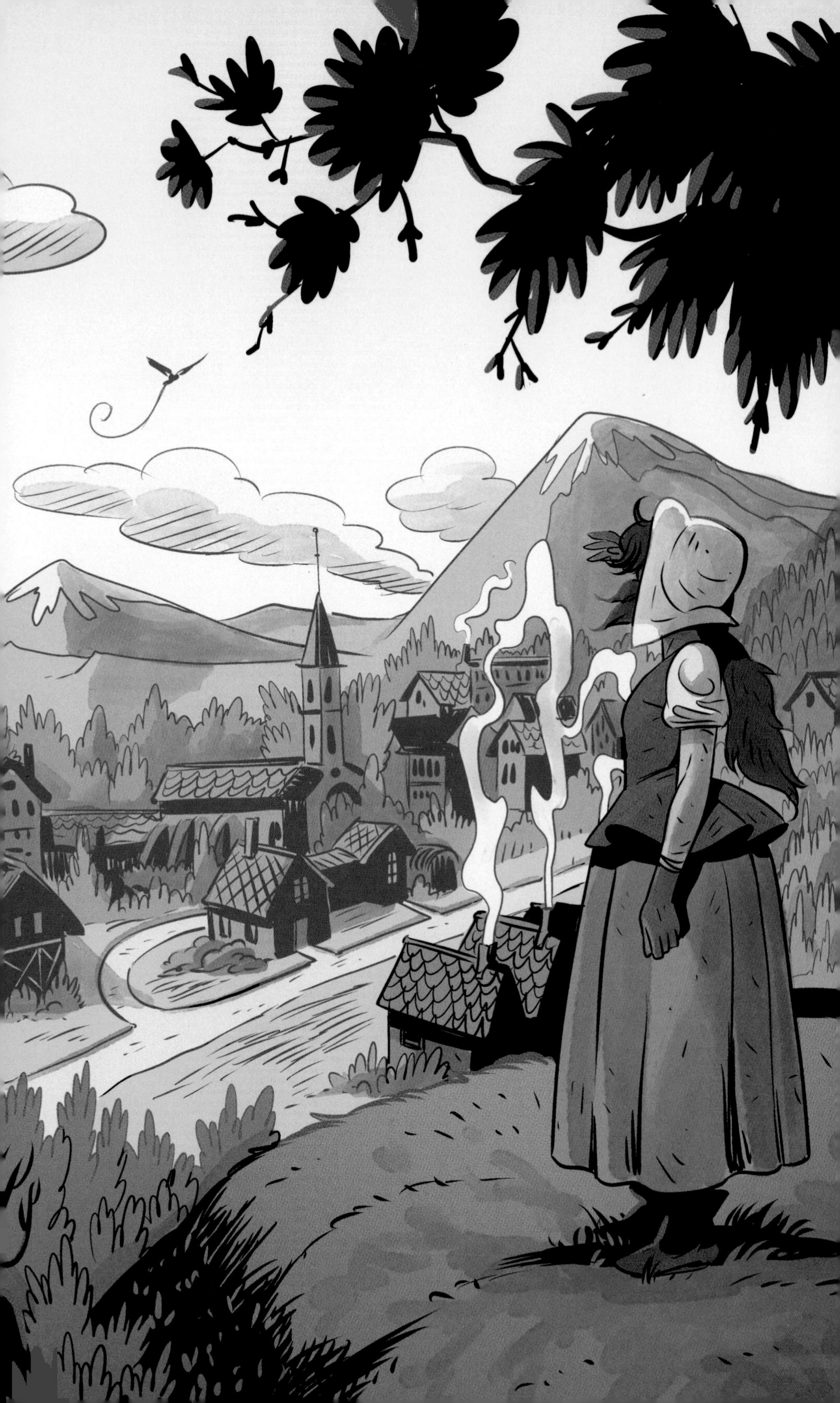

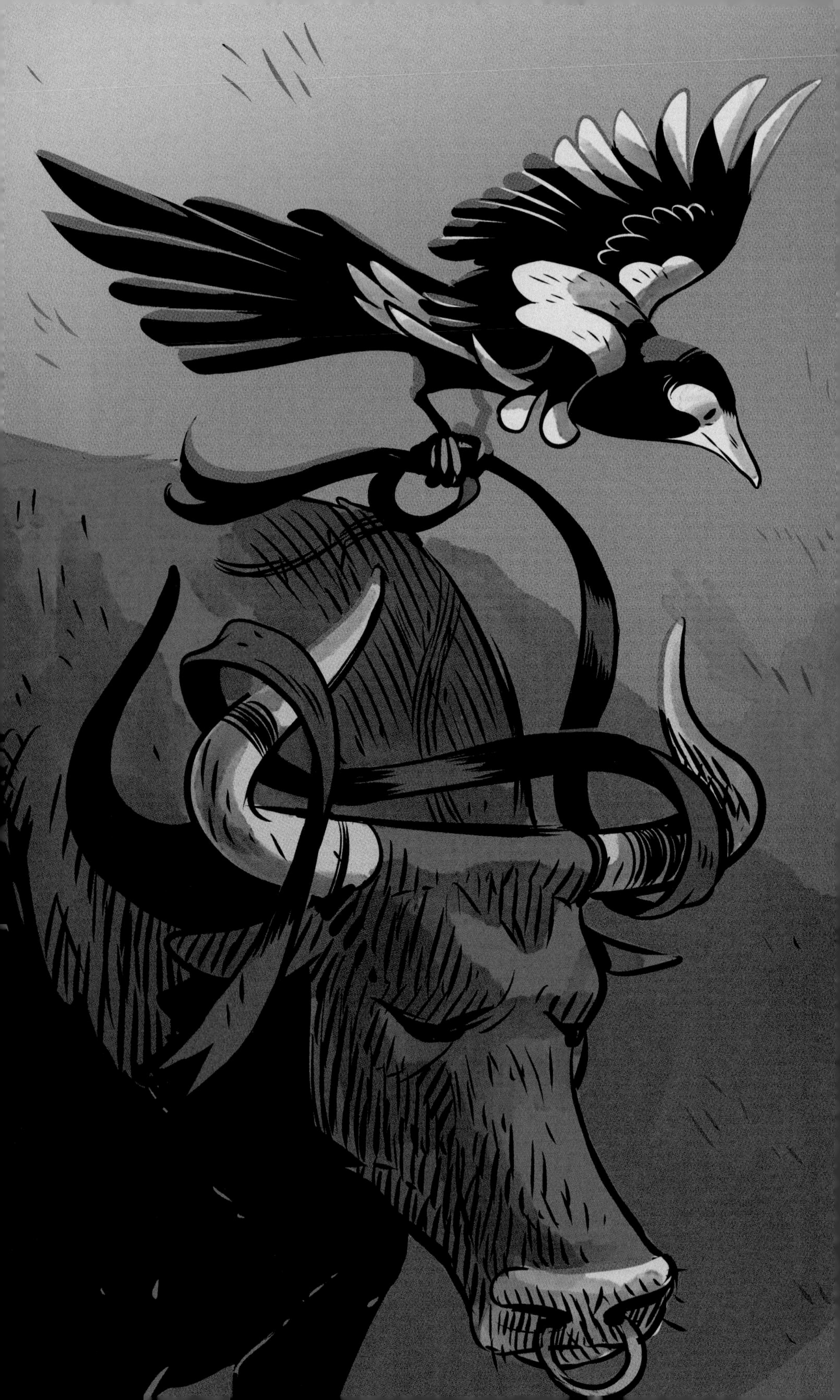

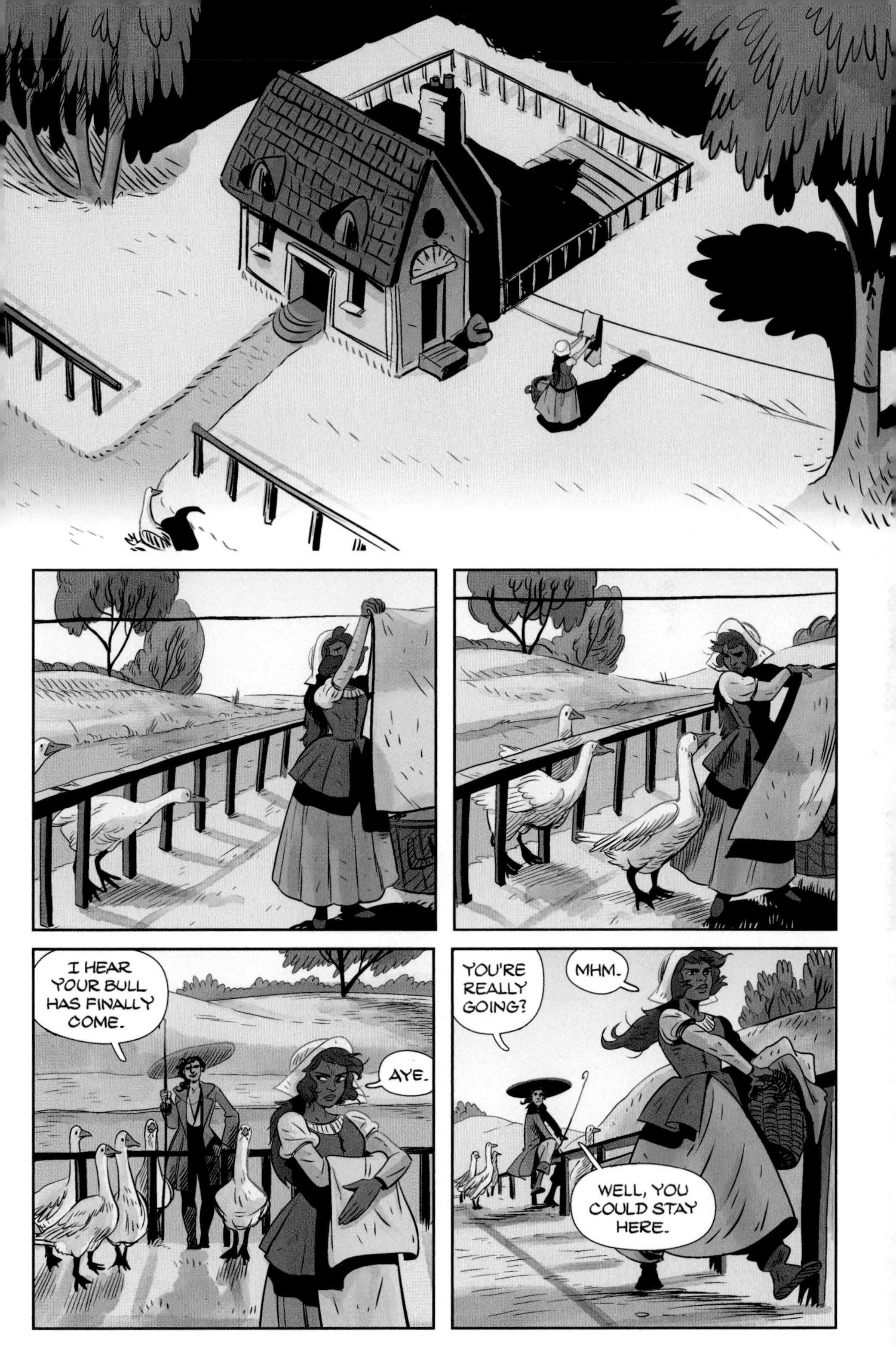
I HEAR YOUR BULL HAS FINALLY COME.
AYE.
YOU'RE REALLY GOING?
MHM.
WELL, YOU COULD STAY HERE.

I'VE SOLD OFF ALL THE ANIMALS. EVEN THE GOAT.

A WOMAN SHOULDN'T BE TENDING ANIMALS ANYHOW.

AND WHAT SHOULD A WOMAN BE DOING?

MARRYING, BEARING CHILDREN.

GOODNESS. I'VE HAD IT WRONG THE WHOLE TIME.

SO YOU'LL MARRY ME INSTEAD?

OH YES. I COULD BE GOOSE BOY'S WIFE.

THE GOOSE LADY.

LADY GOSLING.

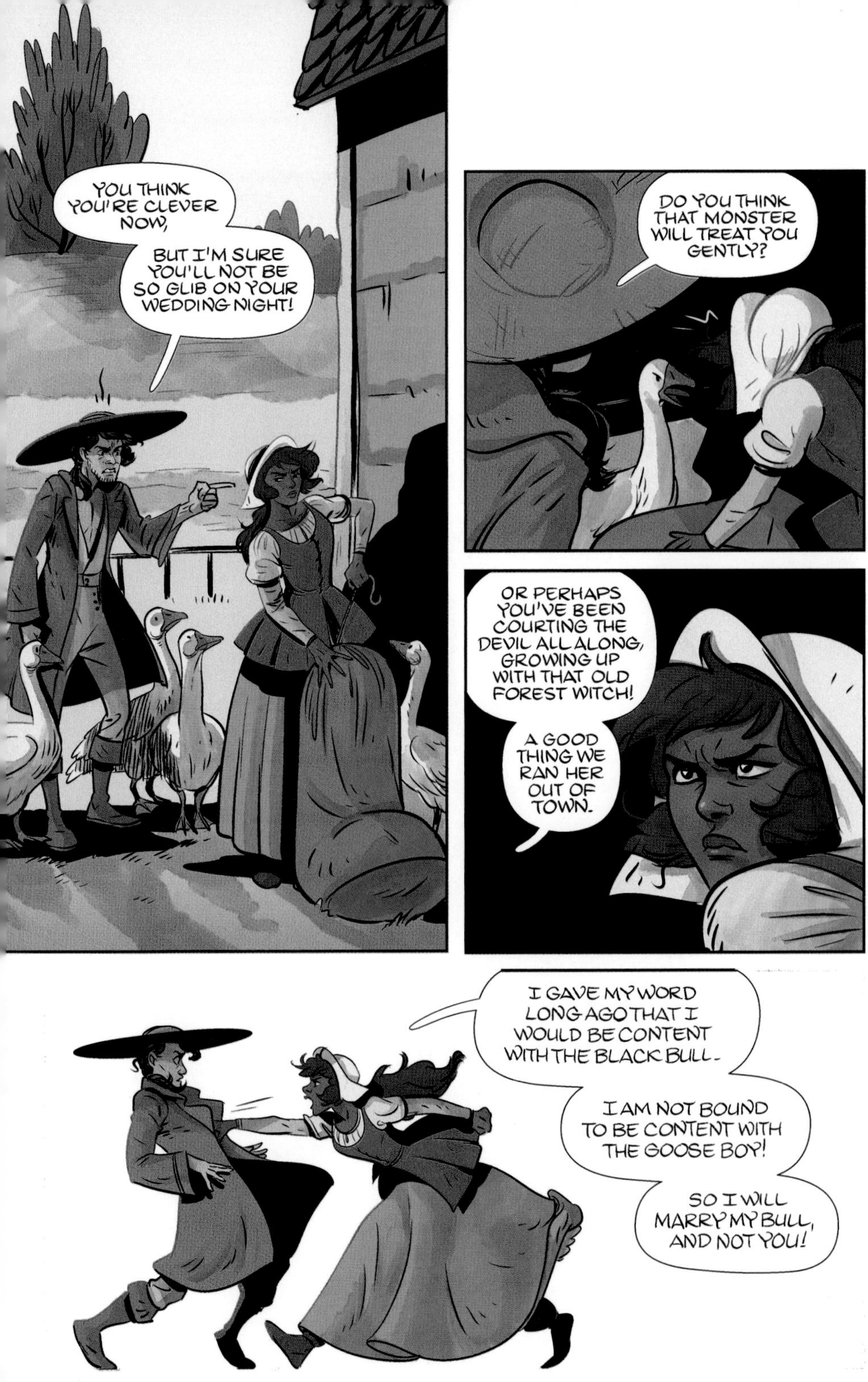
YOU THINK YOU'RE CLEVER NOW,
BUT I'M SURE YOU'LL NOT BE SO GLIB ON YOUR WEDDING NIGHT!
DO YOU THINK THAT MONSTER WILL TREAT YOU GENTLY?
OR PERHAPS YOU'VE BEEN COURTING THE DEVIL ALL ALONG, GROWING UP WITH THAT OLD FOREST WITCH!
A GOOD THING WE RAN HER OUT OF TOWN.
I GAVE MY WORD LONG AGO THAT I WOULD BE CONTENT WITH THE BLACK BULL.
I AM NOT BOUND TO BE CONTENT WITH THE GOOSE BOY!
SO I WILL MARRY MY BULL, AND NOT YOU!

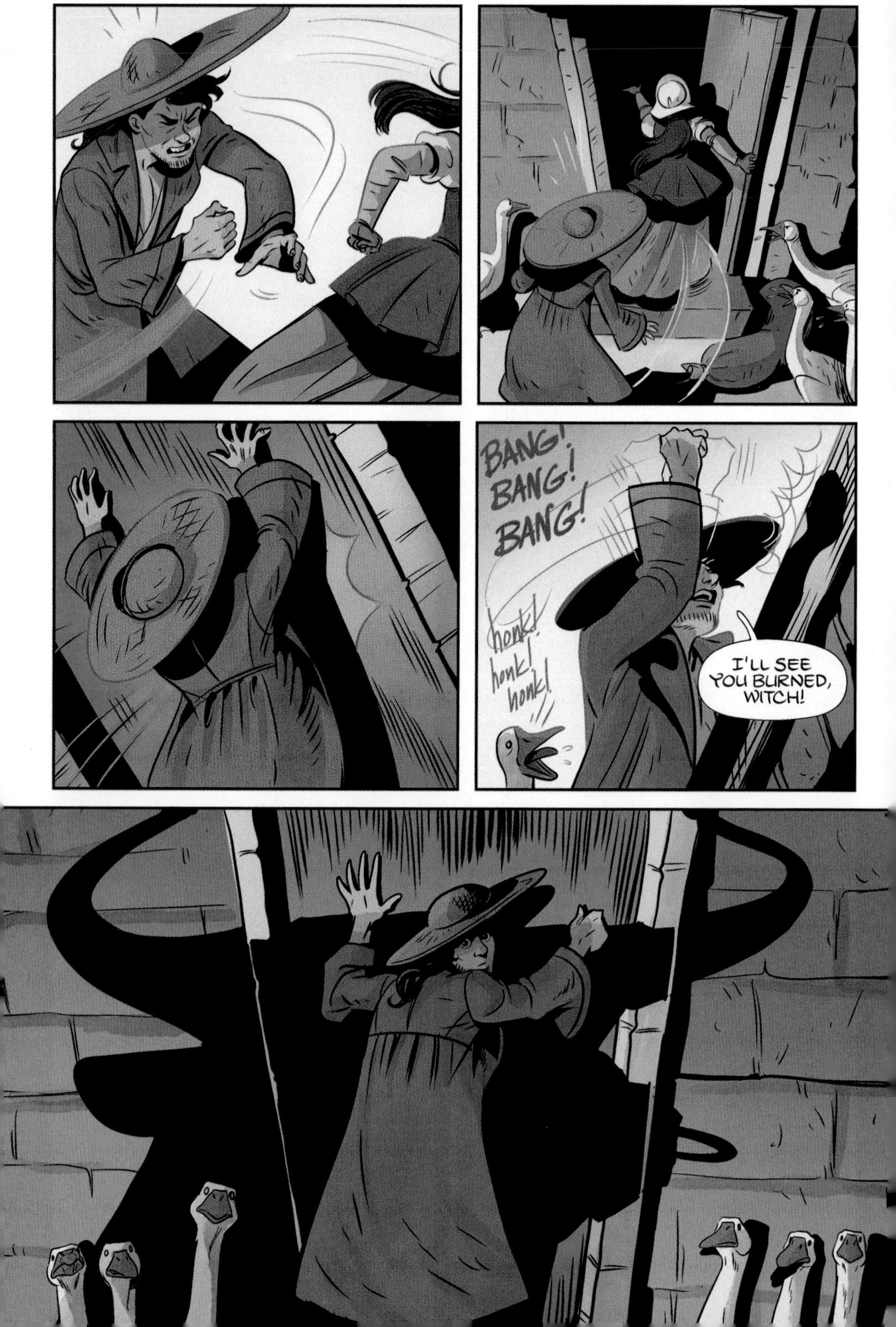
BANG!
BANG!
BANG!
honk!
honk!
honk!
I'LL SEE YOU BURNED, WITCH!

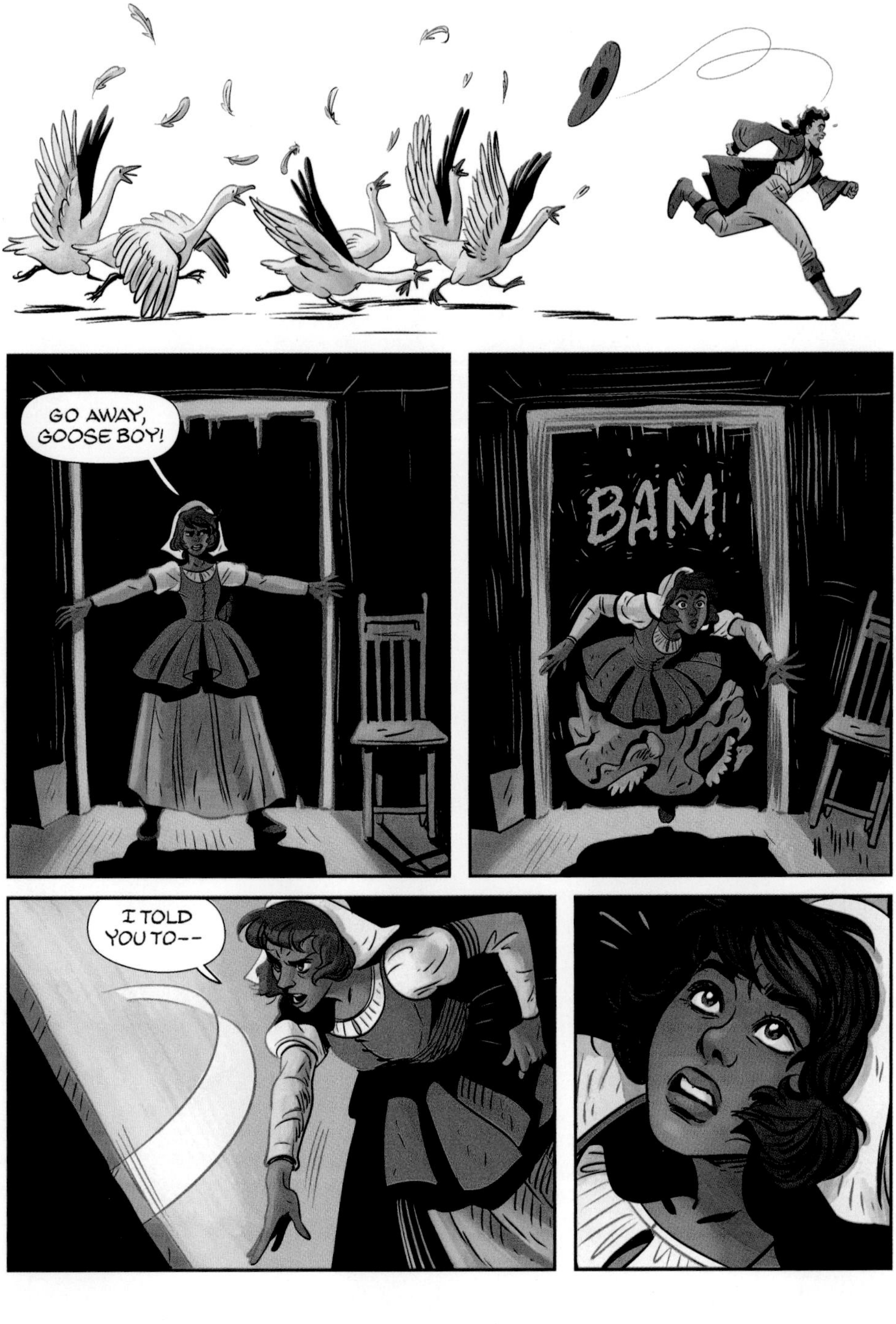
GO AWAY, GOOSE BOY!
BAM
I TOLD YOU TO--

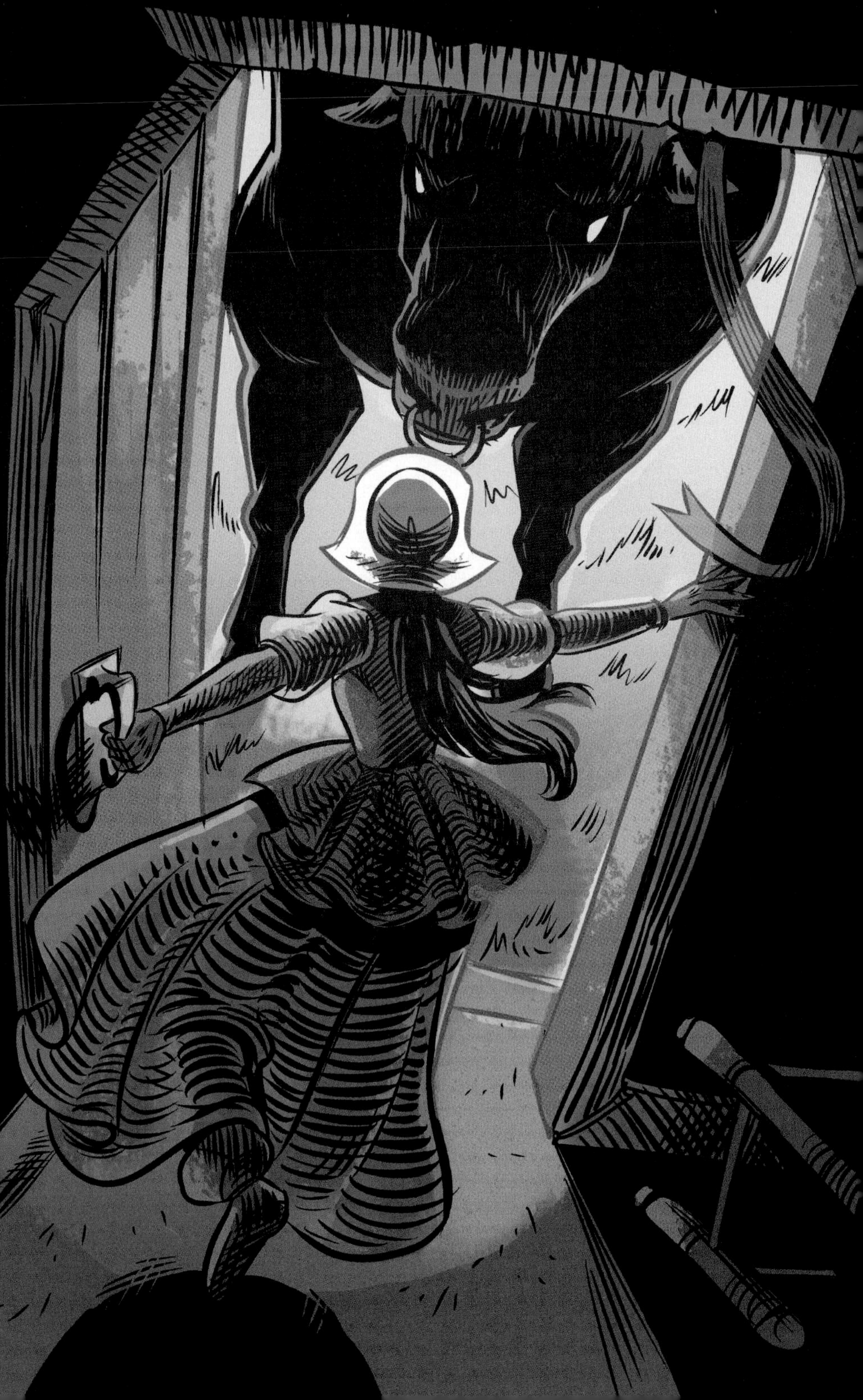

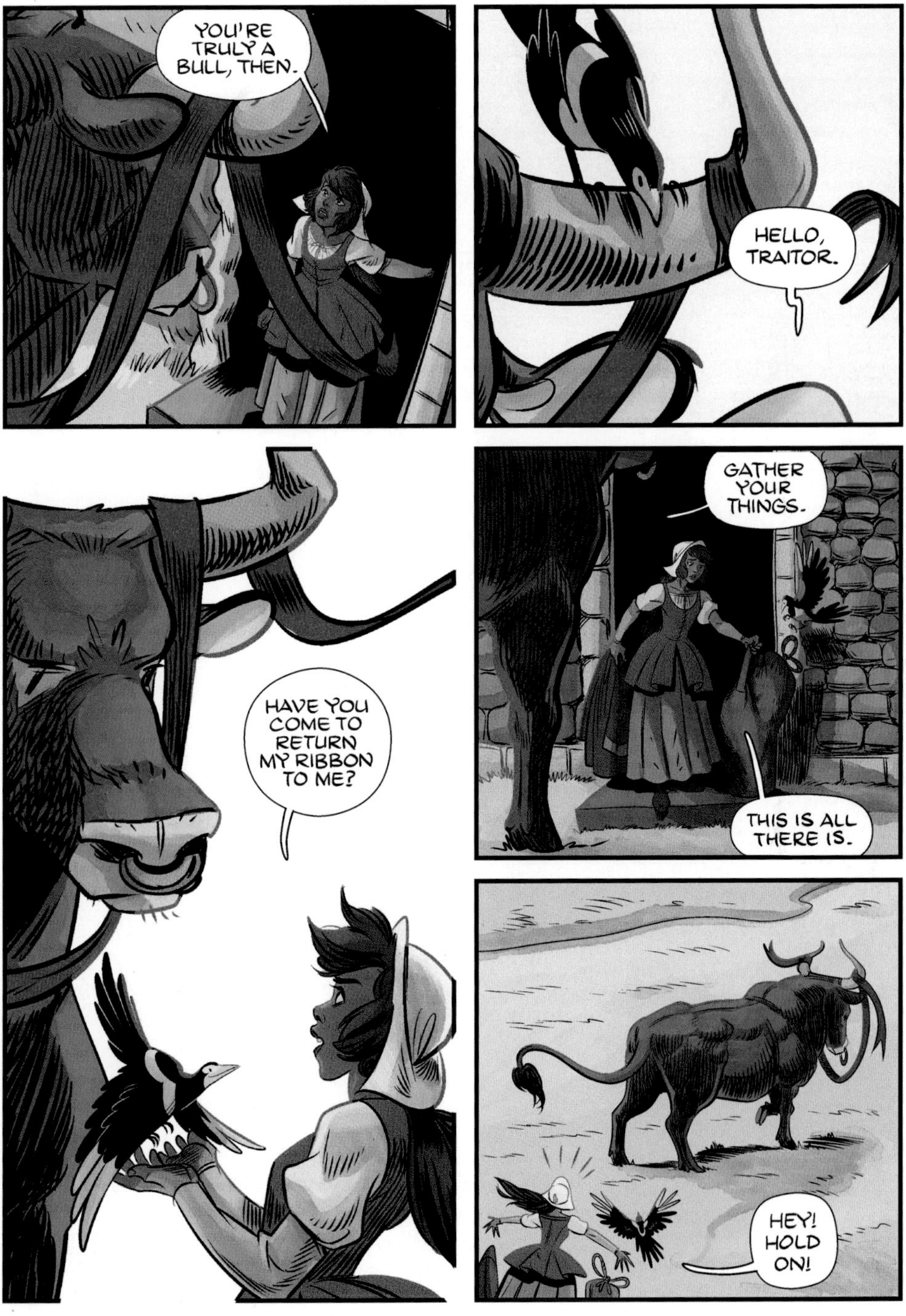
YOU'RE TRULY A BULL, THEN.
HELLO, TRAITOR.
HAVE YOU COME TO RETURN MY RIBBON TO ME?
GATHER YOUR THINGS.
THIS IS ALL THERE IS.
HEY! HOLD ON!

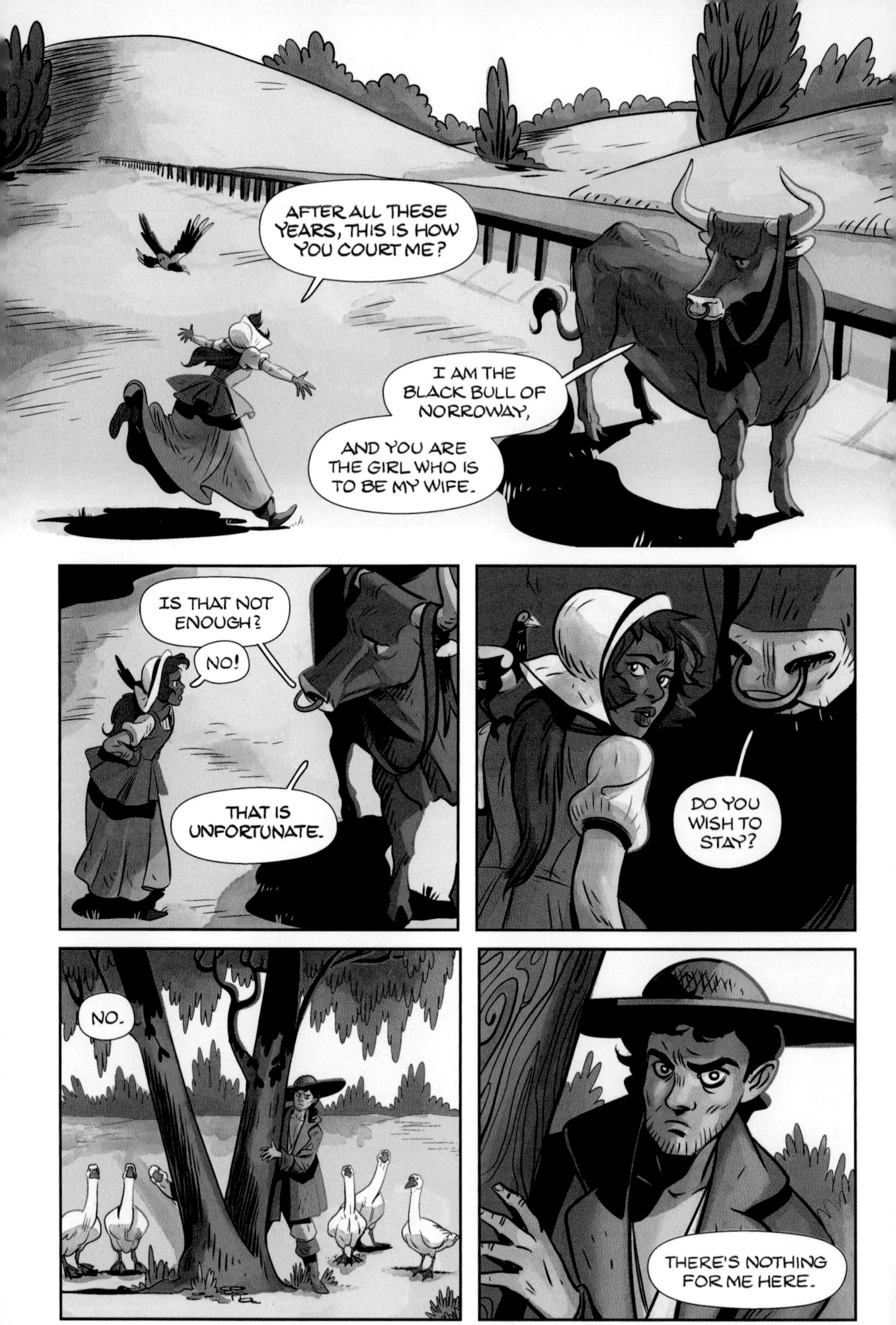
AFTER ALL THESE YEARS, THIS IS HOW YOU COURT ME?
I AM THE BLACK BULL OF NORROWAY,
AND YOU ARE THE GIRL WHO IS TO BE MY WIFE.
IS THAT NOT ENOUGH?
NO!
THAT IS UNFORTUNATE.
DO YOU WISH TO STAY?
NO.
THERE'S NOTHING FOR ME HERE.

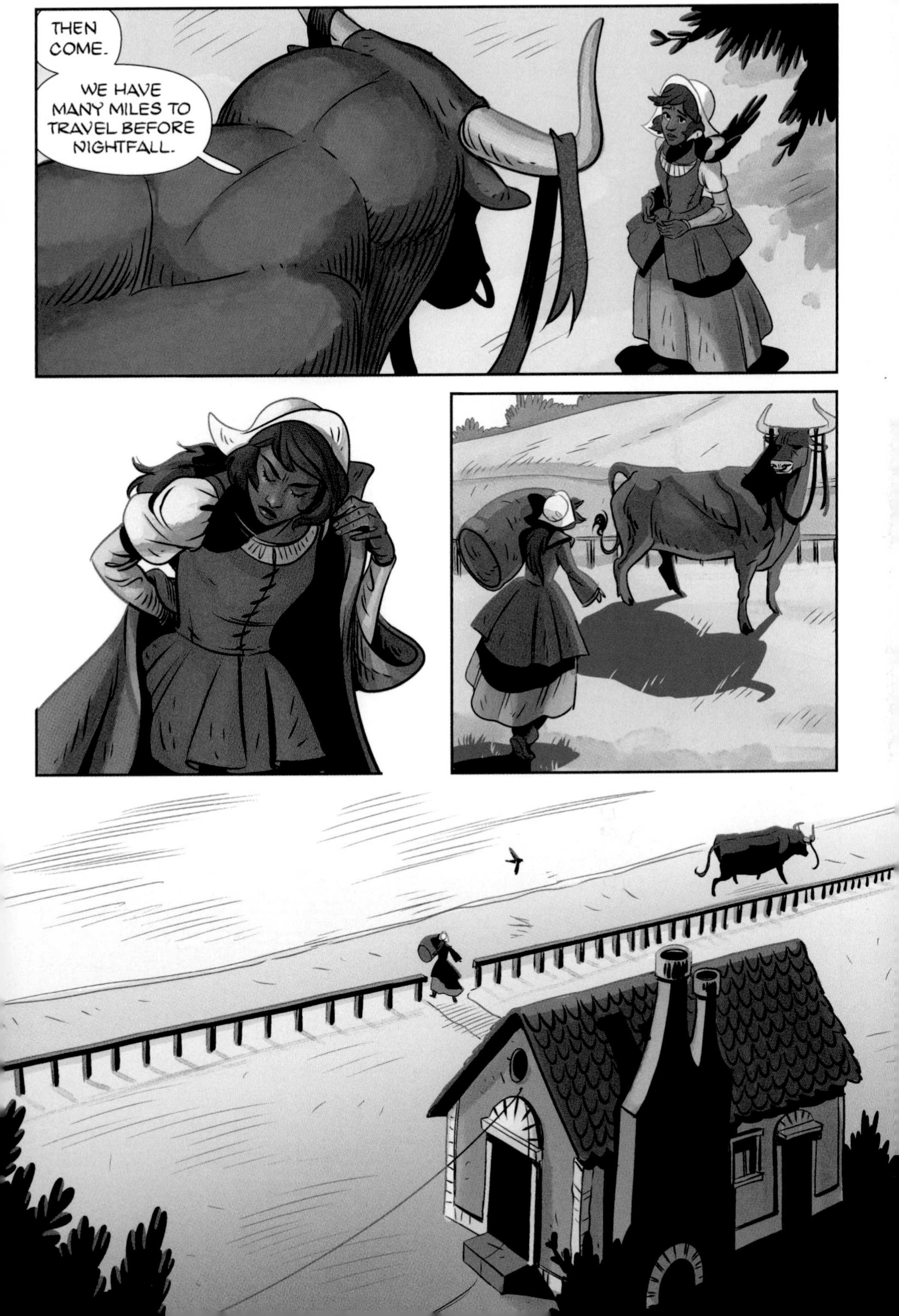
THEN COME.
WE HAVE MANY MILES TO TRAVEL BEFORE NIGHTFALL.

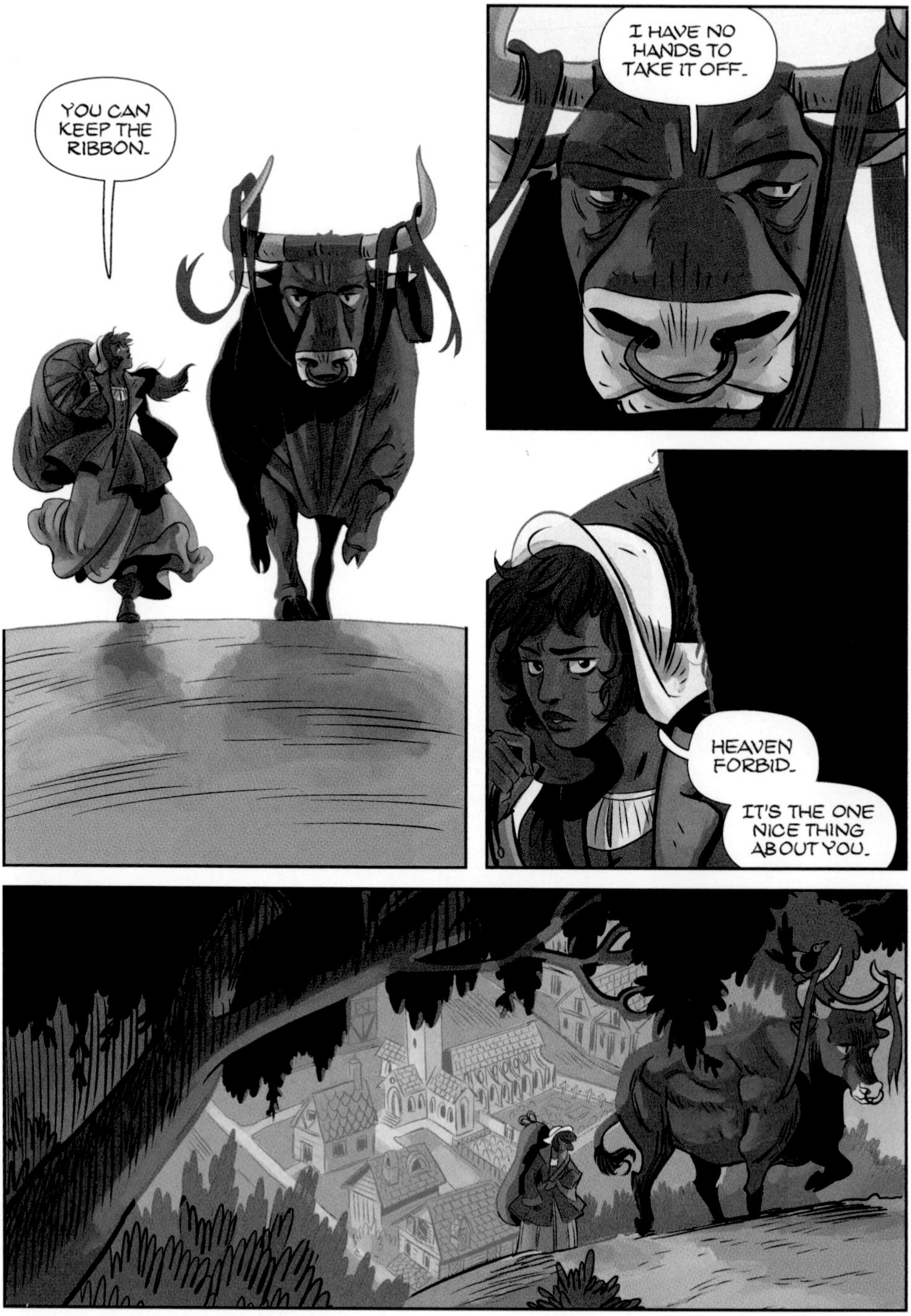
YOU CAN KEEP THE RIBBON.
I HAVE NO HANDS TO TAKE IT OFF.
HEAVEN FORBID.
IT'S THE ONE NICE THING ABOUT YOU.

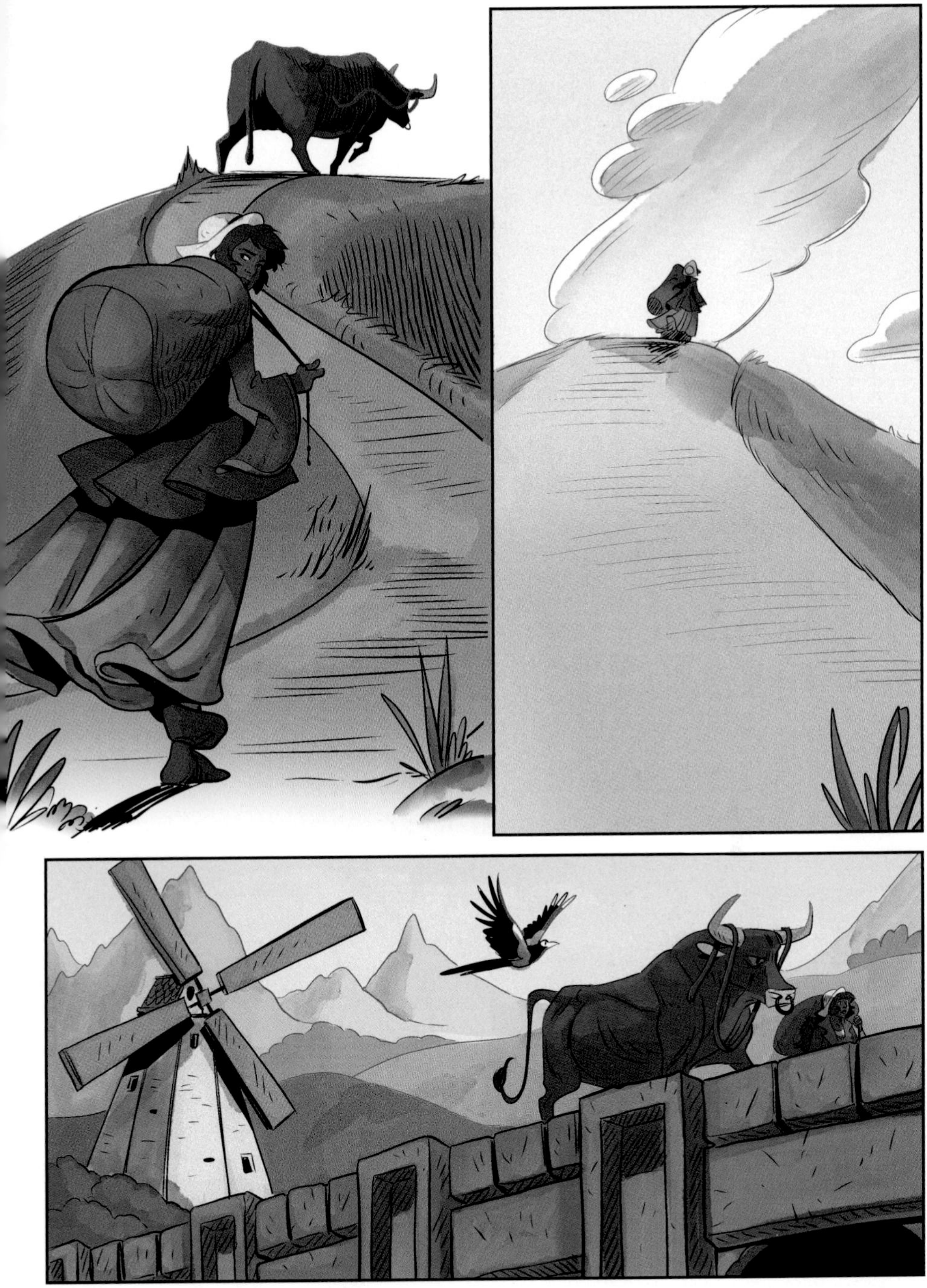

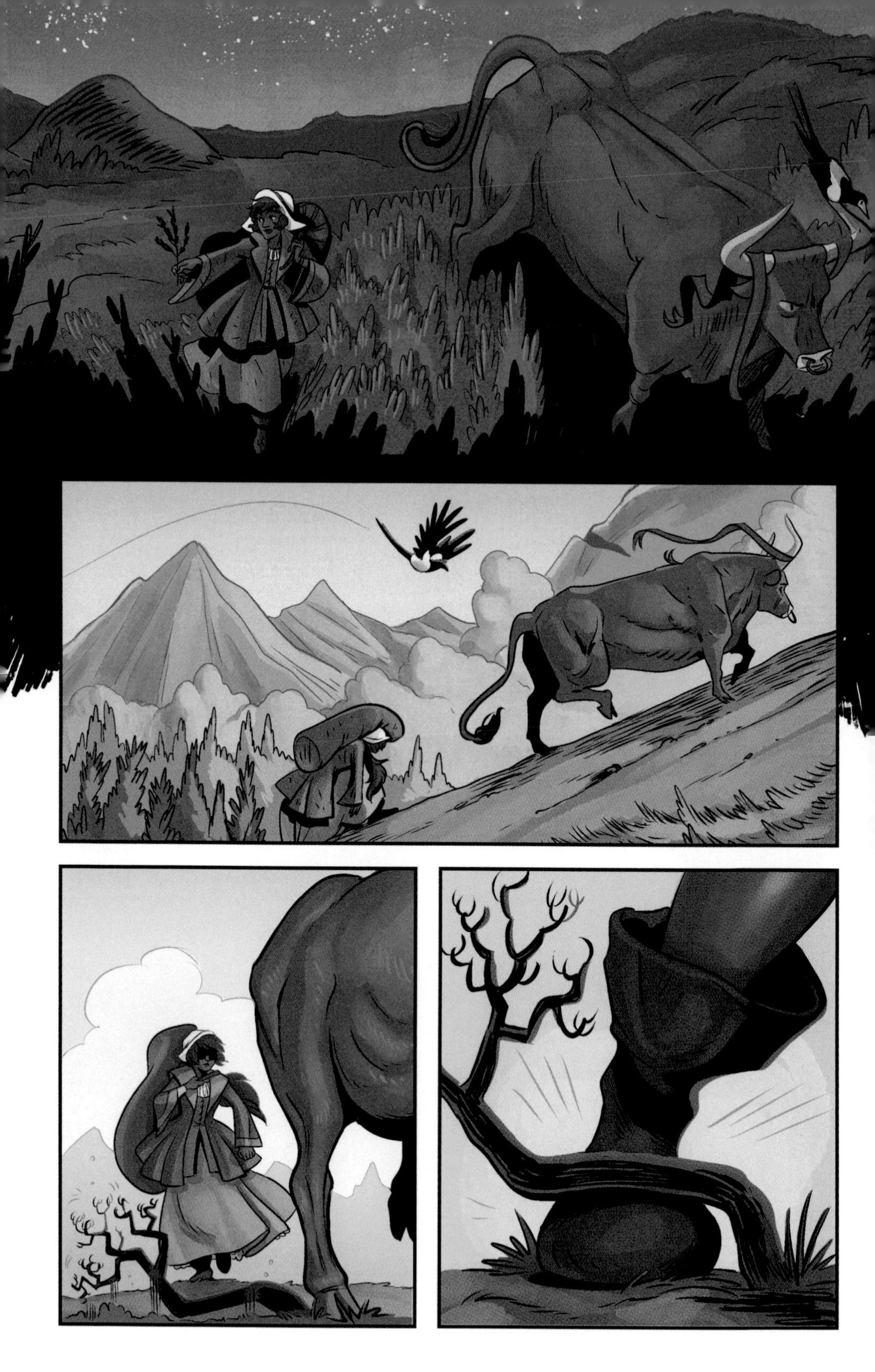

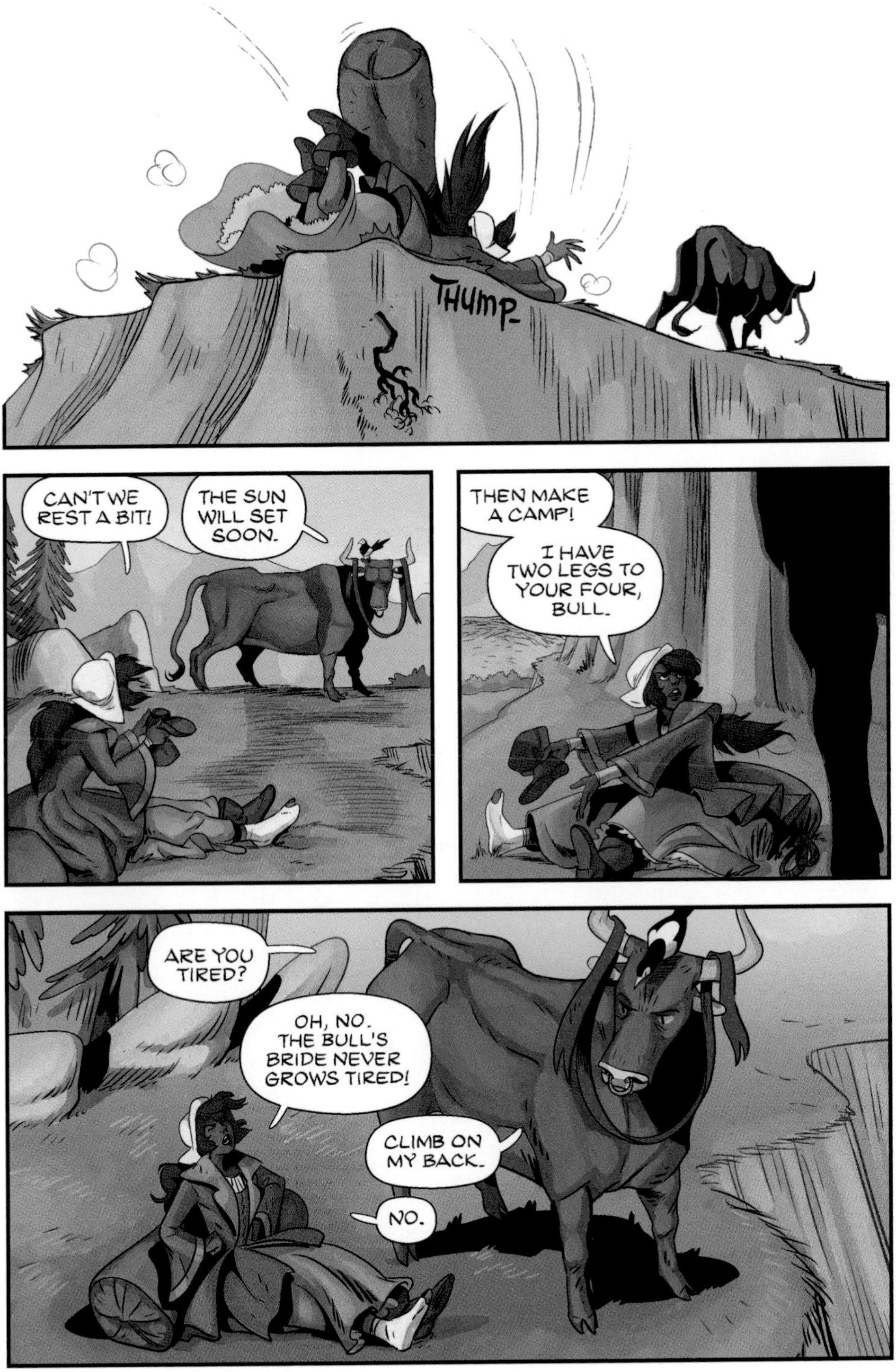
THUMP-
CAN'T WE REST A BIT!
THE SUN WILL SET SOON.
THEN MAKE A CAMP!
I HAVE TWO LEGS TO YOUR FOUR, BULL.
ARE YOU TIRED?
OH, NO. THE BULL'S BRIDE NEVER GROWS TIRED!
CLIMB ON MY BACK.
NO.

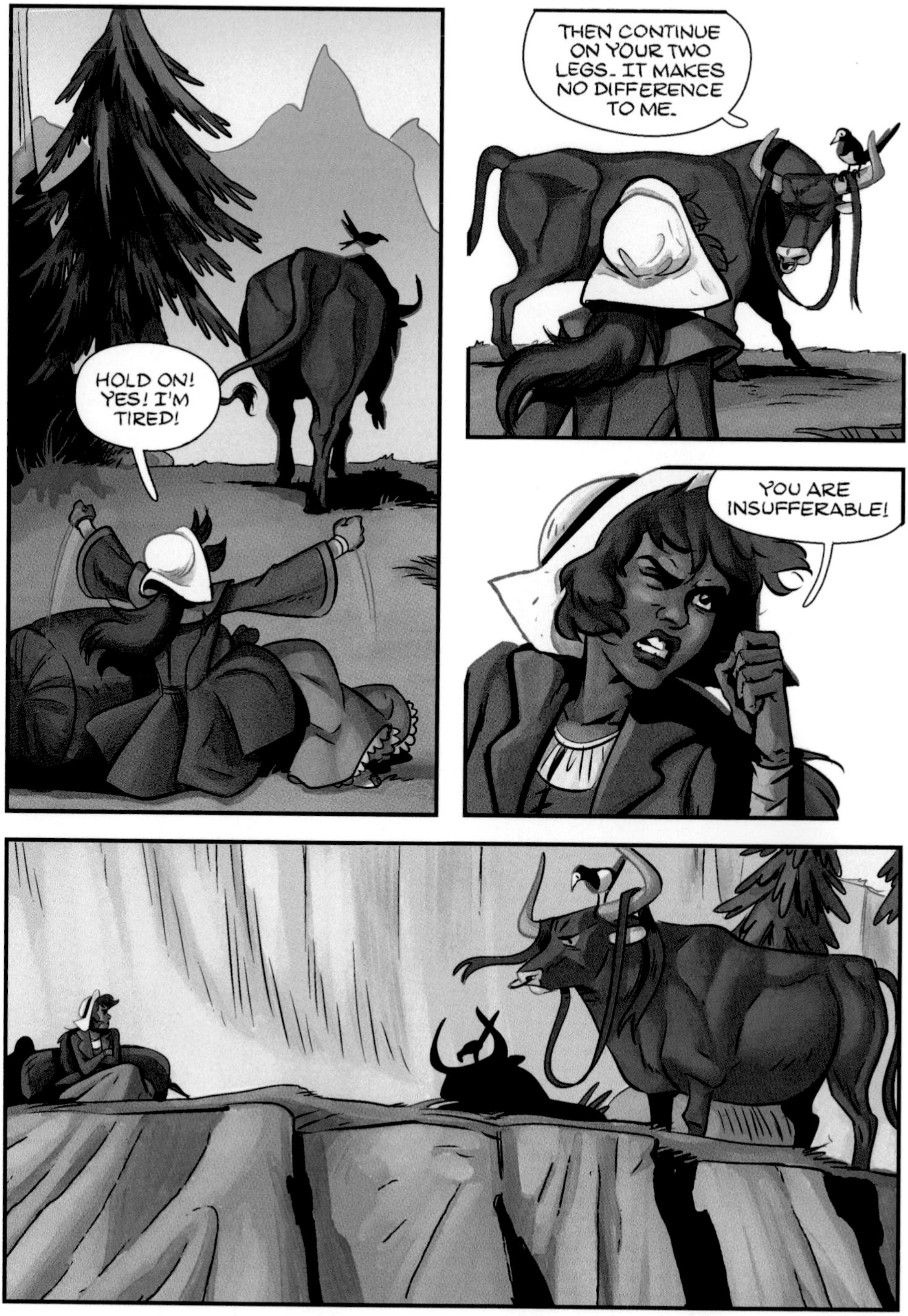
HOLD ON! YES! I'M TIRED!
THEN CONTINUE ON YOUR TWO LEGS. IT MAKES NO DIFFERENCE TO ME.
YOU ARE INSUFFERABLE!

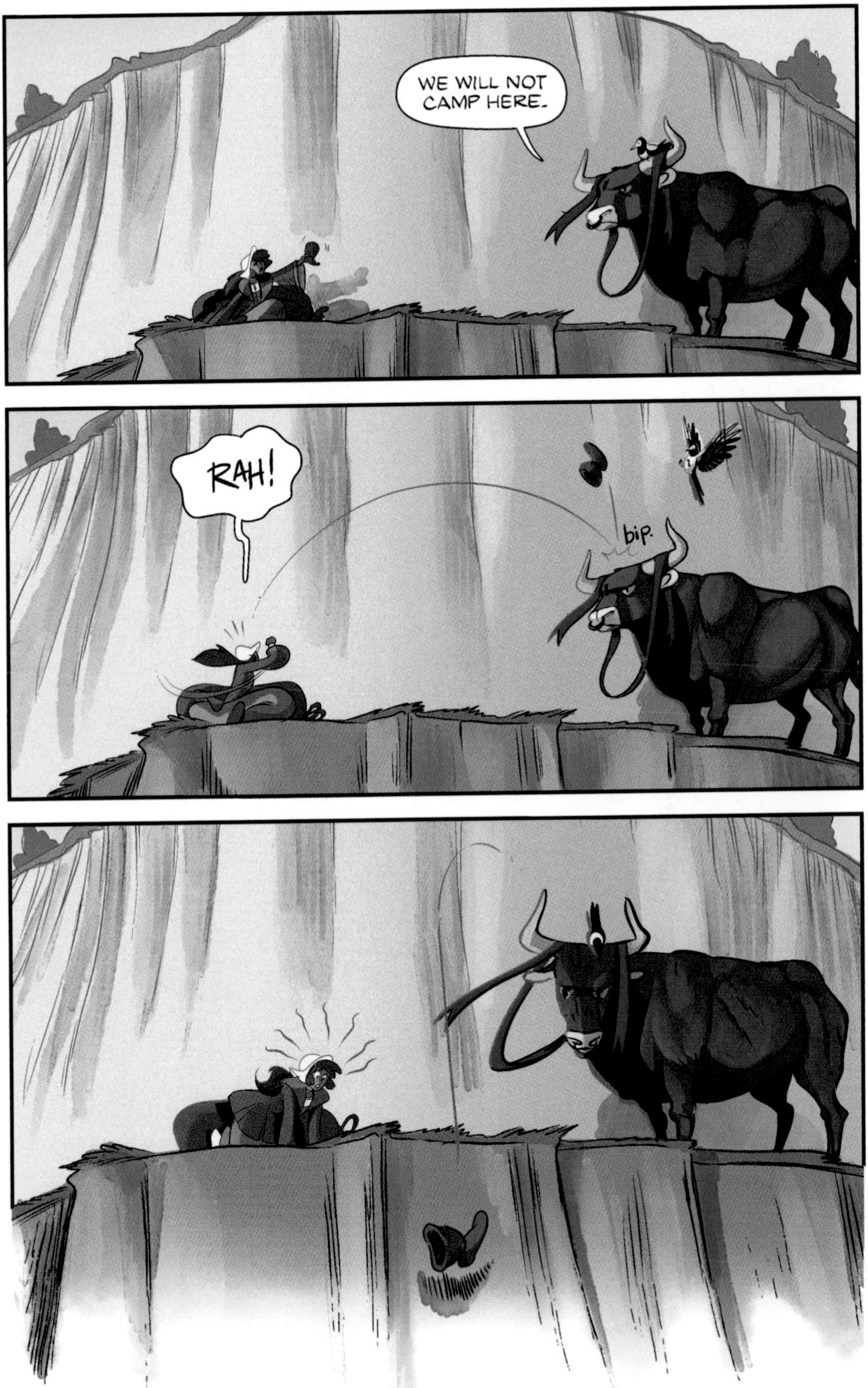
WE WILL NOT CAMP HERE.
RAH!
bip.

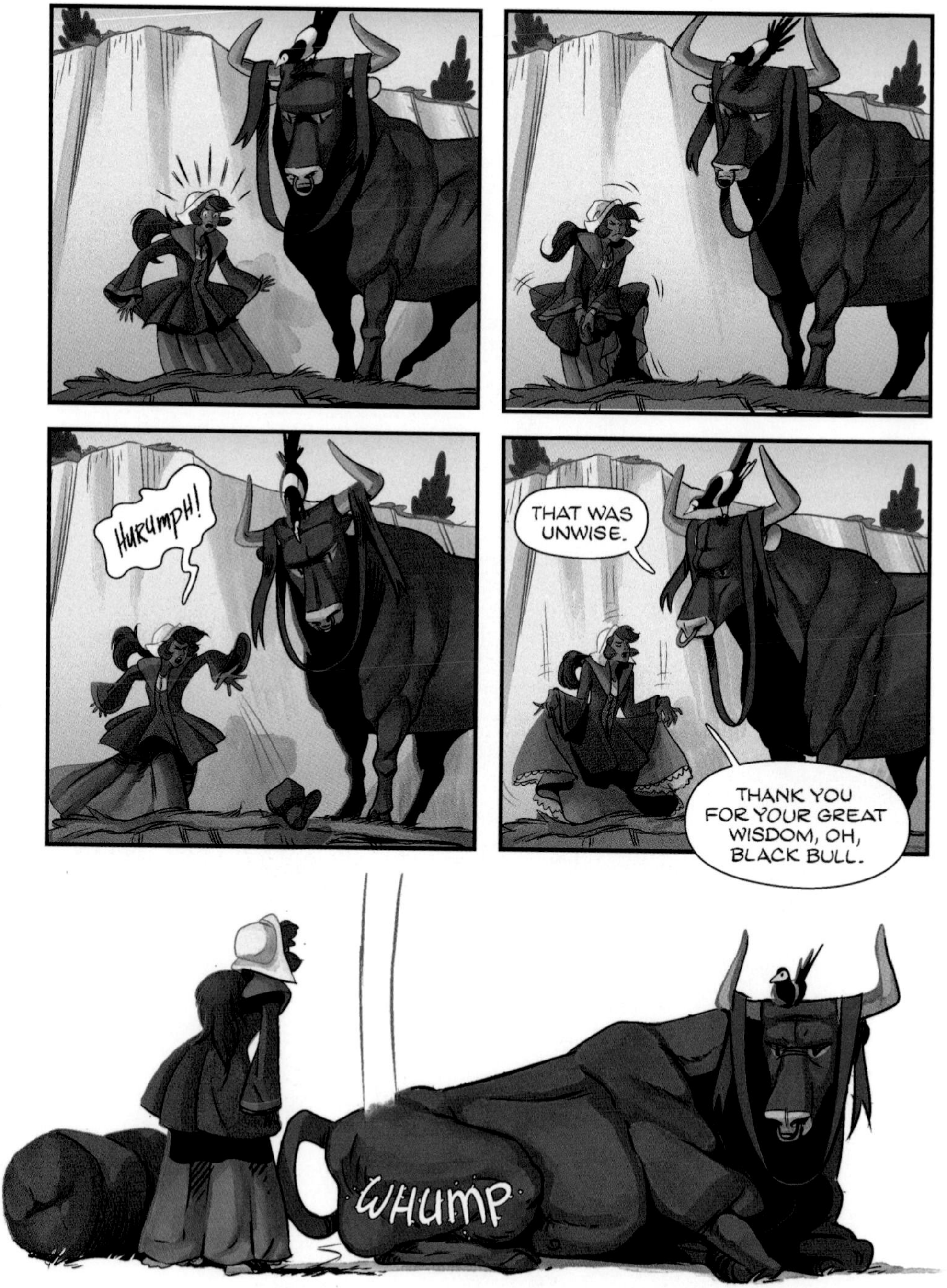
HURUMPH!
THAT WAS UNWISE.
THANK YOU FOR YOUR GREAT WISDOM, OH, BLACK BULL.
WHUMP

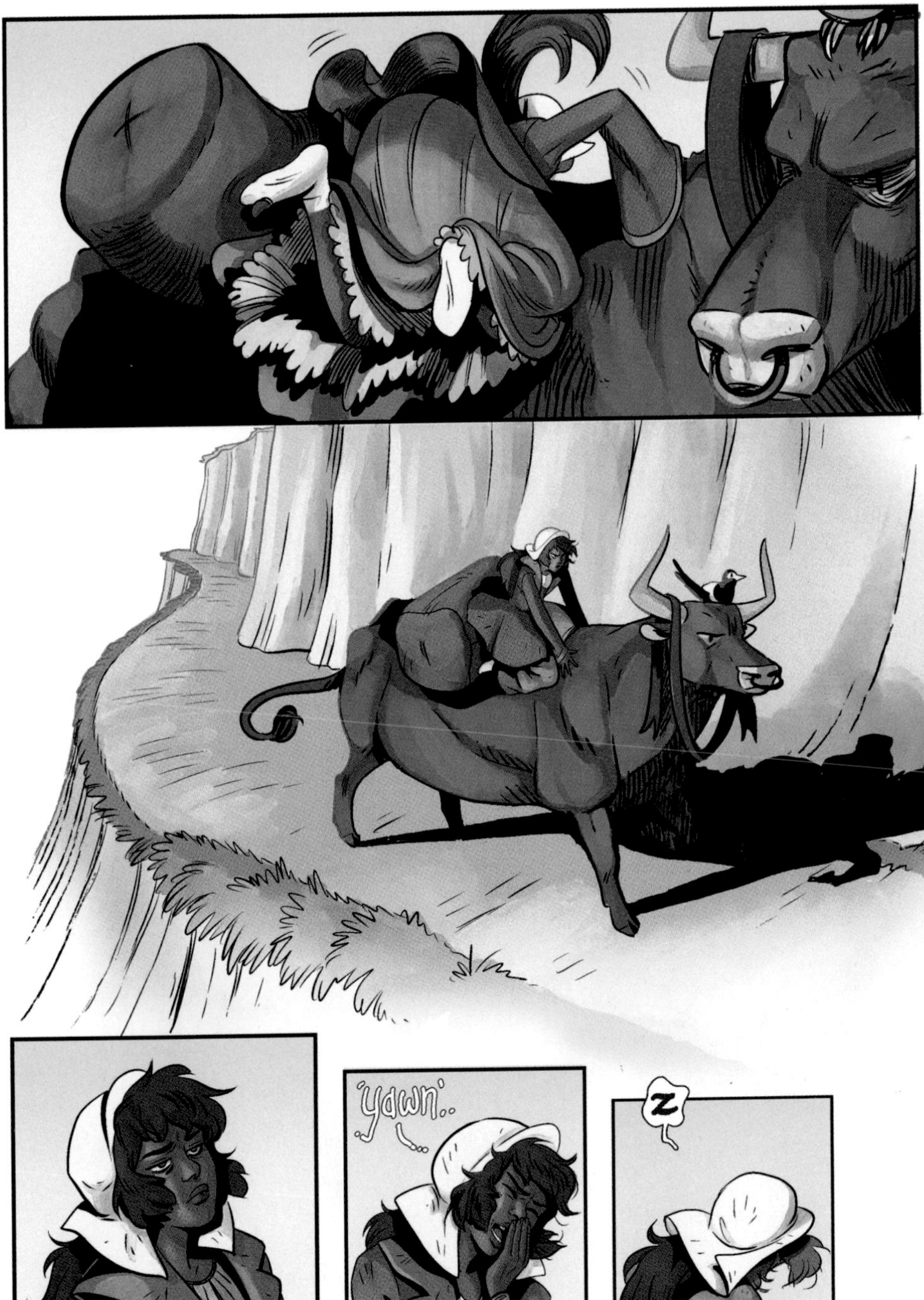
'yawn'..
Z

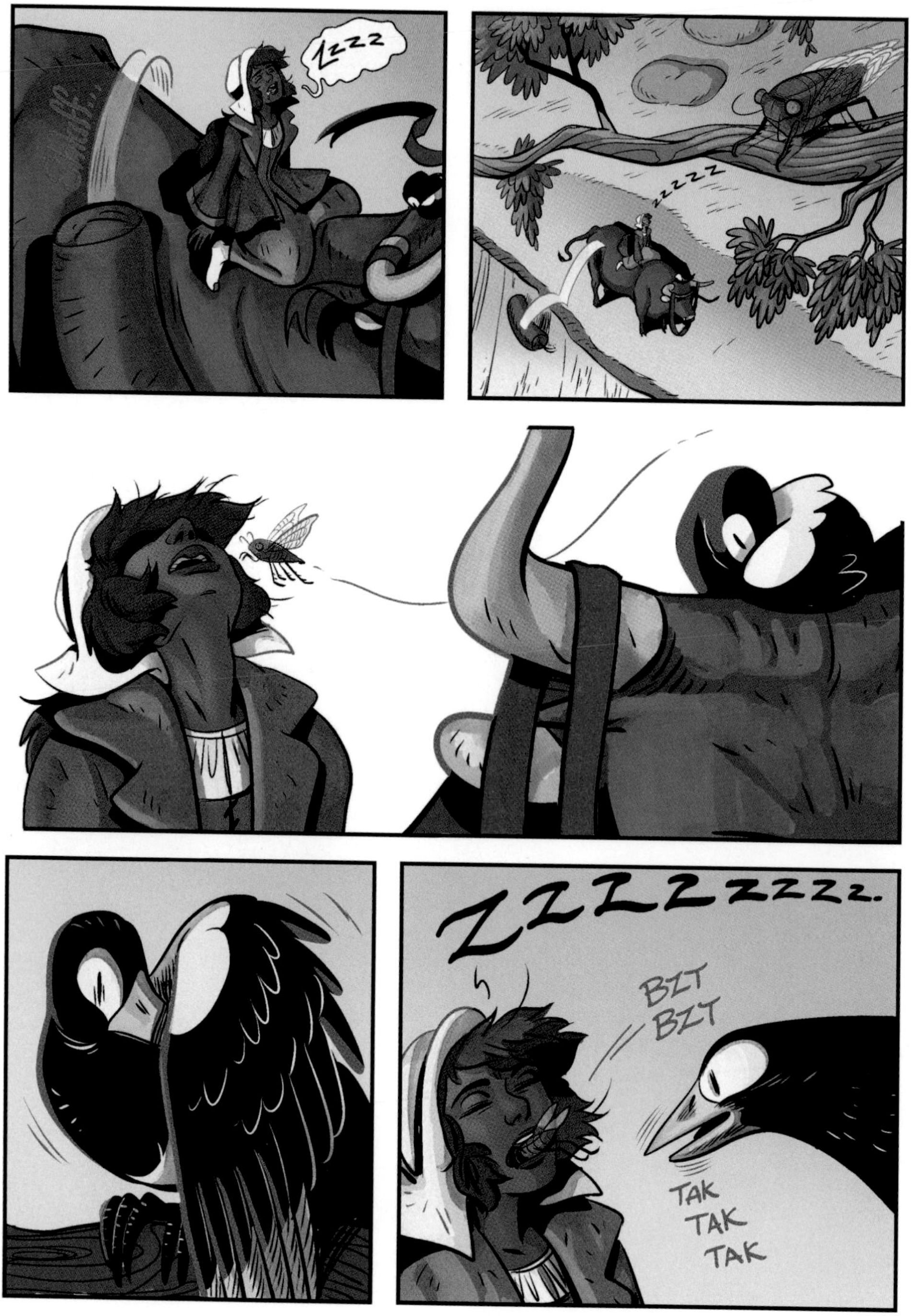
Zzzz
zzzzz
ZZZZZzzzz.
BZT
BZT
TAK
TAK
TAK

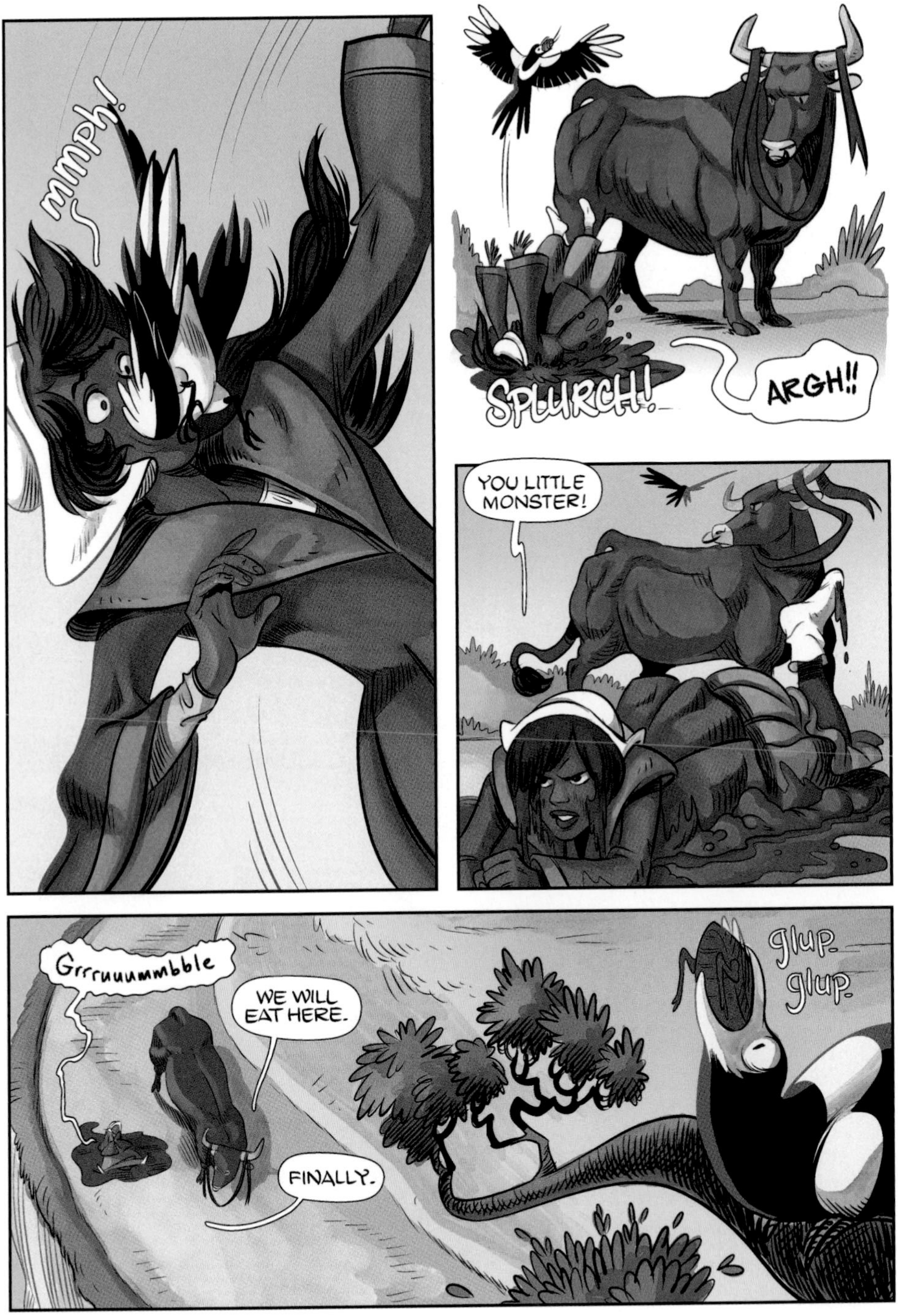
mmph!
SPLURCH!
ARGH!!
YOU LITTLE MONSTER!
Grrruuummbble
WE WILL EAT HERE.
FINALLY.
glup. glup.

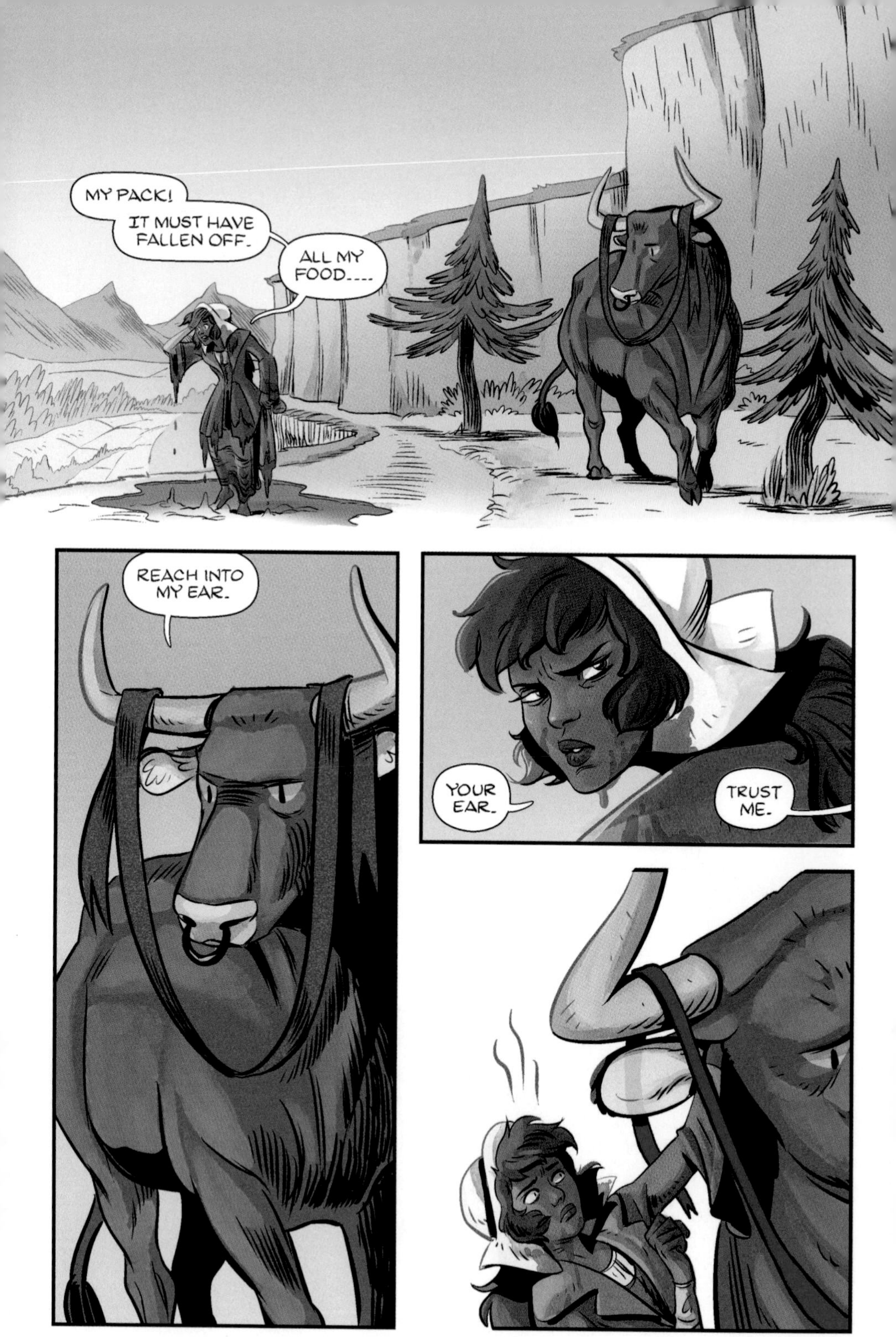
MY PACK!
IT MUST HAVE FALLEN OFF.
ALL MY FOOD....
REACH INTO MY EAR.
YOUR EAR.
TRUST ME.

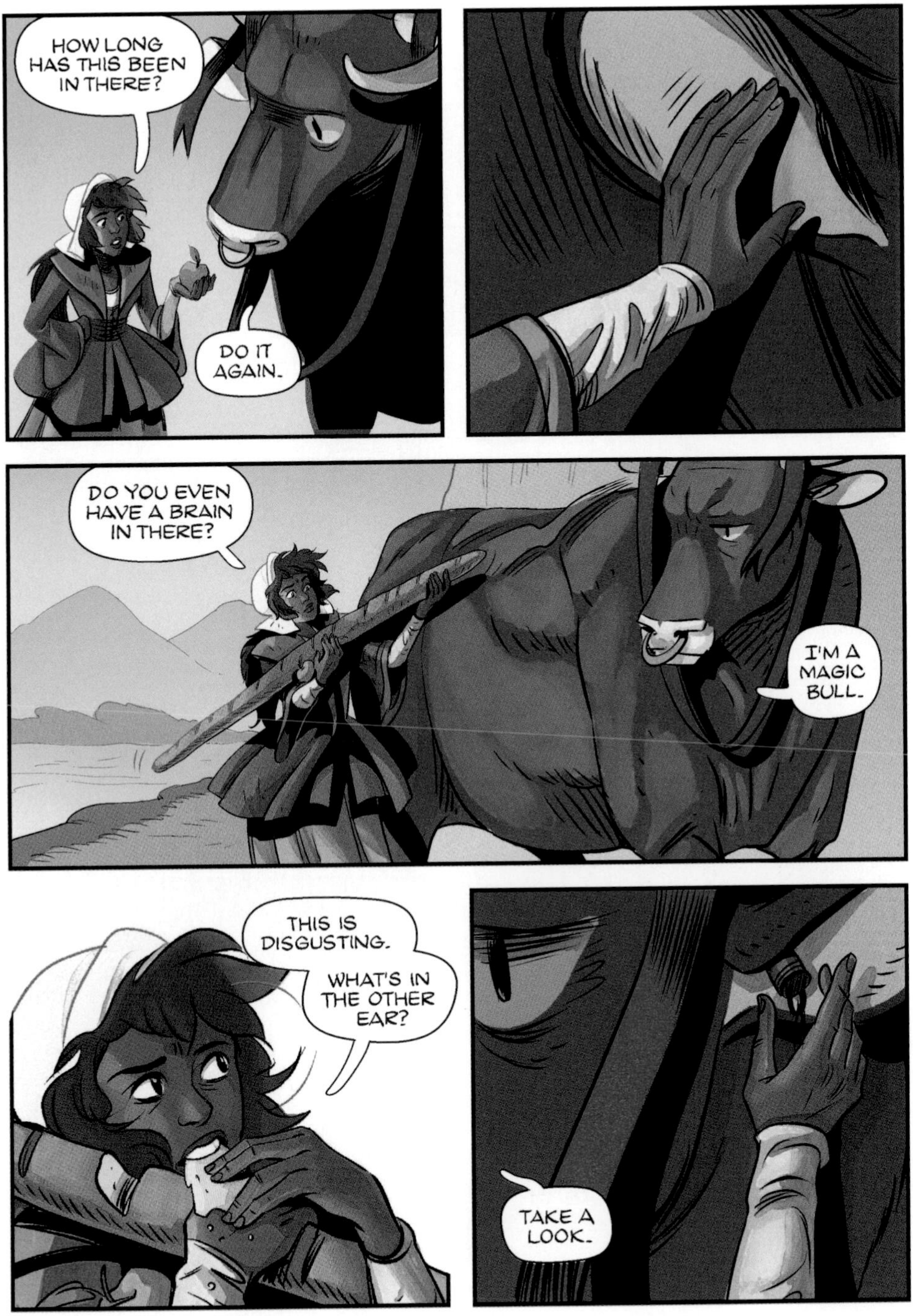
HOW LONG HAS THIS BEEN IN THERE?
DO IT AGAIN.
DO YOU EVEN HAVE A BRAIN IN THERE?
I'M A MAGIC BULL.
THIS IS DISGUSTING.
WHAT'S IN THE OTHER EAR?
TAKE A LOOK.

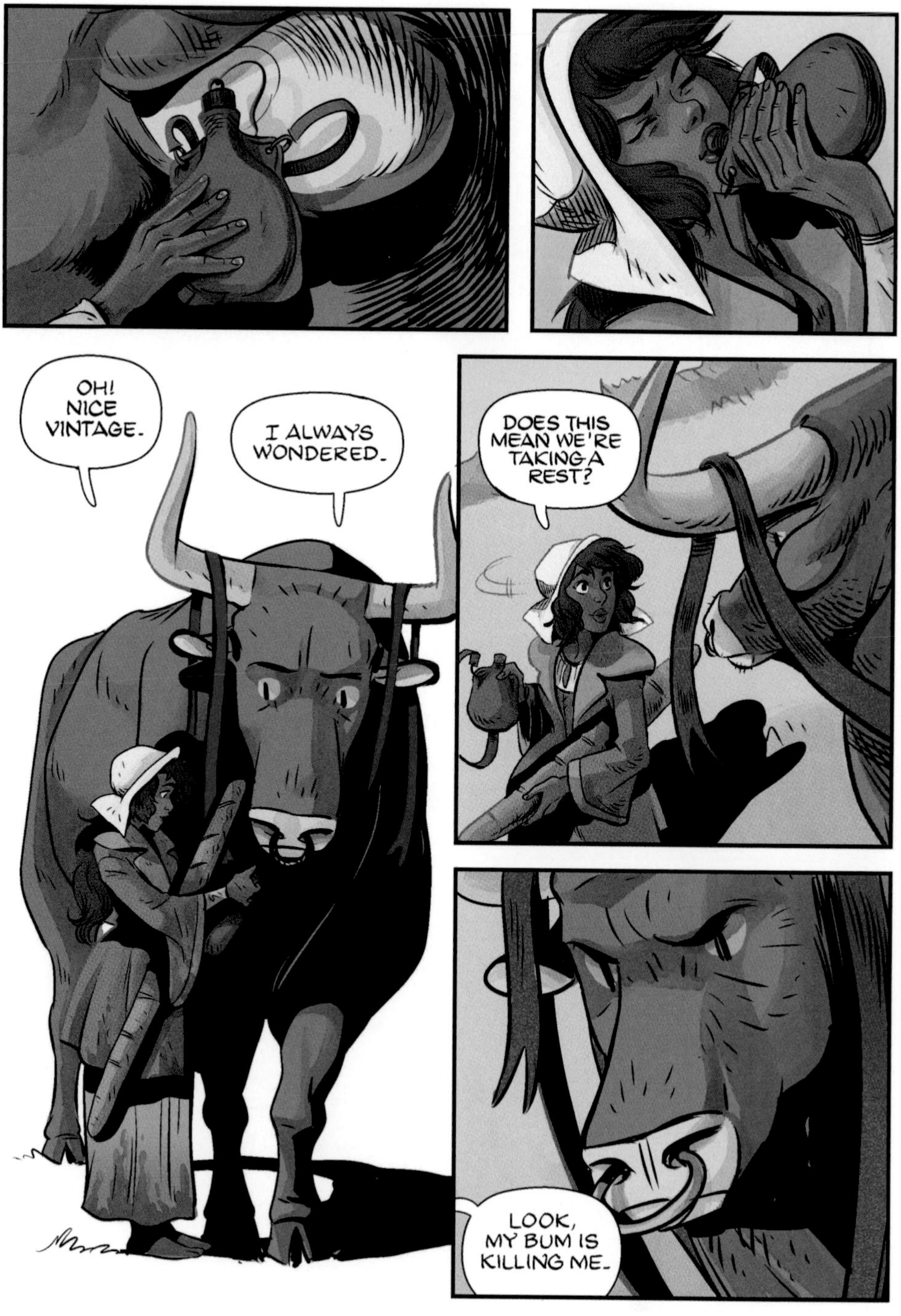
OH! NICE VINTAGE.
I ALWAYS WONDERED.
DOES THIS MEAN WE'RE TAKING A REST?
LOOK, MY BUM IS KILLING ME.

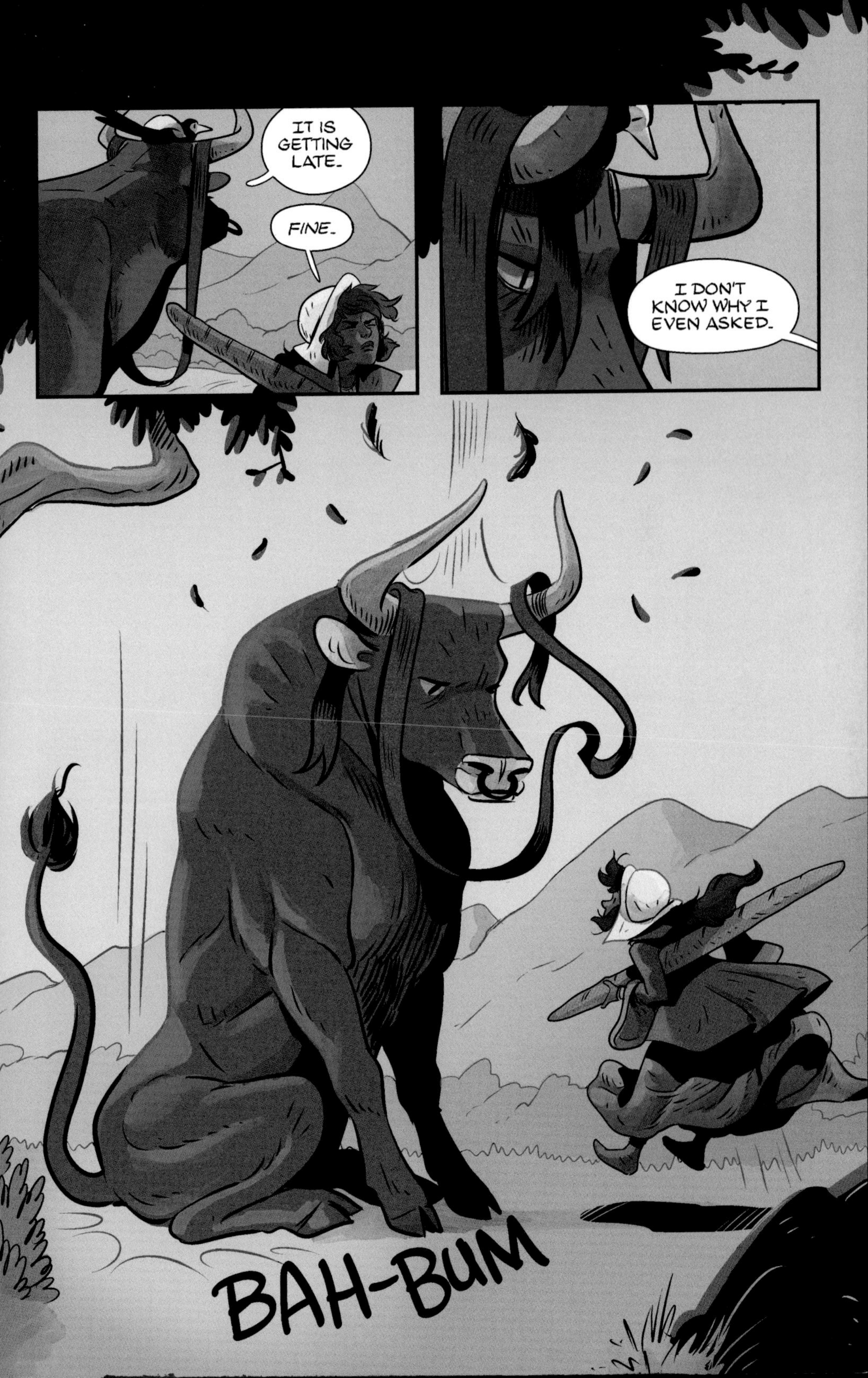
IT IS GETTING LATE.
FINE.
I DON'T KNOW WHY I EVEN ASKED.
BAH-BUM

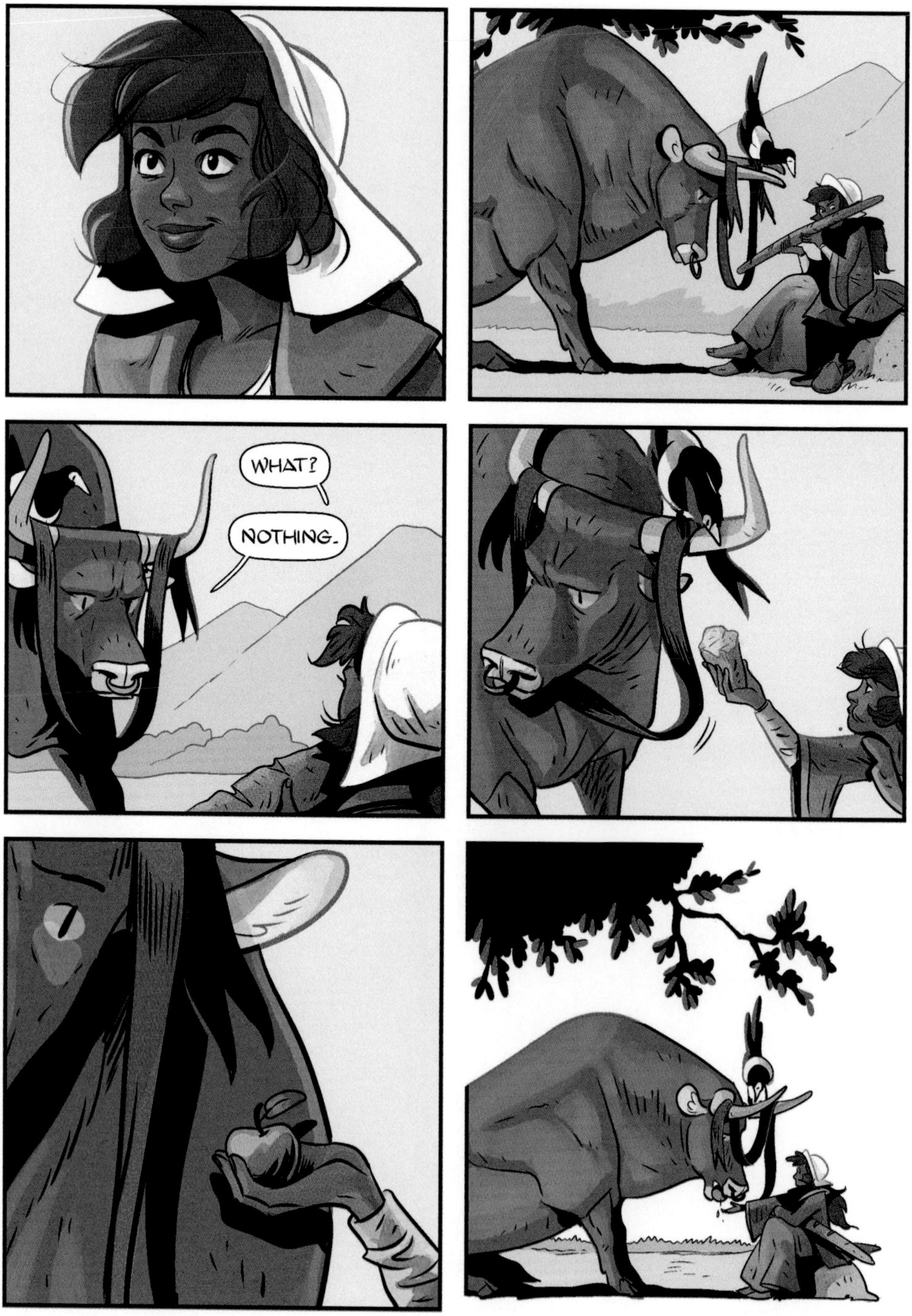
WHAT?
NOTHING.

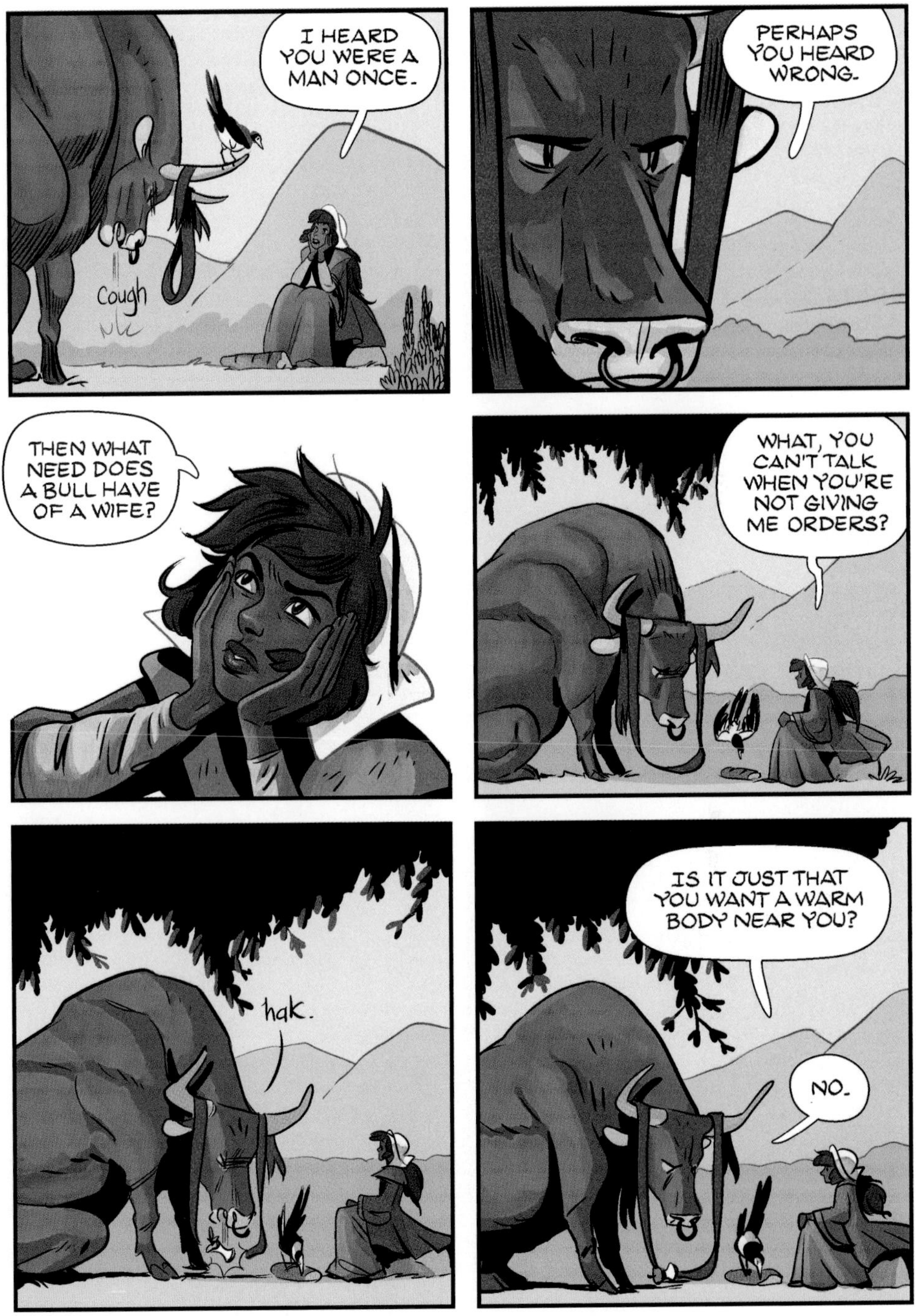
I HEARD YOU WERE A MAN ONCE.
Cough
PERHAPS YOU HEARD WRONG.
THEN WHAT NEED DOES A BULL HAVE OF A WIFE?
WHAT, YOU CAN'T TALK WHEN YOU'RE NOT GIVING ME ORDERS?
hak.
IS IT JUST THAT YOU WANT A WARM BODY NEAR YOU?
NO.

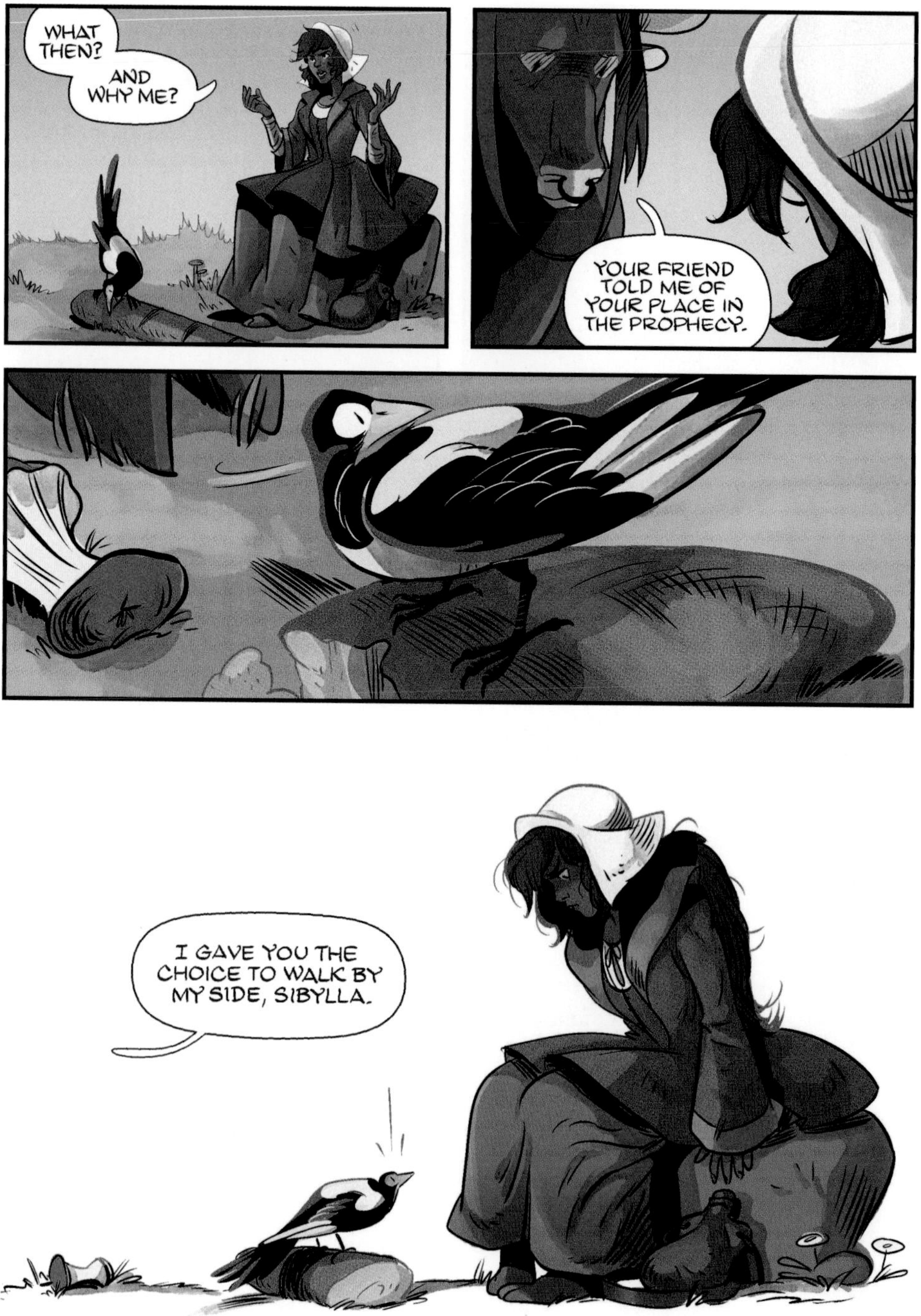
WHAT THEN?
AND WHY ME?
YOUR FRIEND TOLD ME OF YOUR PLACE IN THE PROPHECY.
I GAVE YOU THE CHOICE TO WALK BY MY SIDE, SIBYLLA.

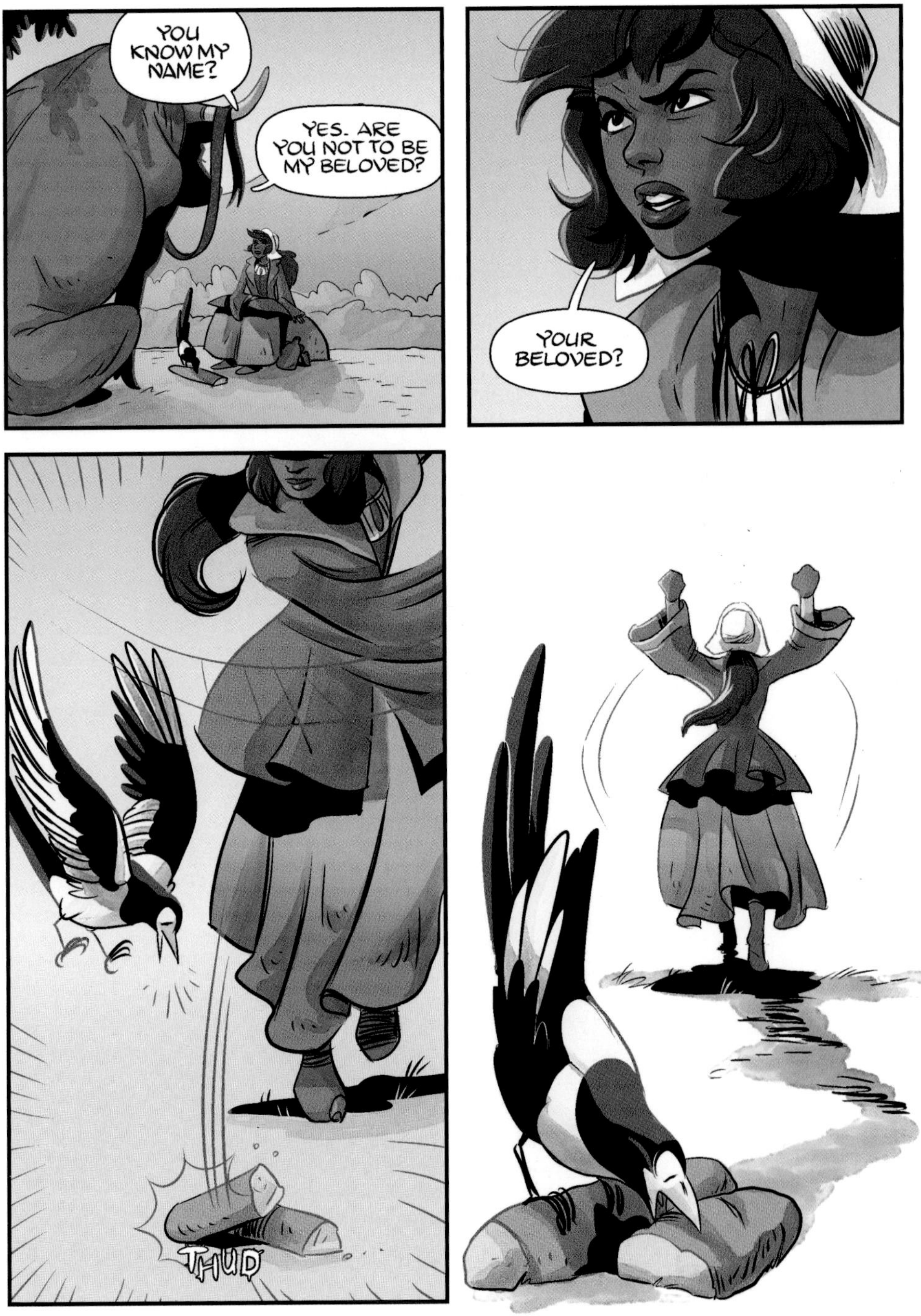
YOU KNOW MY NAME?
YES. ARE YOU NOT TO BE MY BELOVED?
YOUR BELOVED?
THUD

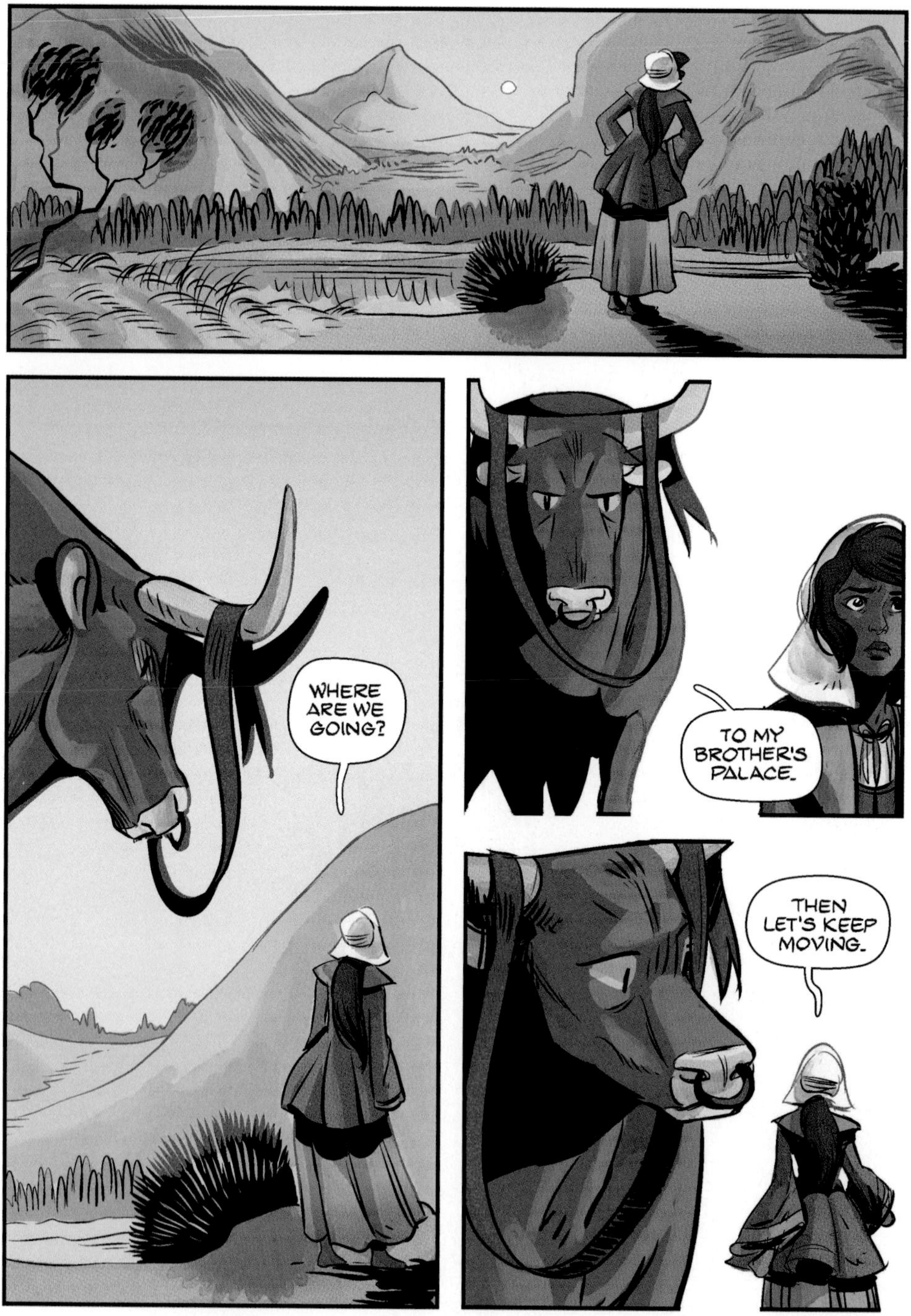
WHERE ARE WE GOING?
TO MY BROTHER'S PALACE.
THEN LET'S KEEP MOVING.

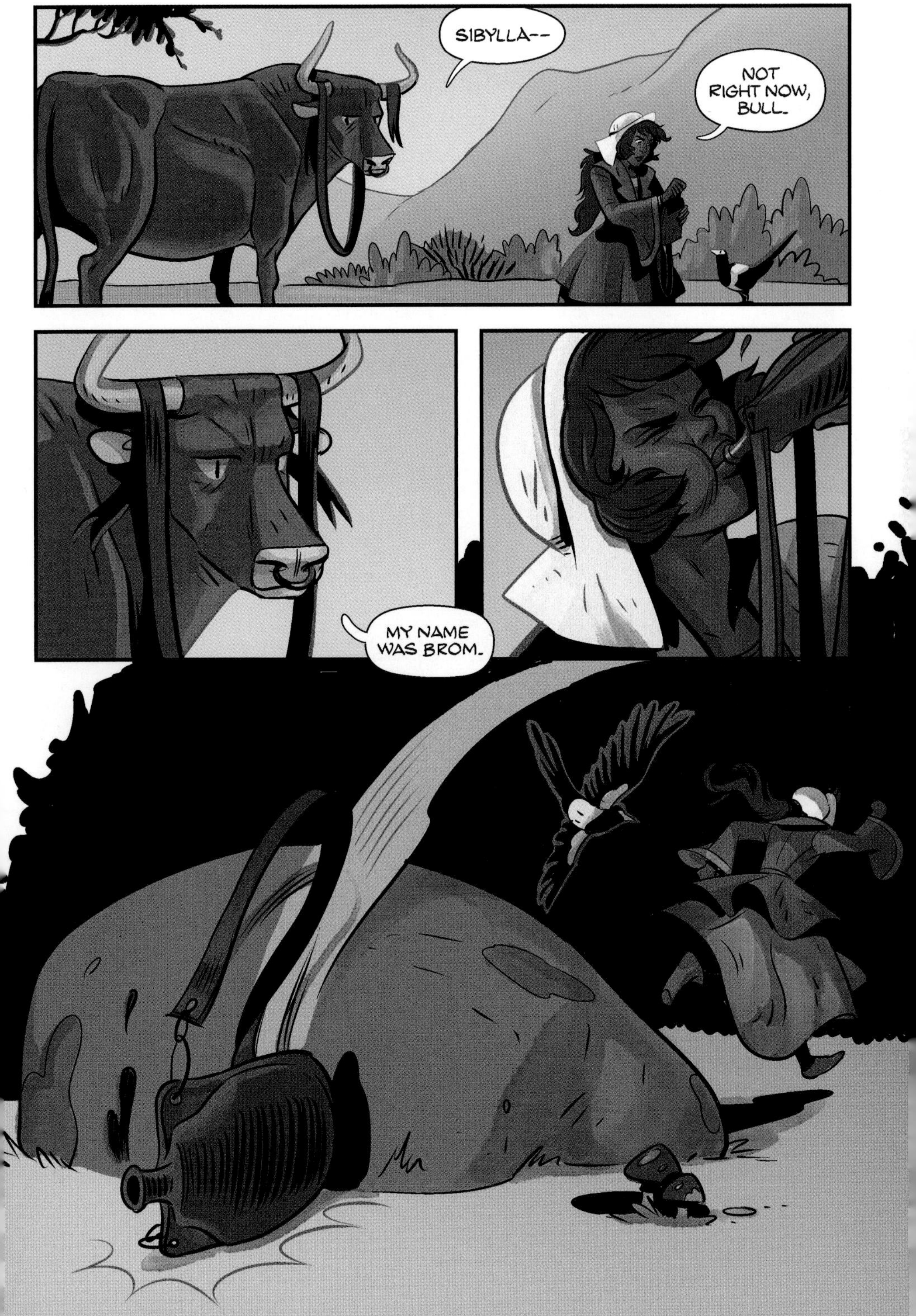
SIBYLLA--
NOT RIGHT NOW, BULL.
MY NAME WAS BROM.

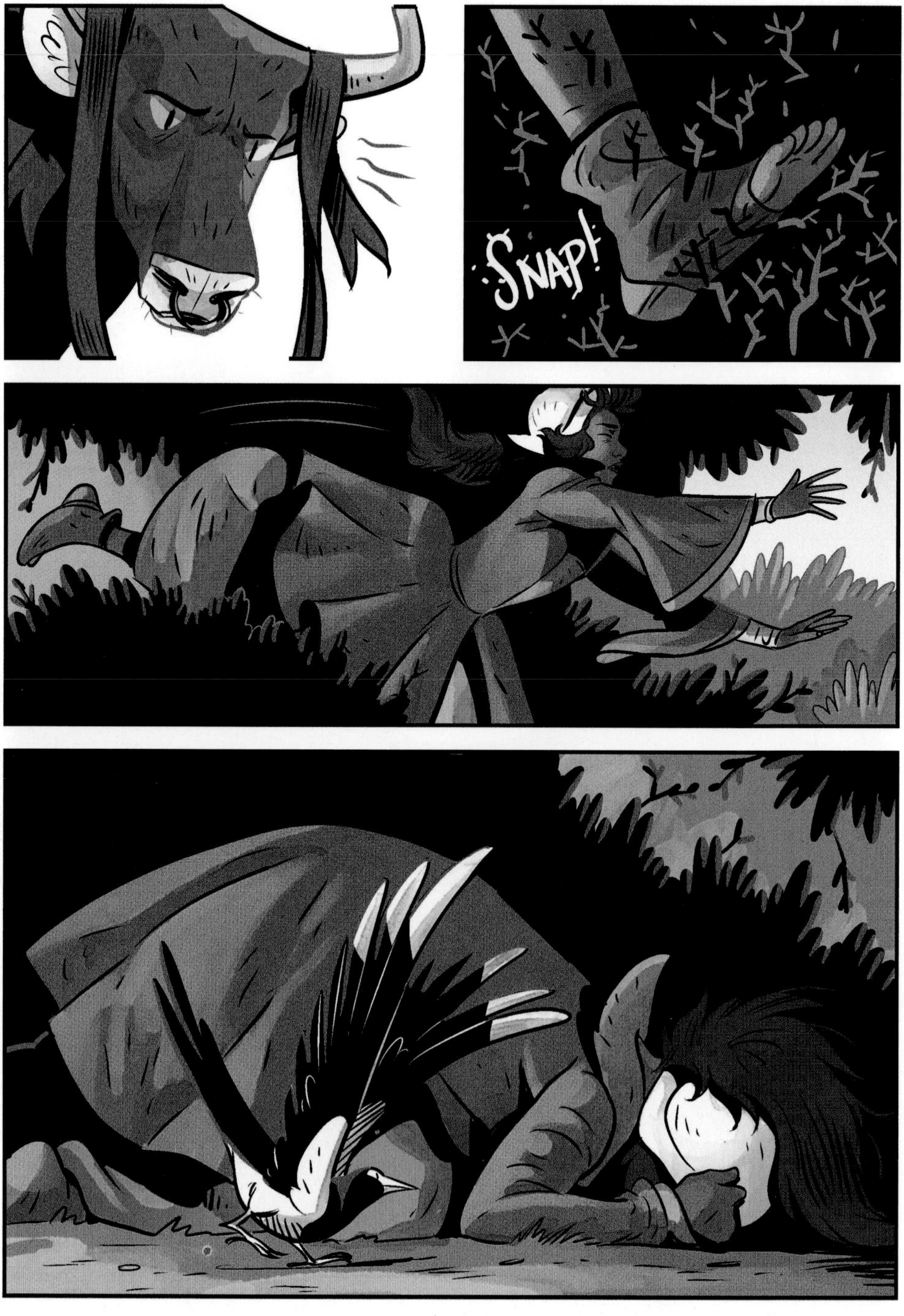
SNAP!

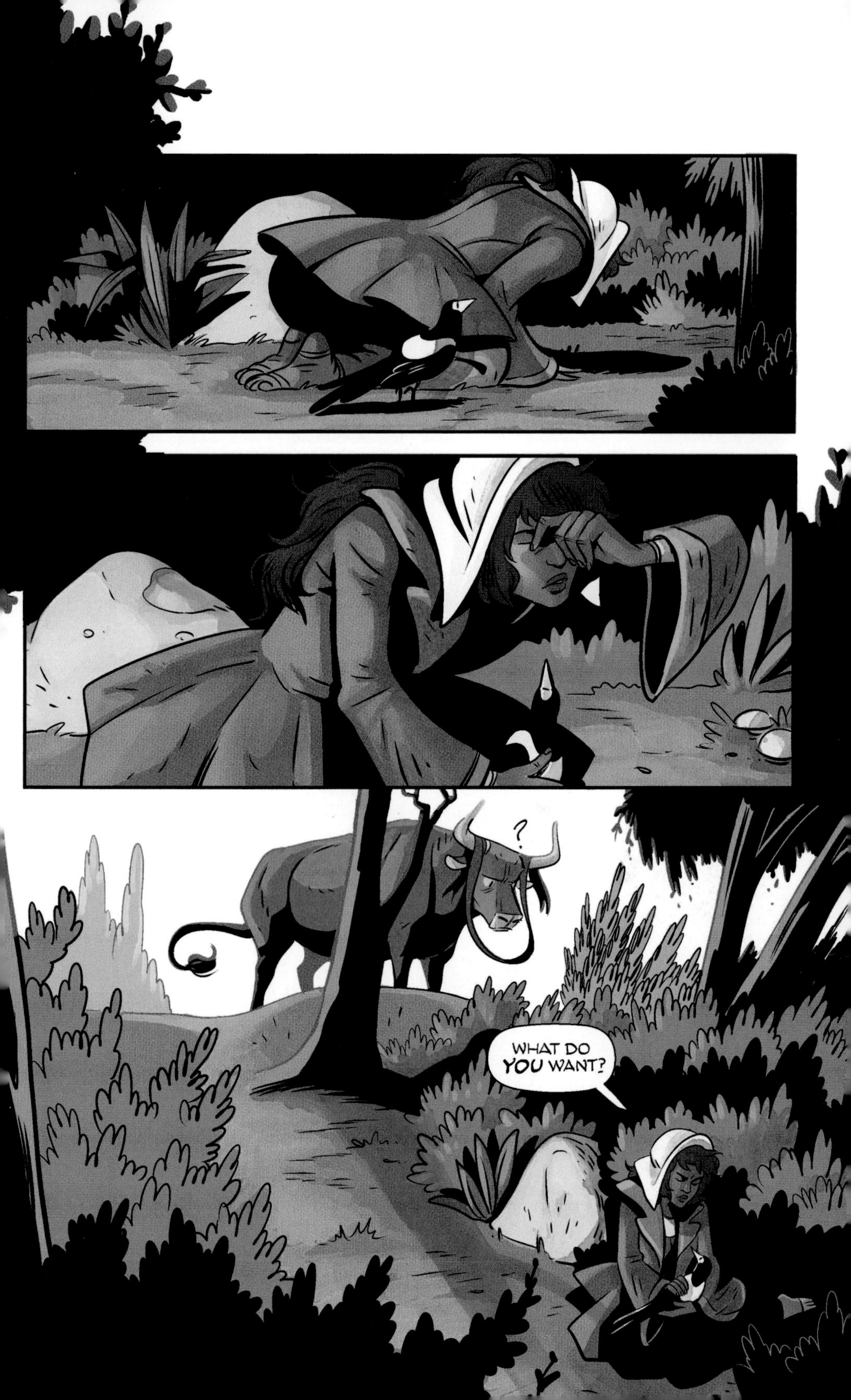
?
WHAT DO YOU WANT?

ARE YOU ALL RIGHT?

DANDY.

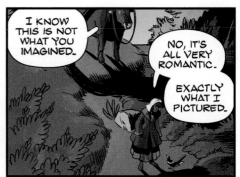

I KNOW THIS IS NOT WHAT YOU IMAGINED.

NO, IT'S ALL VERY ROMANTIC.

EXACTLY WHAT I PICTURED.

IT IS HARD TO BE A MAN WHEN YOU'VE BEEN A BEAST FOR SO LONG.

I NEVER KNEW THERE WAS A DIFFERENCE.

PLEASE, I'M TRYING TO APOLOGIZE.

NO, YOU'RE TRYING TO MAKE EXCUSES.

IF YOU WOULD JUST LET ME SPEAK--

MORE *WORDS!* I AM TIRED OF WORDS!

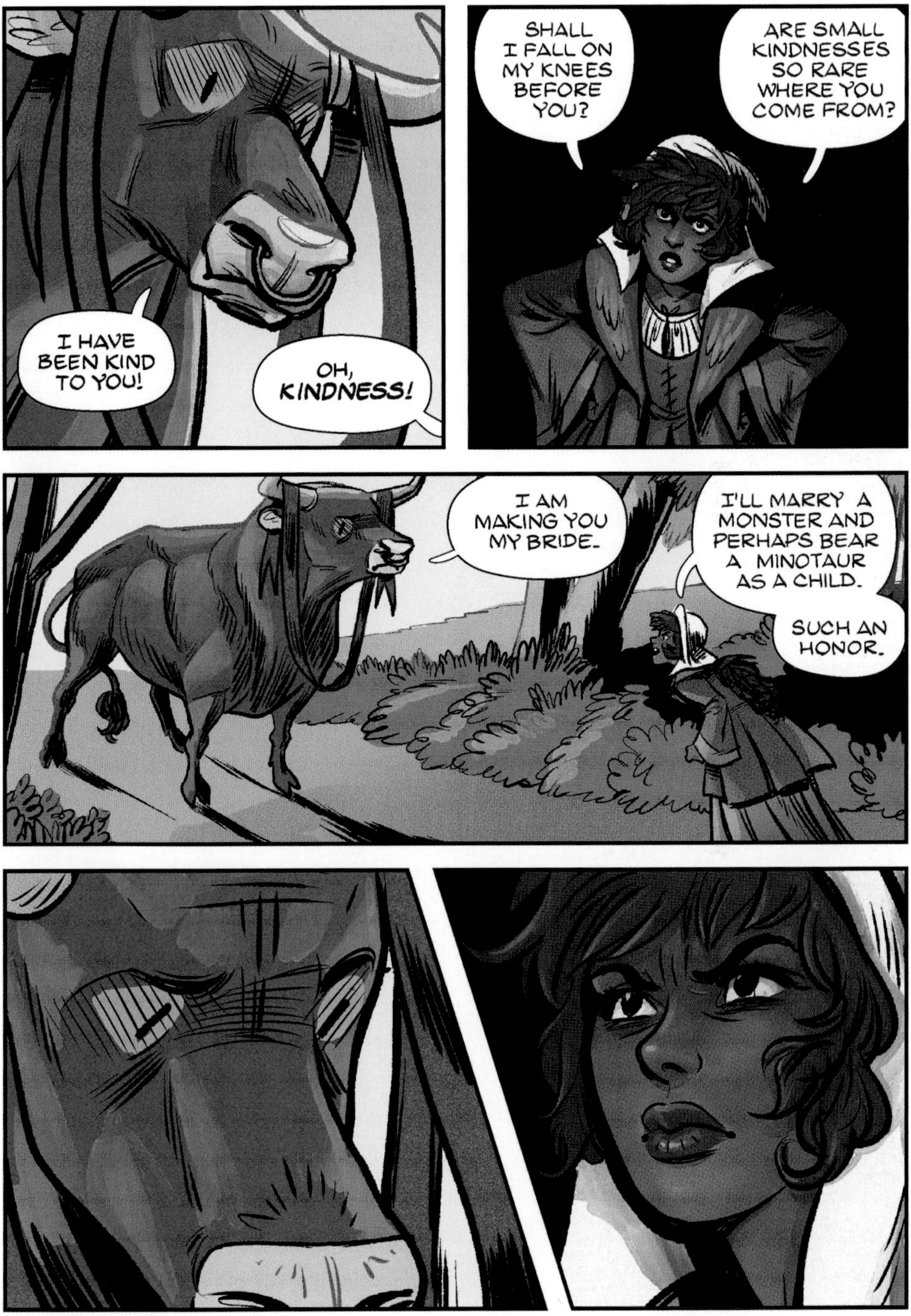
I HAVE BEEN KIND TO YOU!
OH, KINDNESS!
SHALL I FALL ON MY KNEES BEFORE YOU?
ARE SMALL KINDNESSES SO RARE WHERE YOU COME FROM?
I AM MAKING YOU MY BRIDE.
I'LL MARRY A MONSTER AND PERHAPS BEAR A MINOTAUR AS A CHILD.
SUCH AN HONOR.

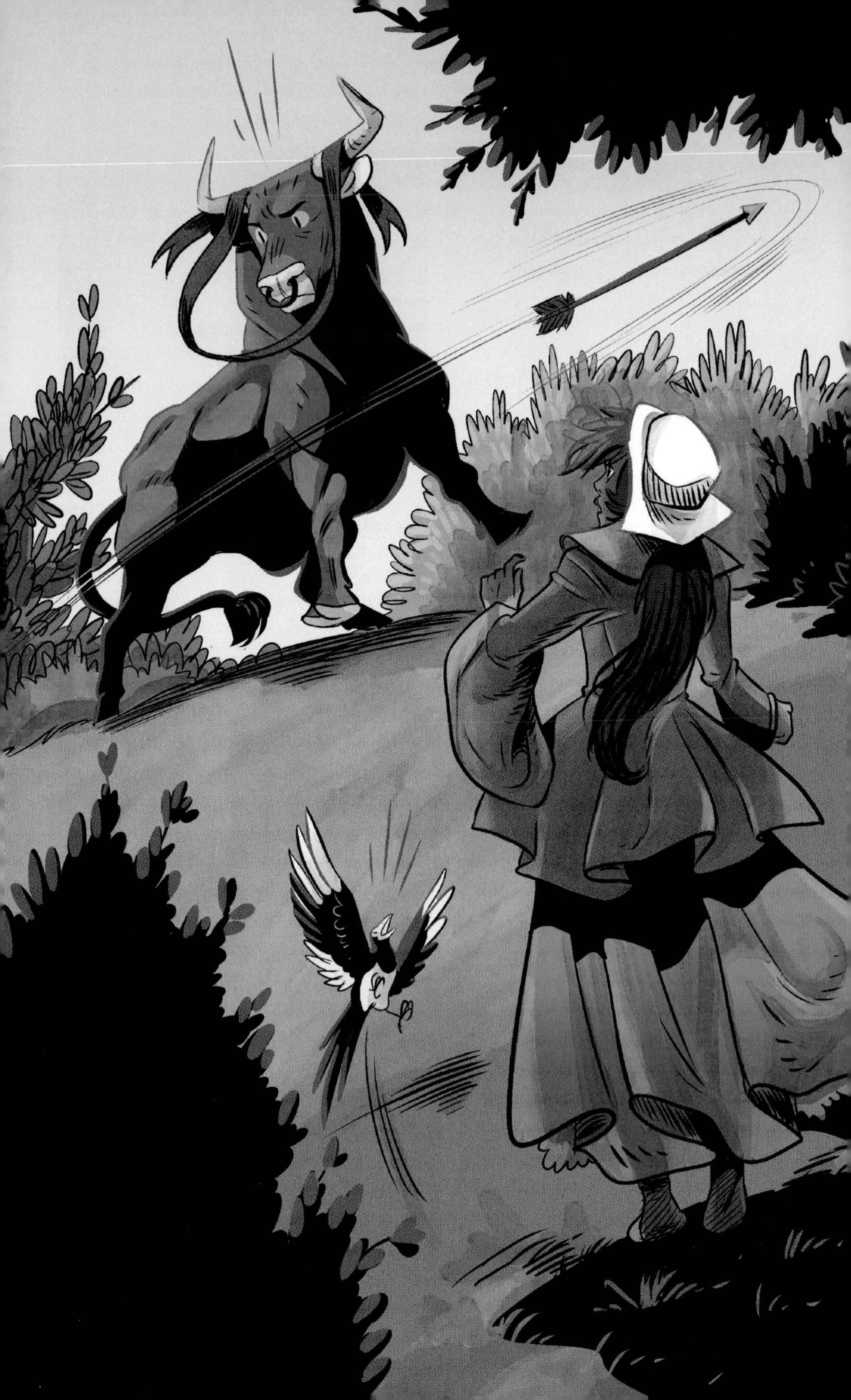

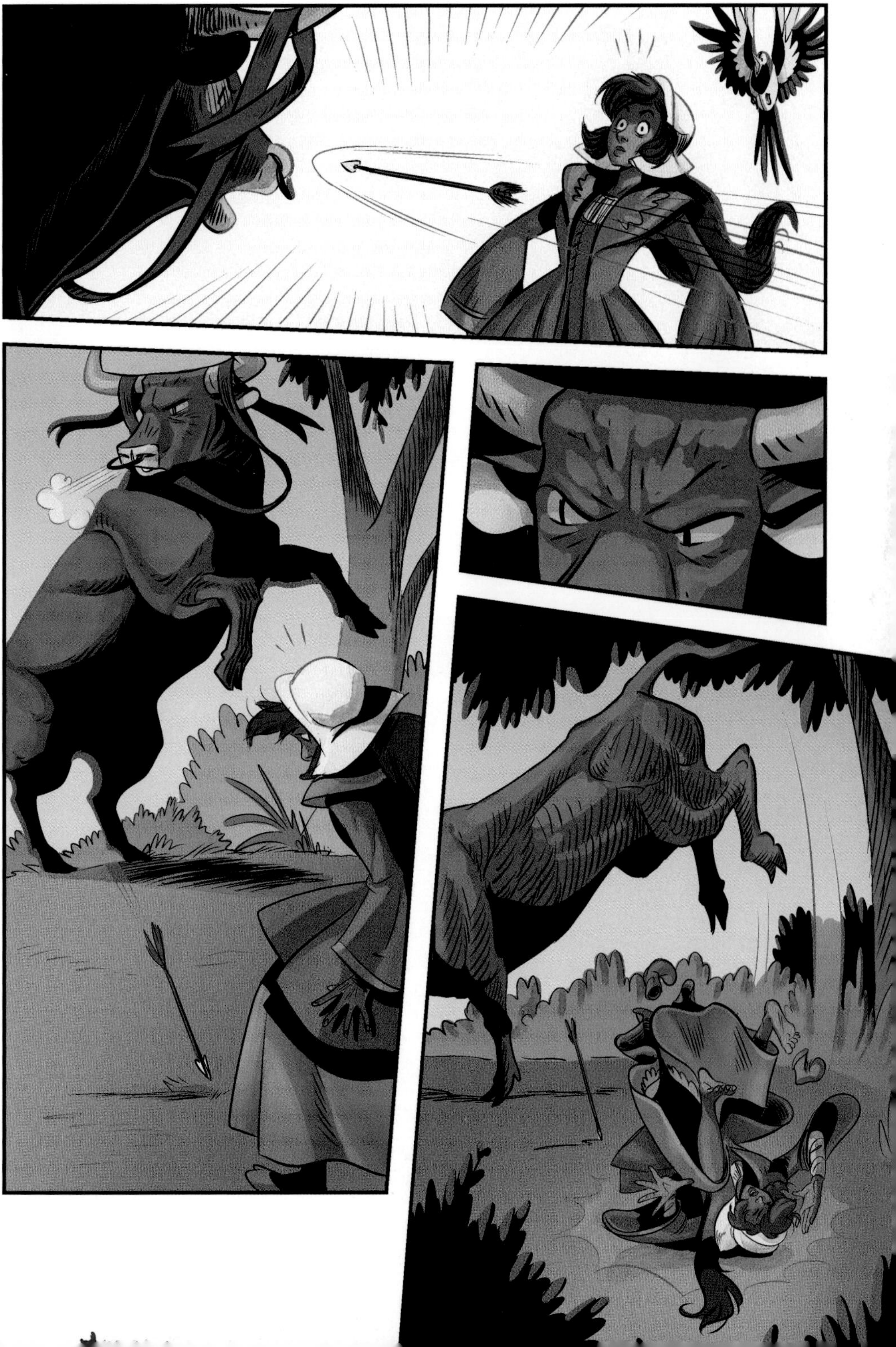

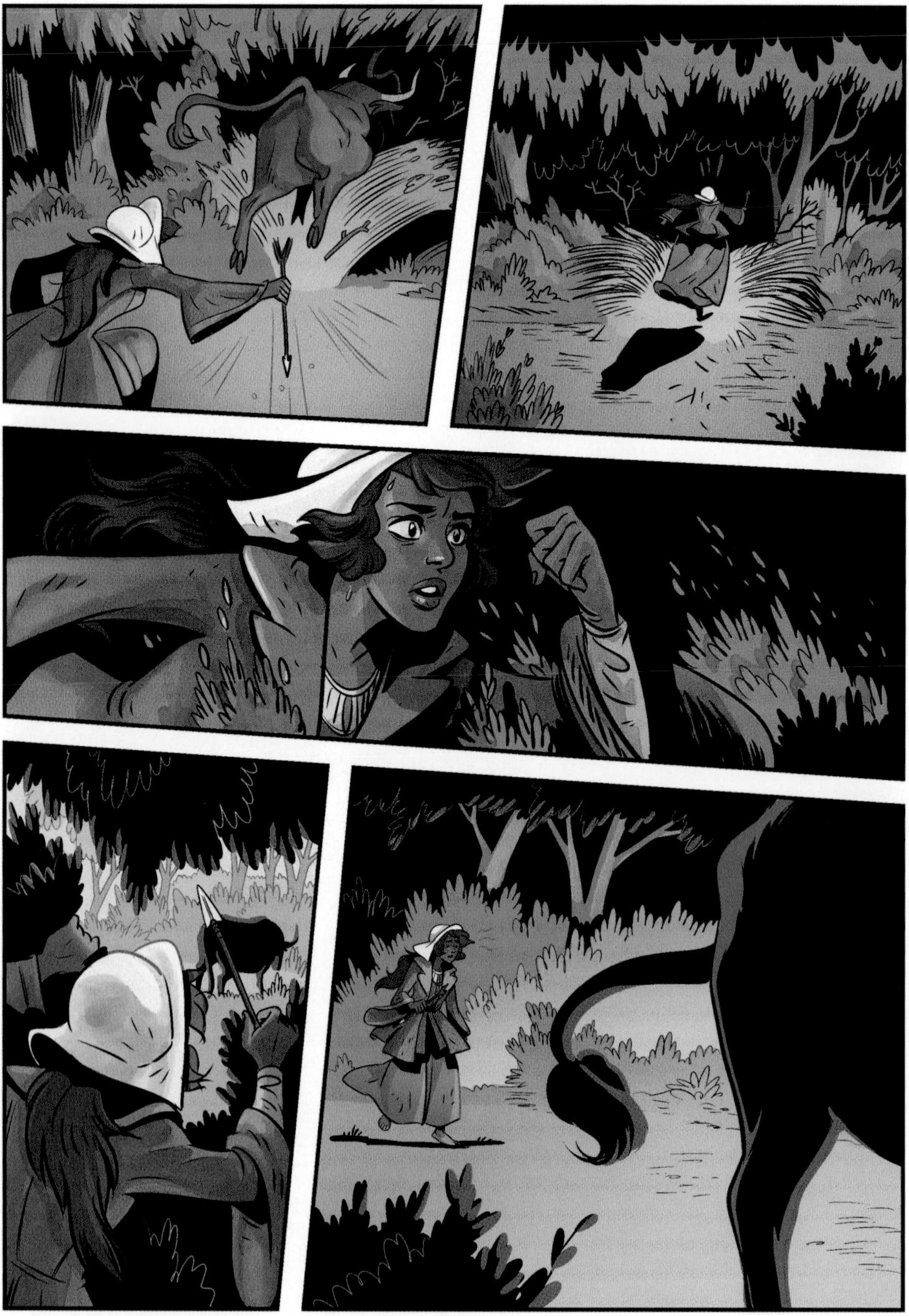

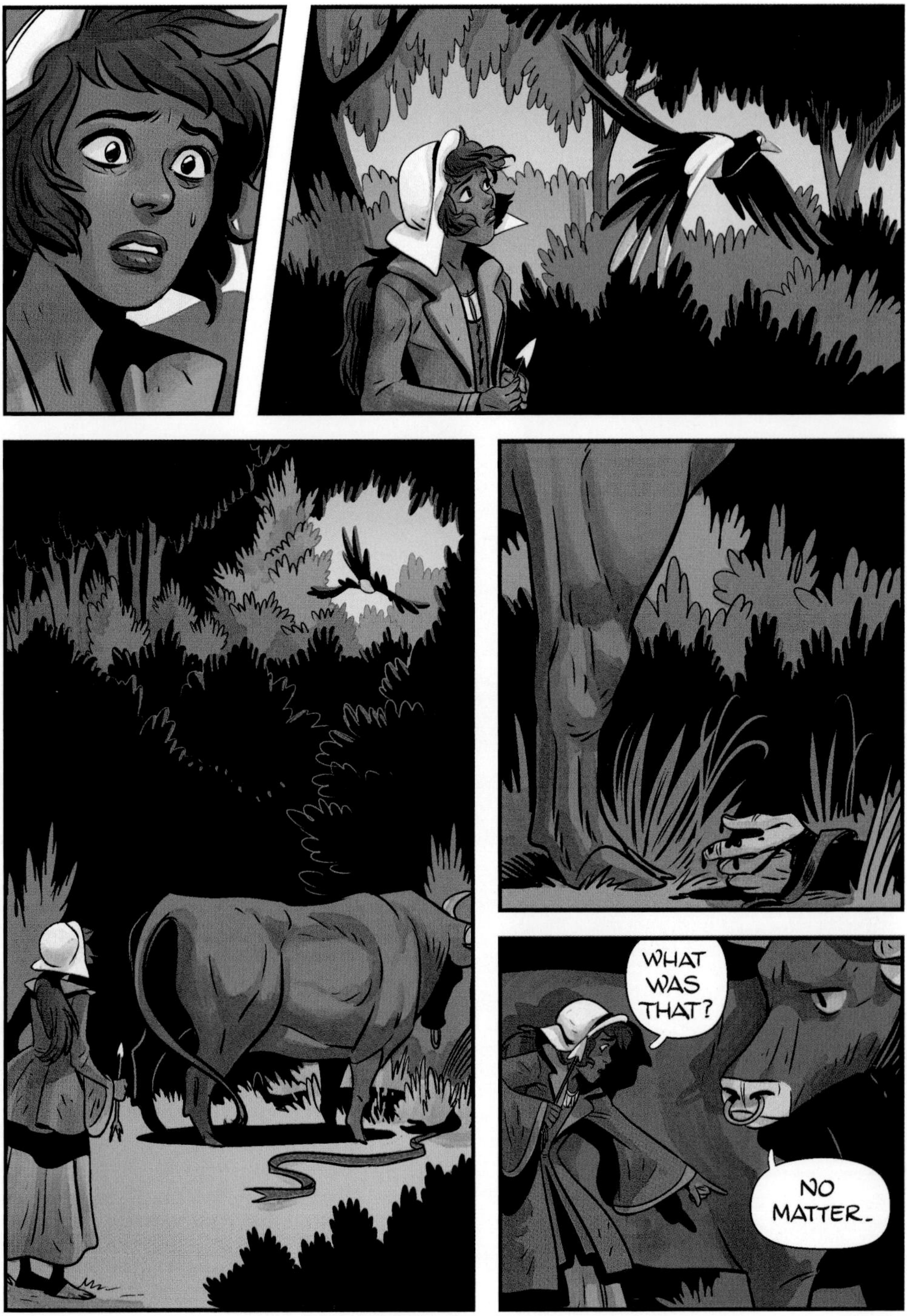
WHAT WAS THAT?
NO MATTER.

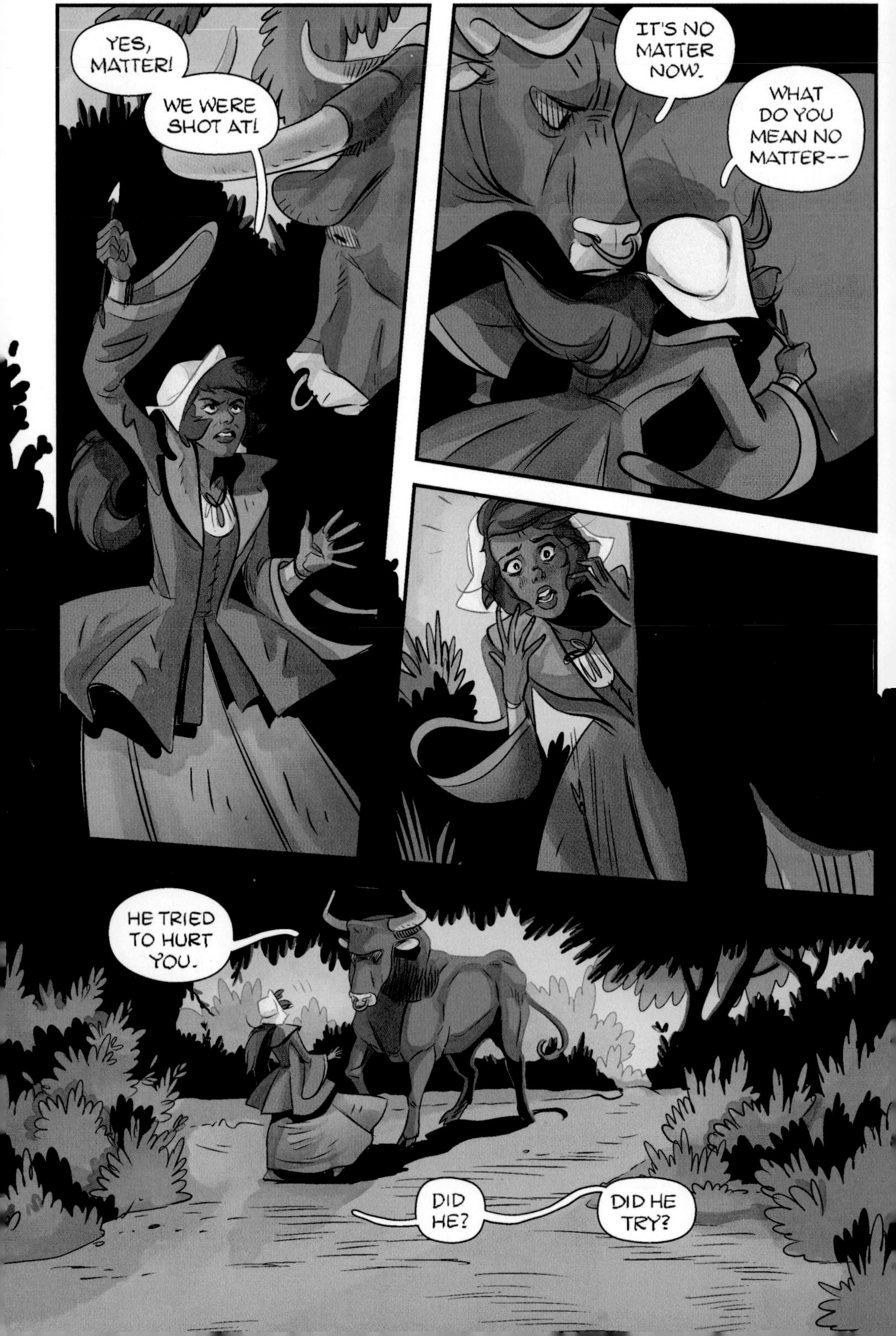
YES, MATTER!
WE WERE SHOT AT!
IT'S NO MATTER NOW.
WHAT DO YOU MEAN NO MATTER--
HE TRIED TO HURT YOU.
DID HE?
DID HE TRY?

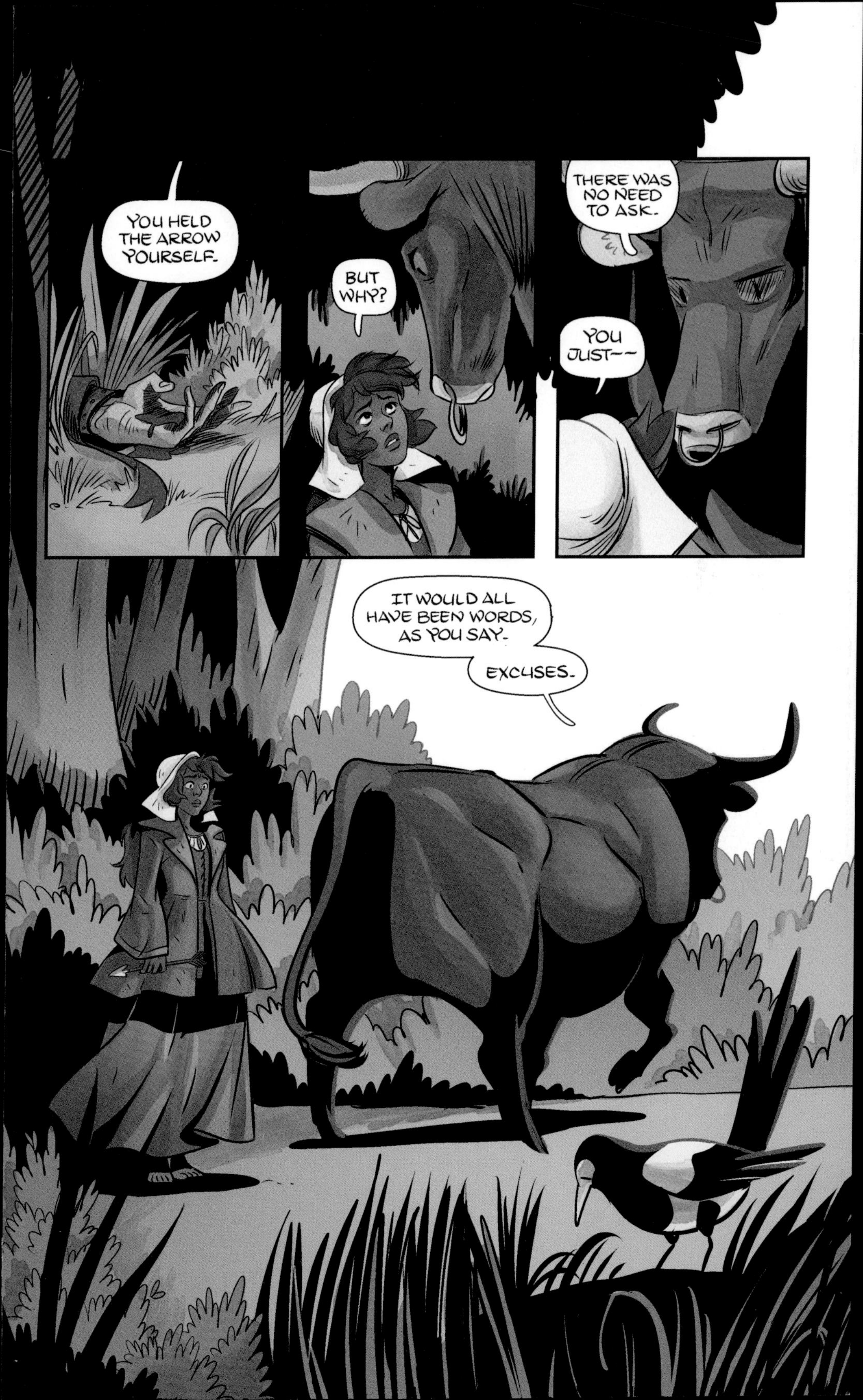
YOU HELD THE ARROW YOURSELF.
BUT WHY?
THERE WAS NO NEED TO ASK.
YOU JUST--
IT WOULD ALL HAVE BEEN WORDS, AS YOU SAY.
EXCUSES.

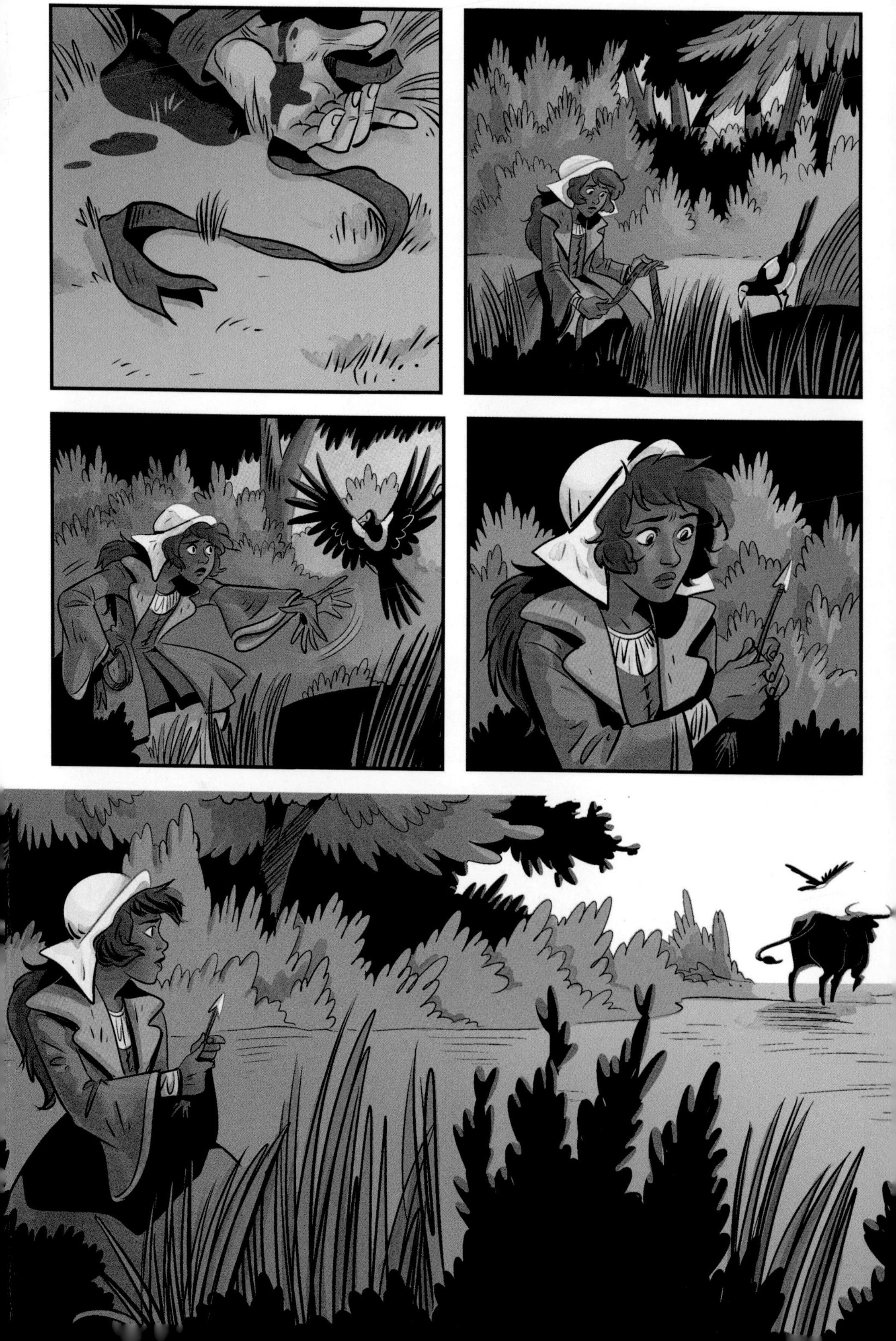

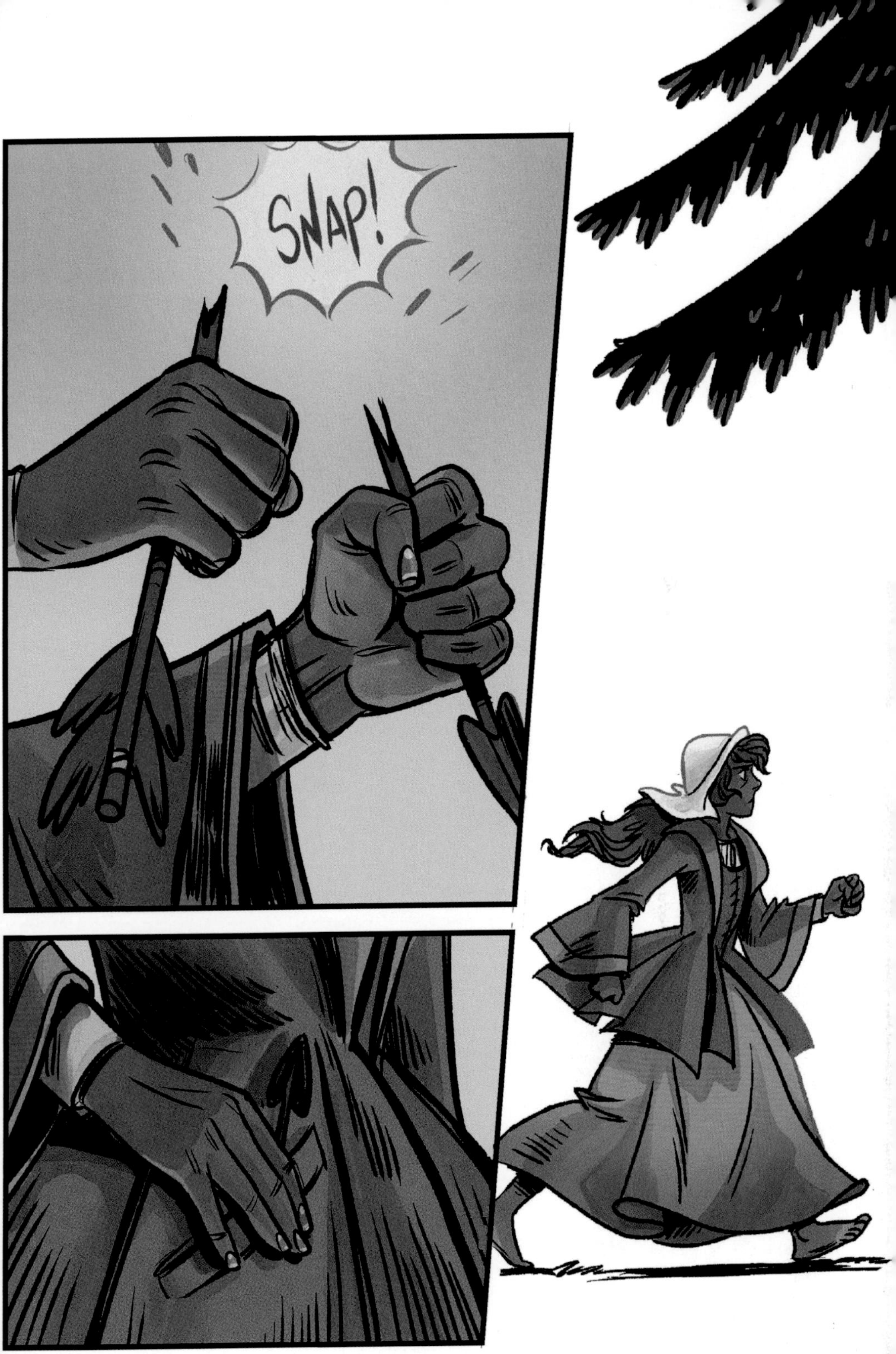
SNAP!

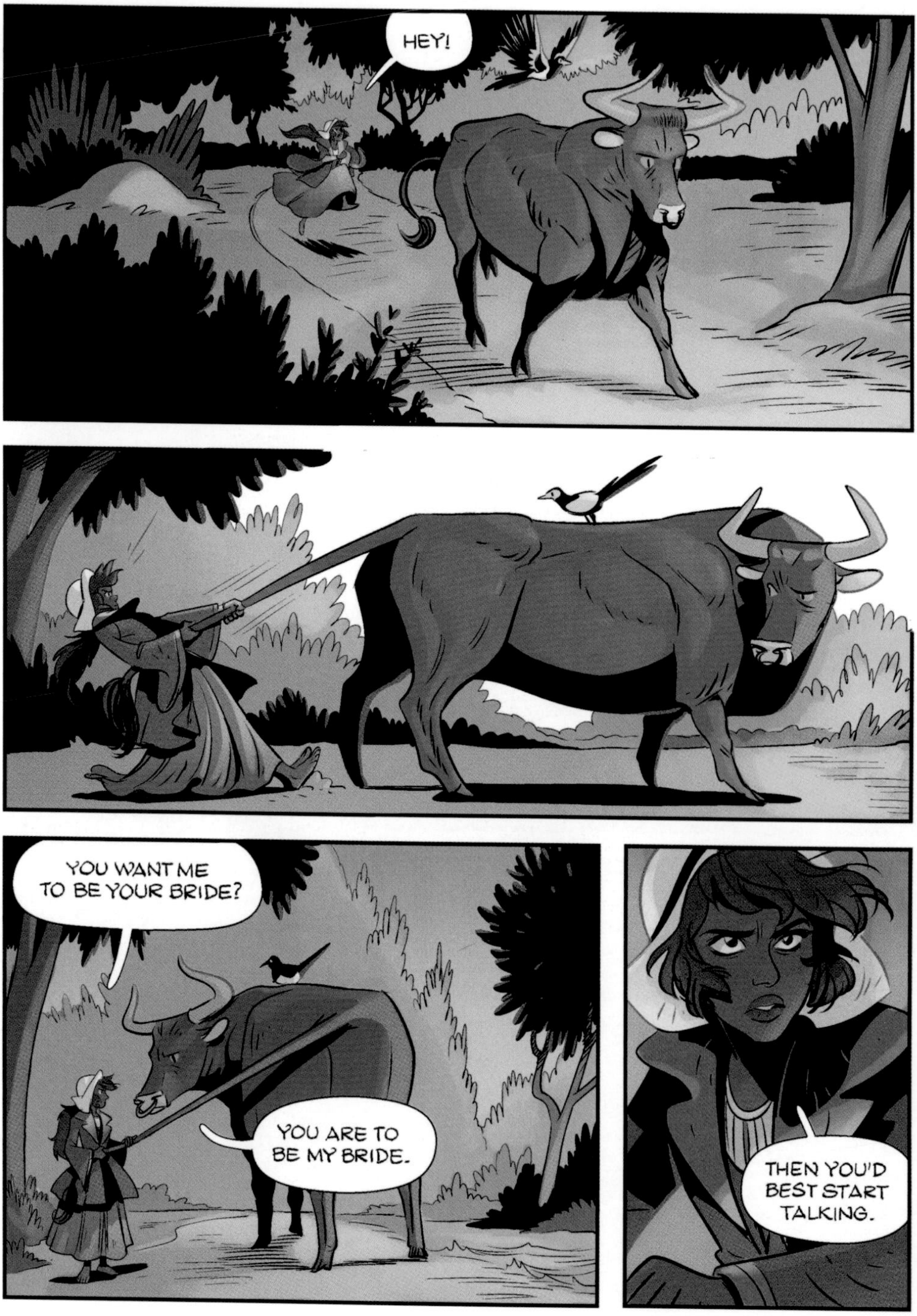
HEY!
YOU WANT ME TO BE YOUR BRIDE?
YOU ARE TO BE MY BRIDE.
THEN YOU'D BEST START TALKING.

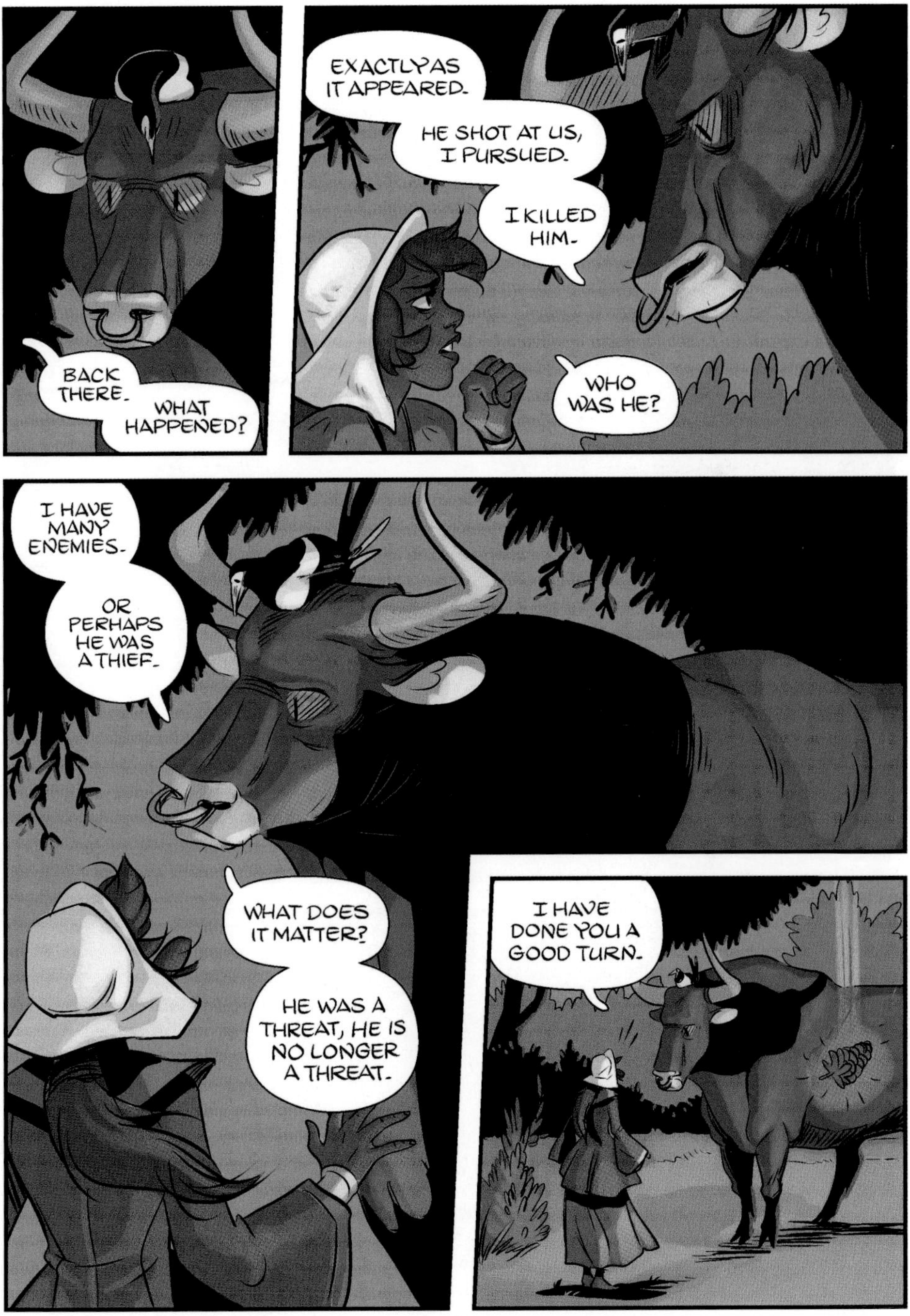
BACK THERE.
WHAT HAPPENED?
EXACTLY AS IT APPEARED.
HE SHOT AT US, I PURSUED.
I KILLED HIM.
WHO WAS HE?
I HAVE MANY ENEMIES.
OR PERHAPS HE WAS A THIEF.
WHAT DOES IT MATTER?
HE WAS A THREAT, HE IS NO LONGER A THREAT.
I HAVE DONE YOU A GOOD TURN.

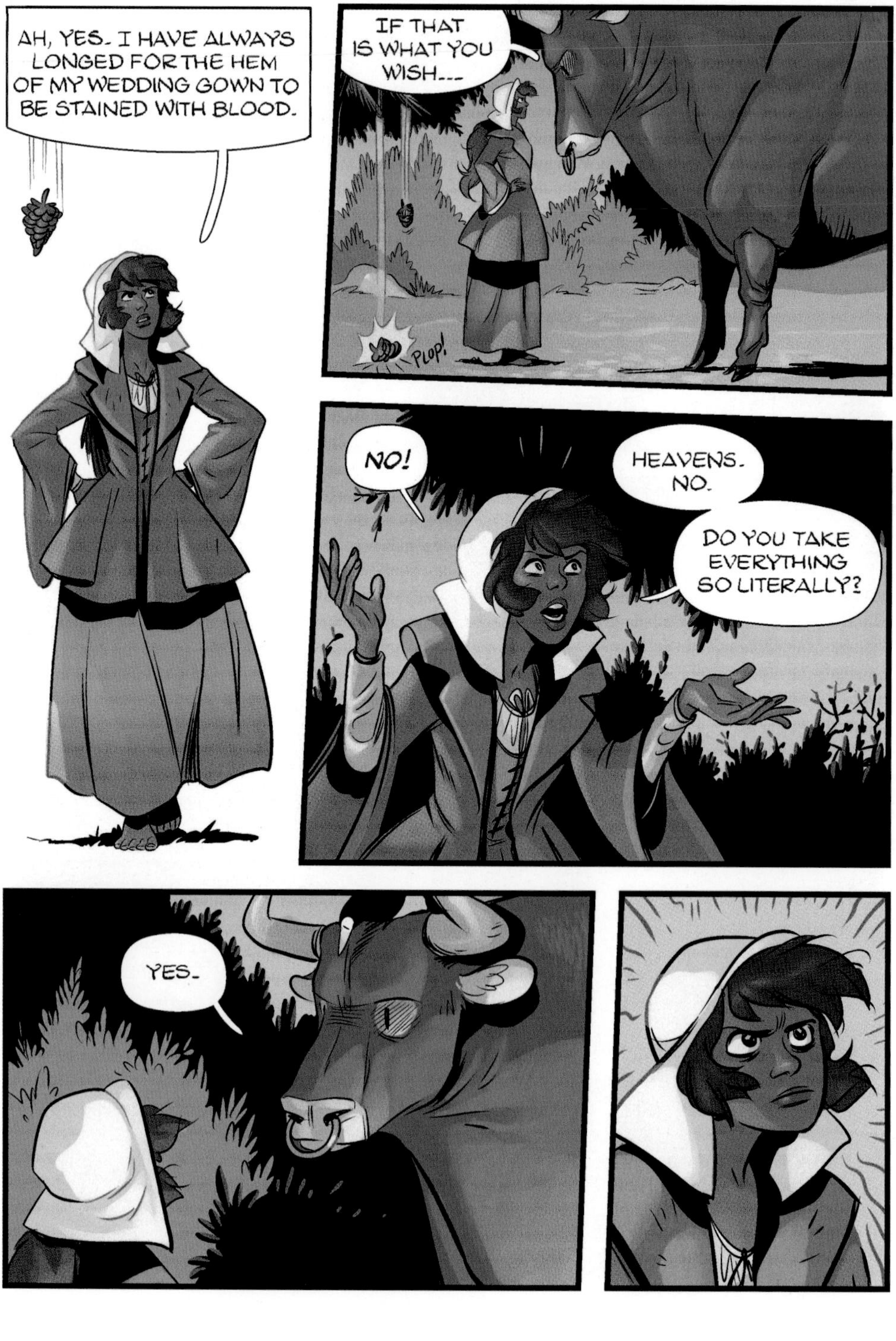
AH, YES. I HAVE ALWAYS LONGED FOR THE HEM OF MY WEDDING GOWN TO BE STAINED WITH BLOOD.
IF THAT IS WHAT YOU WISH...
PLOP!
NO!
HEAVENS. NO.
DO YOU TAKE EVERYTHING SO LITERALLY?
YES.

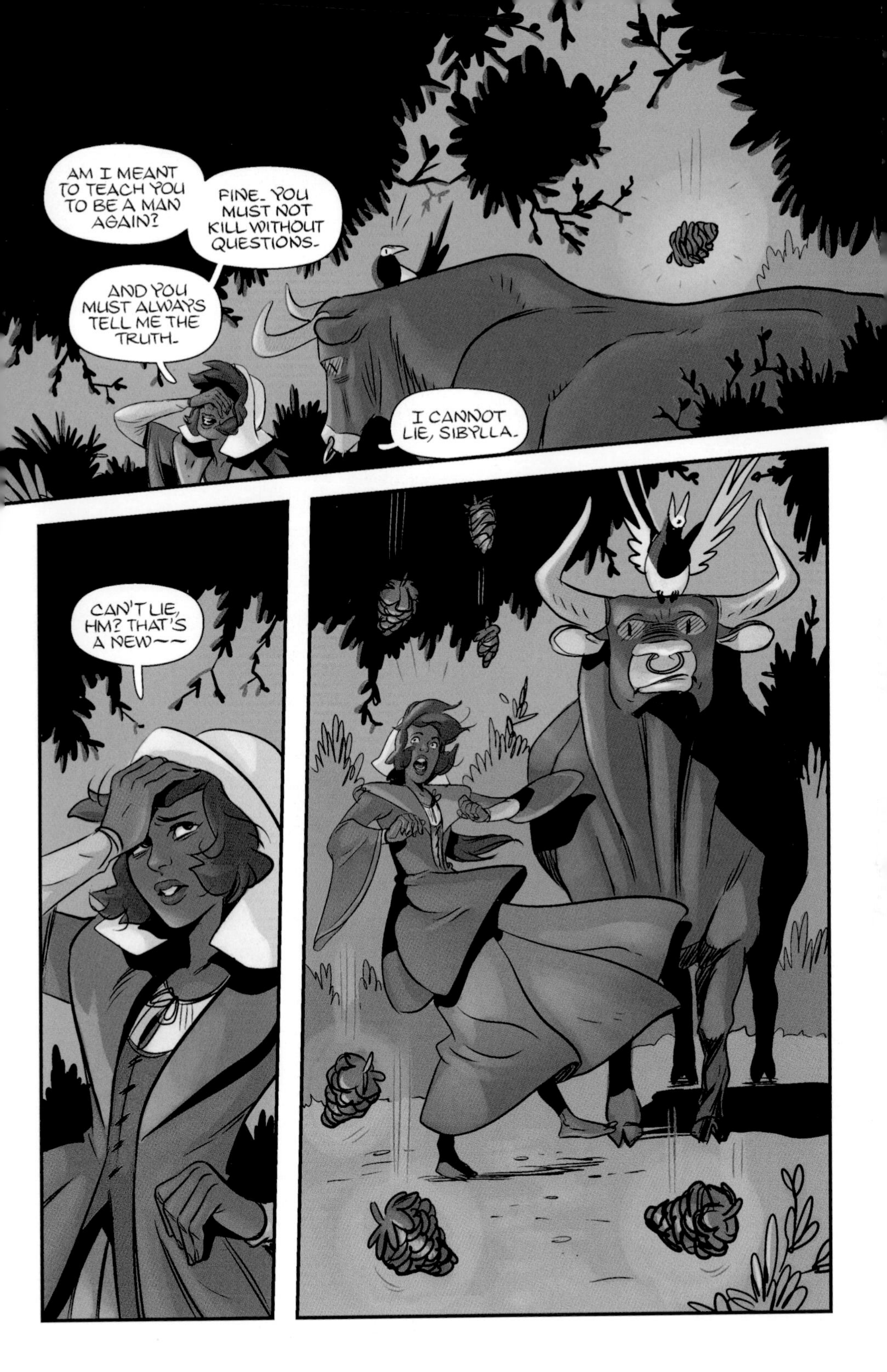
AM I MEANT TO TEACH YOU TO BE A MAN AGAIN?
FINE. YOU MUST NOT KILL WITHOUT QUESTIONS.
AND YOU MUST ALWAYS TELL ME THE TRUTH.
I CANNOT LIE, SIBYLLA.
CAN'T LIE, HM? THAT'S A NEW~~

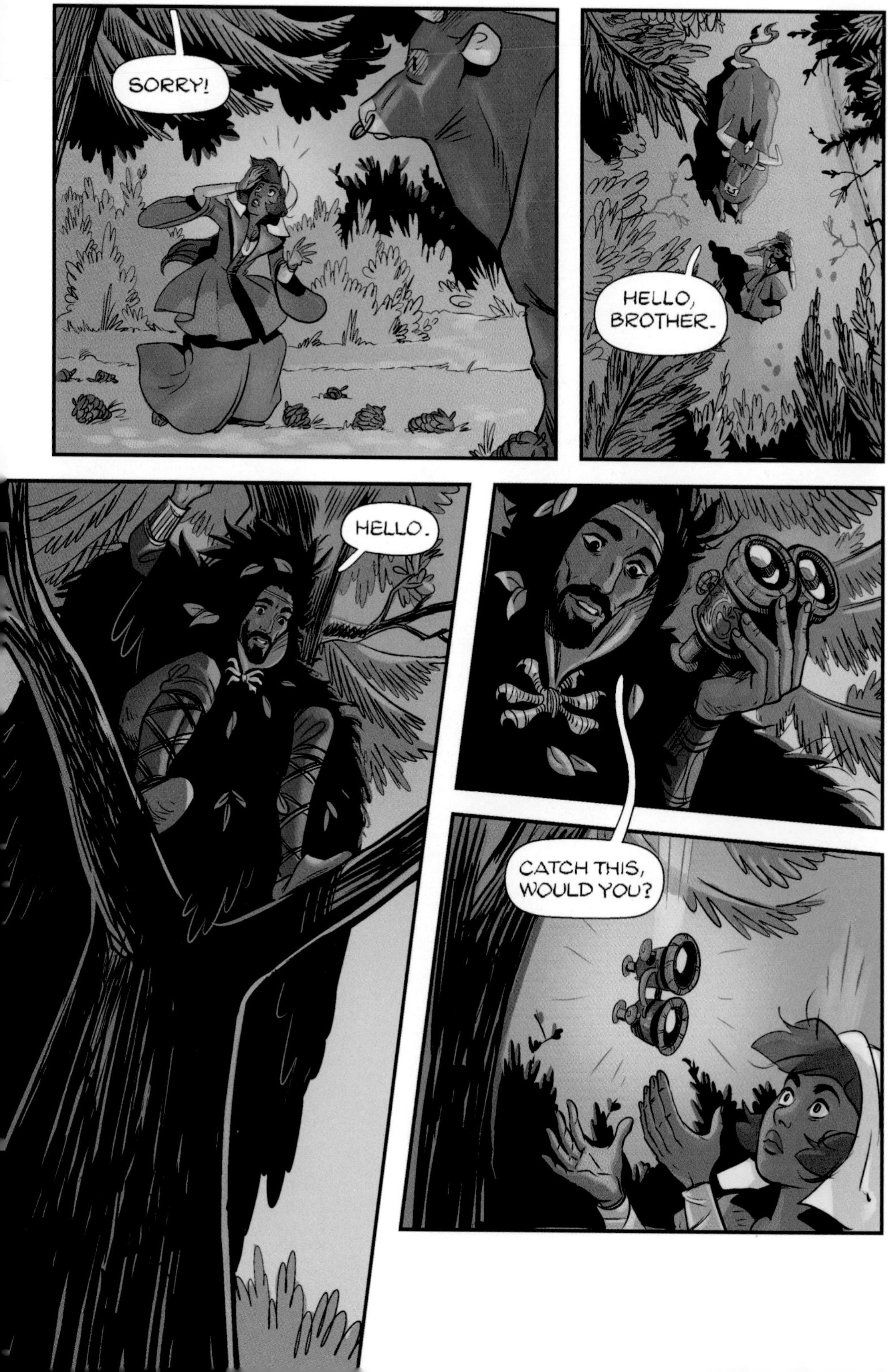
SORRY!
HELLO, BROTHER.
HELLO.
CATCH THIS, WOULD YOU?

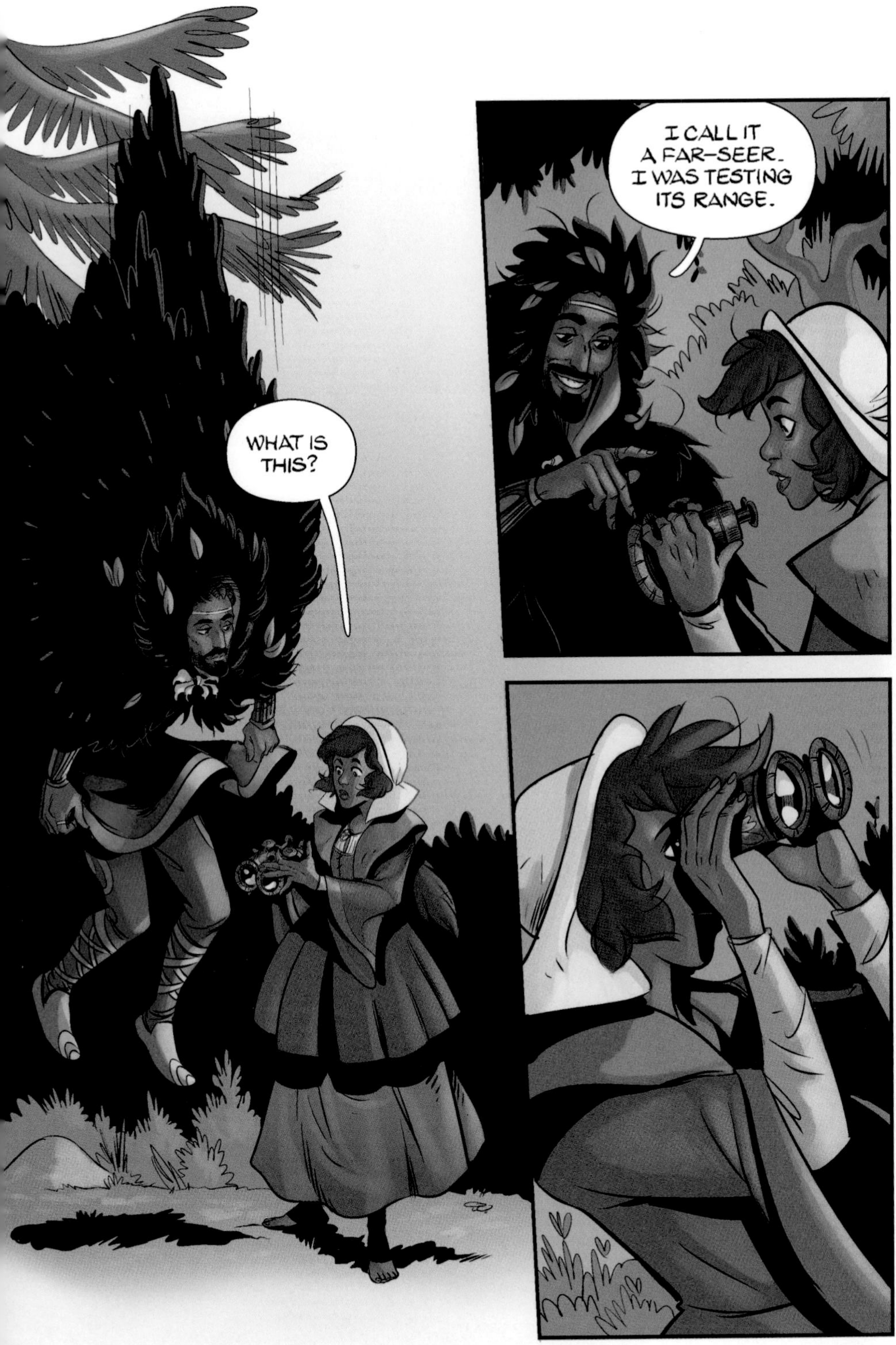
WHAT IS THIS?
I CALL IT A FAR-SEER. I WAS TESTING ITS RANGE.

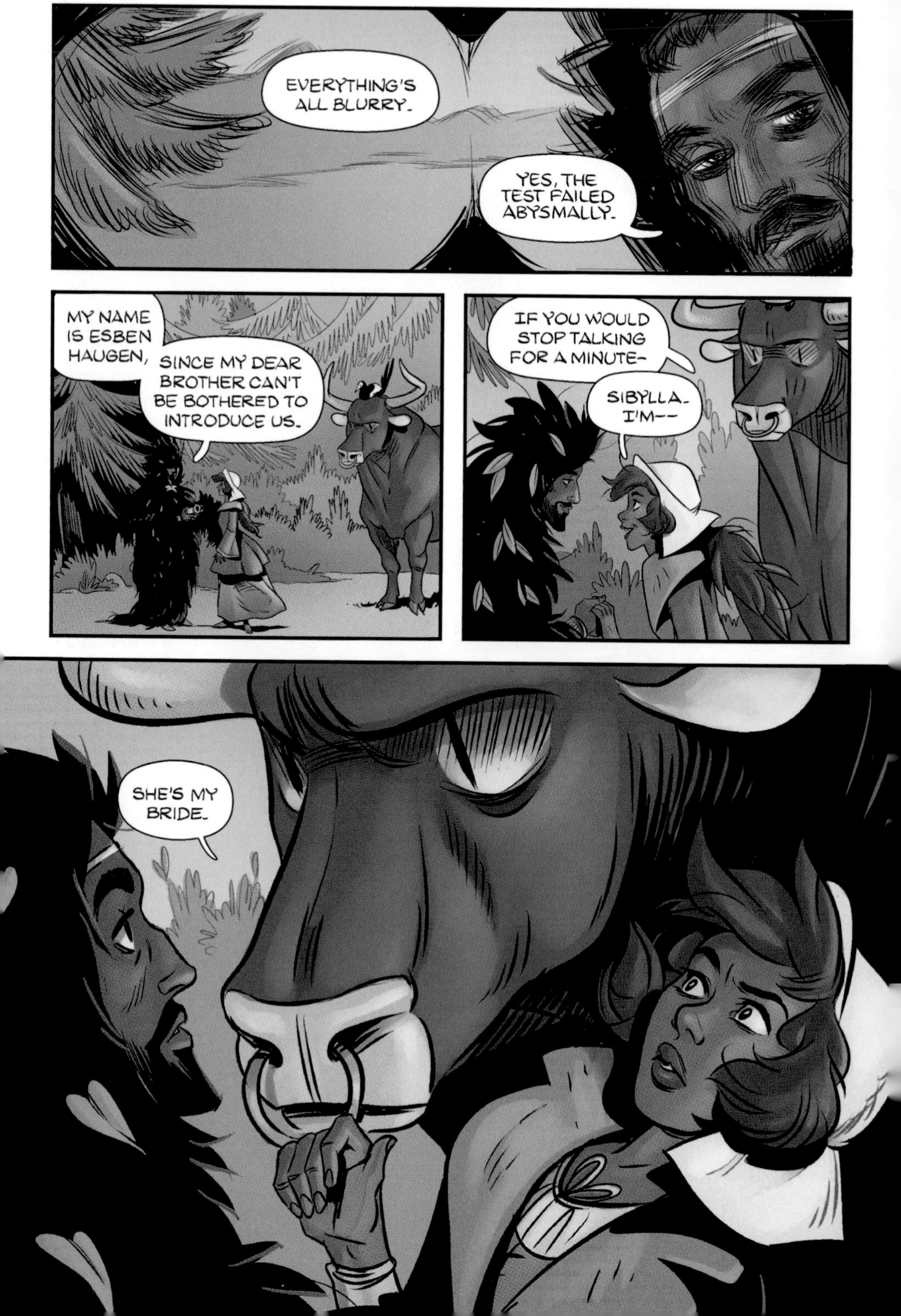
EVERYTHING'S ALL BLURRY.
YES, THE TEST FAILED ABYSMALLY.
MY NAME IS ESBEN HAUGEN,
SINCE MY DEAR BROTHER CAN'T BE BOTHERED TO INTRODUCE US.
IF YOU WOULD STOP TALKING FOR A MINUTE-
SIBYLLA. I'M--
SHE'S MY BRIDE.

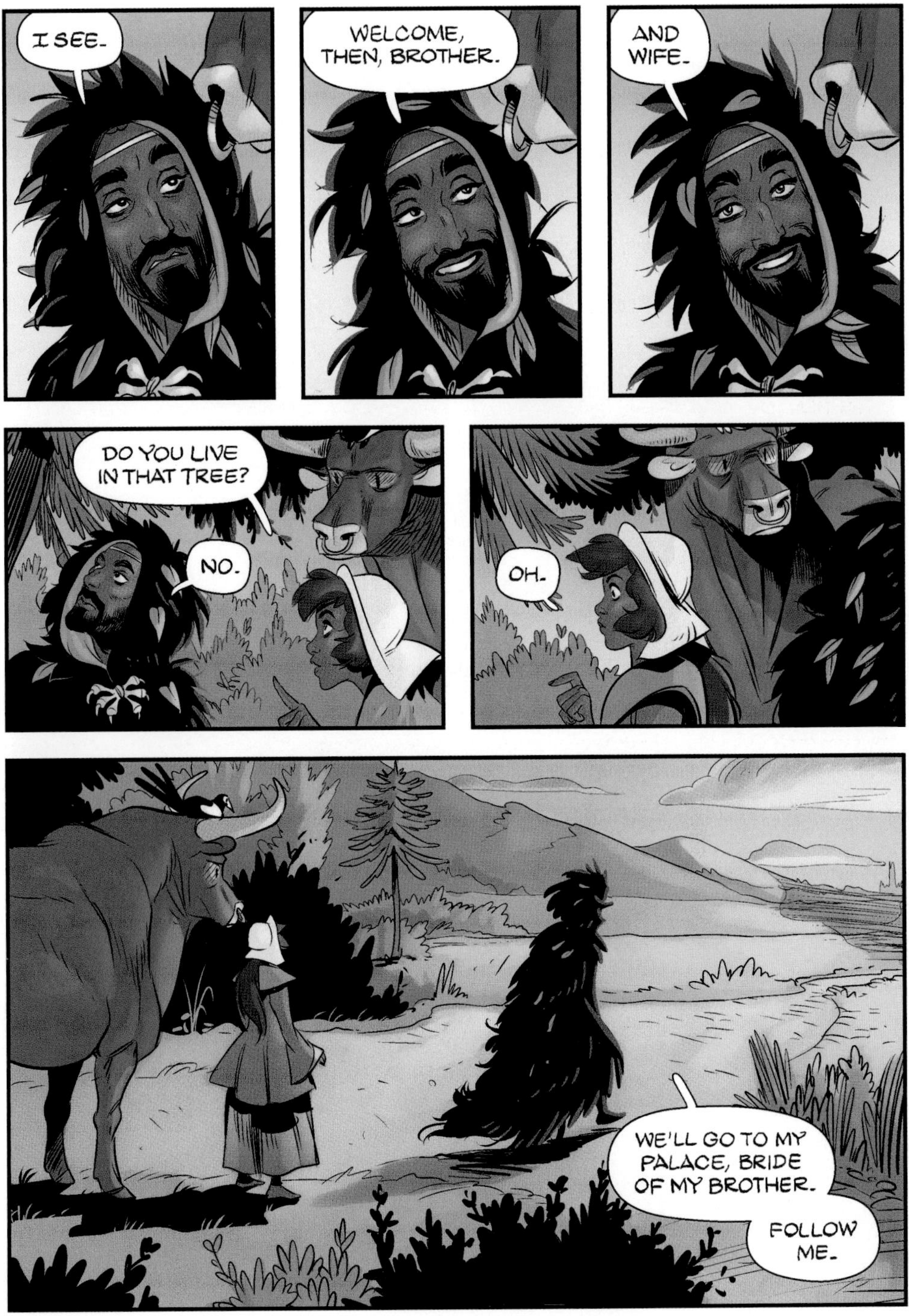
I SEE.
WELCOME, THEN, BROTHER.
AND WIFE.
DO YOU LIVE IN THAT TREE?
NO.
OH.
WE'LL GO TO MY PALACE, BRIDE OF MY BROTHER.
FOLLOW ME.

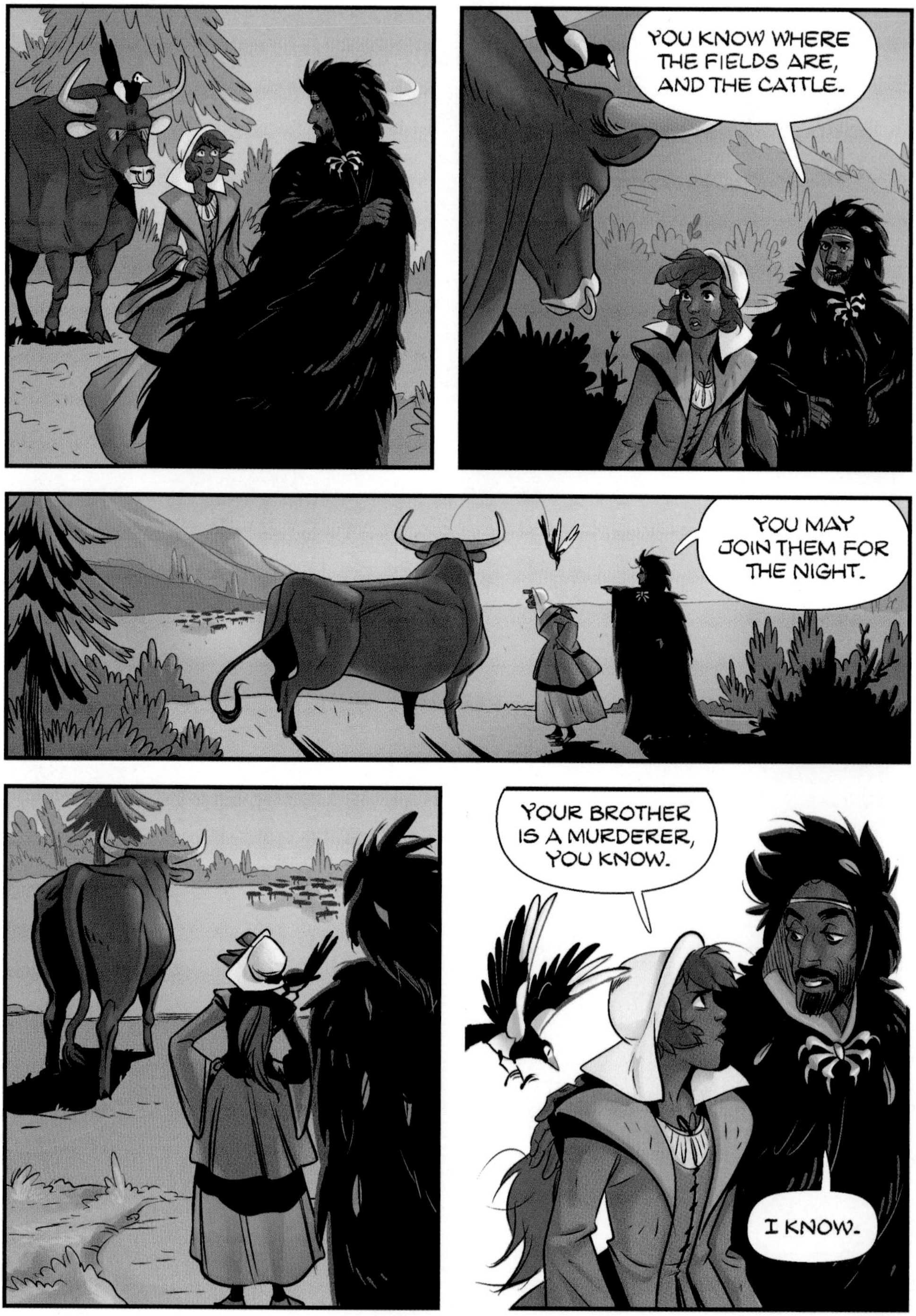
YOU KNOW WHERE THE FIELDS ARE, AND THE CATTLE.
YOU MAY JOIN THEM FOR THE NIGHT.
YOUR BROTHER IS A MURDERER, YOU KNOW.
I KNOW.

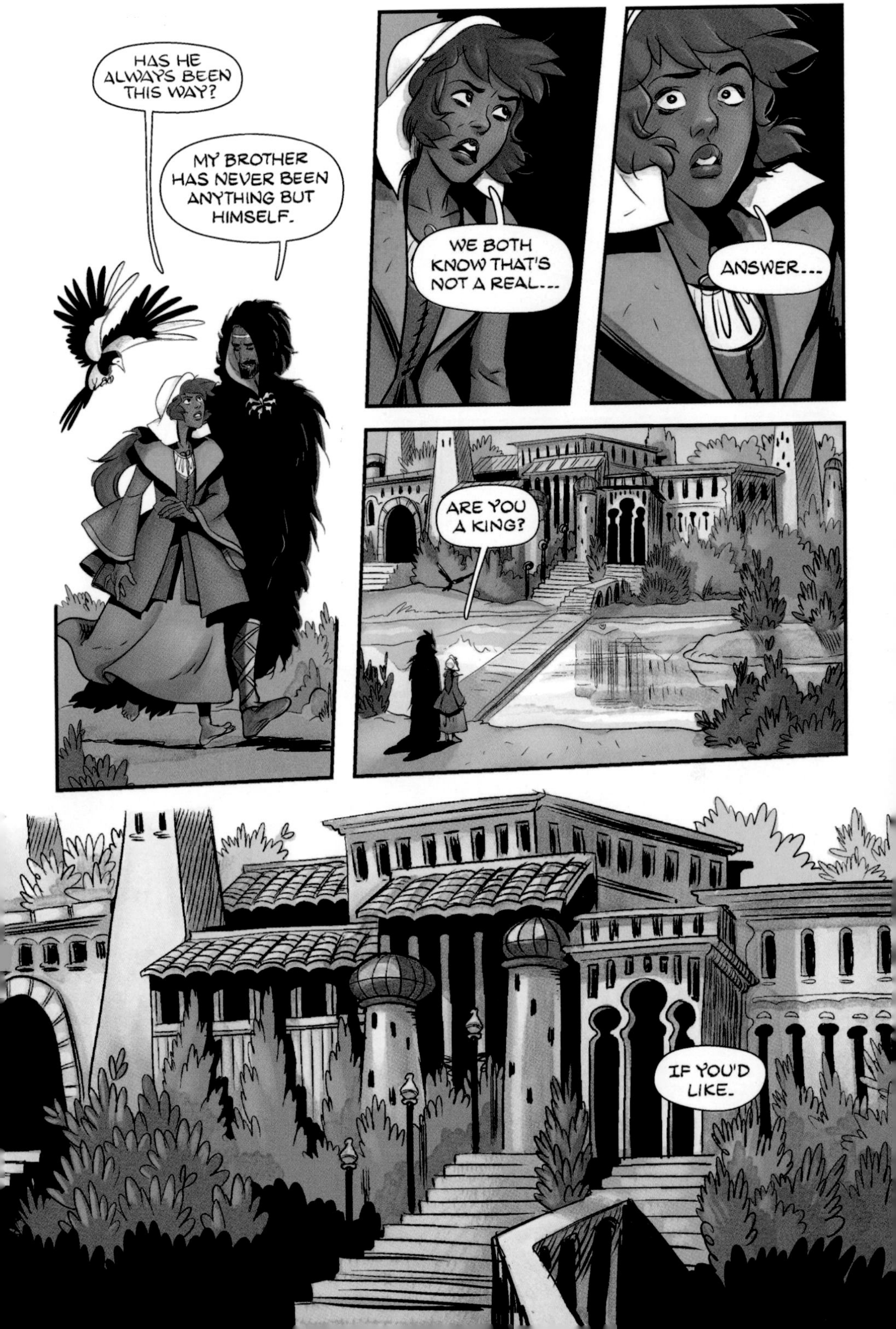
HAS HE ALWAYS BEEN THIS WAY?
MY BROTHER HAS NEVER BEEN ANYTHING BUT HIMSELF.
WE BOTH KNOW THAT'S NOT A REAL...
ANSWER...
ARE YOU A KING?
IF YOU'D LIKE.

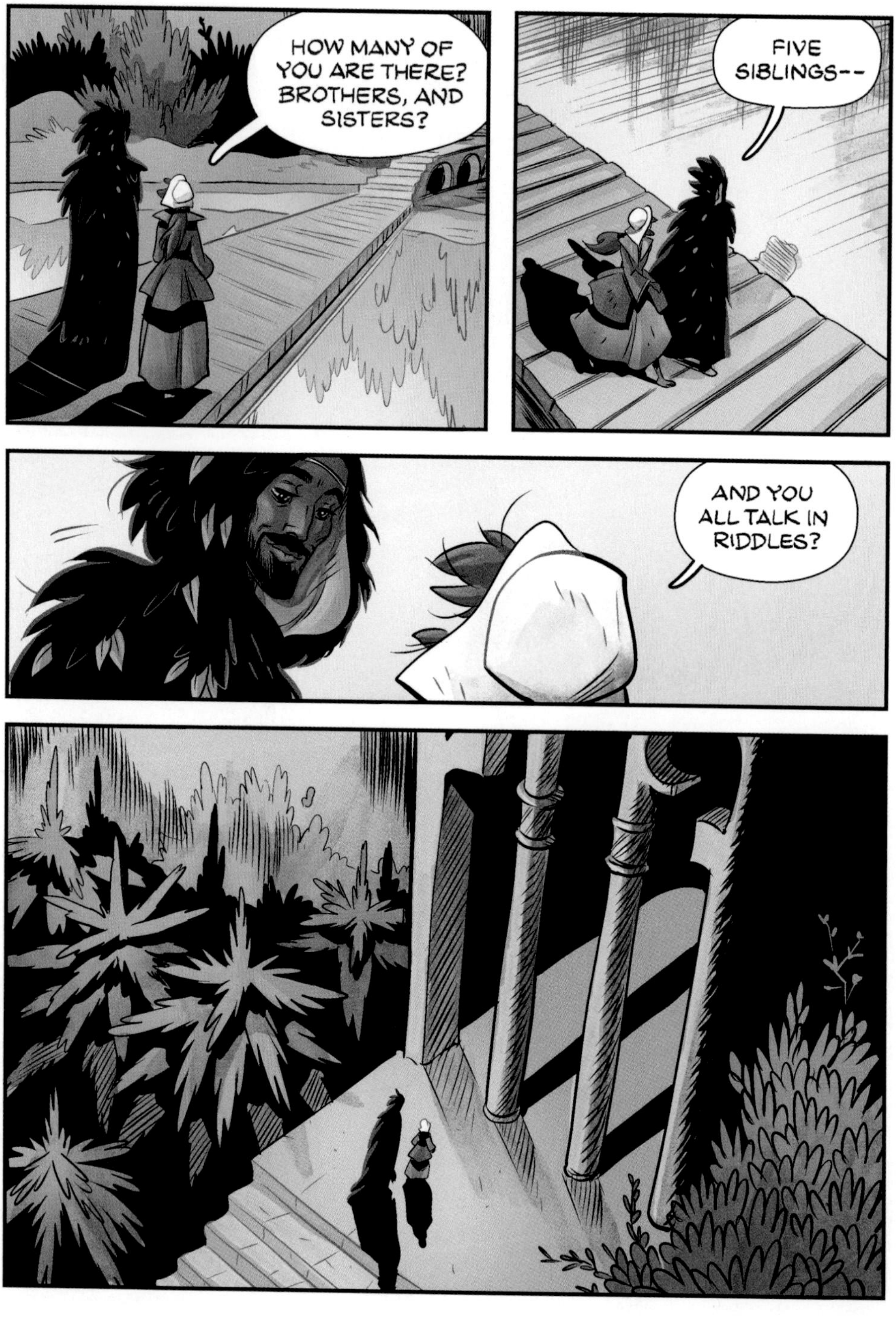
HOW MANY OF YOU ARE THERE? BROTHERS, AND SISTERS?
FIVE SIBLINGS--
AND YOU ALL TALK IN RIDDLES?

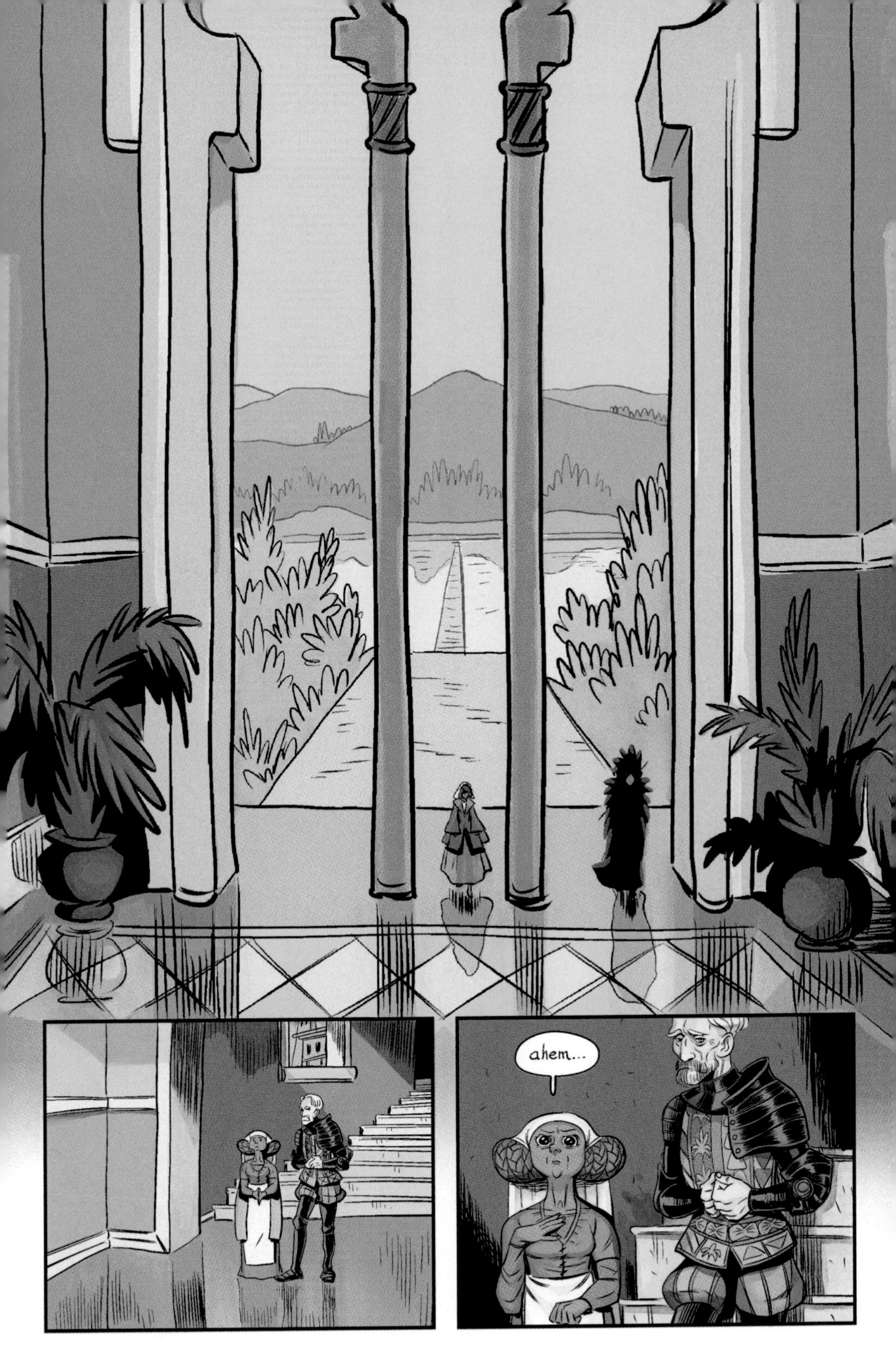
ahem...

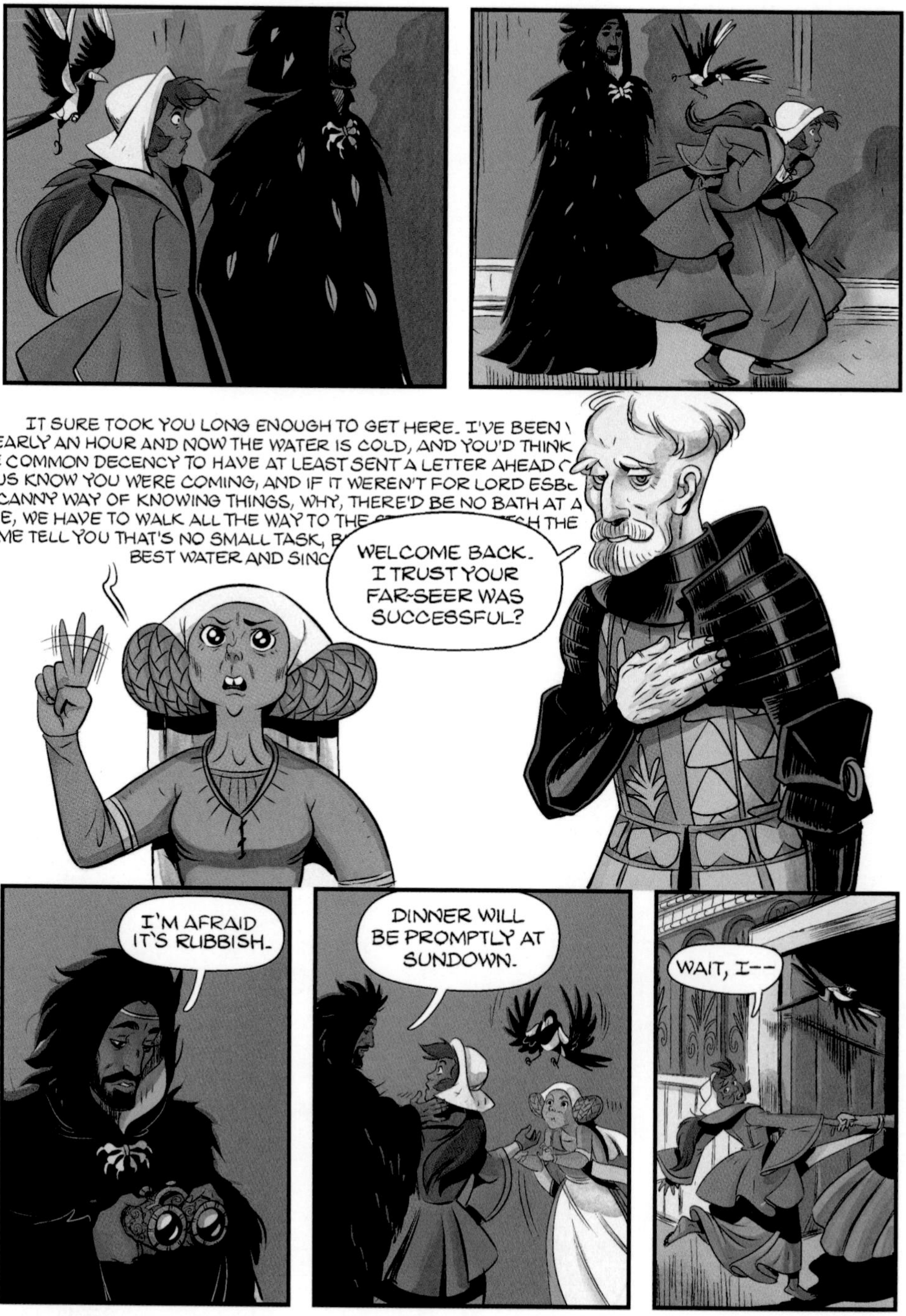
IT SURE TOOK YOU LONG ENOUGH TO GET HERE. I'VE BEEN
NEARLY AN HOUR AND NOW THE WATER IS COLD, AND YOU'D THINK
THE COMMON DECENCY TO HAVE AT LEAST SENT A LETTER AHEAD
US KNOW YOU WERE COMING, AND IF IT WEREN'T FOR LORD
UNCANNY WAY OF KNOWING THINGS, WHY, THERE'D BE NO BATH AT
SEE, WE HAVE TO WALK ALL THE WAY TO THE
LET ME TELL YOU THAT'S NO SMALL TASK,
BEST WATER AND
WELCOME BACK. I TRUST YOUR FAR-SEER WAS SUCCESSFUL?
I'M AFRAID IT'S RUBBISH.
DINNER WILL BE PROMPTLY AT SUNDOWN.
WAIT, I--

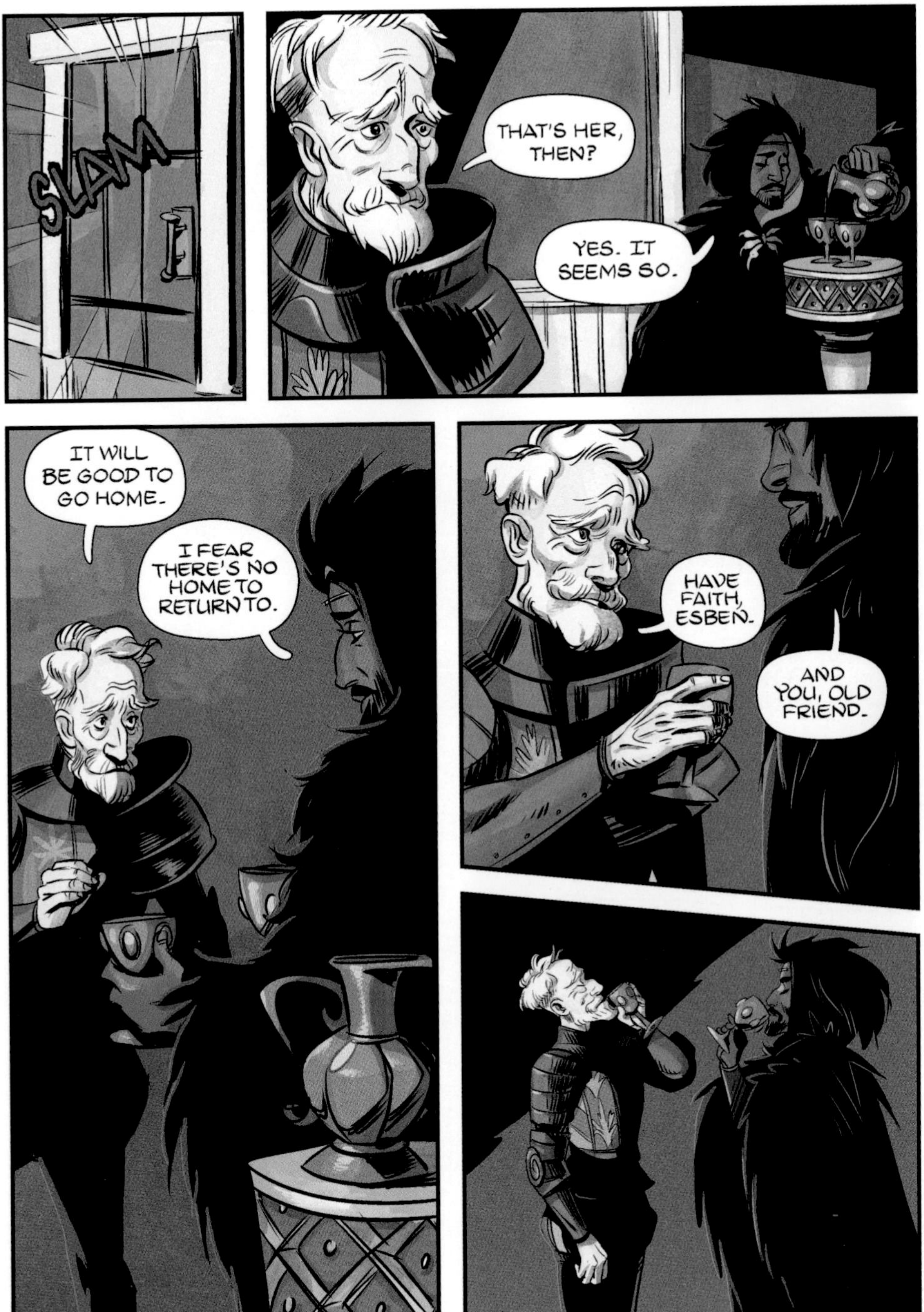
SLAM
THAT'S HER, THEN?
YES. IT SEEMS SO.
IT WILL BE GOOD TO GO HOME.
I FEAR THERE'S NO HOME TO RETURN TO.
HAVE FAITH, ESBEN.
AND YOU, OLD FRIEND.

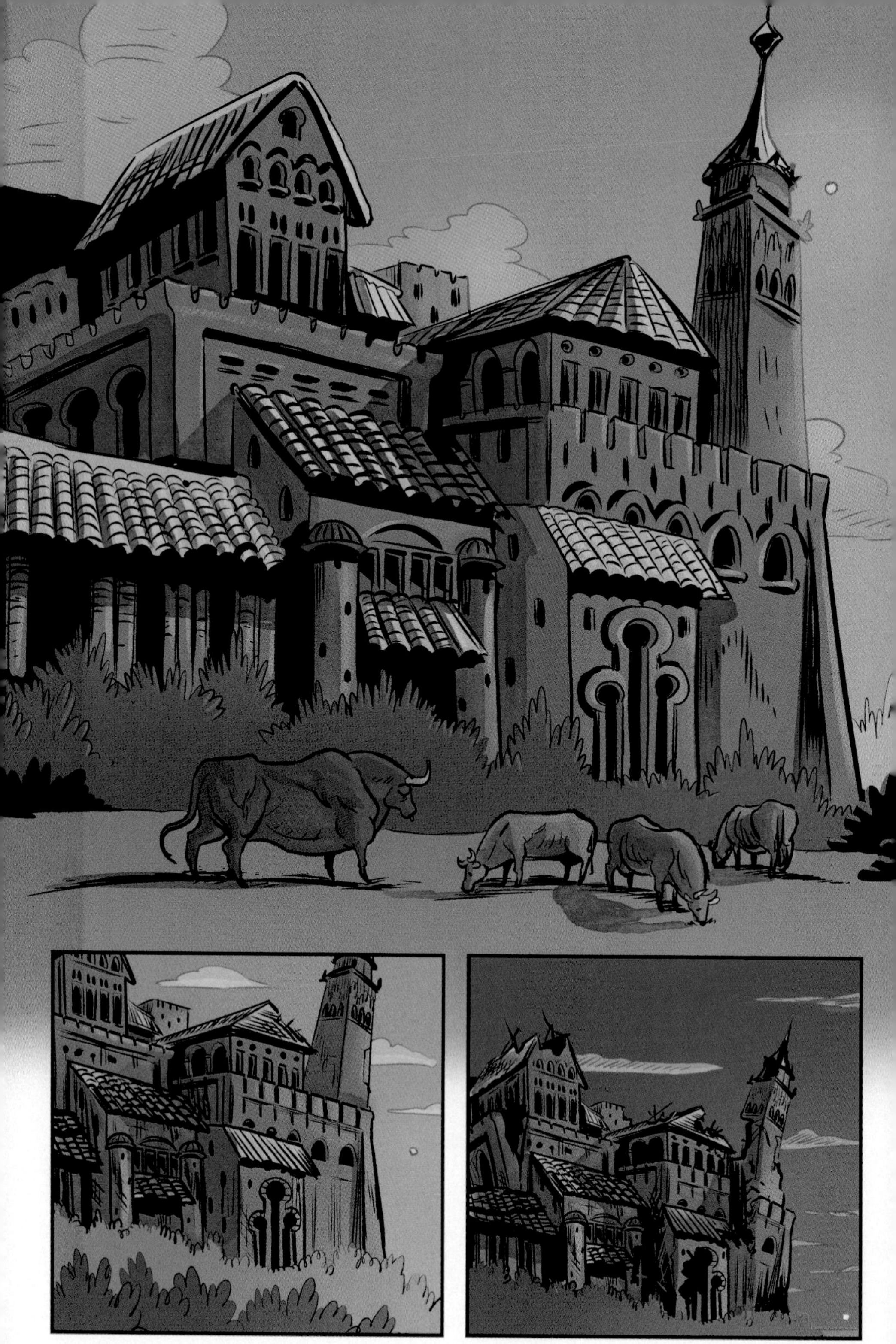

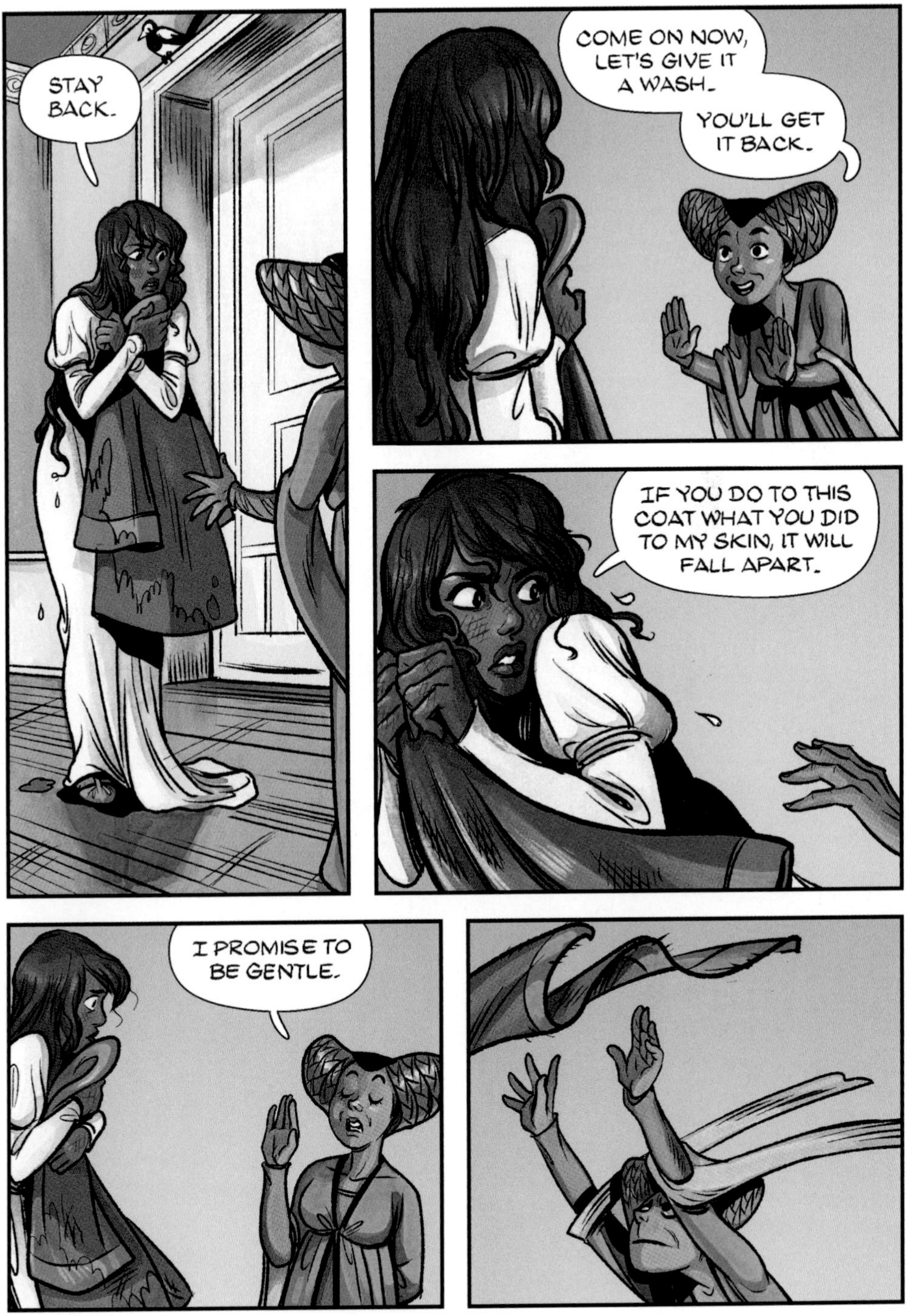
STAY BACK.
COME ON NOW, LET'S GIVE IT A WASH.
YOU'LL GET IT BACK.
IF YOU DO TO THIS COAT WHAT YOU DID TO MY SKIN, IT WILL FALL APART.
I PROMISE TO BE GENTLE.

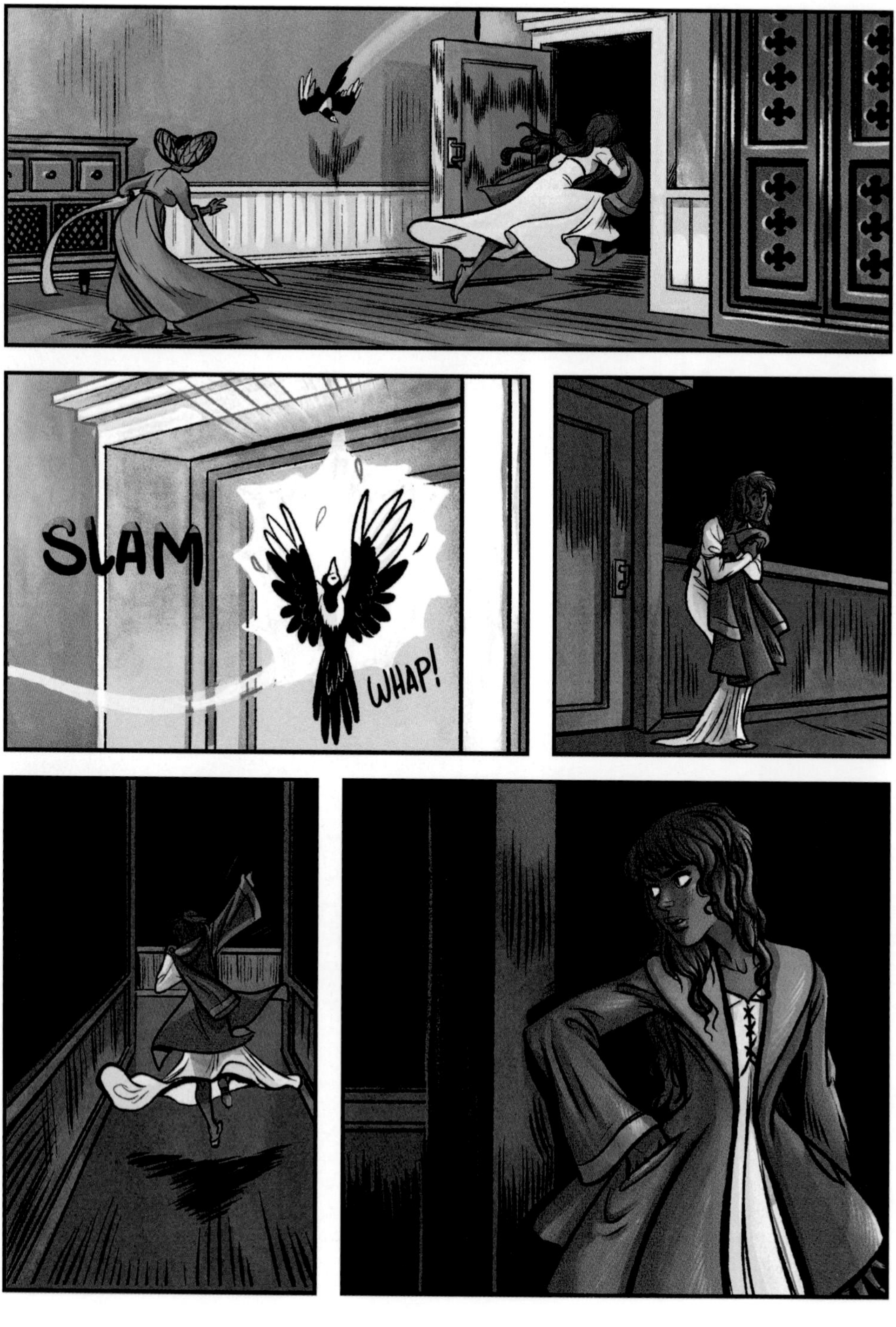
SLAM
WHAP!

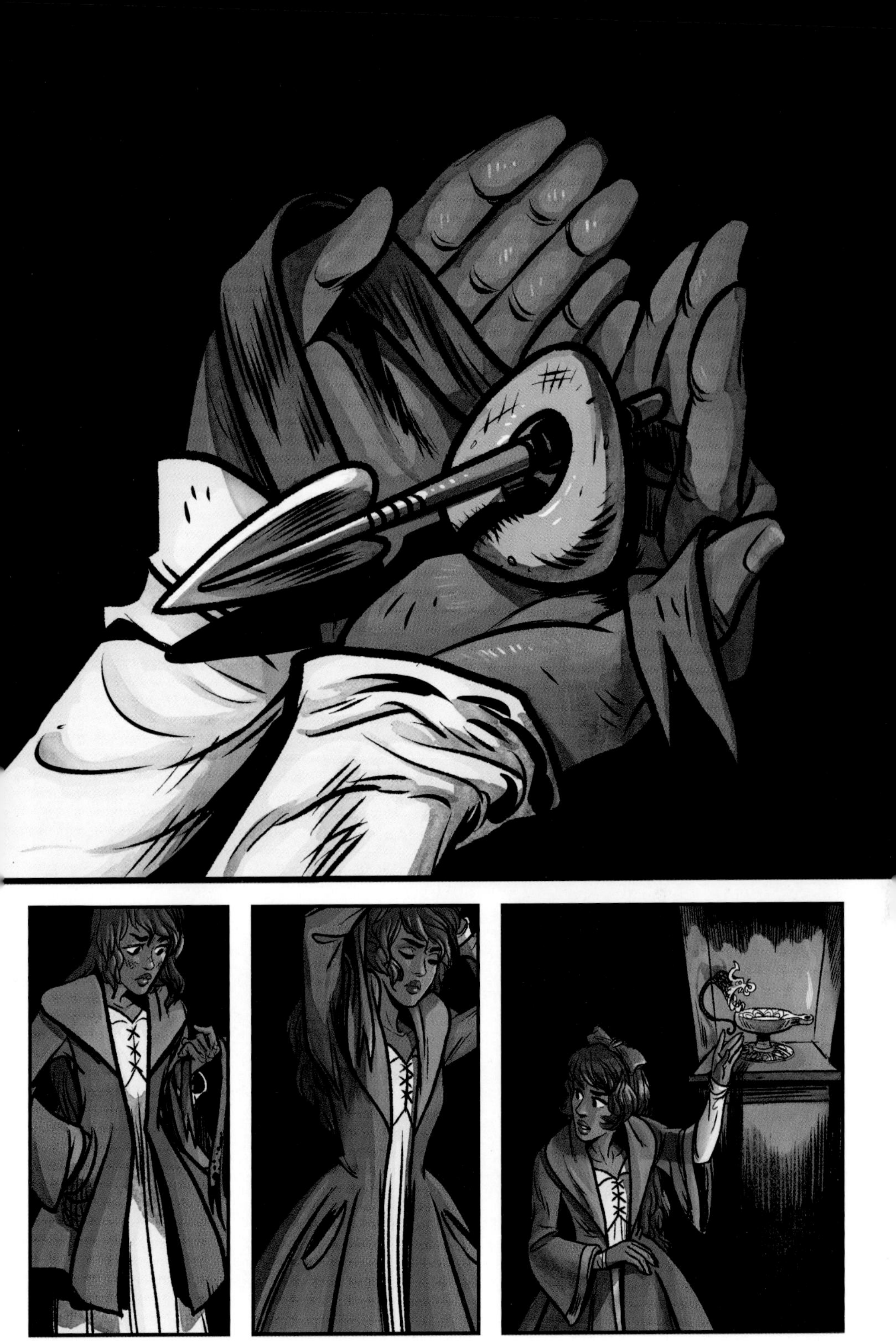

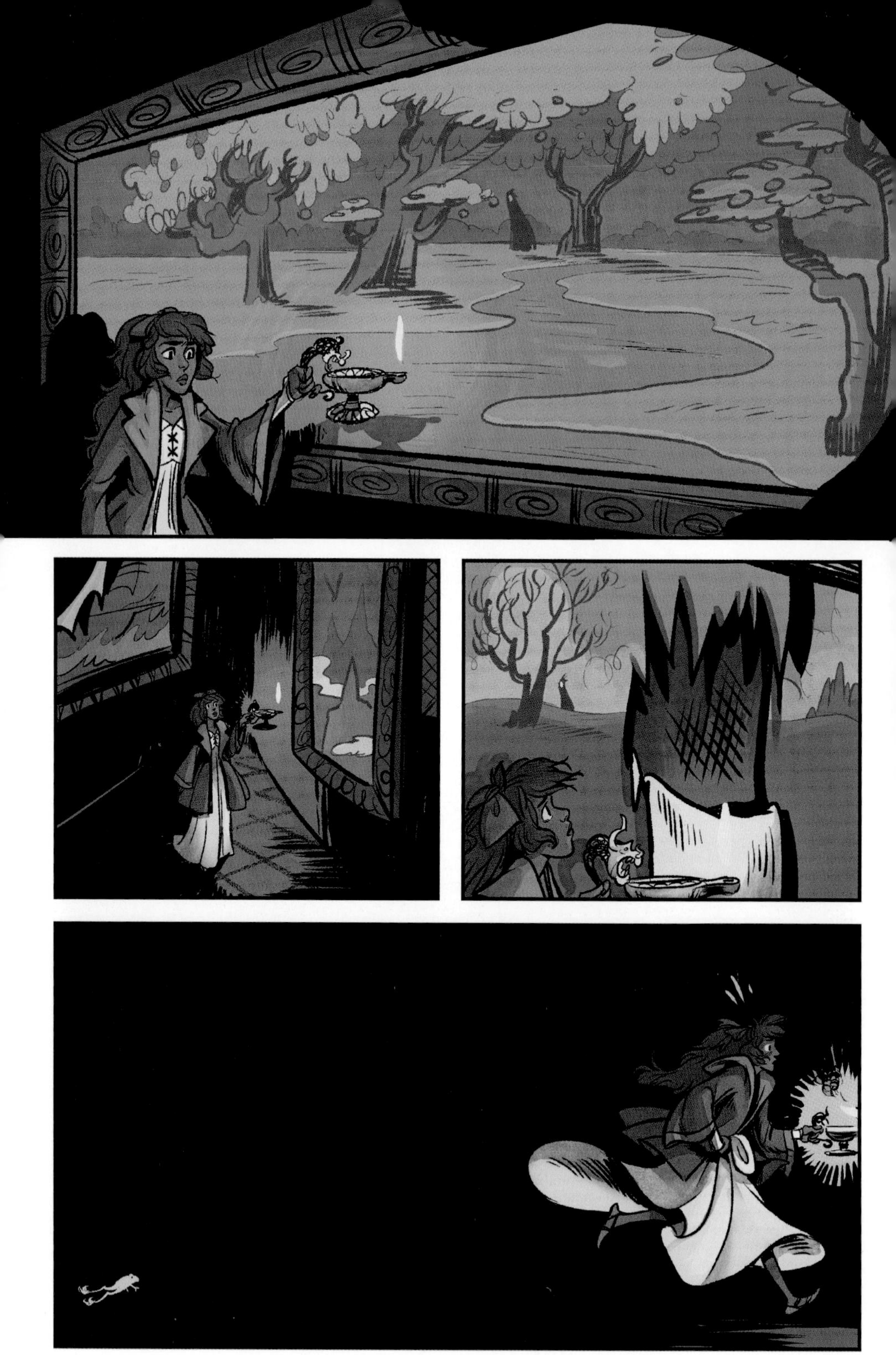

THE SUN'S ALMOST SET, MY DEAR. YOU'LL BE LATE FOR DINNER.

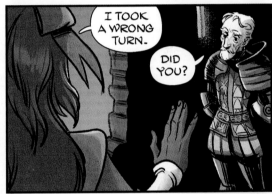
I TOOK A WRONG TURN.

DID YOU?

IT LOOKS LIKE NO ONE EVER COMES BACK THIS WAY.

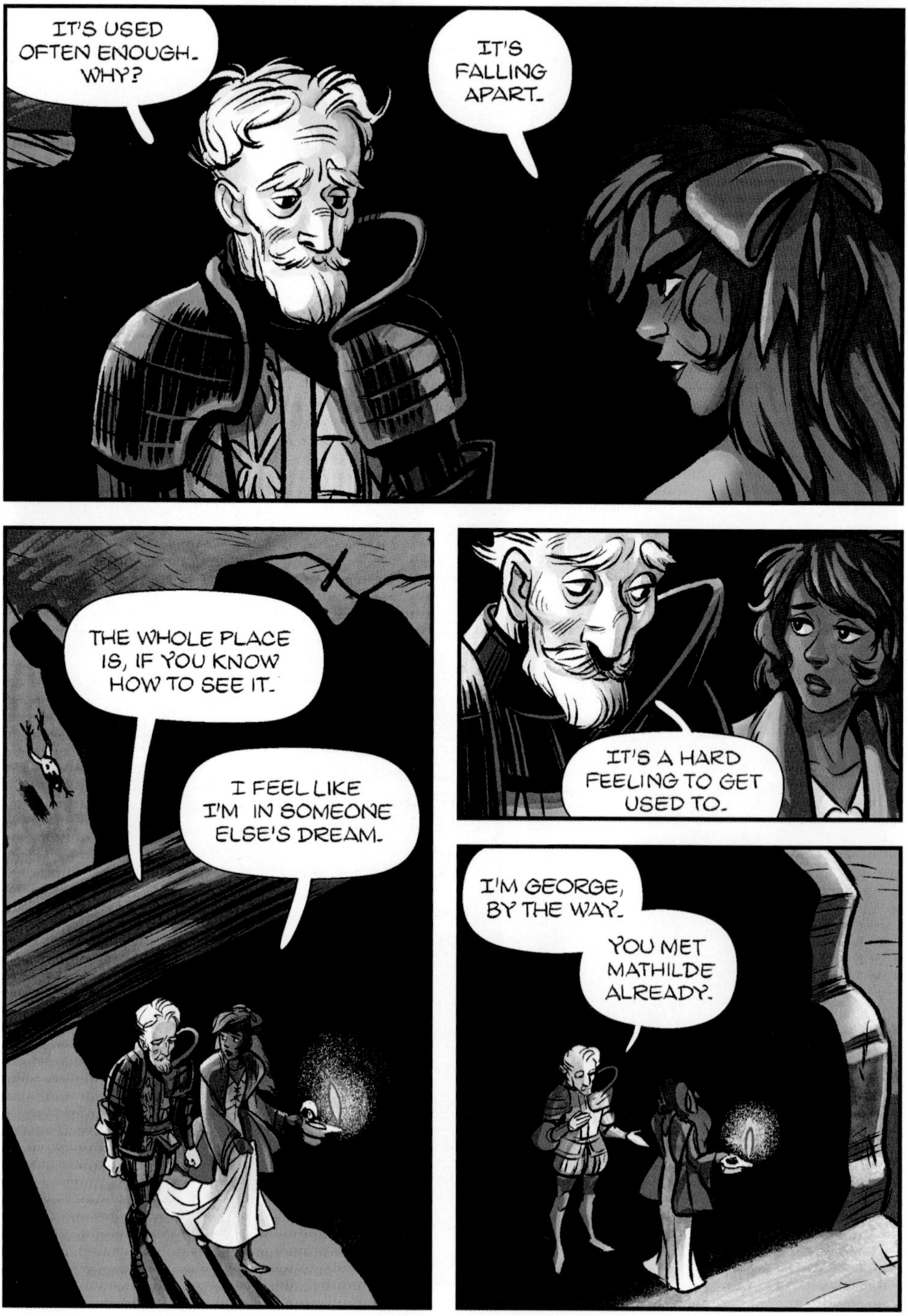
IT'S USED OFTEN ENOUGH. WHY?
IT'S FALLING APART.
THE WHOLE PLACE IS, IF YOU KNOW HOW TO SEE IT.
I FEEL LIKE I'M IN SOMEONE ELSE'S DREAM.
IT'S A HARD FEELING TO GET USED TO.
I'M GEORGE, BY THE WAY.
YOU MET MATHILDE ALREADY.

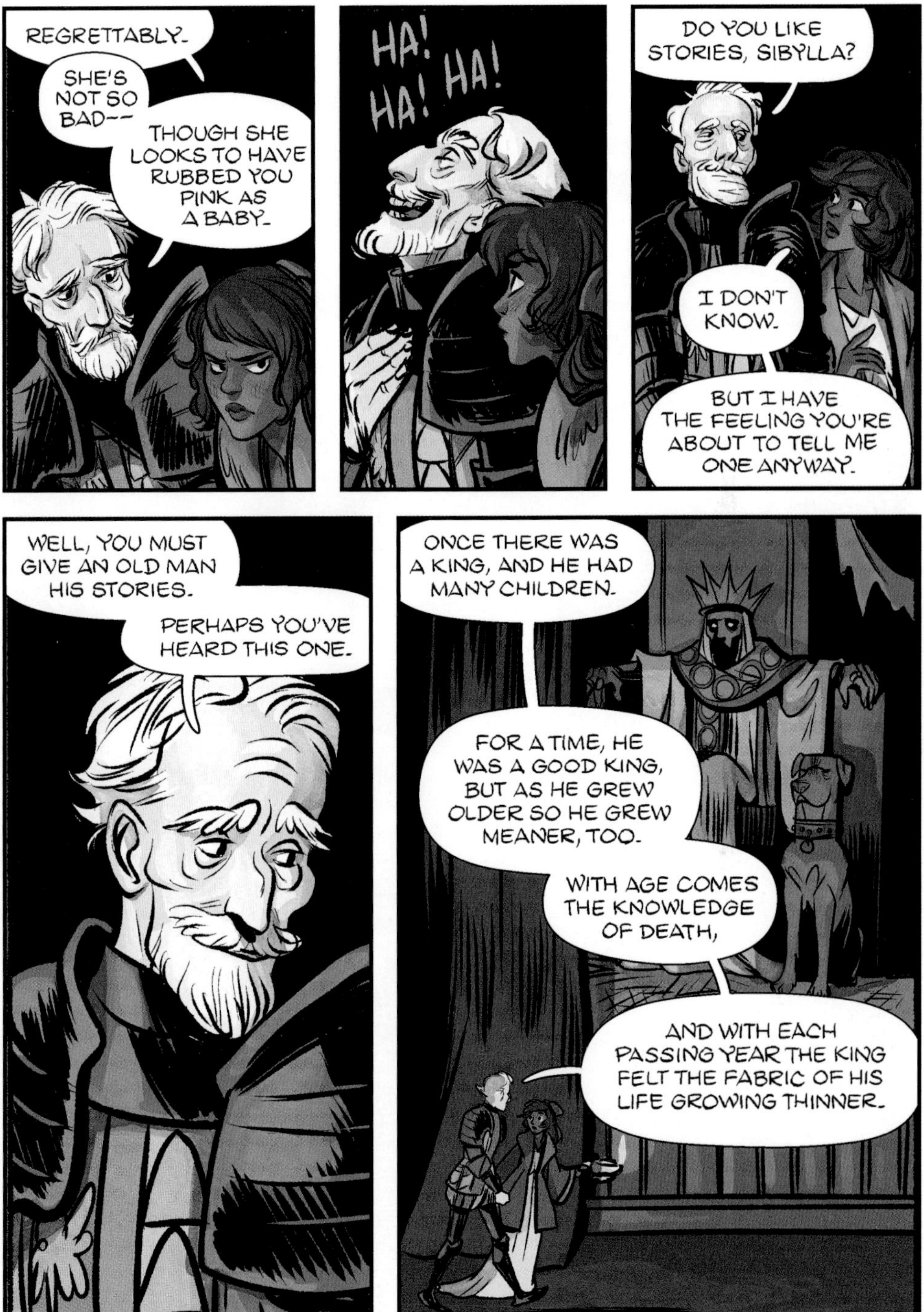

REGRETTABLY.
SHE'S NOT SO BAD--
THOUGH SHE LOOKS TO HAVE RUBBED YOU PINK AS A BABY.
HA! HA! HA!
DO YOU LIKE STORIES, SIBYLLA?
I DON'T KNOW.
BUT I HAVE THE FEELING YOU'RE ABOUT TO TELL ME ONE ANYWAY.
WELL, YOU MUST GIVE AN OLD MAN HIS STORIES.
PERHAPS YOU'VE HEARD THIS ONE.
ONCE THERE WAS A KING, AND HE HAD MANY CHILDREN.
FOR A TIME, HE WAS A GOOD KING, BUT AS HE GREW OLDER SO HE GREW MEANER, TOO.
WITH AGE COMES THE KNOWLEDGE OF DEATH,
AND WITH EACH PASSING YEAR THE KING FELT THE FABRIC OF HIS LIFE GROWING THINNER.

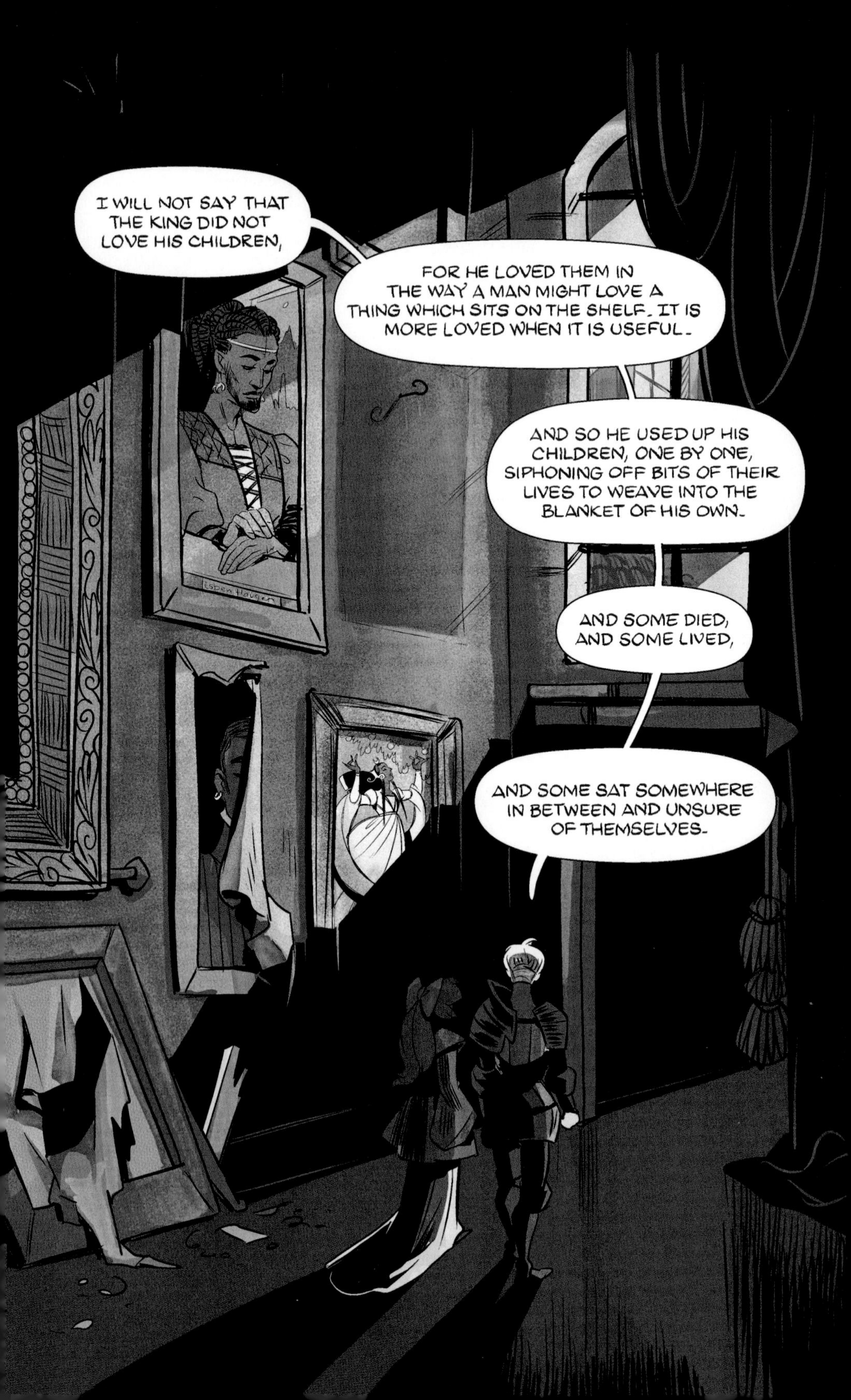
I WILL NOT SAY THAT THE KING DID NOT LOVE HIS CHILDREN,
FOR HE LOVED THEM IN THE WAY A MAN MIGHT LOVE A THING WHICH SITS ON THE SHELF. IT IS MORE LOVED WHEN IT IS USEFUL.
AND SO HE USED UP HIS CHILDREN, ONE BY ONE, SIPHONING OFF BITS OF THEIR LIVES TO WEAVE INTO THE BLANKET OF HIS OWN.
AND SOME DIED, AND SOME LIVED,
AND SOME SAT SOMEWHERE IN BETWEEN AND UNSURE OF THEMSELVES.

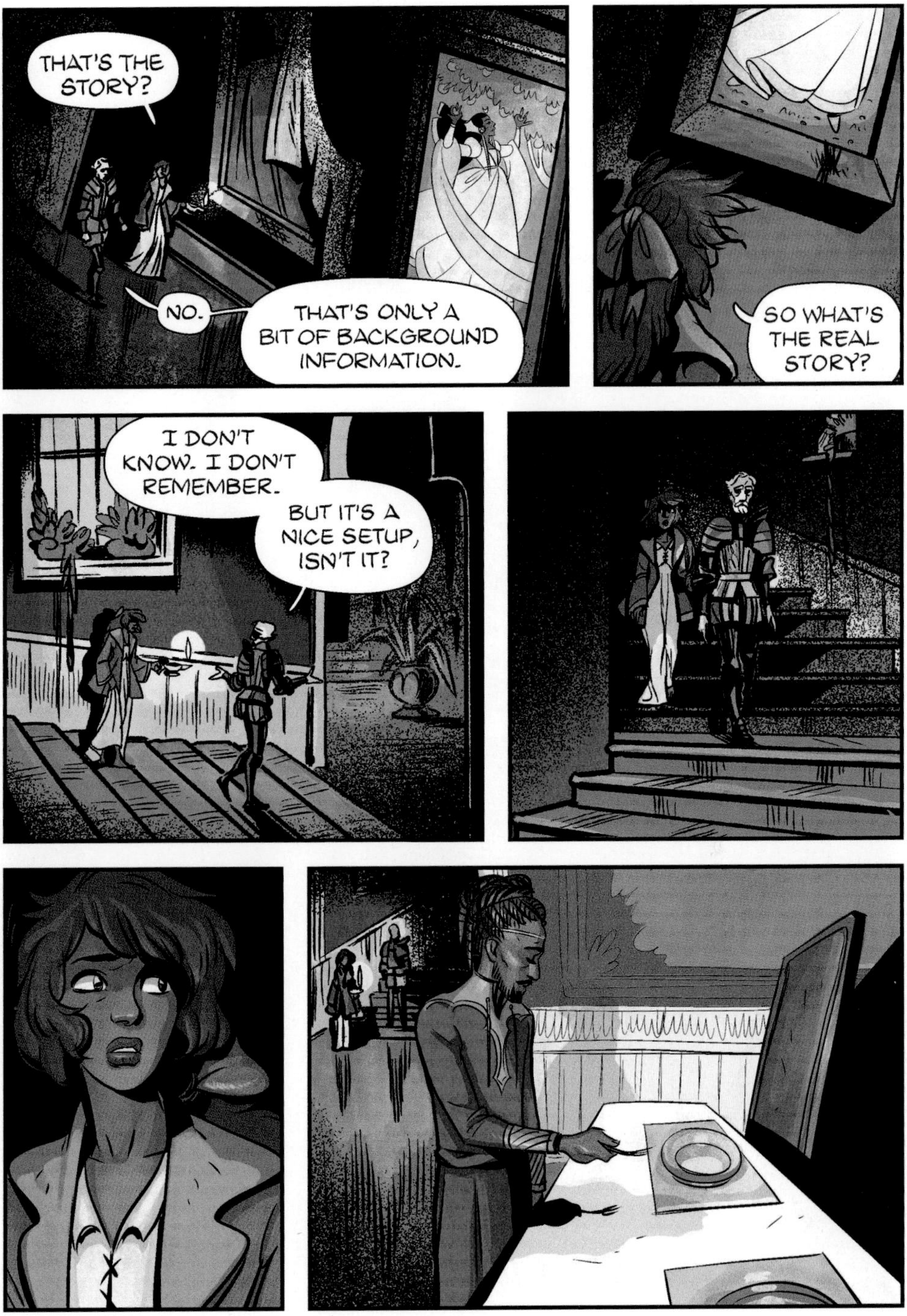
THAT'S THE STORY?
NO.
THAT'S ONLY A BIT OF BACKGROUND INFORMATION.
SO WHAT'S THE REAL STORY?
I DON'T KNOW. I DON'T REMEMBER.
BUT IT'S A NICE SETUP, ISN'T IT?

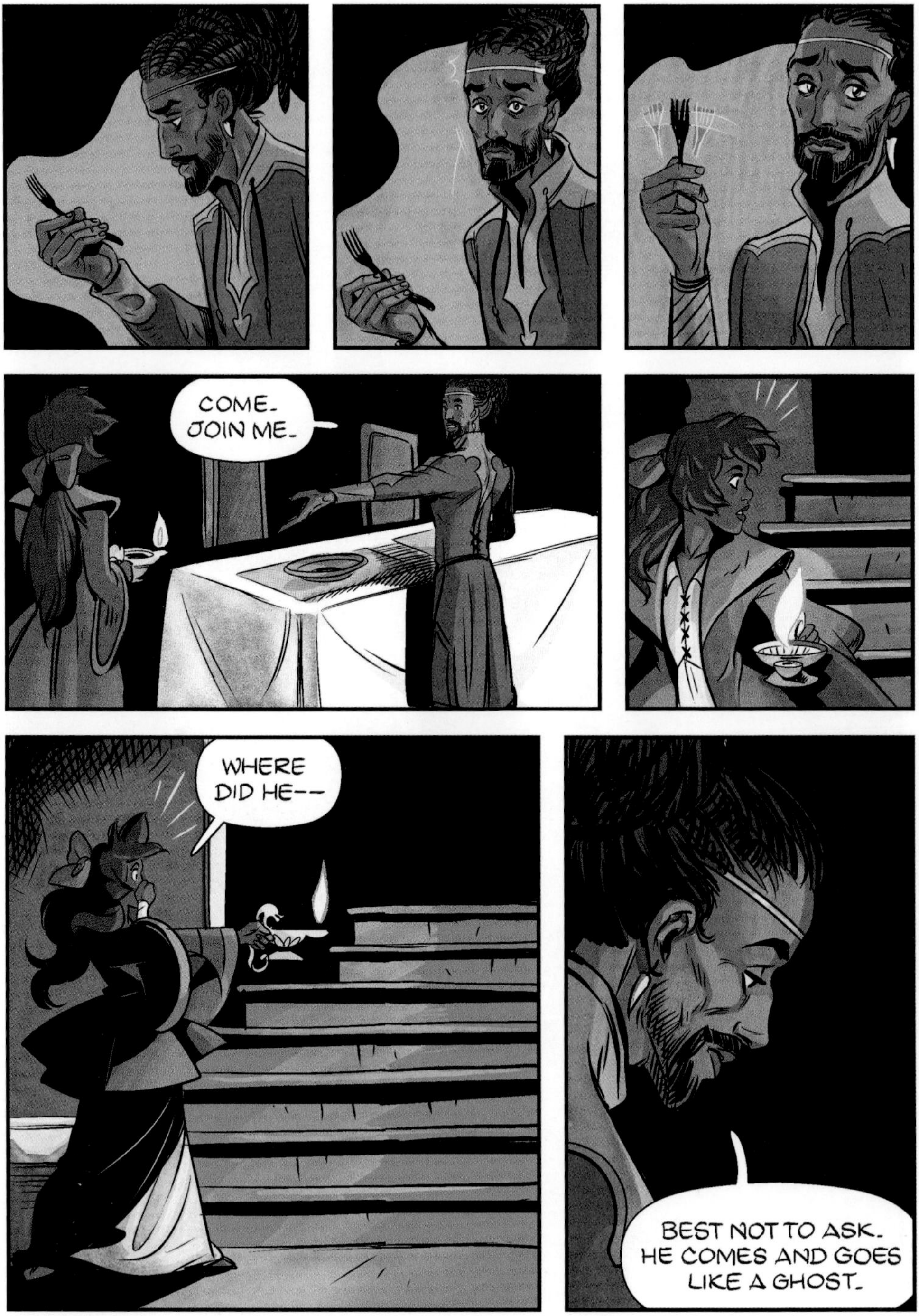
COME. JOIN ME.
WHERE DID HE--
BEST NOT TO ASK. HE COMES AND GOES LIKE A GHOST.

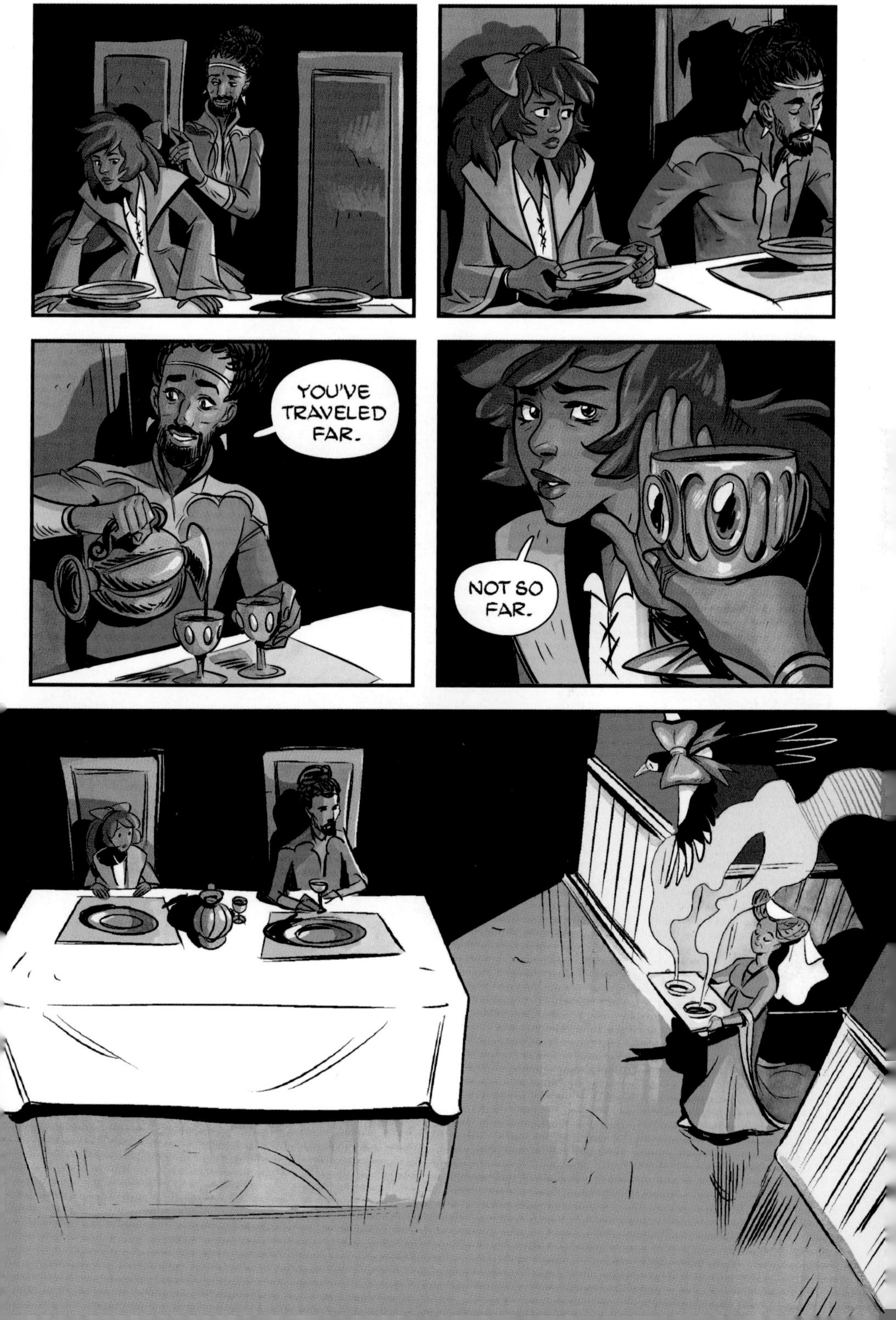
YOU'VE TRAVELED FAR.
NOT SO FAR.

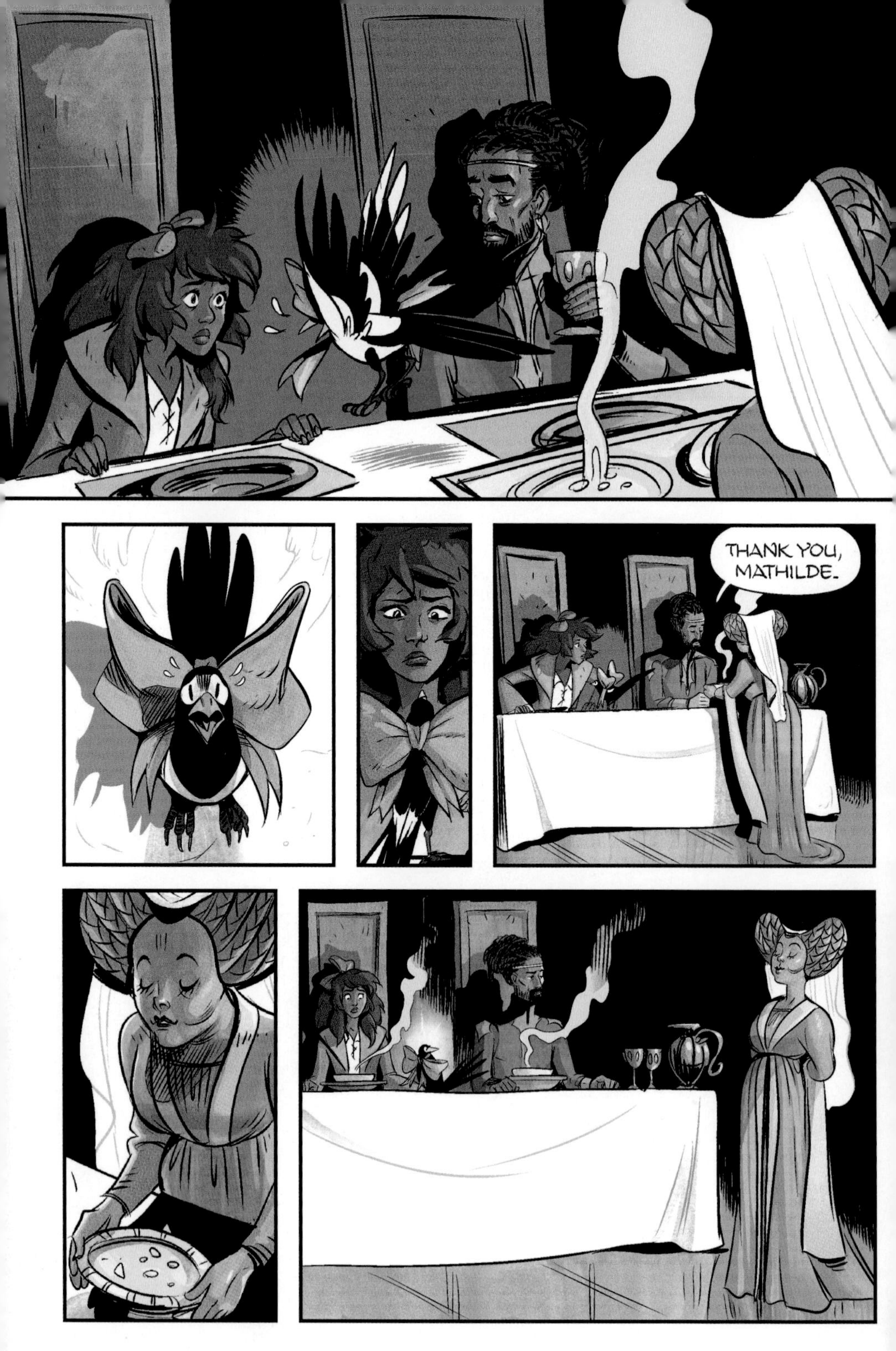
THANK YOU, MATHILDE.

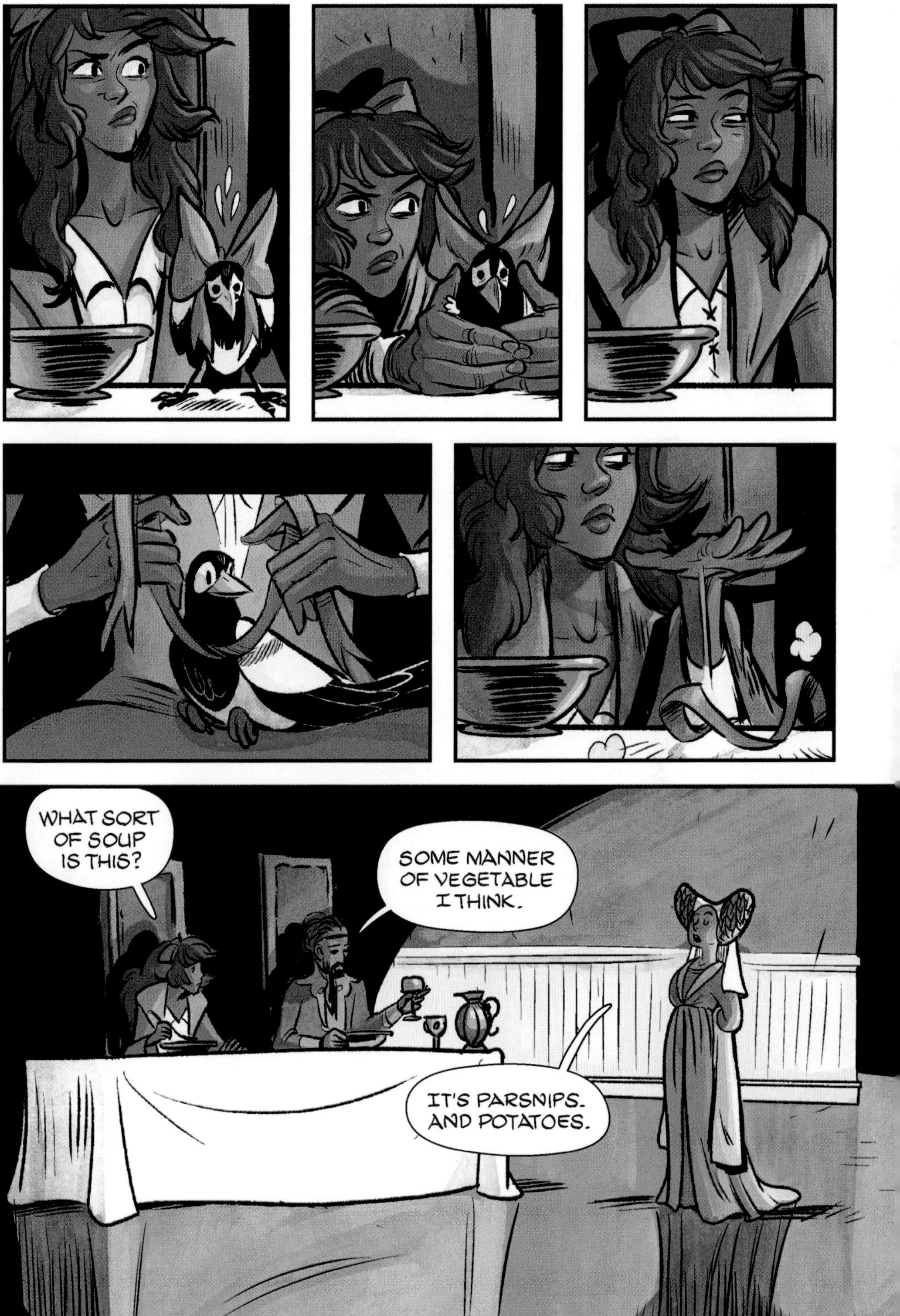
WHAT SORT OF SOUP IS THIS?
SOME MANNER OF VEGETABLE I THINK.
IT'S PARSNIPS. AND POTATOES.

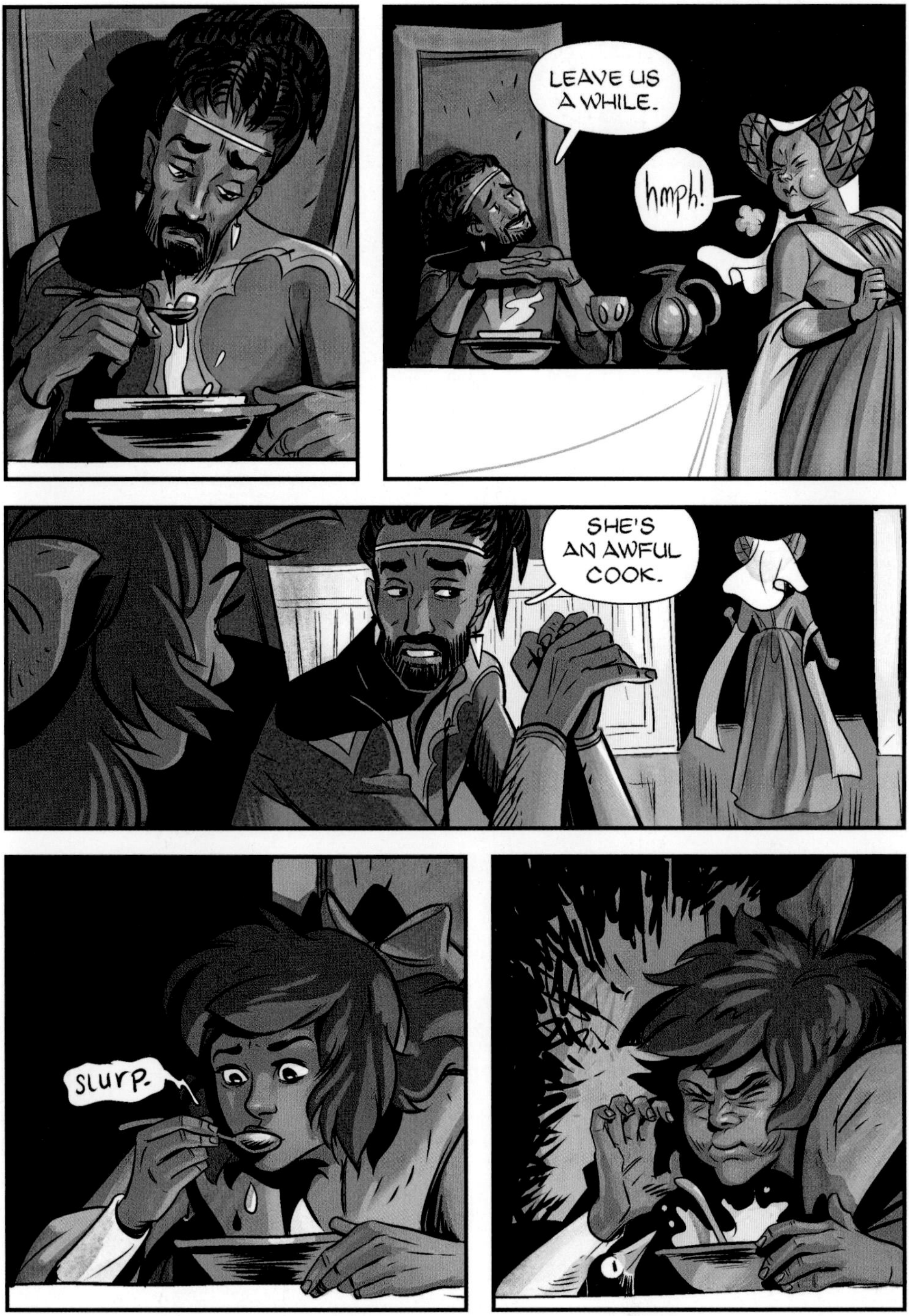
LEAVE US A WHILE.
hmph!
SHE'S AN AWFUL COOK.
slurp.

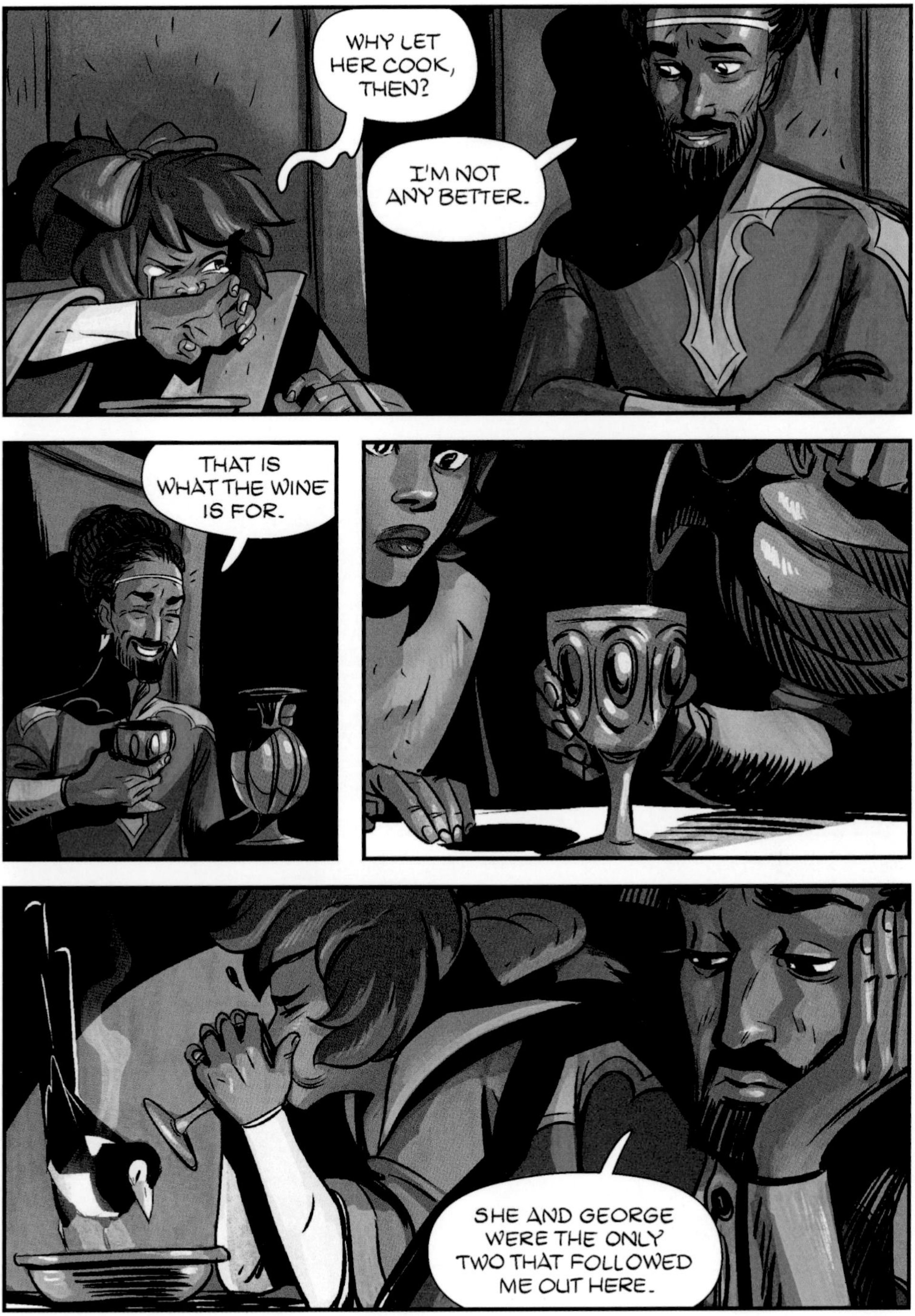
WHY LET HER COOK, THEN?
I'M NOT ANY BETTER.
THAT IS WHAT THE WINE IS FOR.
SHE AND GEORGE WERE THE ONLY TWO THAT FOLLOWED ME OUT HERE.

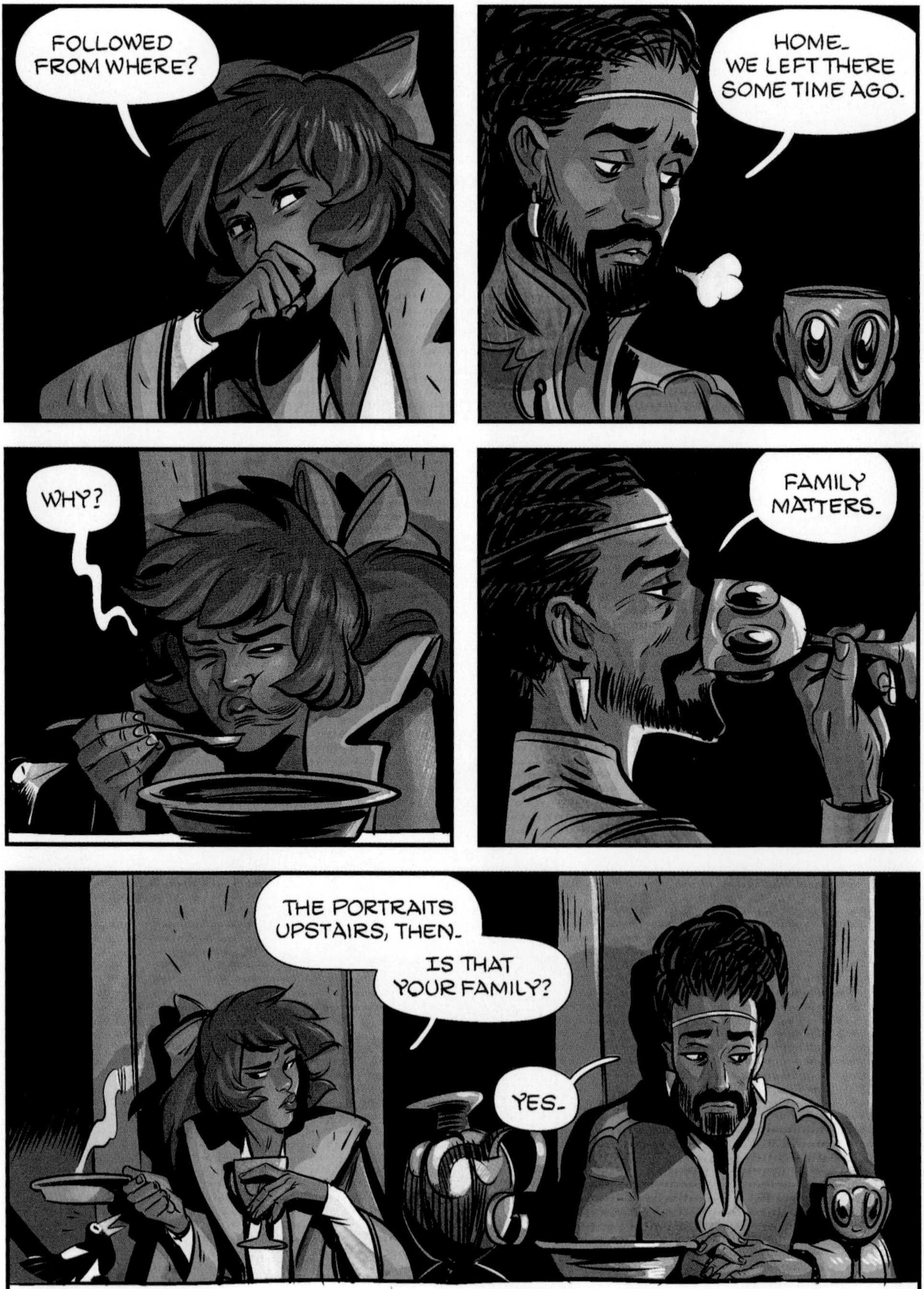
FOLLOWED FROM WHERE?
HOME. WE LEFT THERE SOME TIME AGO.
WHY?
FAMILY MATTERS.
THE PORTRAITS UPSTAIRS, THEN.
IS THAT YOUR FAMILY?
YES.

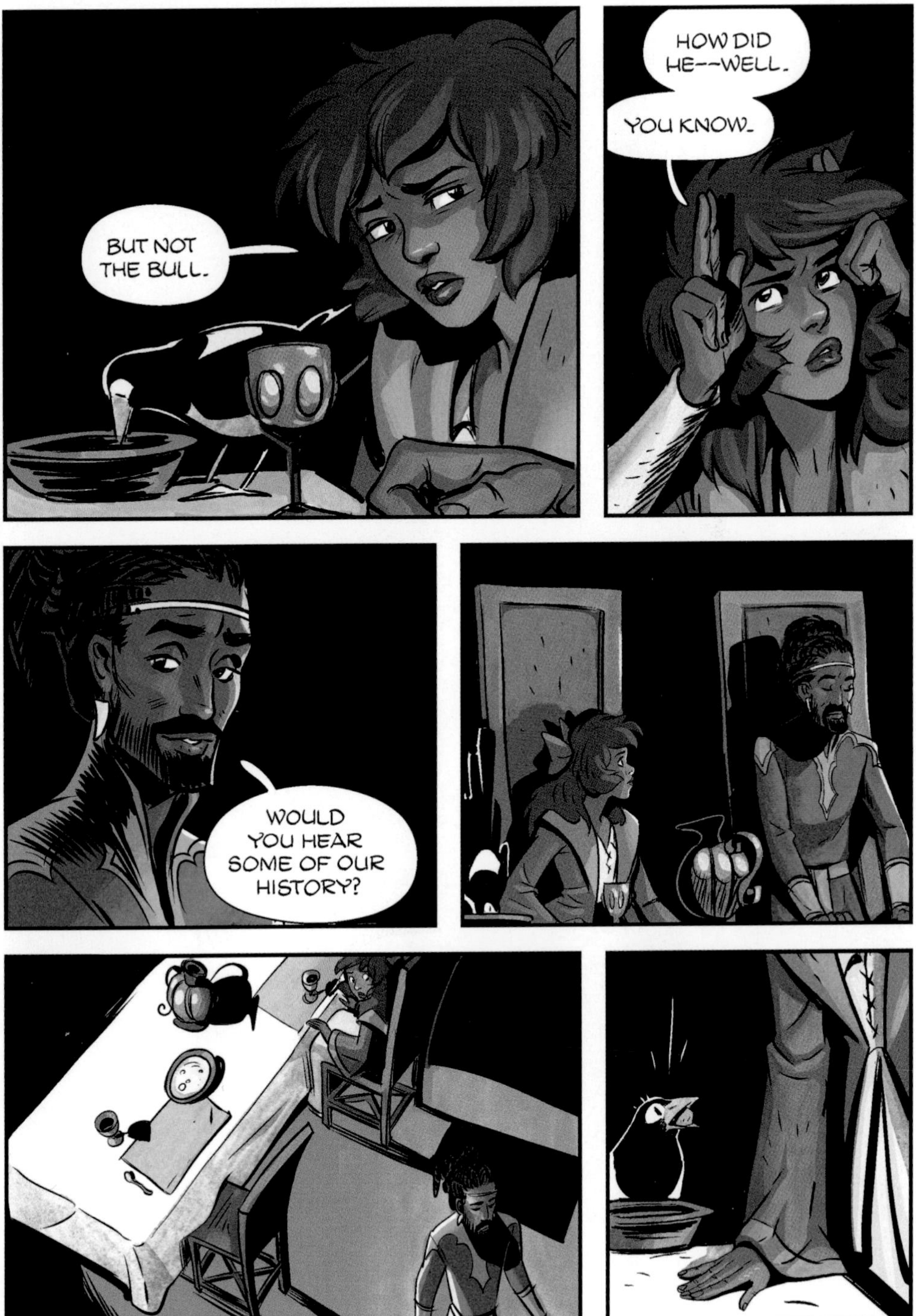
BUT NOT THE BULL.
HOW DID HE--WELL.
YOU KNOW.
WOULD YOU HEAR SOME OF OUR HISTORY?

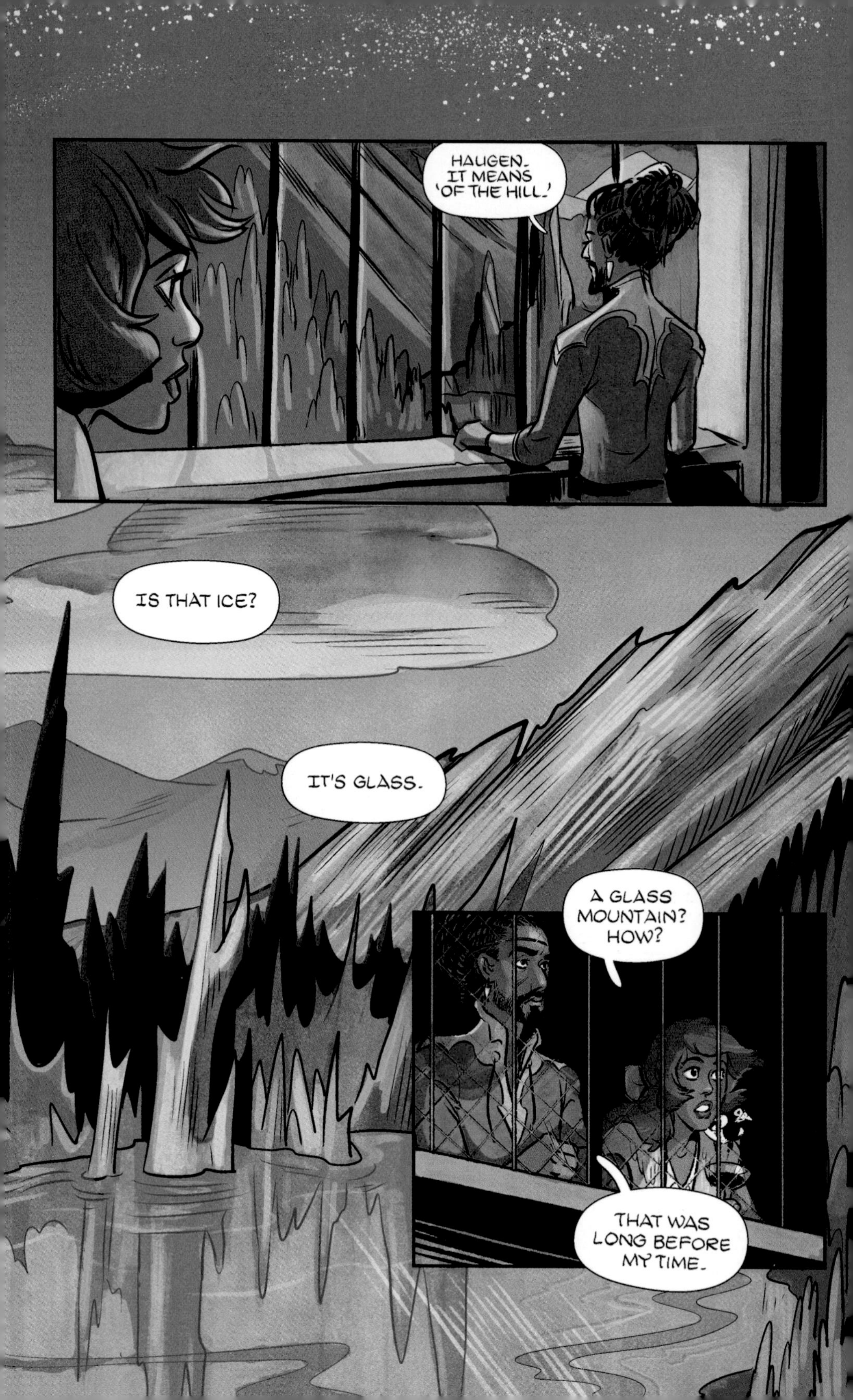
HAUGEN. IT MEANS 'OF THE HILL.'
IS THAT ICE?
IT'S GLASS.
A GLASS MOUNTAIN? HOW?
THAT WAS LONG BEFORE MY TIME.

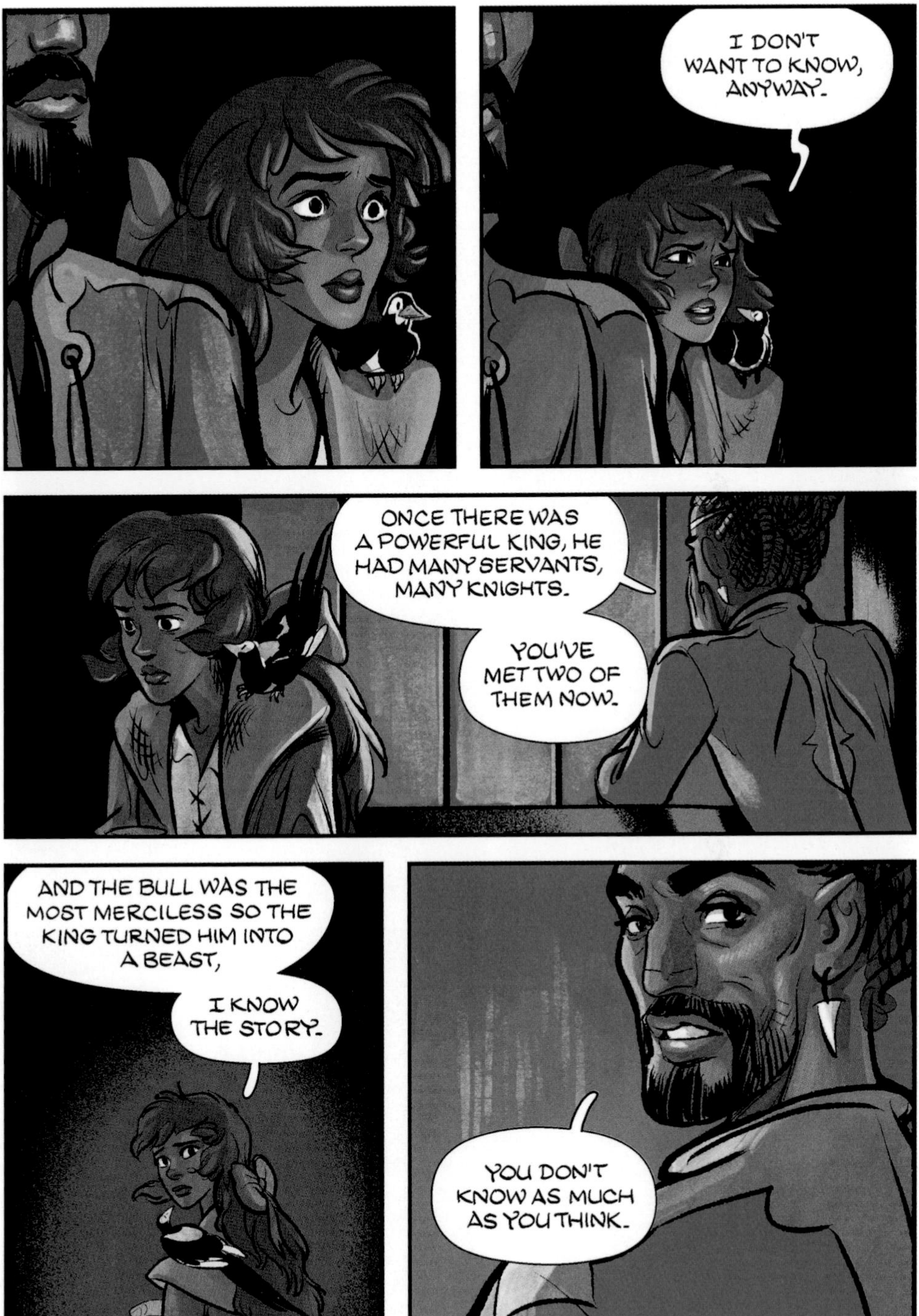
I DON'T WANT TO KNOW, ANYWAY.
ONCE THERE WAS A POWERFUL KING, HE HAD MANY SERVANTS, MANY KNIGHTS.
YOU'VE MET TWO OF THEM NOW.
AND THE BULL WAS THE MOST MERCILESS SO THE KING TURNED HIM INTO A BEAST,
I KNOW THE STORY.
YOU DON'T KNOW AS MUCH AS YOU THINK.

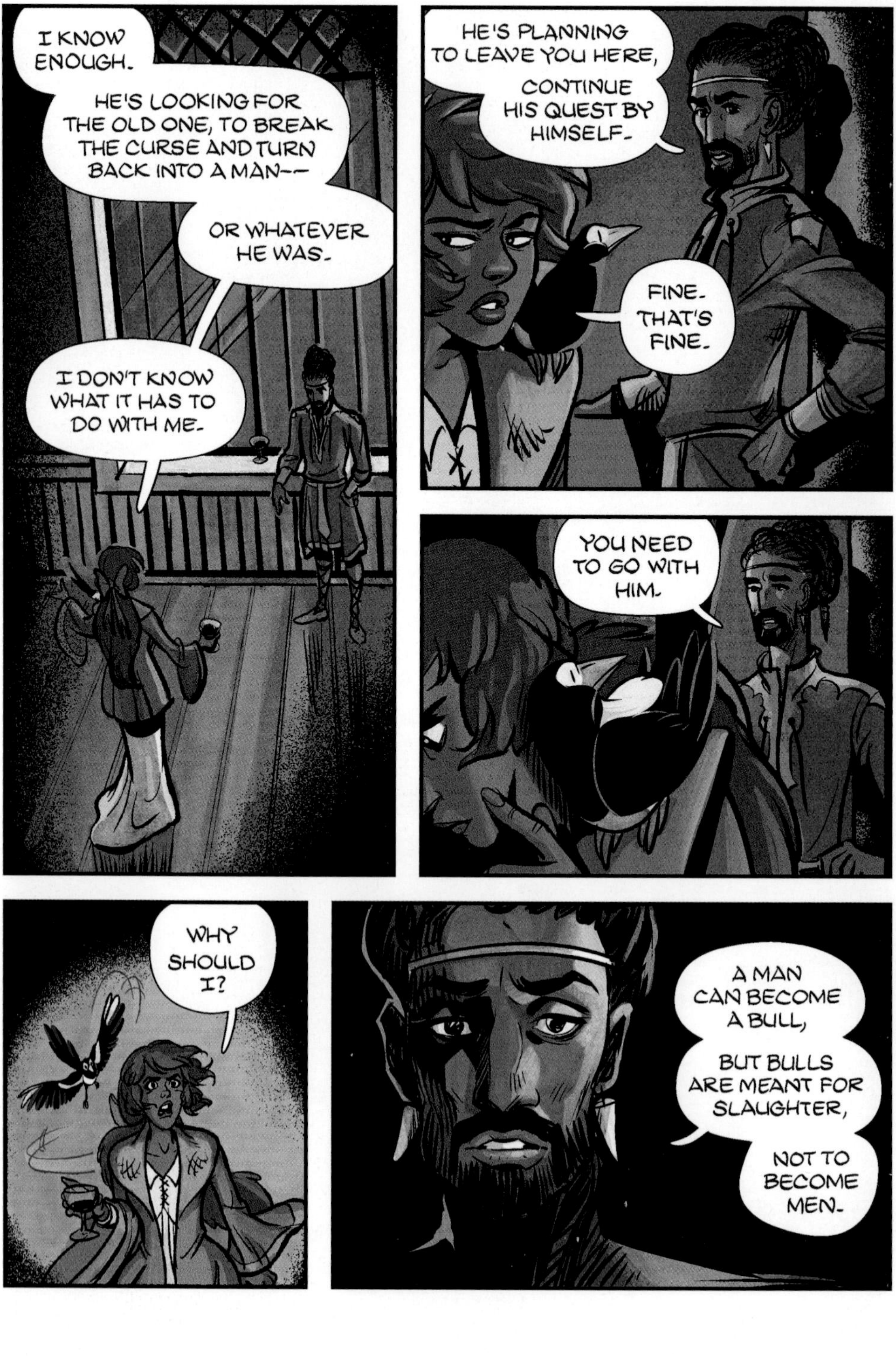
I KNOW ENOUGH.
HE'S LOOKING FOR THE OLD ONE, TO BREAK THE CURSE AND TURN BACK INTO A MAN--
OR WHATEVER HE WAS.
I DON'T KNOW WHAT IT HAS TO DO WITH ME.
HE'S PLANNING TO LEAVE YOU HERE,
CONTINUE HIS QUEST BY HIMSELF.
FINE. THAT'S FINE.
YOU NEED TO GO WITH HIM.
WHY SHOULD I?
A MAN CAN BECOME A BULL,
BUT BULLS ARE MEANT FOR SLAUGHTER,
NOT TO BECOME MEN.

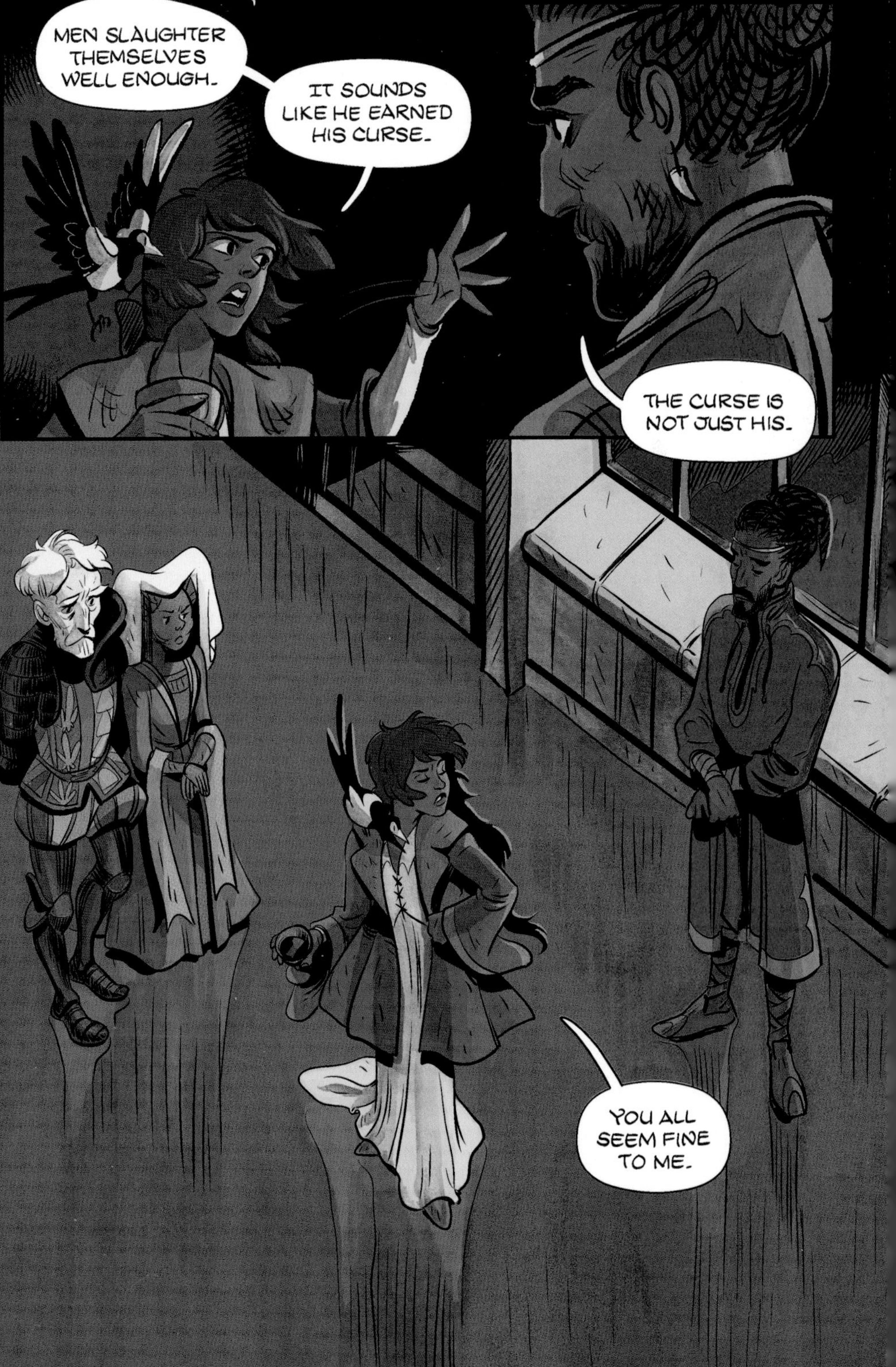
MEN SLAUGHTER THEMSELVES WELL ENOUGH.
IT SOUNDS LIKE HE EARNED HIS CURSE.
THE CURSE IS NOT JUST HIS.
YOU ALL SEEM FINE TO ME.

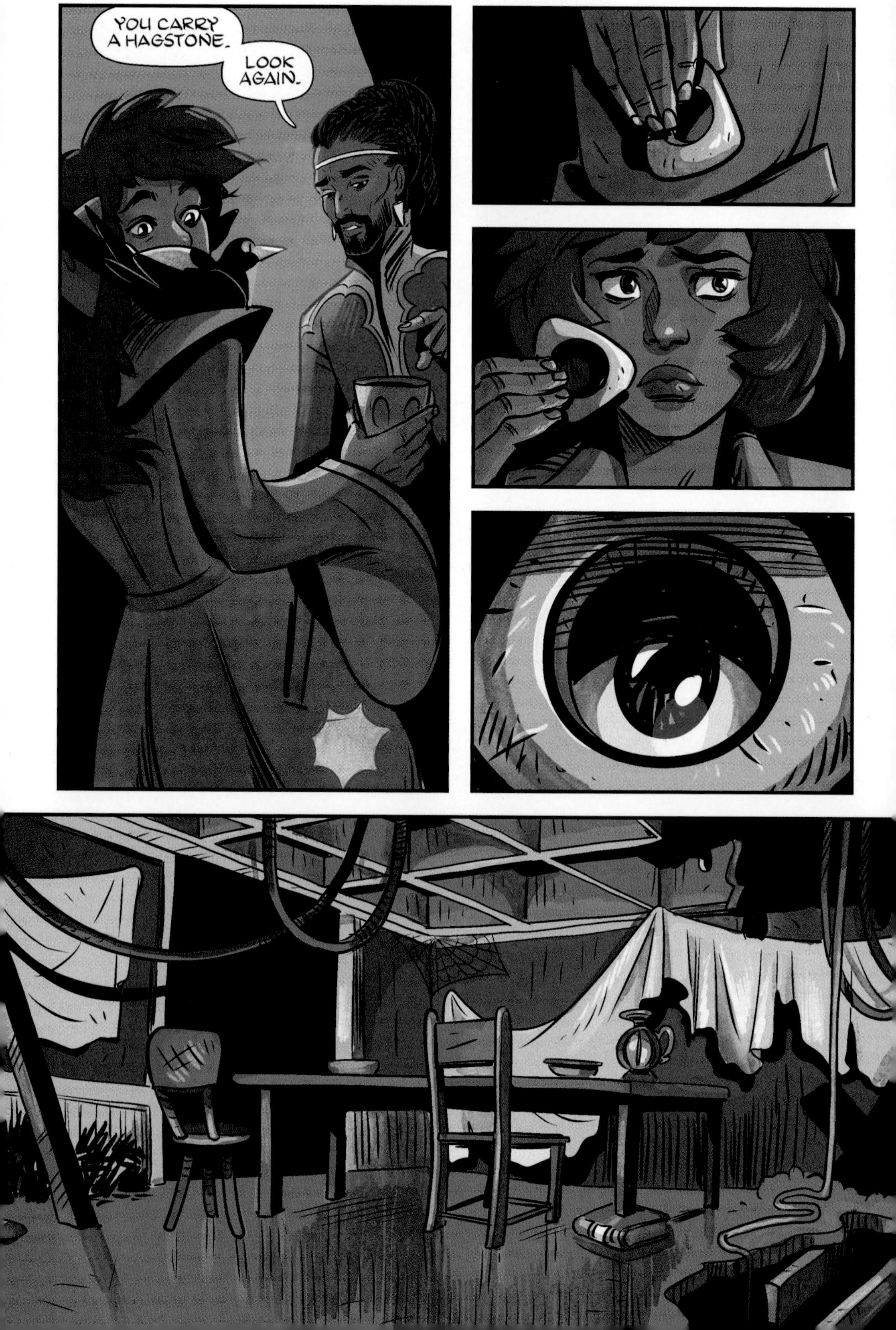

YOU CARRY A HAGSTONE.
LOOK AGAIN.

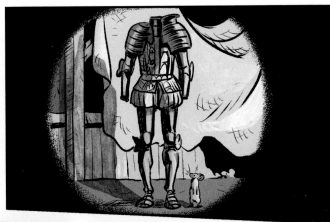

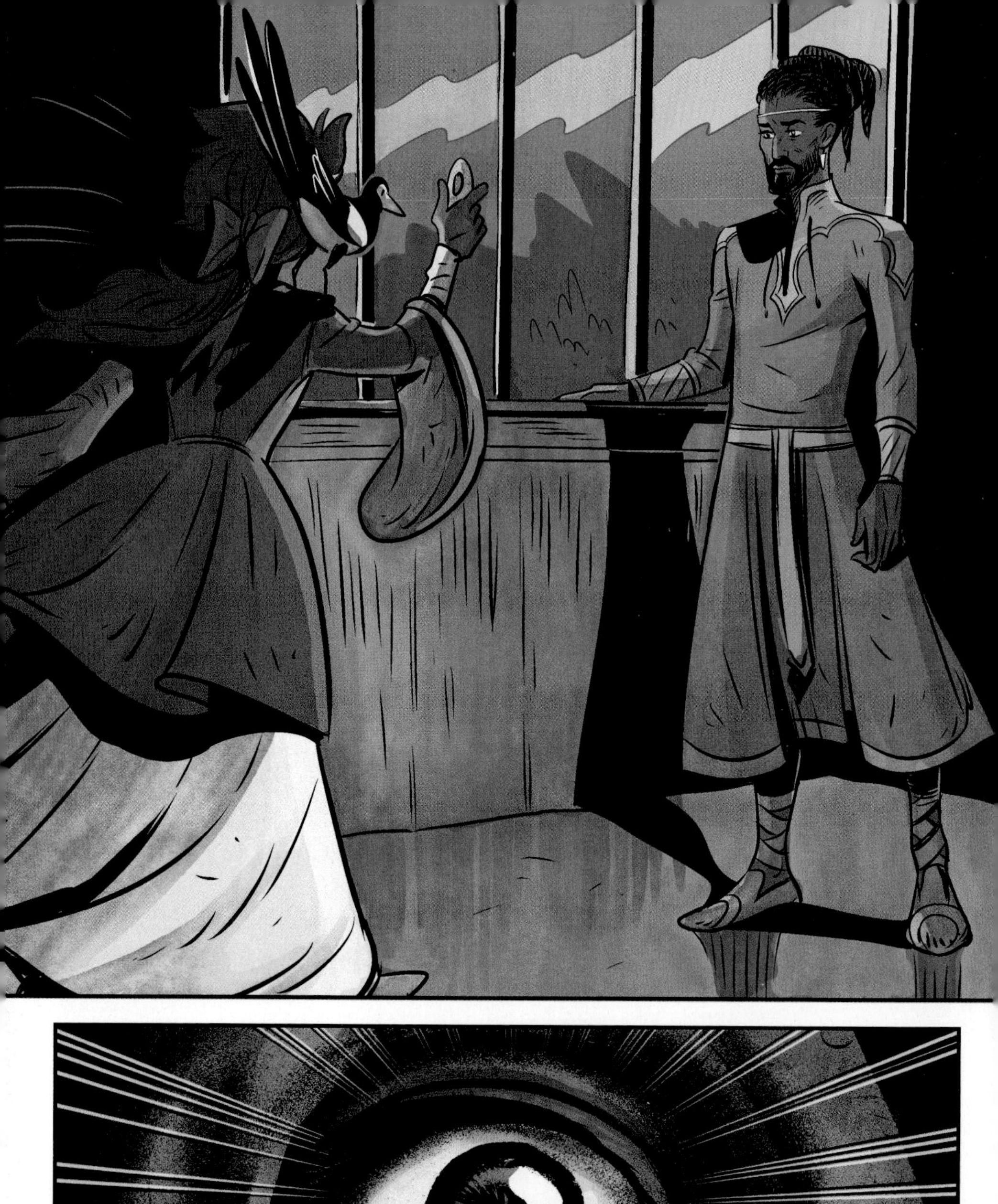

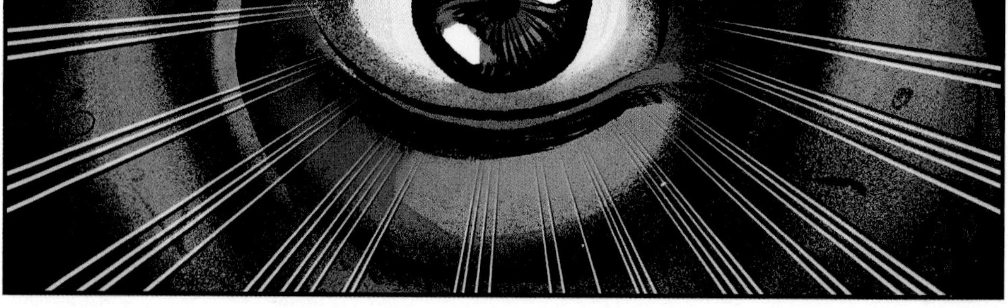

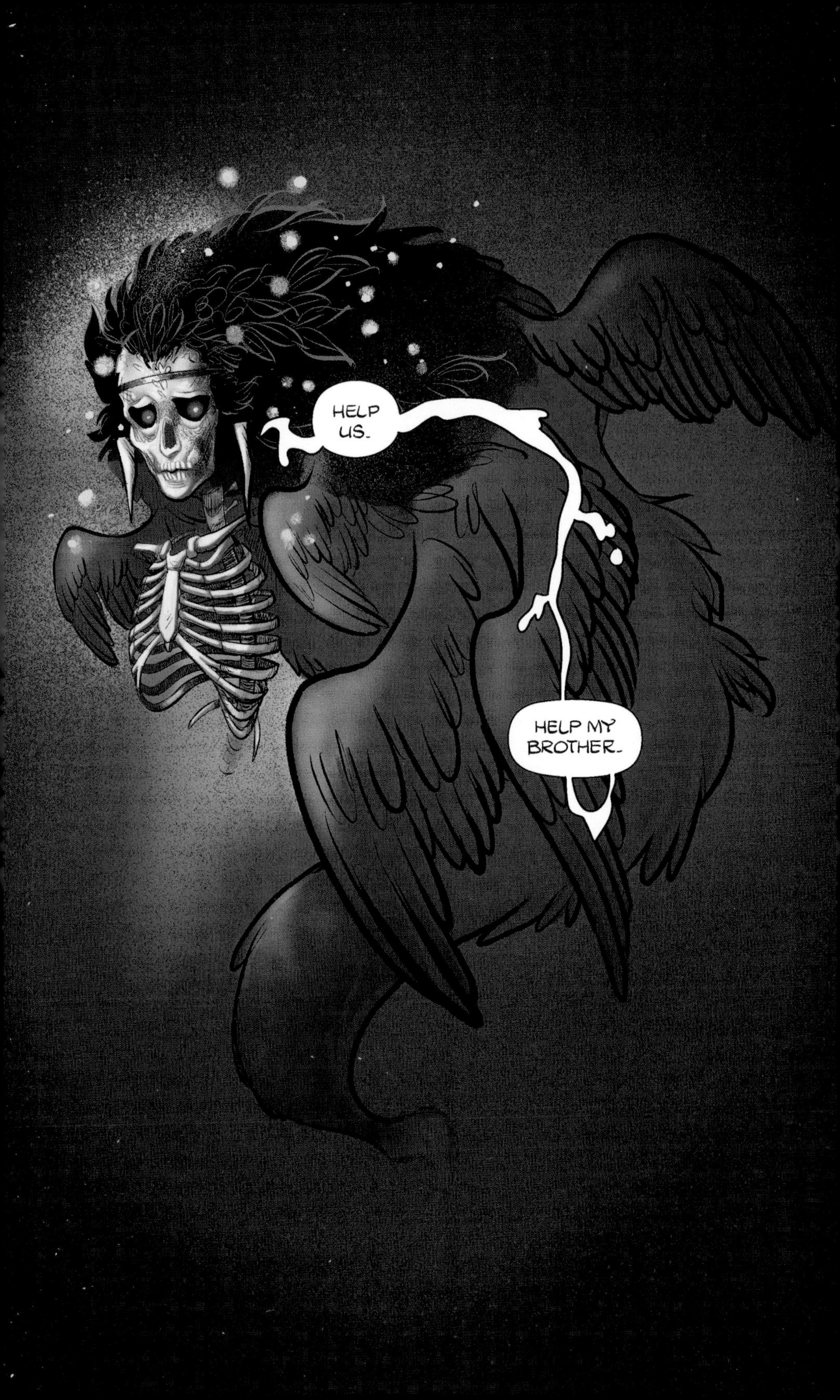
HELP US.
HELP MY BROTHER.

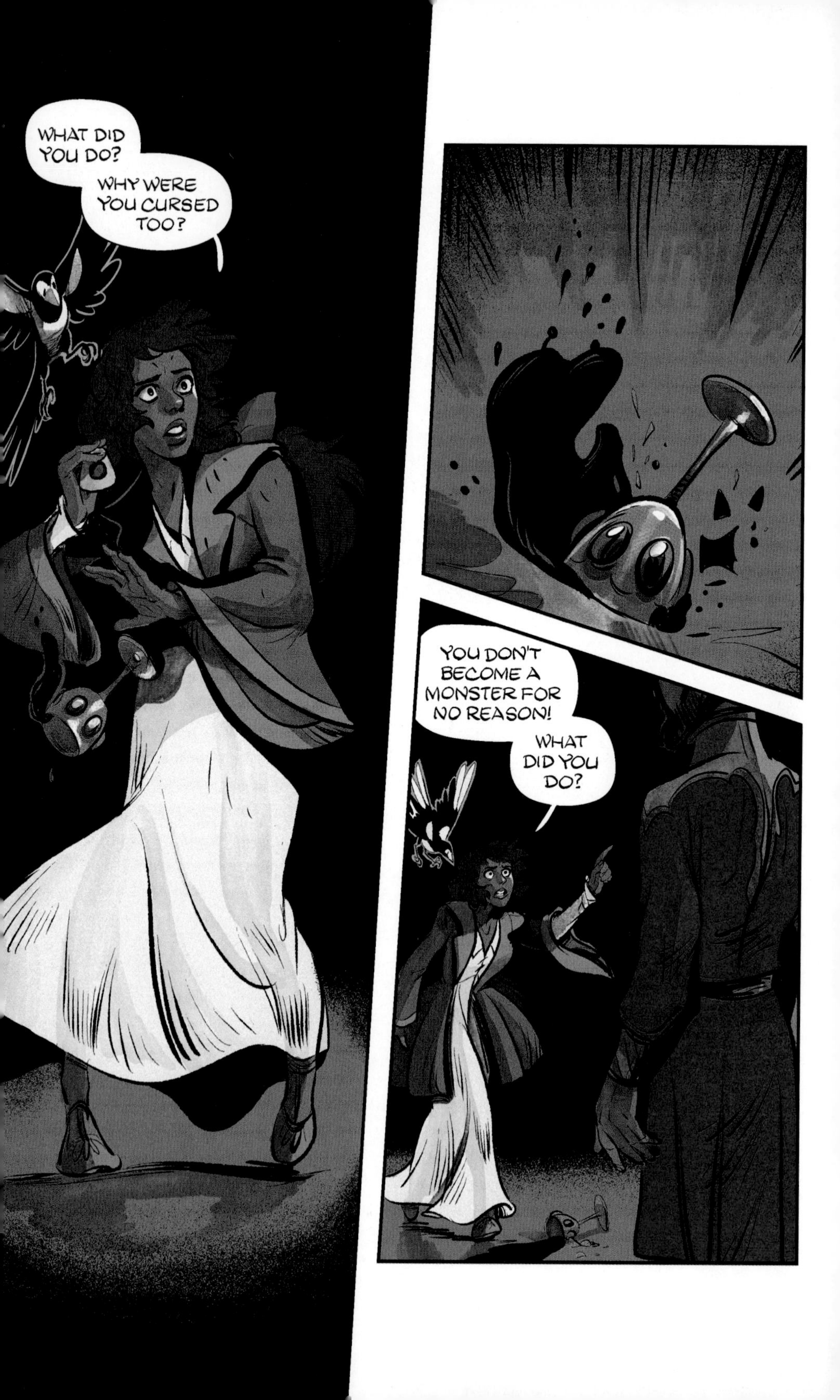
WHAT DID YOU DO?
WHY WERE YOU CURSED TOO?
YOU DON'T BECOME A MONSTER FOR NO REASON!
WHAT DID YOU DO?

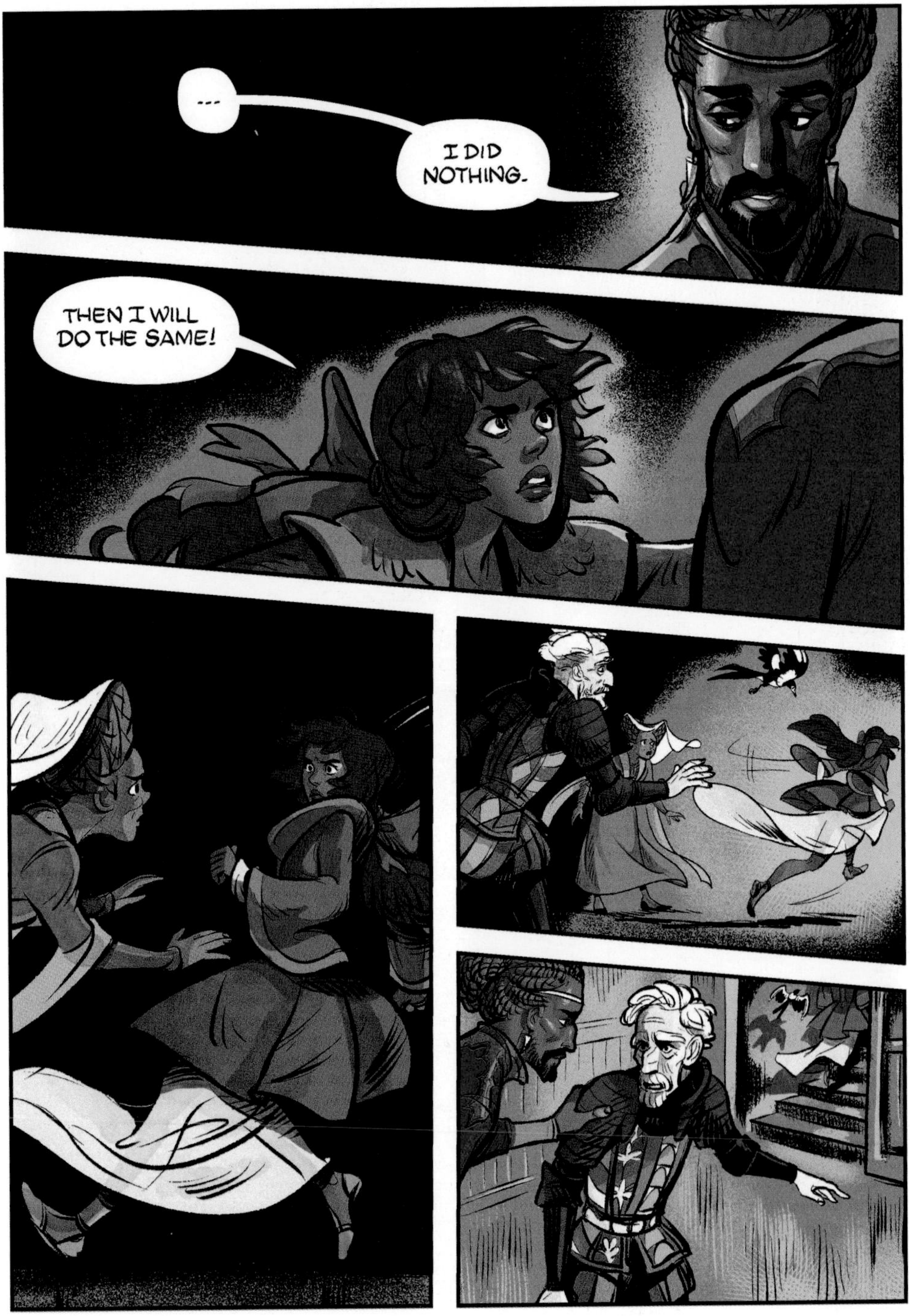
...
I DID NOTHING.
THEN I WILL DO THE SAME!

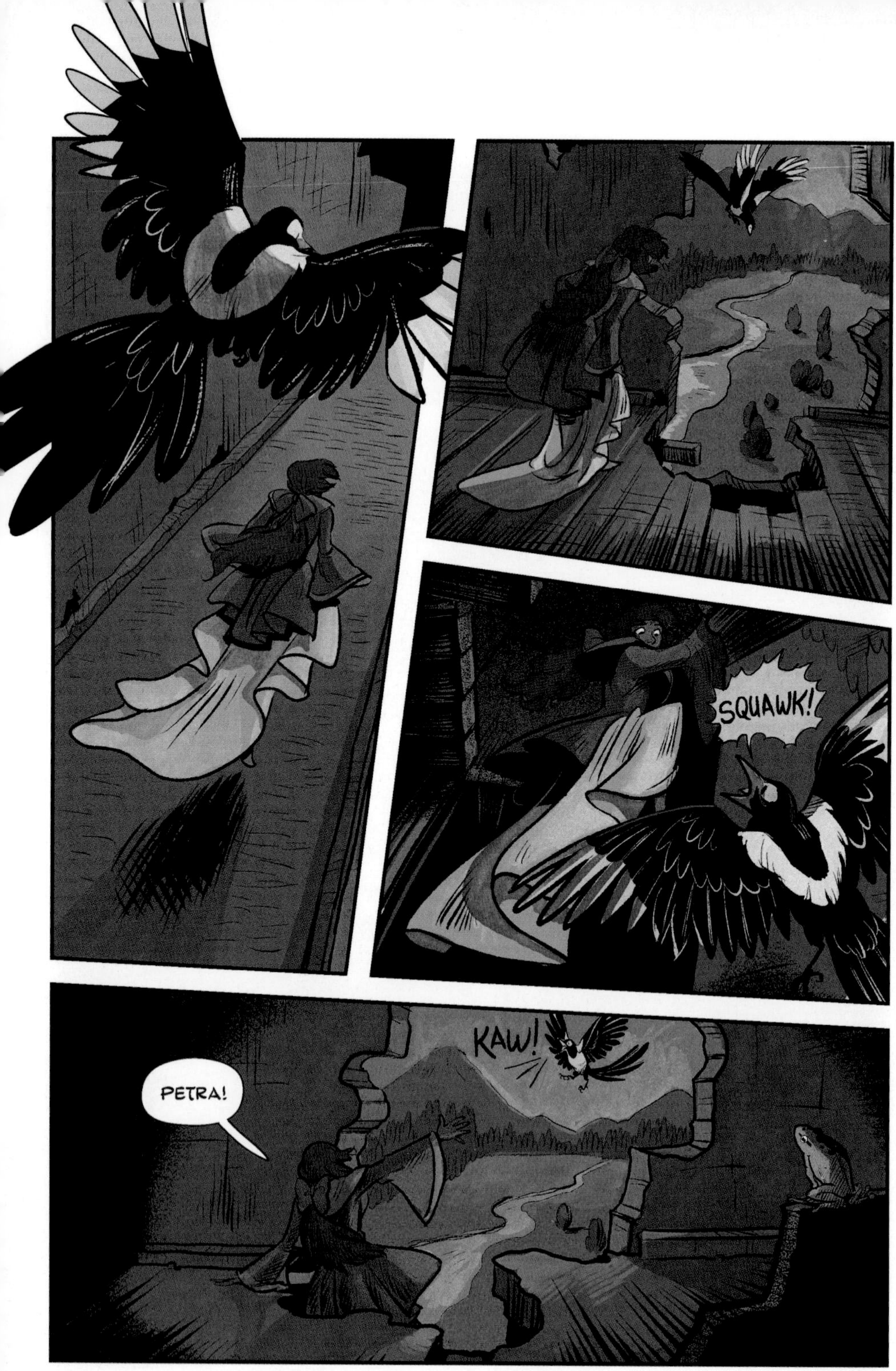
SQUAWK!
KAW!
PETRA!

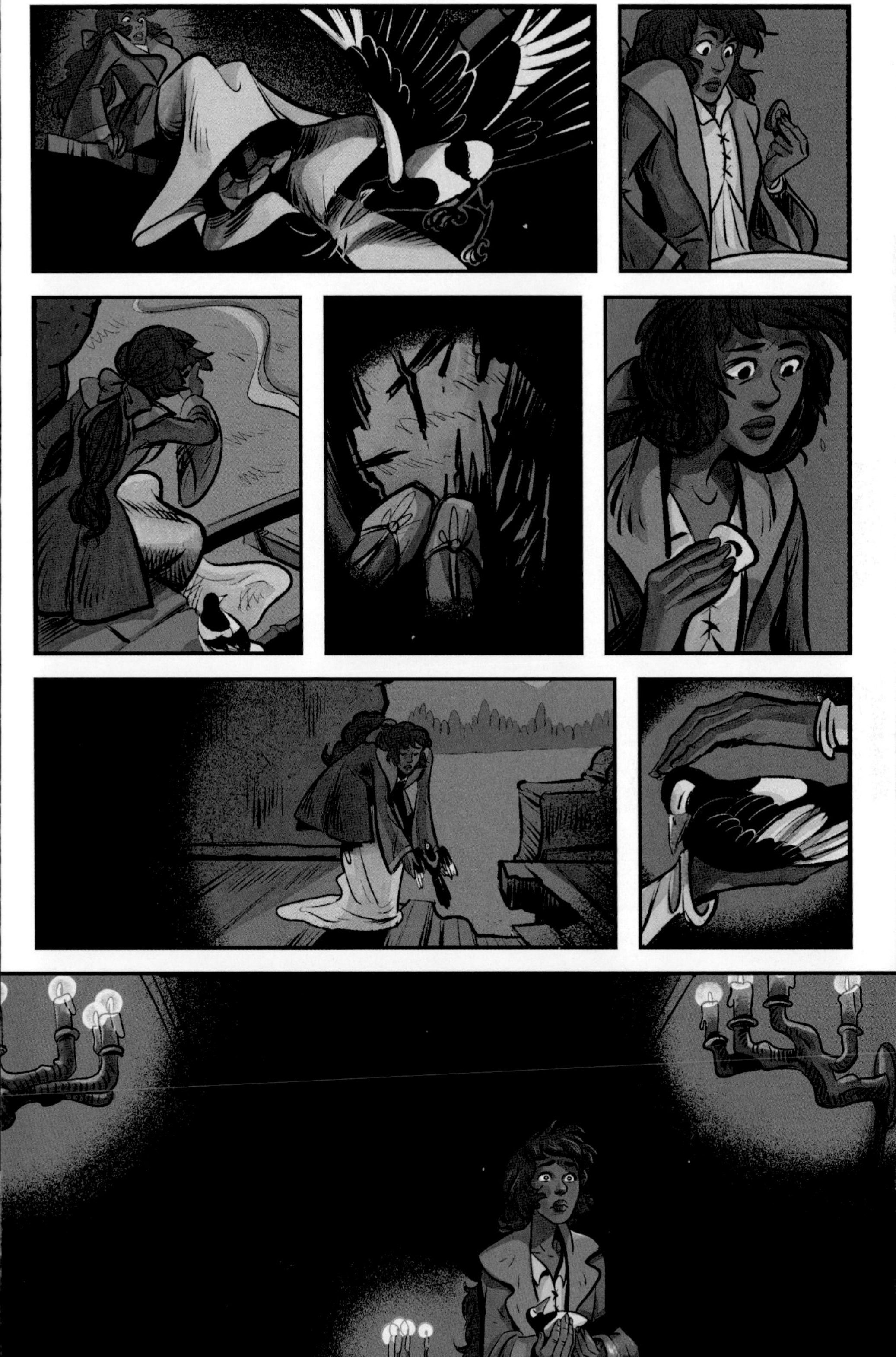

fsh
fsh
fsh
fsh
fwoooosh

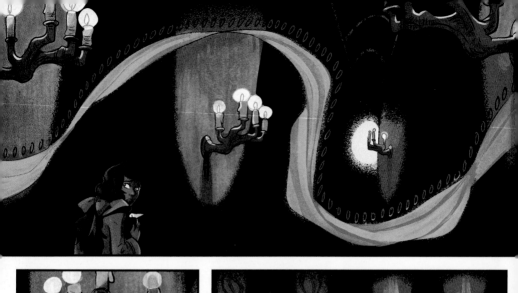

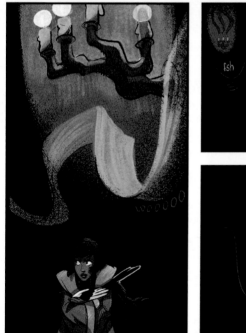

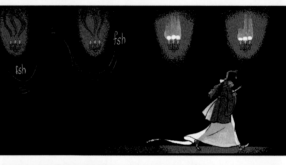

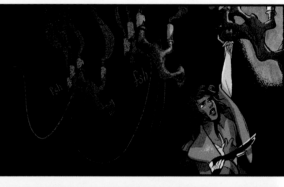

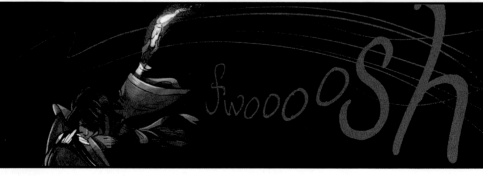

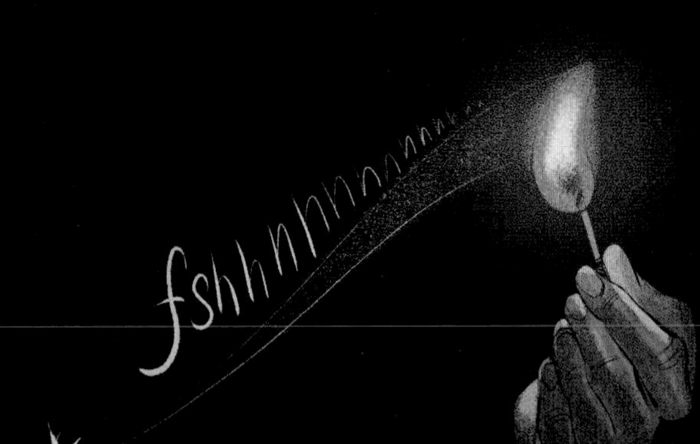
fshhhhhhhhhhh

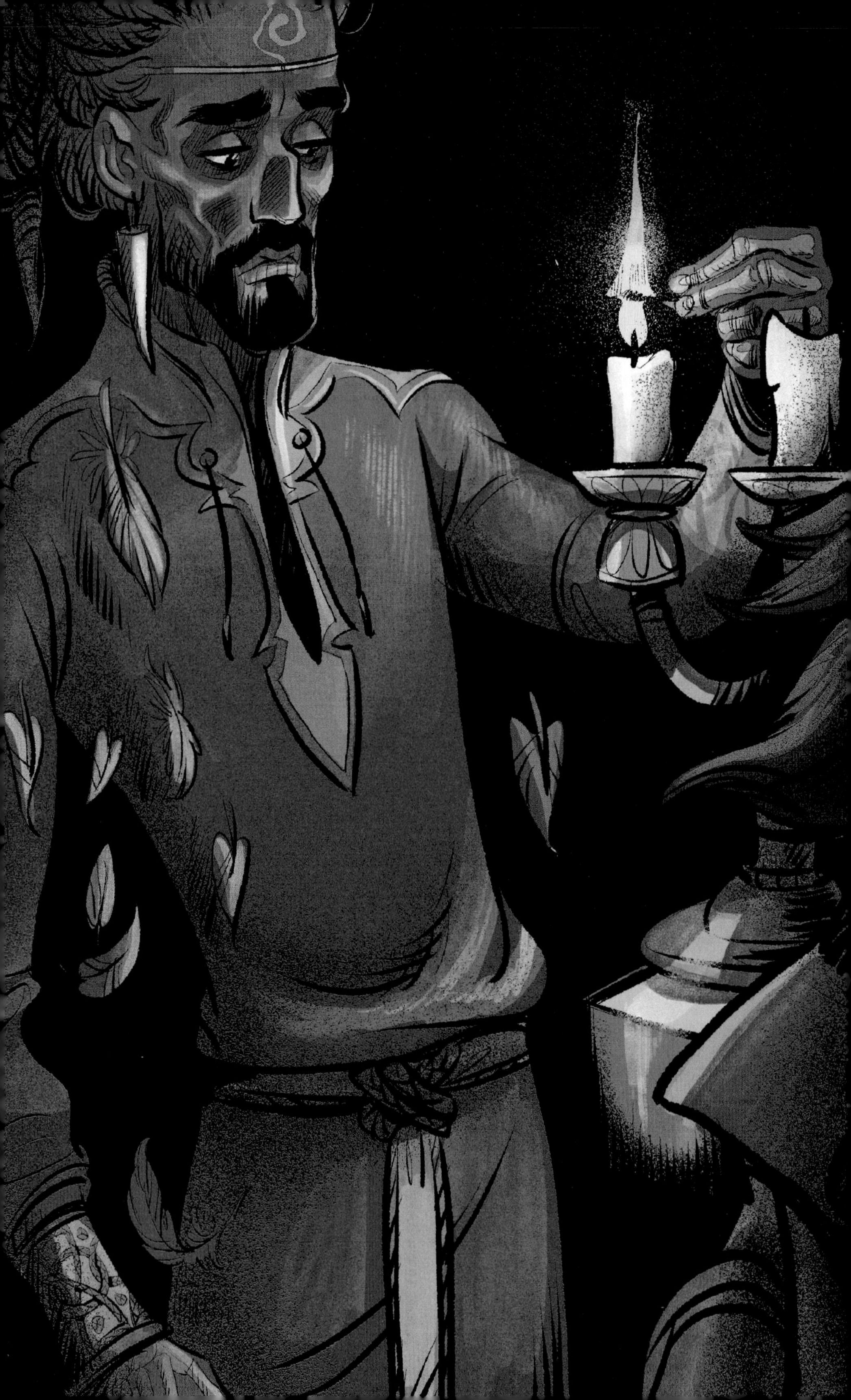

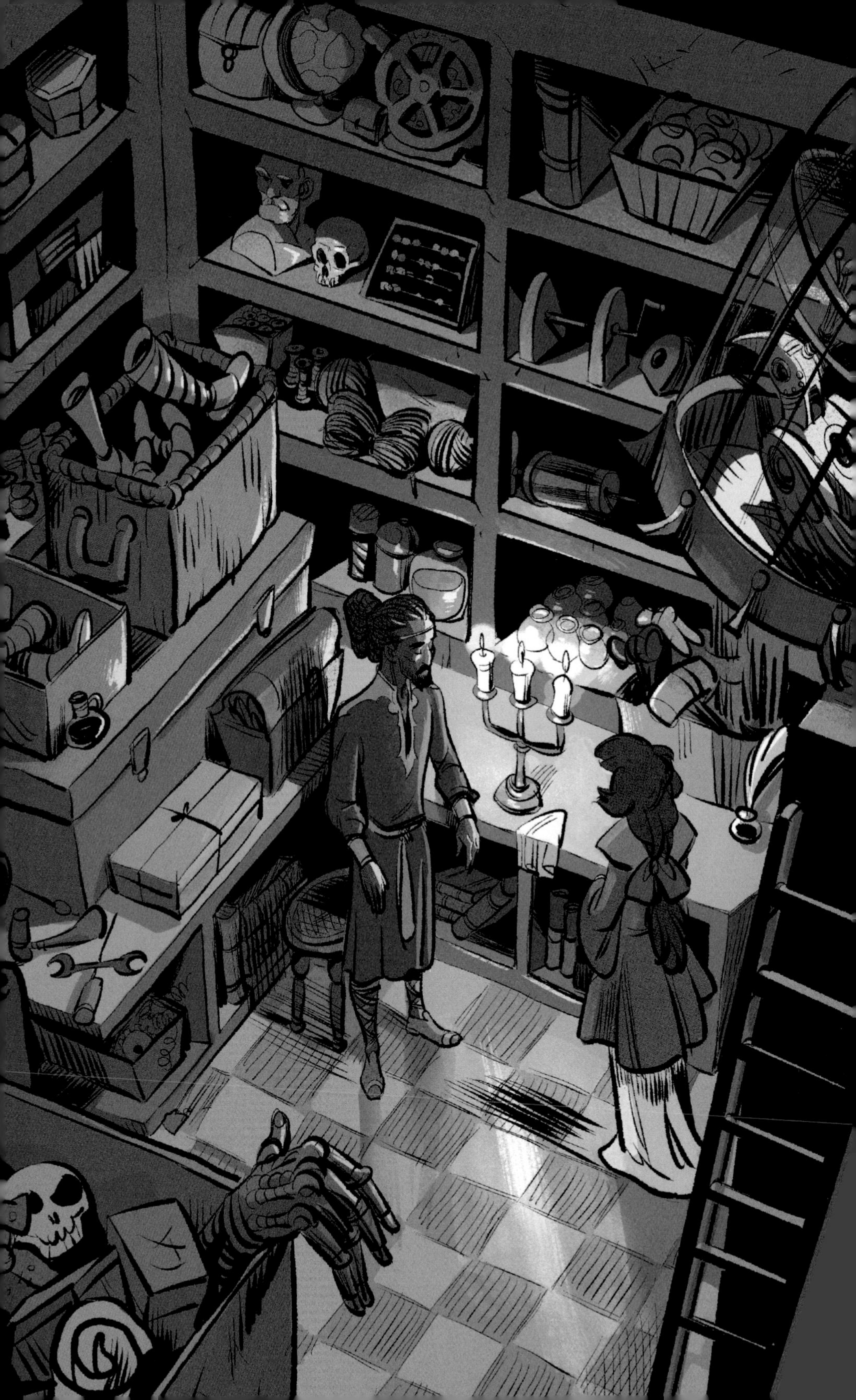

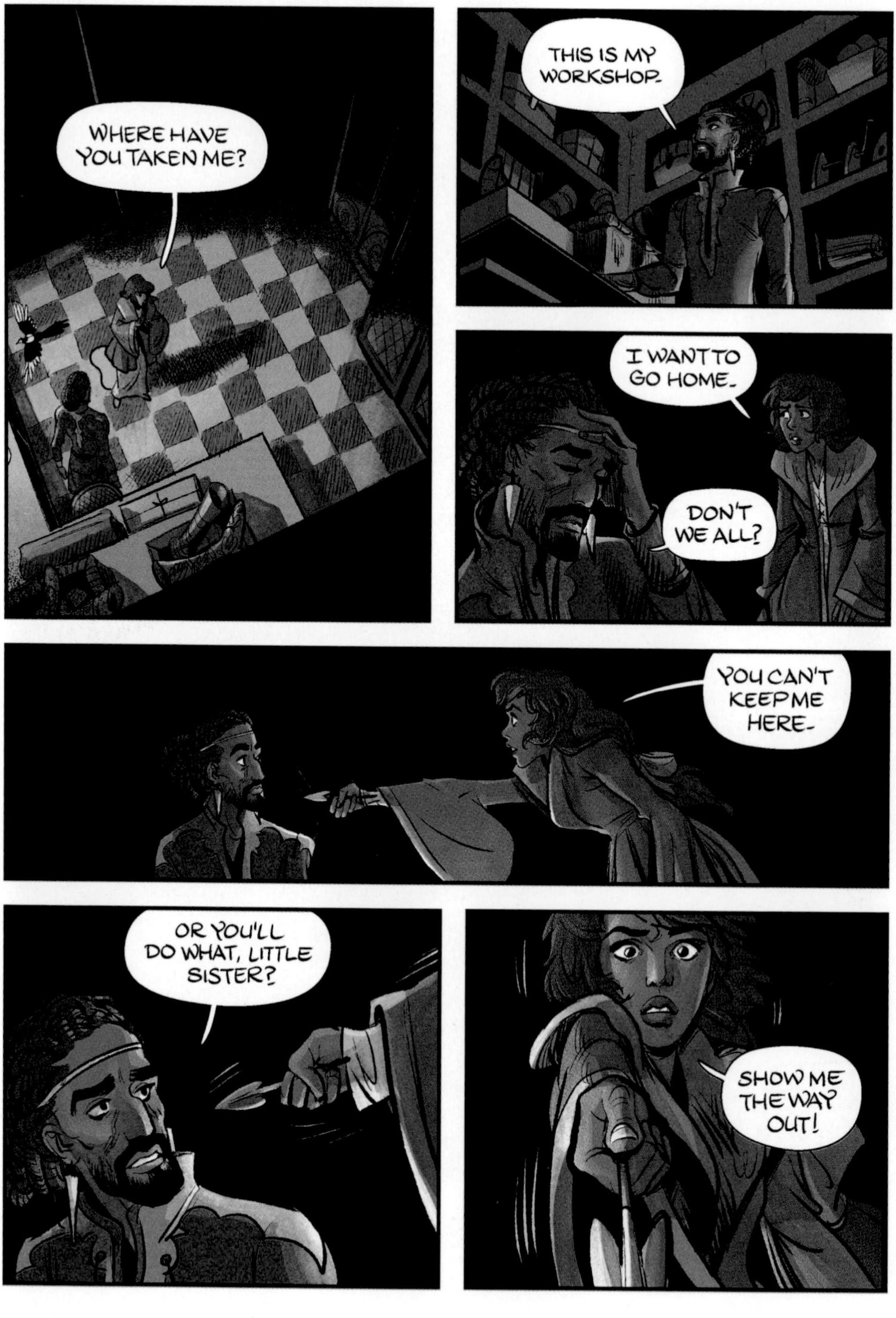
WHERE HAVE YOU TAKEN ME?
THIS IS MY WORKSHOP.
I WANT TO GO HOME.
DON'T WE ALL?
YOU CAN'T KEEP ME HERE.
OR YOU'LL DO WHAT, LITTLE SISTER?
SHOW ME THE WAY OUT!

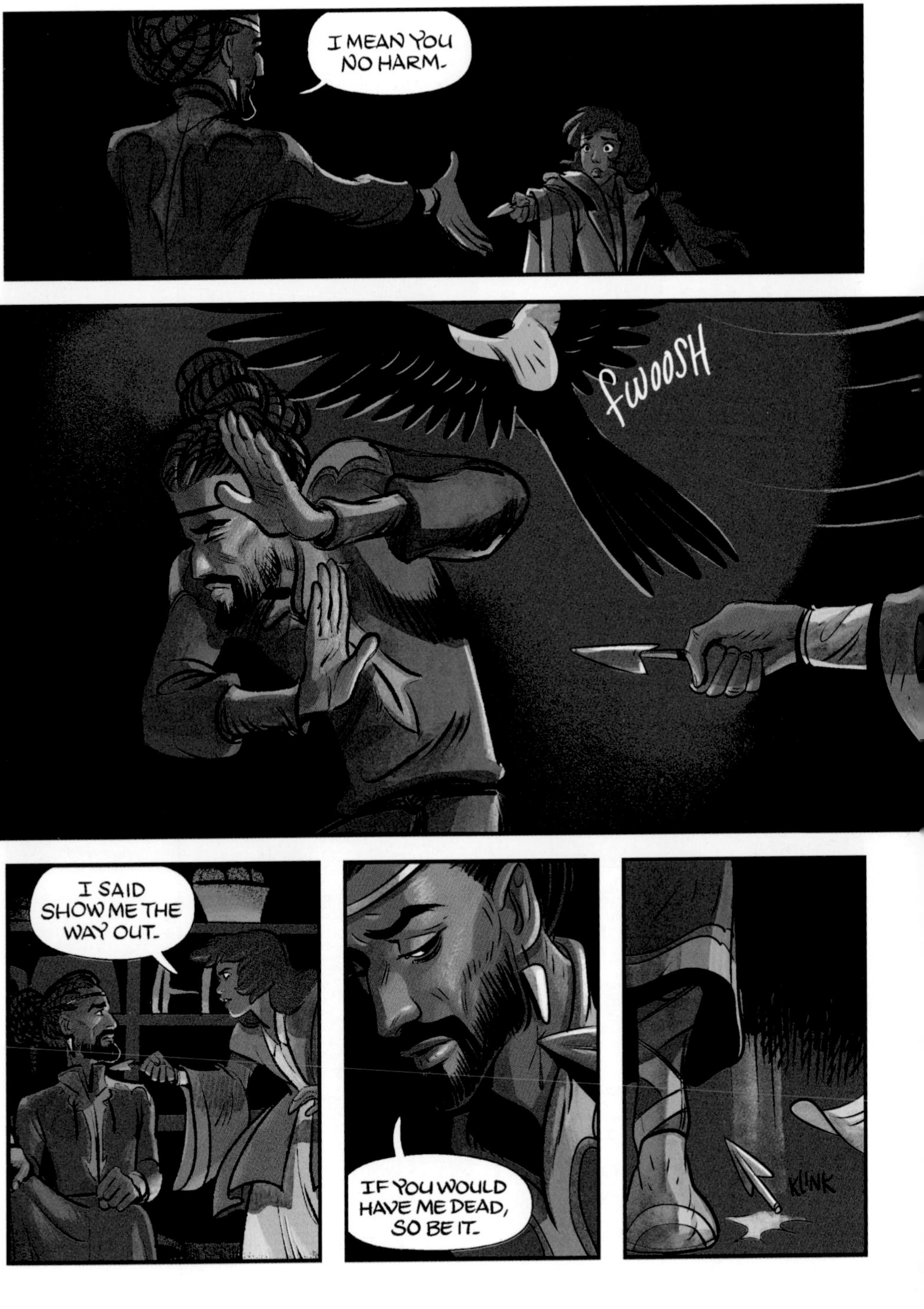
I MEAN YOU NO HARM.
FWOOSH
I SAID SHOW ME THE WAY OUT.
IF YOU WOULD HAVE ME DEAD, SO BE IT.
KLINK

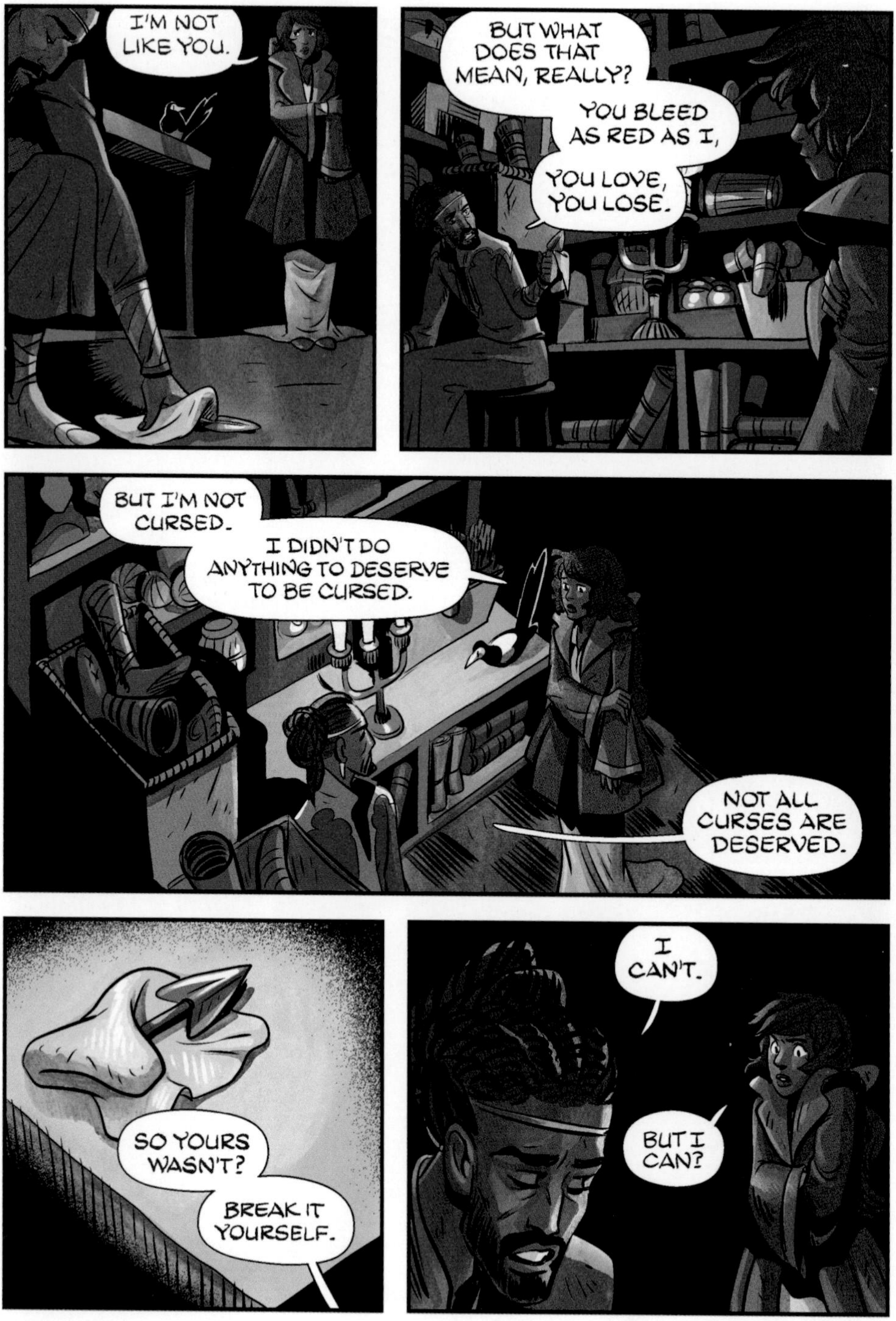
I'M NOT LIKE YOU.
BUT WHAT DOES THAT MEAN, REALLY?
YOU BLEED AS RED AS I,
YOU LOVE, YOU LOSE.
BUT I'M NOT CURSED.
I DIDN'T DO ANYTHING TO DESERVE TO BE CURSED.
NOT ALL CURSES ARE DESERVED.
SO YOURS WASN'T?
BREAK IT YOURSELF.
I CAN'T.
BUT I CAN?

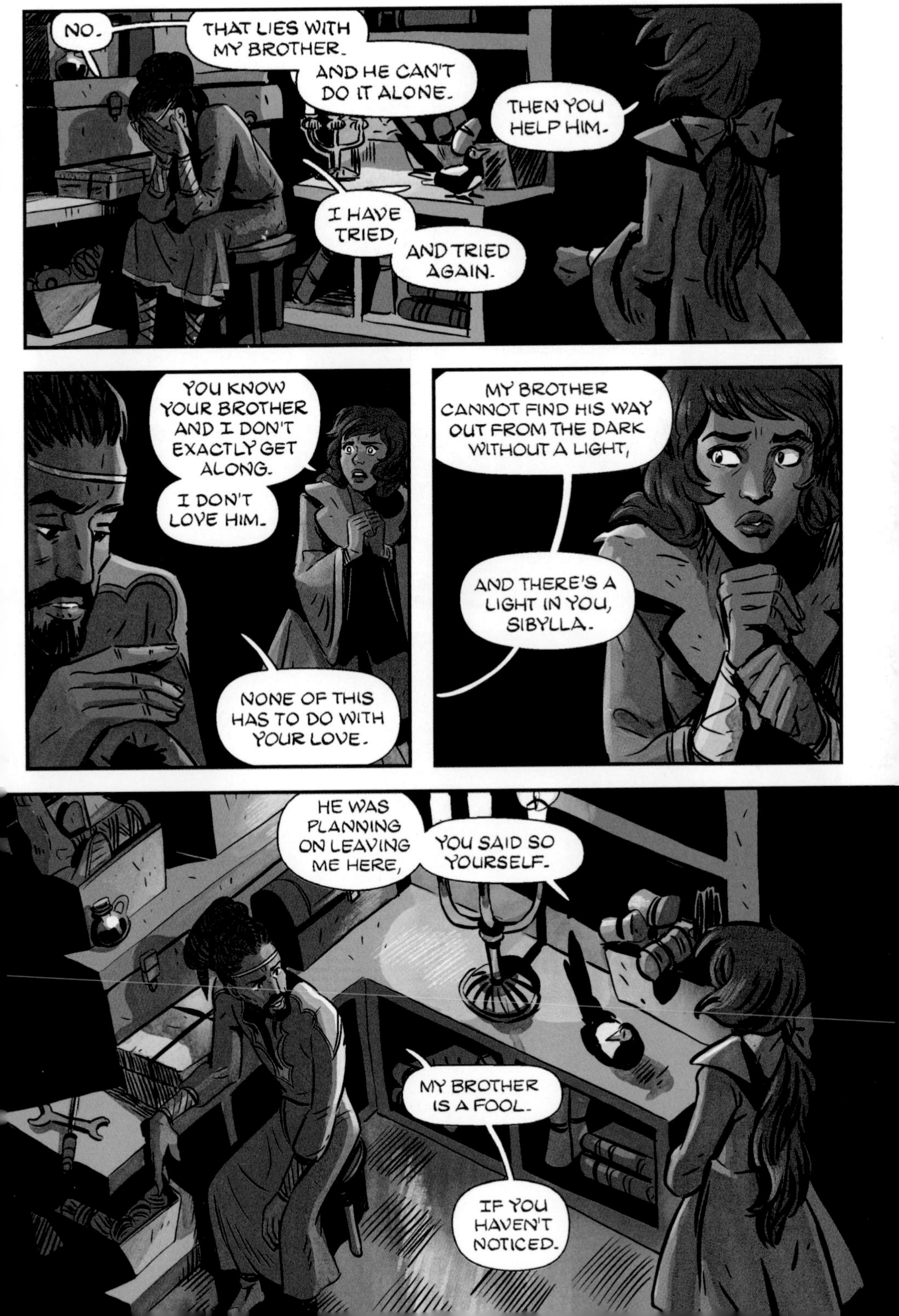
NO.
THAT LIES WITH MY BROTHER.
AND HE CAN'T DO IT ALONE.
THEN YOU HELP HIM.
I HAVE TRIED,
AND TRIED AGAIN.
YOU KNOW YOUR BROTHER AND I DON'T EXACTLY GET ALONG.
I DON'T LOVE HIM.
NONE OF THIS HAS TO DO WITH YOUR LOVE.
MY BROTHER CANNOT FIND HIS WAY OUT FROM THE DARK WITHOUT A LIGHT,
AND THERE'S A LIGHT IN YOU, SIBYLLA.
HE WAS PLANNING ON LEAVING ME HERE,
YOU SAID SO YOURSELF.
MY BROTHER IS A FOOL.
IF YOU HAVEN'T NOTICED.

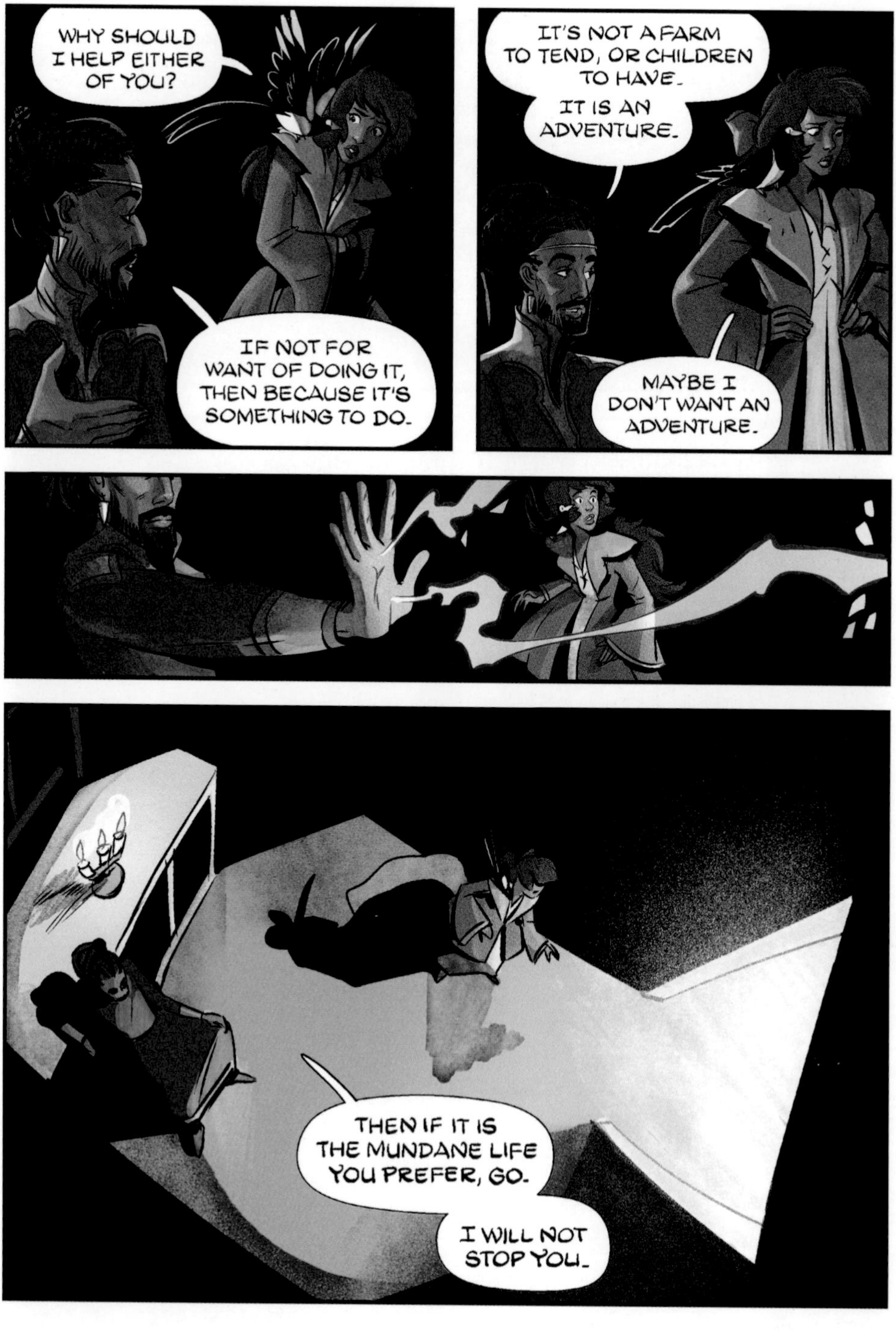
WHY SHOULD I HELP EITHER OF YOU?
IF NOT FOR WANT OF DOING IT, THEN BECAUSE IT'S SOMETHING TO DO.
IT'S NOT A FARM TO TEND, OR CHILDREN TO HAVE.
IT IS AN ADVENTURE.
MAYBE I DON'T WANT AN ADVENTURE.
THEN IF IT IS THE MUNDANE LIFE YOU PREFER, GO.
I WILL NOT STOP YOU.

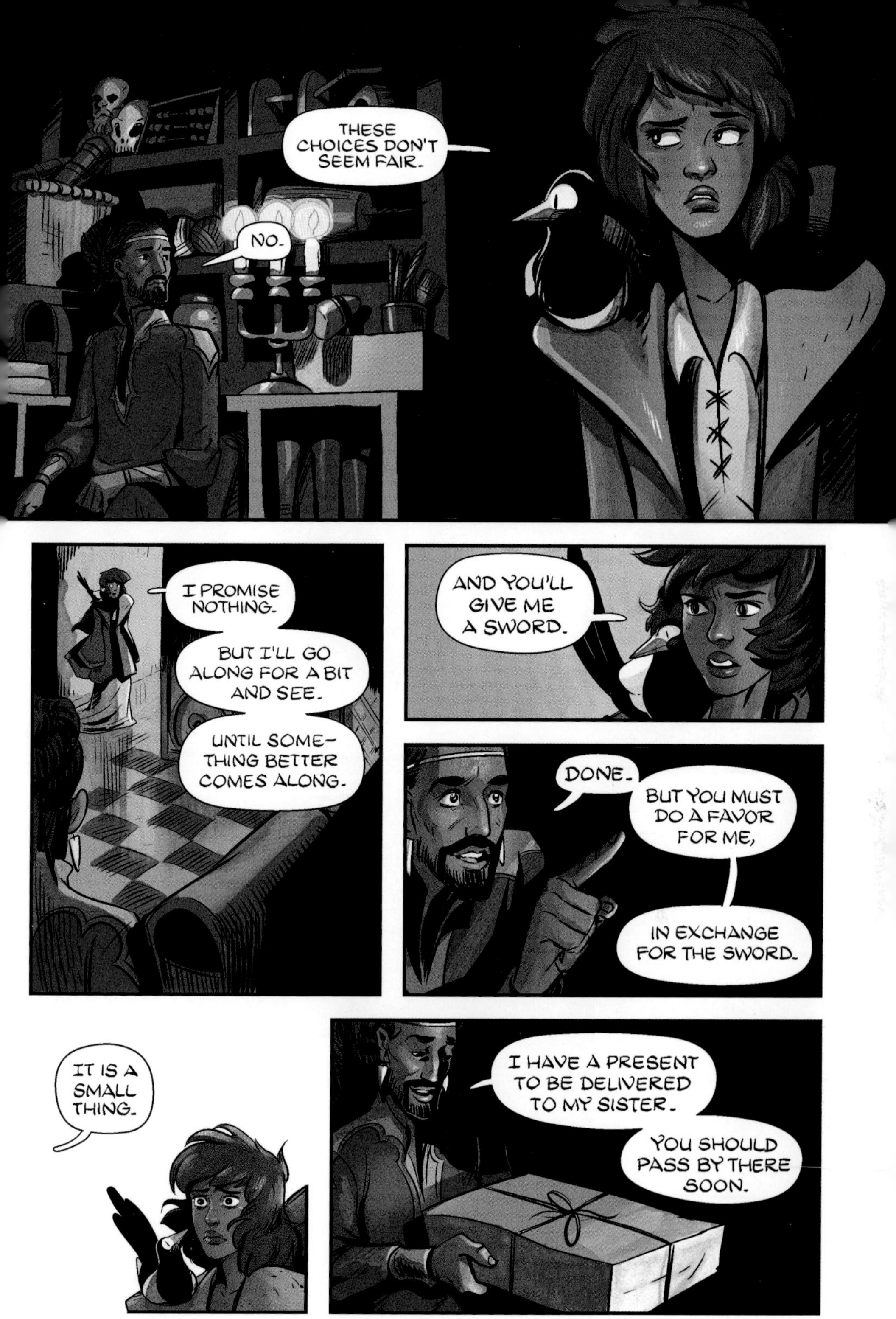
THESE CHOICES DON'T SEEM FAIR.
NO.
I PROMISE NOTHING.
BUT I'LL GO ALONG FOR A BIT AND SEE.
UNTIL SOME-THING BETTER COMES ALONG.
AND YOU'LL GIVE ME A SWORD.
DONE.
BUT YOU MUST DO A FAVOR FOR ME,
IN EXCHANGE FOR THE SWORD.
IT IS A SMALL THING.
I HAVE A PRESENT TO BE DELIVERED TO MY SISTER.
YOU SHOULD PASS BY THERE SOON.

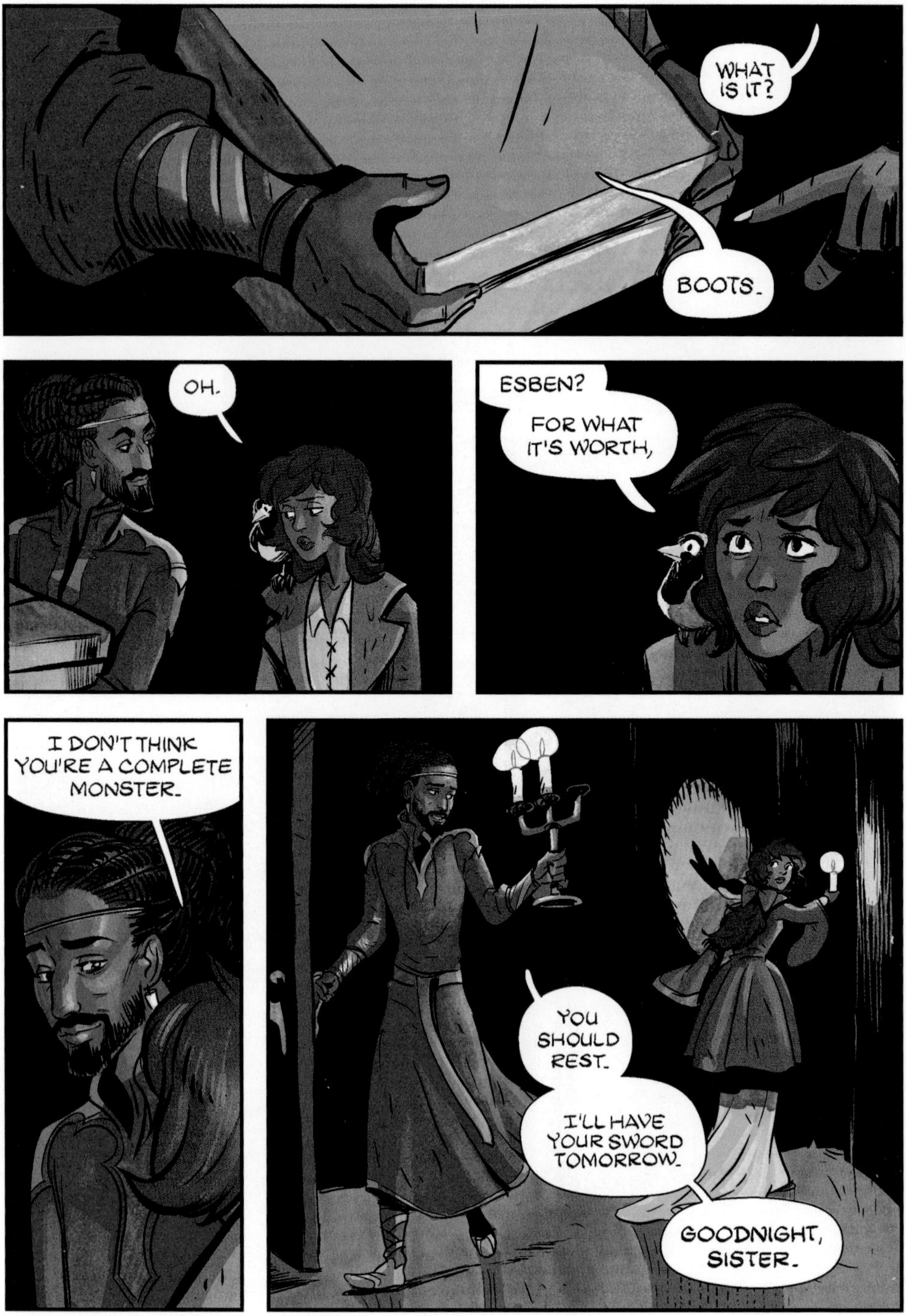
WHAT IS IT?
BOOTS.
OH.
ESBEN?
FOR WHAT IT'S WORTH,
I DON'T THINK YOU'RE A COMPLETE MONSTER.
YOU SHOULD REST.
I'LL HAVE YOUR SWORD TOMORROW.
GOODNIGHT, SISTER.

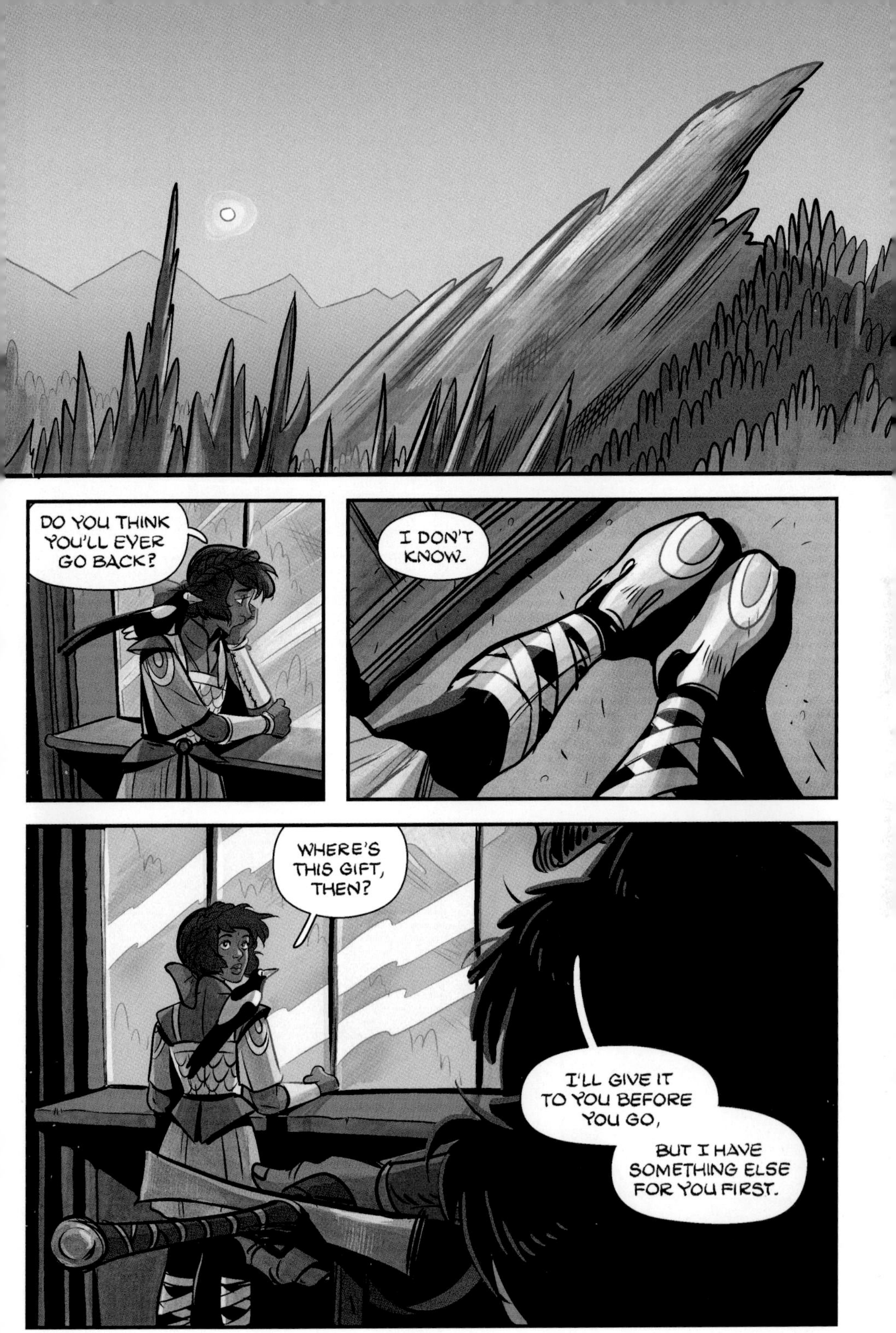
DO YOU THINK YOU'LL EVER GO BACK?
I DON'T KNOW.
WHERE'S THIS GIFT, THEN?
I'LL GIVE IT TO YOU BEFORE YOU GO,
BUT I HAVE SOMETHING ELSE FOR YOU FIRST.

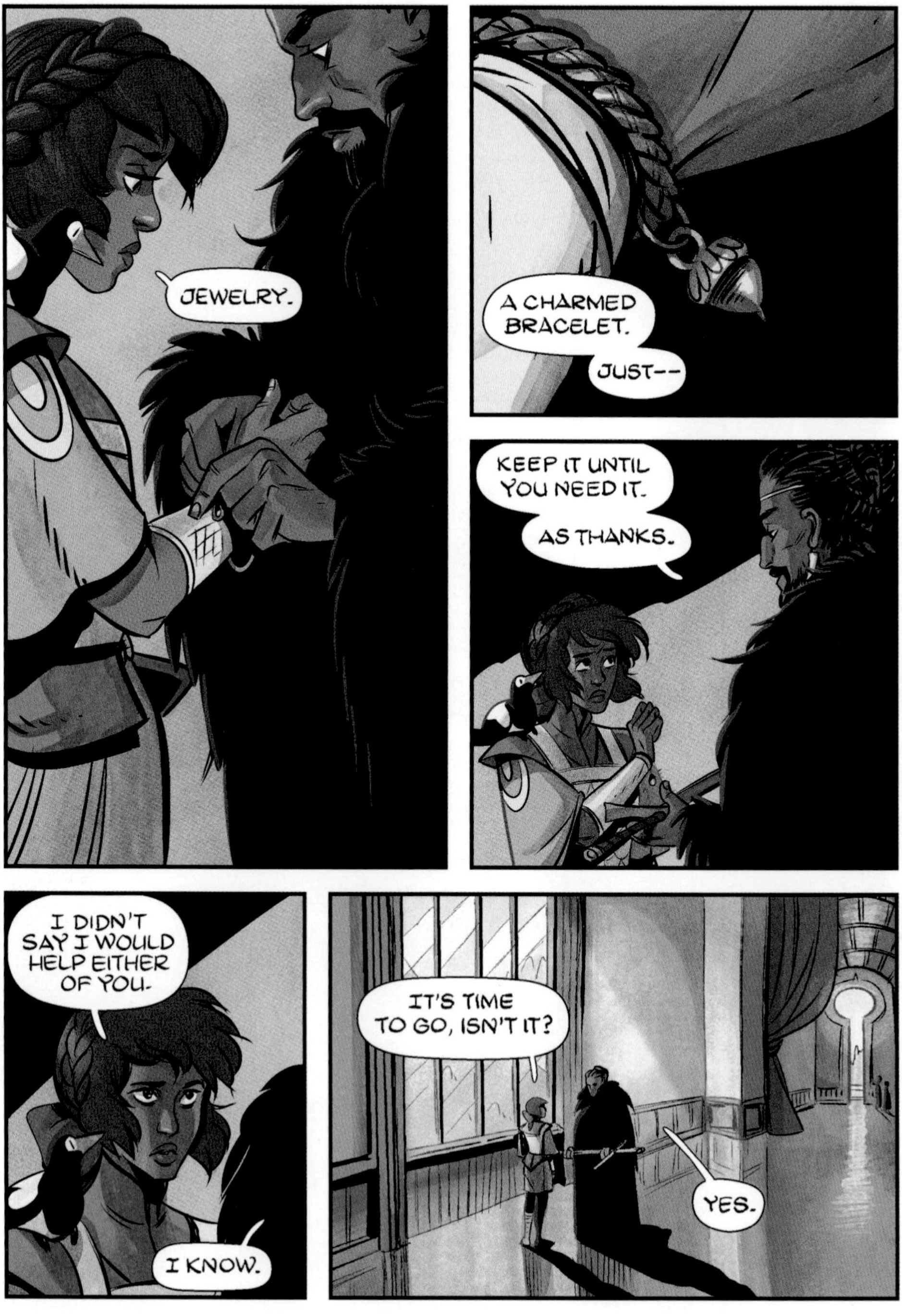
JEWELRY.
A CHARMED BRACELET.
JUST--
KEEP IT UNTIL YOU NEED IT.
AS THANKS.
I DIDN'T SAY I WOULD HELP EITHER OF YOU.
I KNOW.
IT'S TIME TO GO, ISN'T IT?
YES.

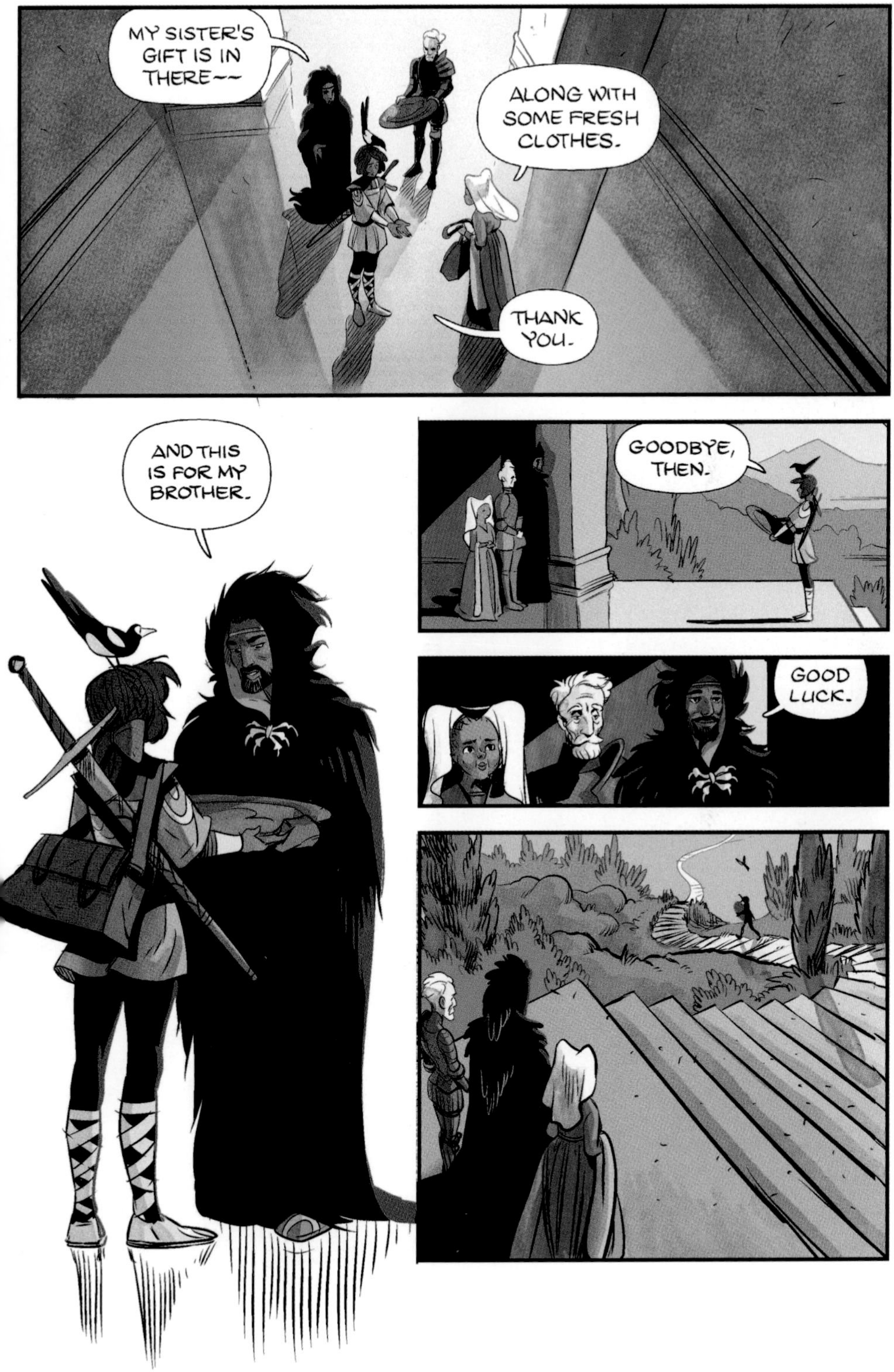
MY SISTER'S GIFT IS IN THERE--
ALONG WITH SOME FRESH CLOTHES.
THANK YOU.
AND THIS IS FOR MY BROTHER.
GOODBYE, THEN.
GOOD LUCK.

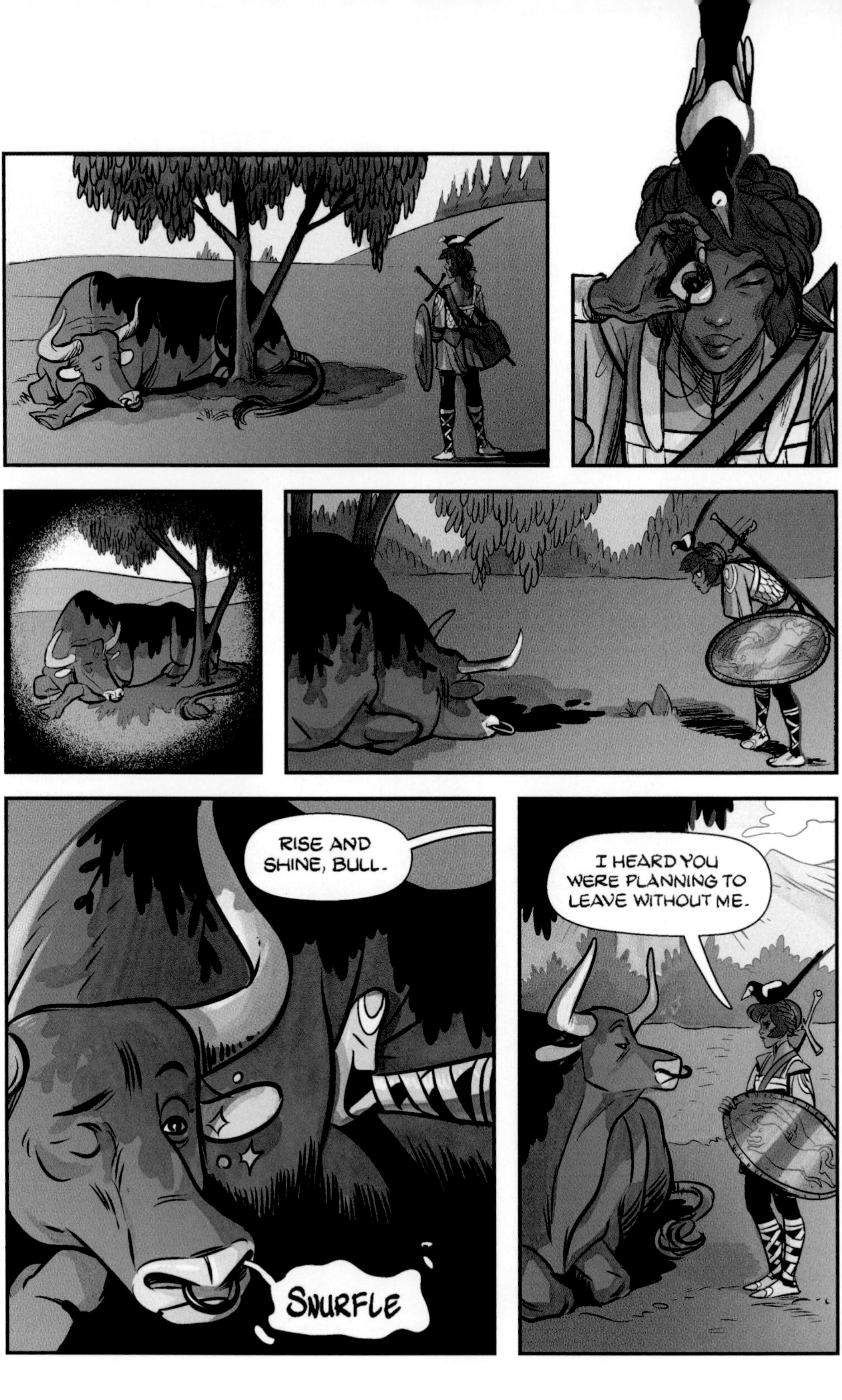
RISE AND SHINE, BULL.
SNURFLE
I HEARD YOU WERE PLANNING TO LEAVE WITHOUT ME.

YOU HAVE A SWORD.

YOUR BROTHER TOLD ME TO USE IT ON YOU IF YOU GOT TOO OUT OF HAND.

YOU AIM TO COME, THEN?

AYE. FOR A WHILE.

IT WOULD BE BETTER IF YOU STAYED HERE, AND WAITED FOR ME.

NO.

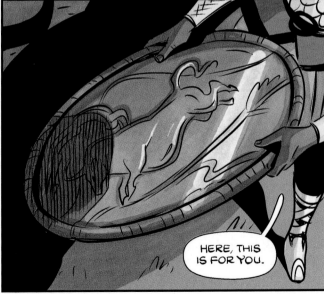

HERE, THIS IS FOR YOU.

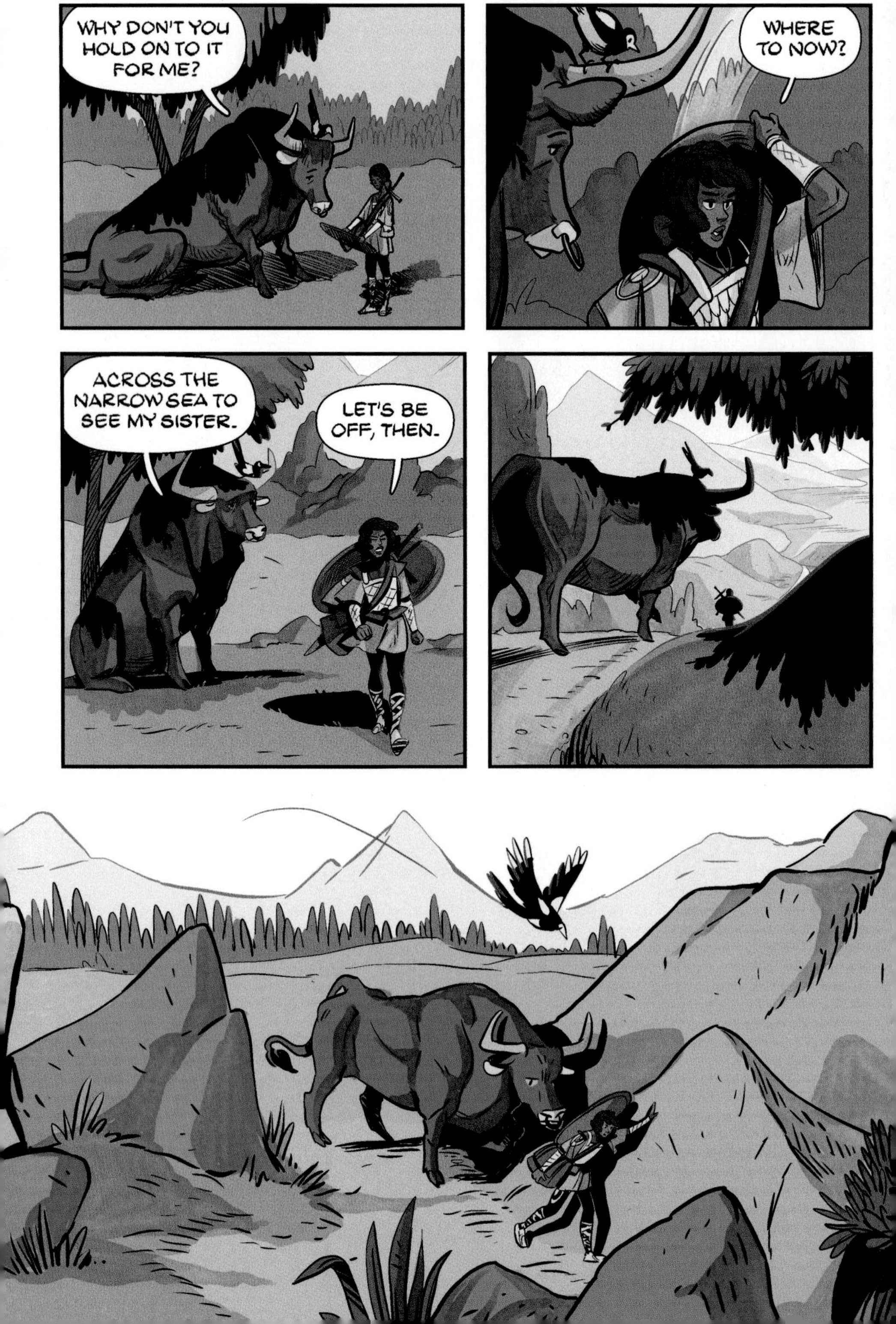
WHY DON'T YOU HOLD ON TO IT FOR ME?
WHERE TO NOW?
ACROSS THE NARROW SEA TO SEE MY SISTER.
LET'S BE OFF, THEN.

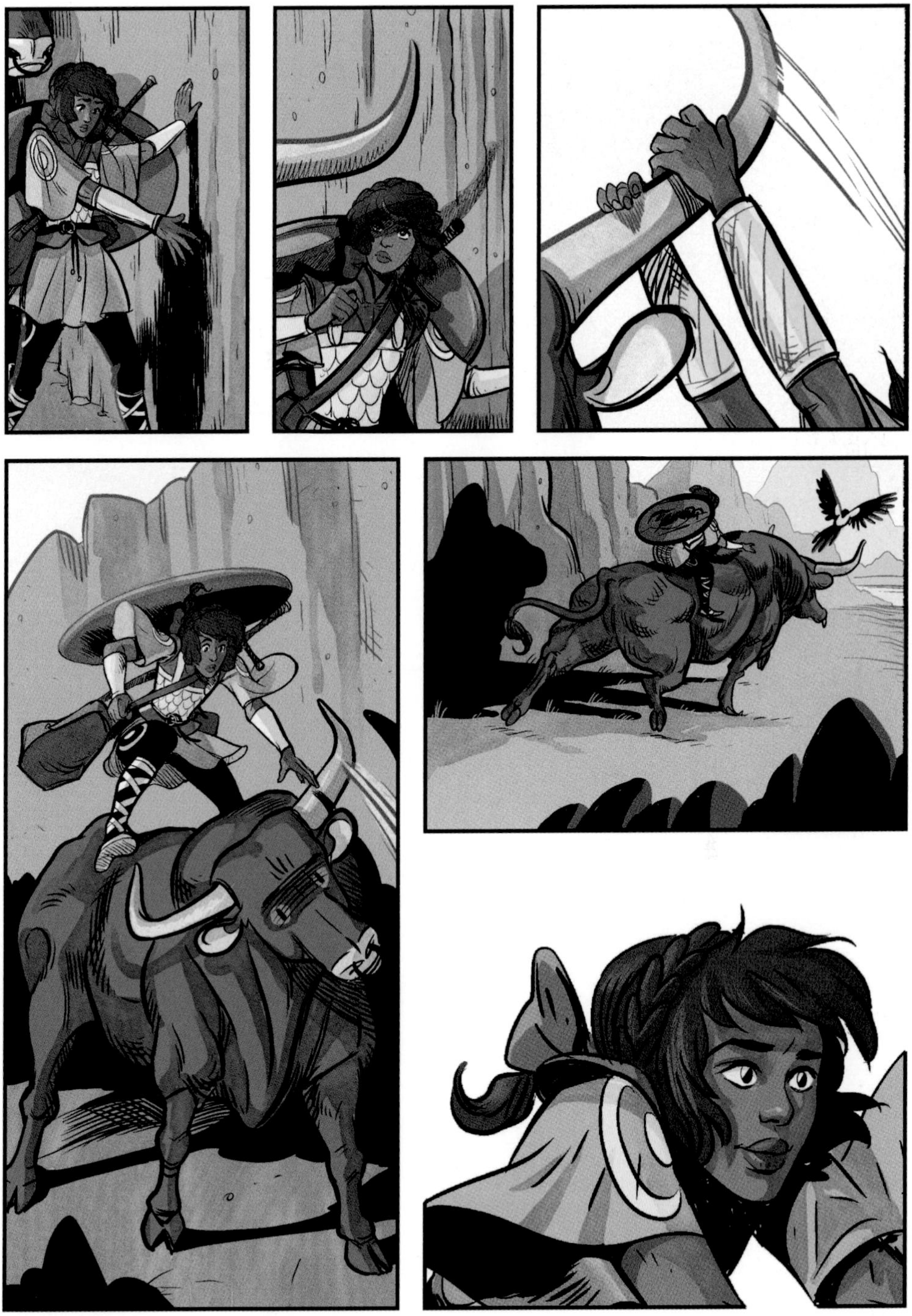

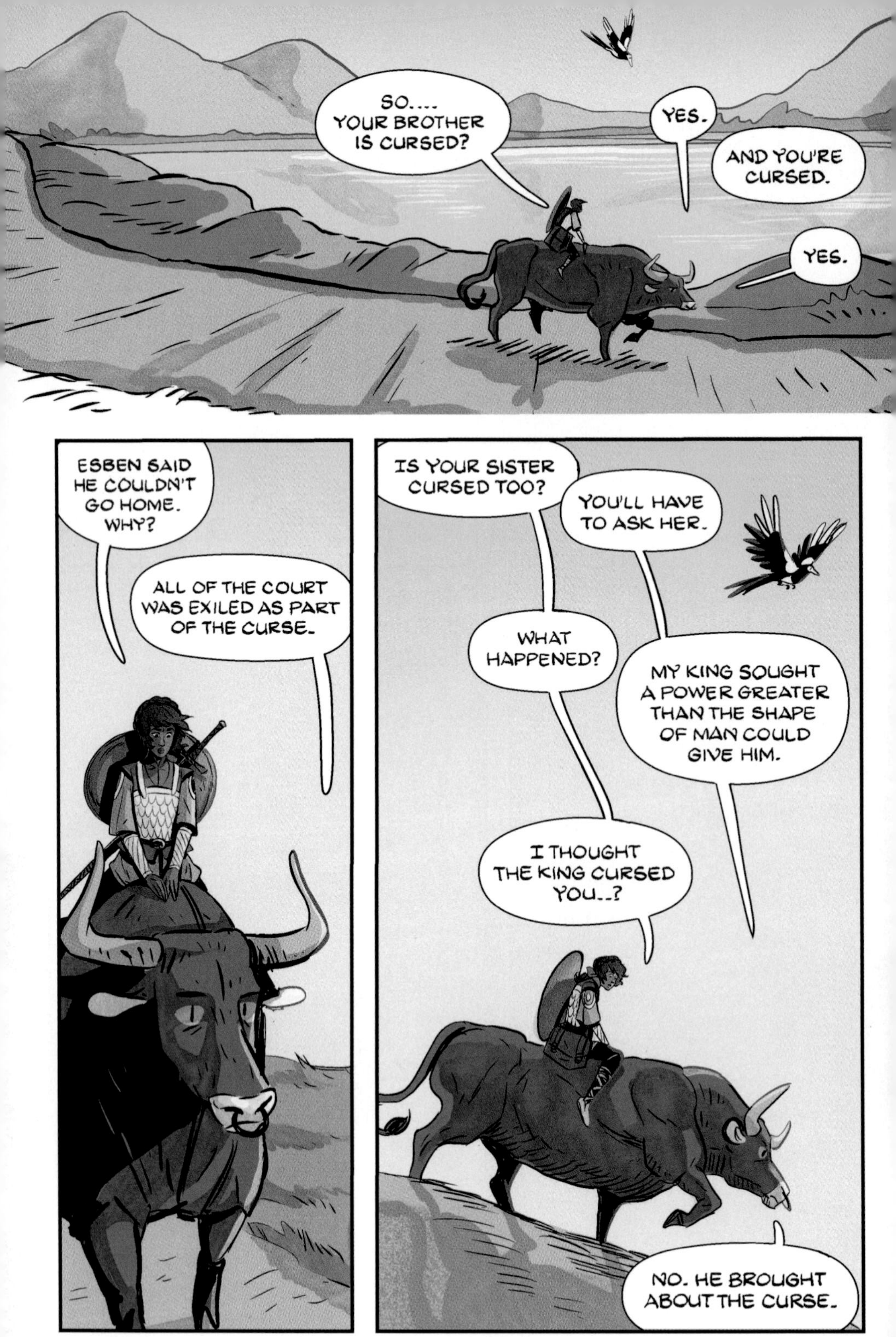
SO.... YOUR BROTHER IS CURSED?
YES.
AND YOU'RE CURSED.
YES.
ESBEN SAID HE COULDN'T GO HOME. WHY?
ALL OF THE COURT WAS EXILED AS PART OF THE CURSE.
IS YOUR SISTER CURSED TOO?
YOU'LL HAVE TO ASK HER.
WHAT HAPPENED?
MY KING SOUGHT A POWER GREATER THAN THE SHAPE OF MAN COULD GIVE HIM.
I THOUGHT THE KING CURSED YOU..?
NO. HE BROUGHT ABOUT THE CURSE.

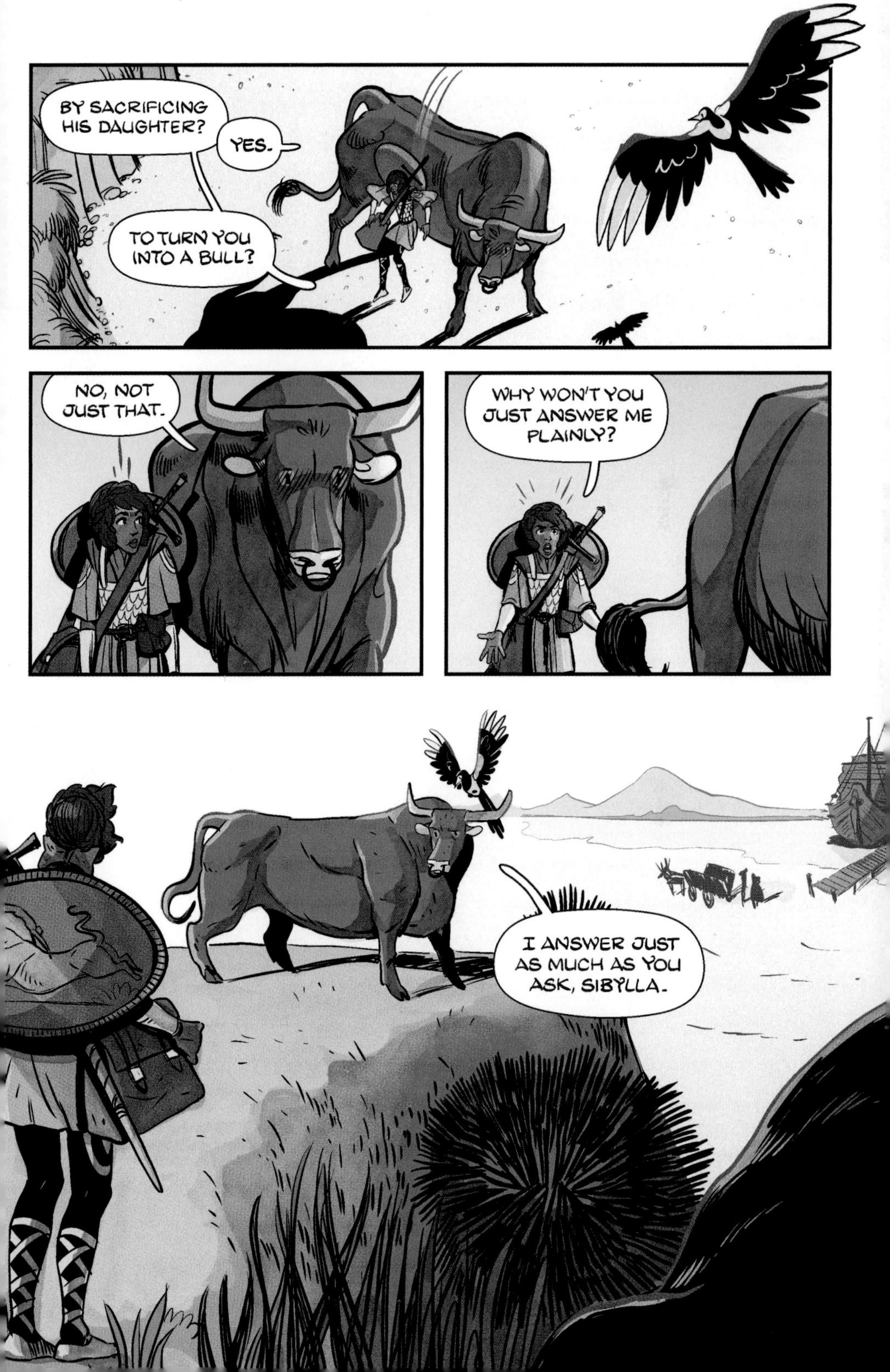
BY SACRIFICING HIS DAUGHTER?
YES.
TO TURN YOU INTO A BULL?
NO, NOT JUST THAT.
WHY WON'T YOU JUST ANSWER ME PLAINLY?
I ANSWER JUST AS MUCH AS YOU ASK, SIBYLLA.

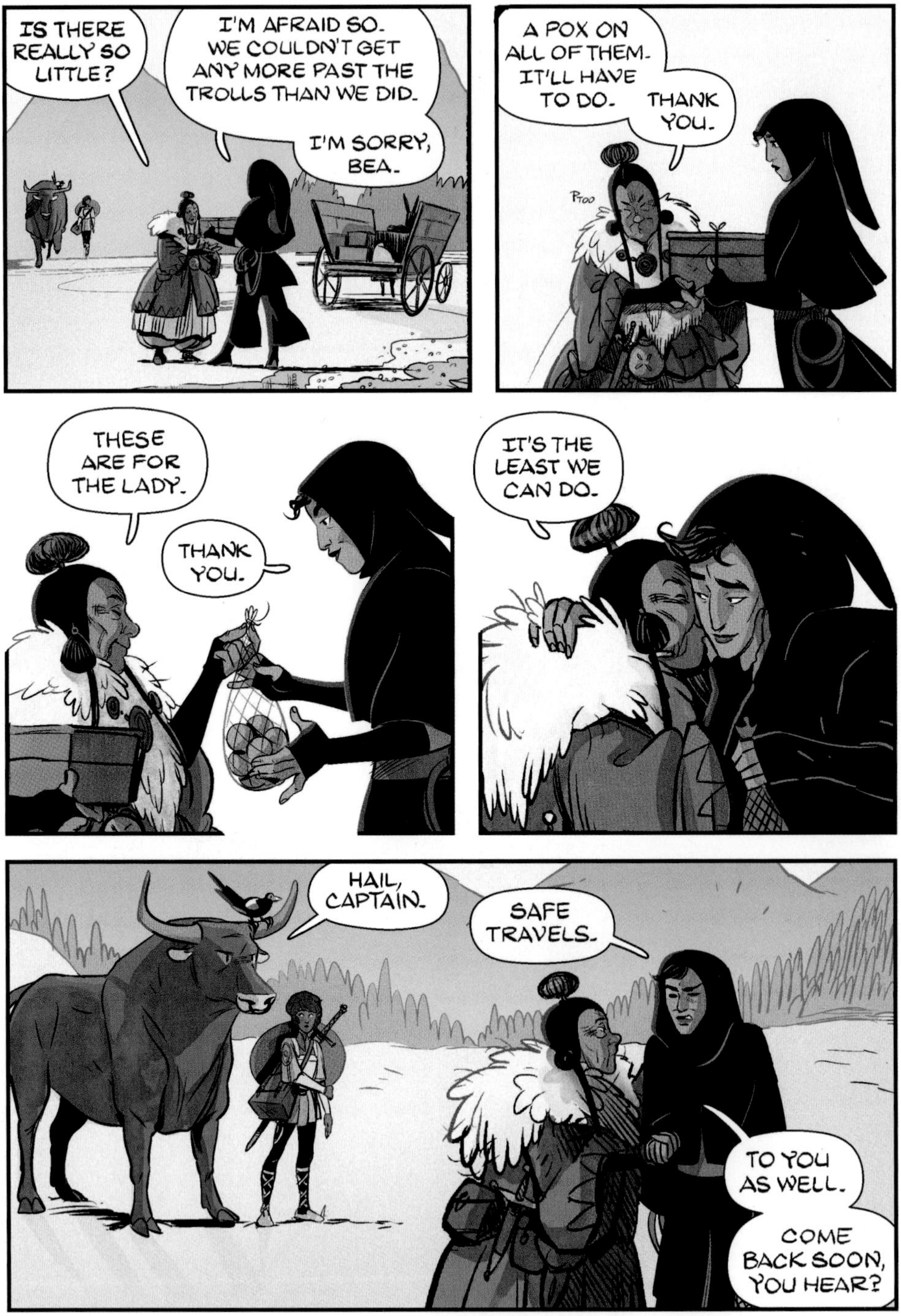
IS THERE REALLY SO LITTLE?
I'M AFRAID SO. WE COULDN'T GET ANY MORE PAST THE TROLLS THAN WE DID.
I'M SORRY, BEA.
A POX ON ALL OF THEM. IT'LL HAVE TO DO.
THANK YOU.
PTOO
THESE ARE FOR THE LADY.
THANK YOU.
IT'S THE LEAST WE CAN DO.
HAIL, CAPTAIN.
SAFE TRAVELS.
TO YOU AS WELL.
COME BACK SOON, YOU HEAR?

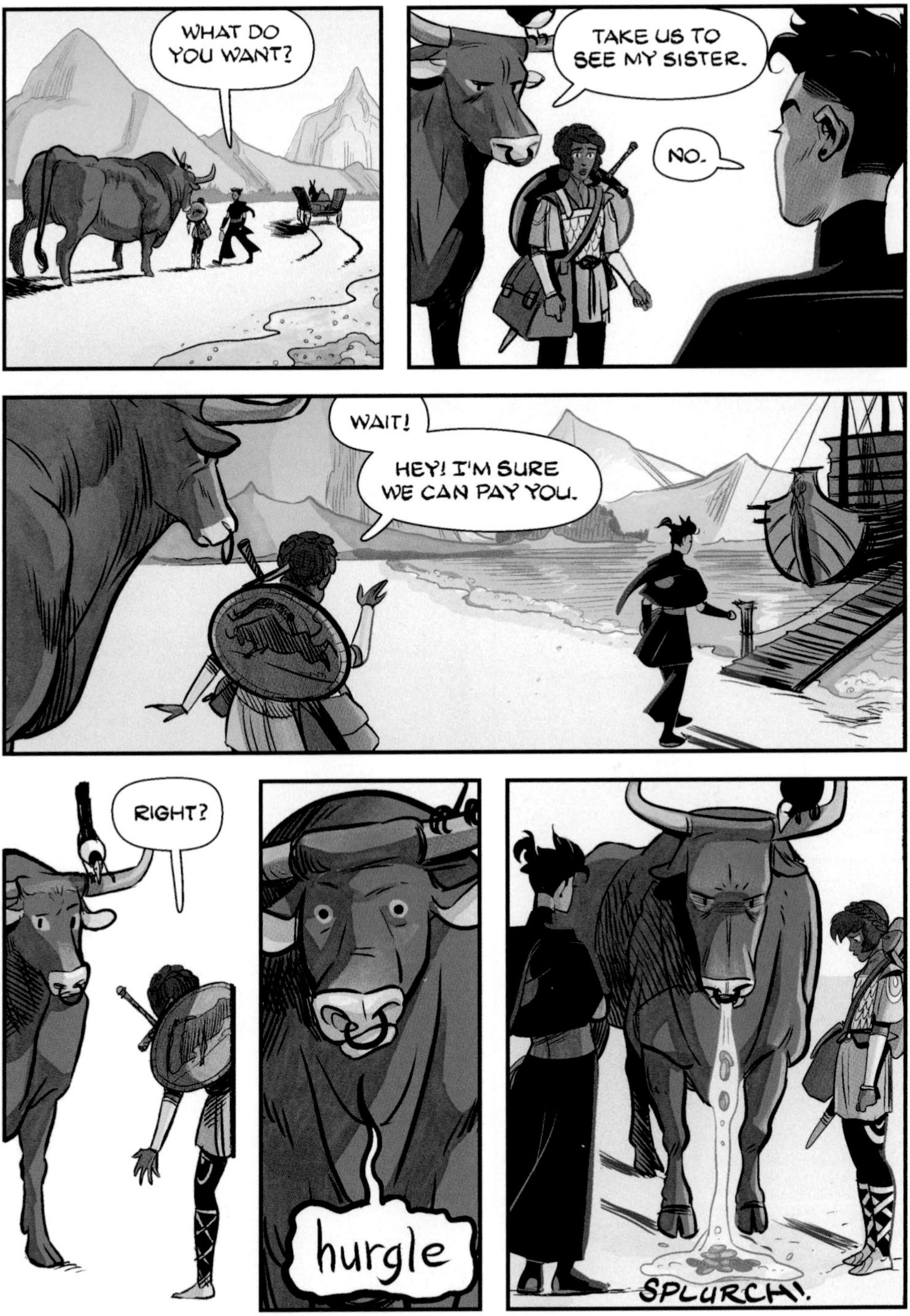
WHAT DO YOU WANT?
TAKE US TO SEE MY SISTER.
NO.
WAIT!
HEY! I'M SURE WE CAN PAY YOU.
RIGHT?
hurgle
SPLURCH!

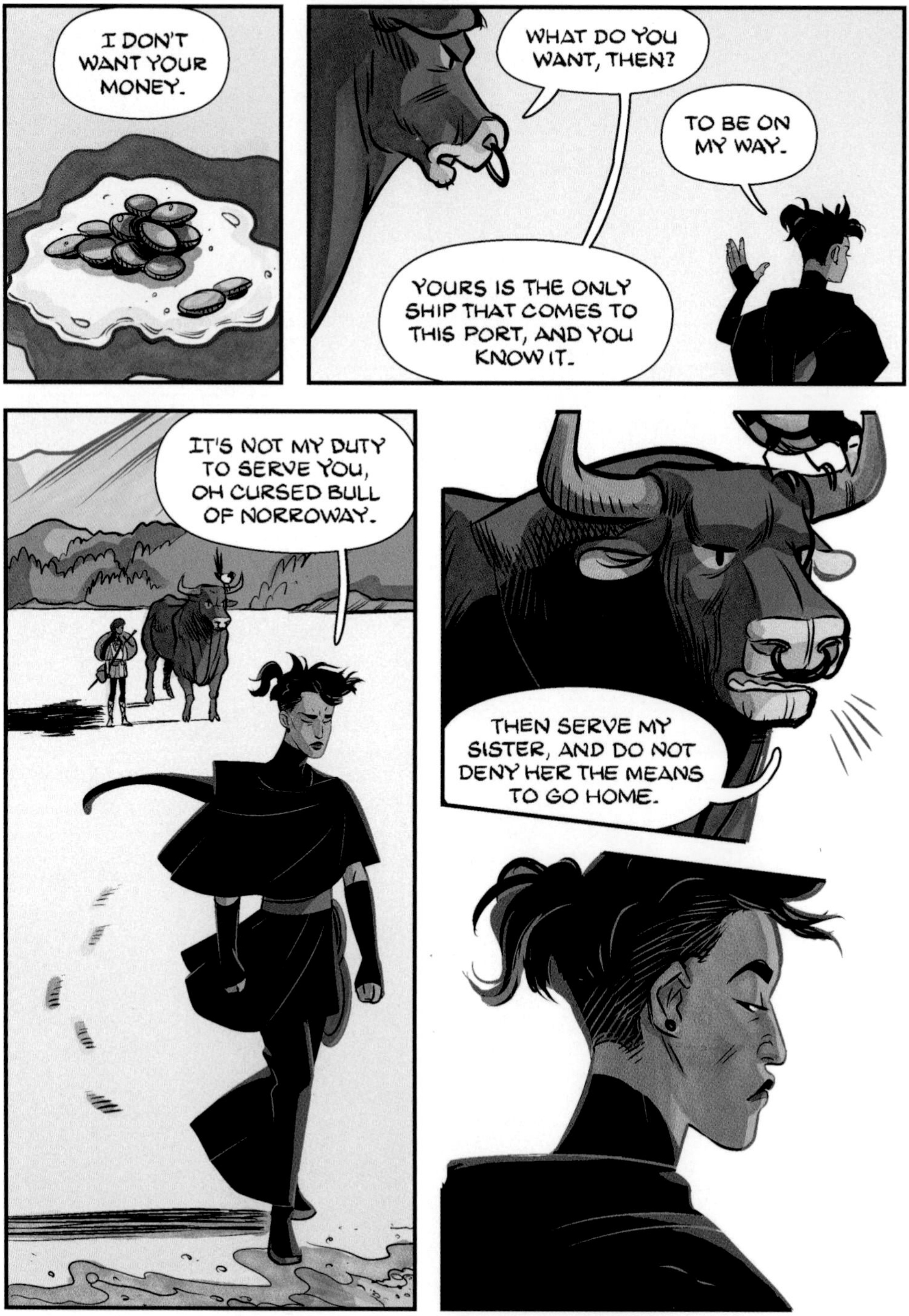
I DON'T WANT YOUR MONEY.
WHAT DO YOU WANT, THEN?
TO BE ON MY WAY.
YOURS IS THE ONLY SHIP THAT COMES TO THIS PORT, AND YOU KNOW IT.
IT'S NOT MY DUTY TO SERVE YOU, OH CURSED BULL OF NORROWAY.
THEN SERVE MY SISTER, AND DO NOT DENY HER THE MEANS TO GO HOME.

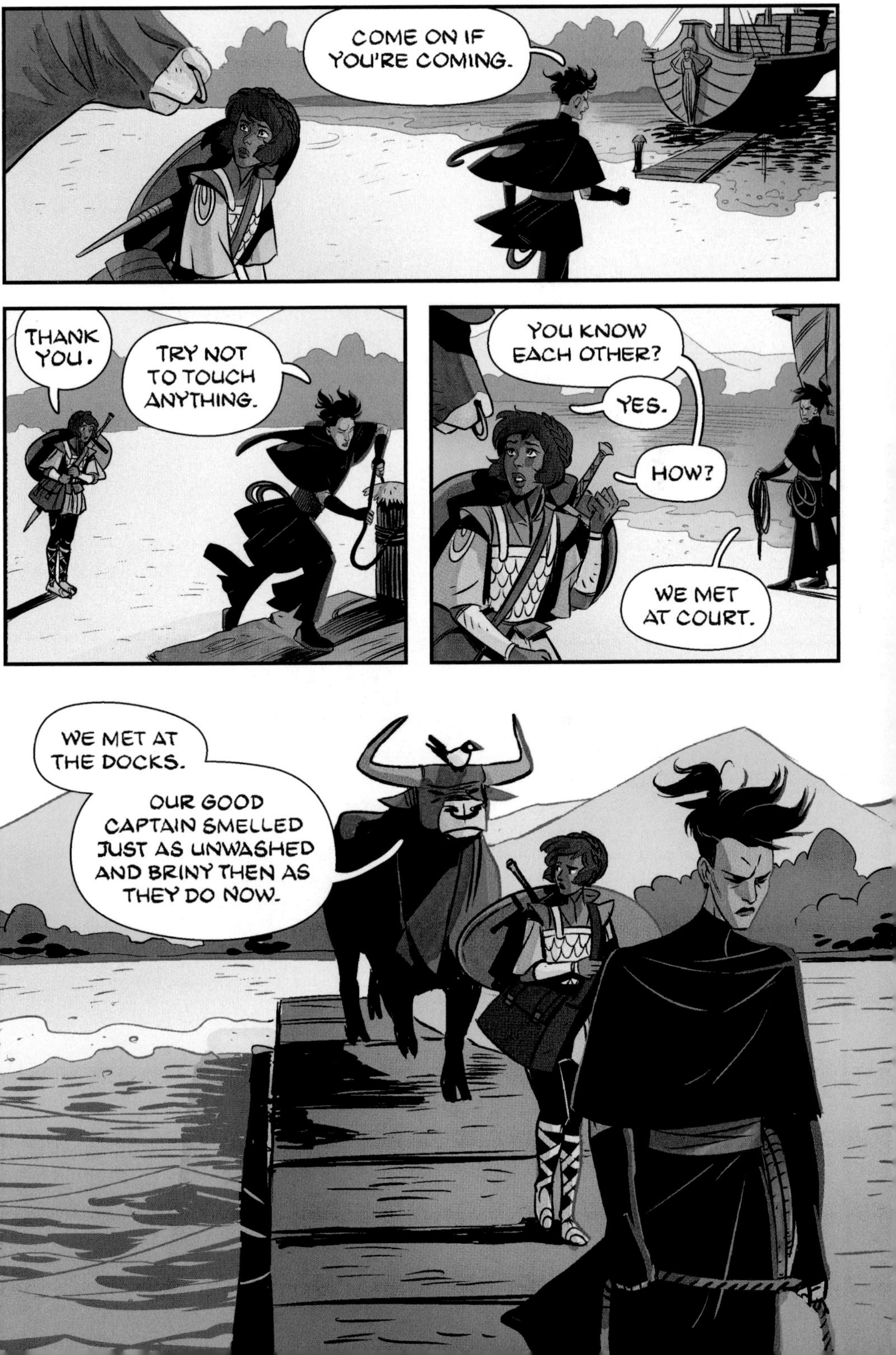
COME ON IF YOU'RE COMING.
THANK YOU.
TRY NOT TO TOUCH ANYTHING.
YOU KNOW EACH OTHER?
YES.
HOW?
WE MET AT COURT.
WE MET AT THE DOCKS.
OUR GOOD CAPTAIN SMELLED JUST AS UNWASHED AND BRINY THEN AS THEY DO NOW.

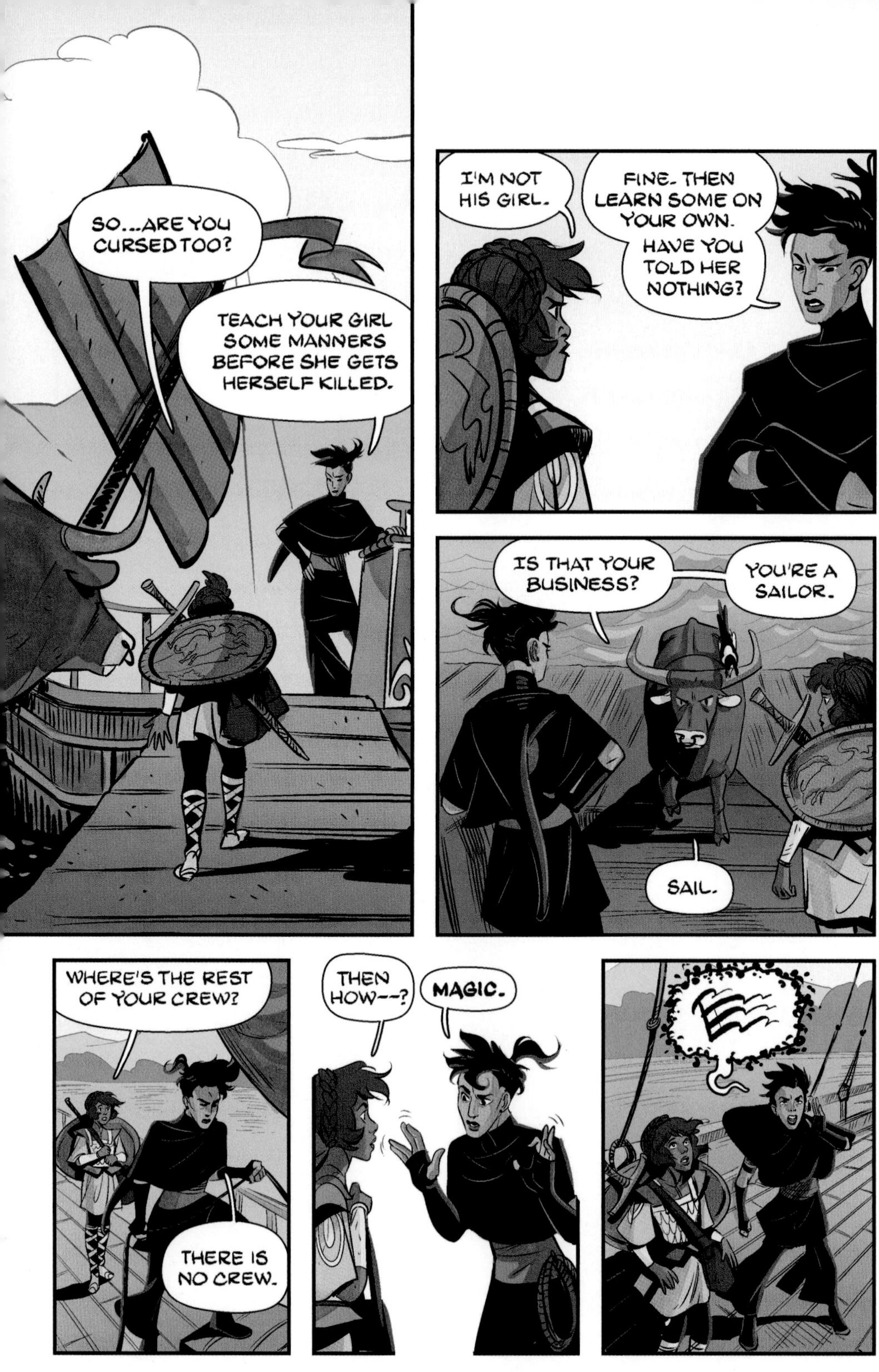
SO...ARE YOU CURSED TOO?
TEACH YOUR GIRL SOME MANNERS BEFORE SHE GETS HERSELF KILLED.
I'M NOT HIS GIRL.
FINE. THEN LEARN SOME ON YOUR OWN.
HAVE YOU TOLD HER NOTHING?
IS THAT YOUR BUSINESS?
YOU'RE A SAILOR.
SAIL.
WHERE'S THE REST OF YOUR CREW?
THERE IS NO CREW.
THEN HOW--?
MAGIC.

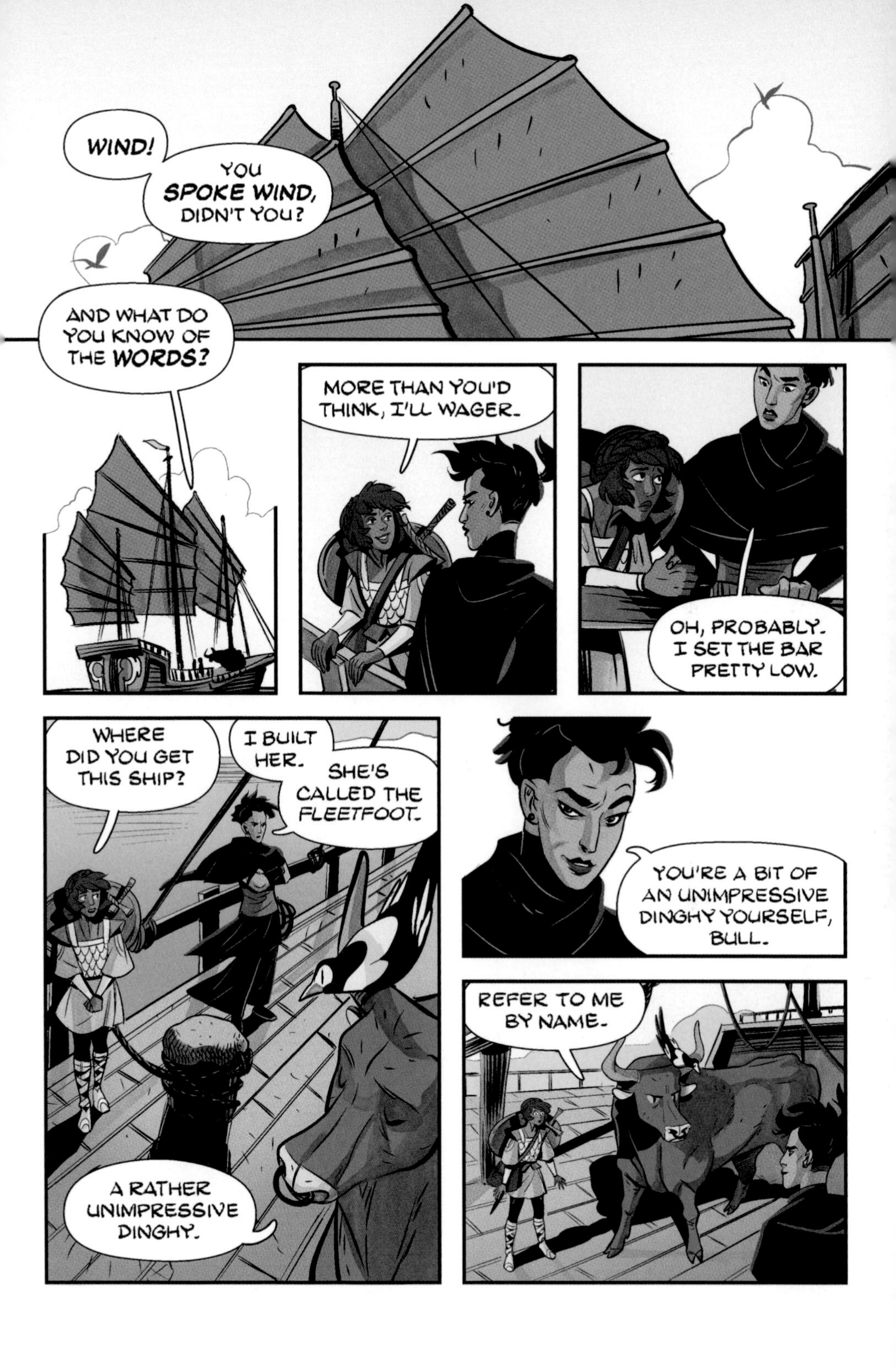
WIND!
YOU SPOKE WIND, DIDN'T YOU?
AND WHAT DO YOU KNOW OF THE WORDS?
MORE THAN YOU'D THINK, I'LL WAGER.
OH, PROBABLY. I SET THE BAR PRETTY LOW.
WHERE DID YOU GET THIS SHIP?
I BUILT HER.
SHE'S CALLED THE FLEETFOOT.
A RATHER UNIMPRESSIVE DINGHY.
YOU'RE A BIT OF AN UNIMPRESSIVE DINGHY YOURSELF, BULL.
REFER TO ME BY NAME.

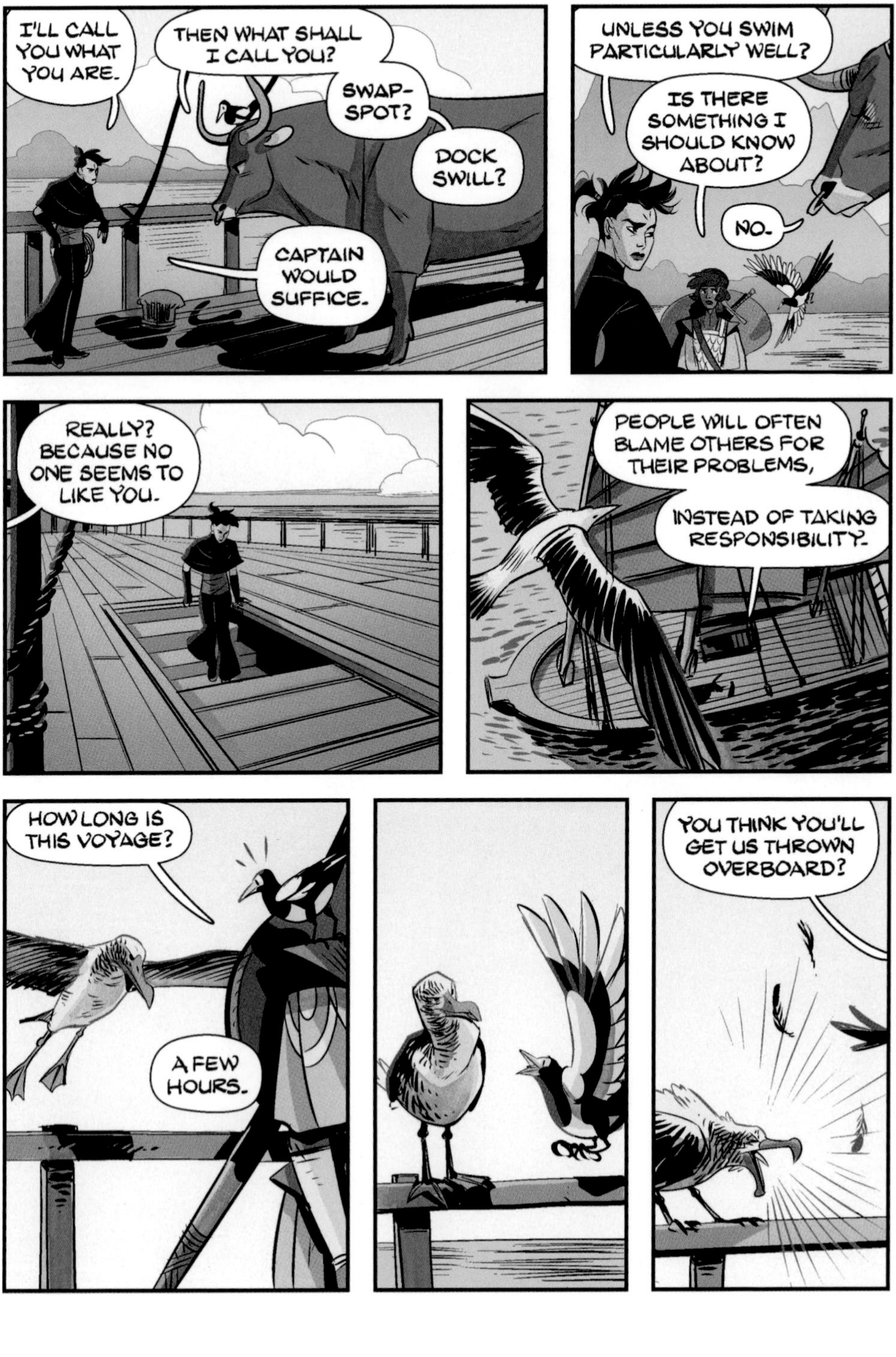
I'LL CALL YOU WHAT YOU ARE.
THEN WHAT SHALL I CALL YOU?
SWAP-SPOT?
DOCK SWILL?
CAPTAIN WOULD SUFFICE.
UNLESS YOU SWIM PARTICULARLY WELL?
IS THERE SOMETHING I SHOULD KNOW ABOUT?
NO.
REALLY? BECAUSE NO ONE SEEMS TO LIKE YOU.
PEOPLE WILL OFTEN BLAME OTHERS FOR THEIR PROBLEMS,
INSTEAD OF TAKING RESPONSIBILITY.
HOW LONG IS THIS VOYAGE?
A FEW HOURS.
YOU THINK YOU'LL GET US THROWN OVERBOARD?

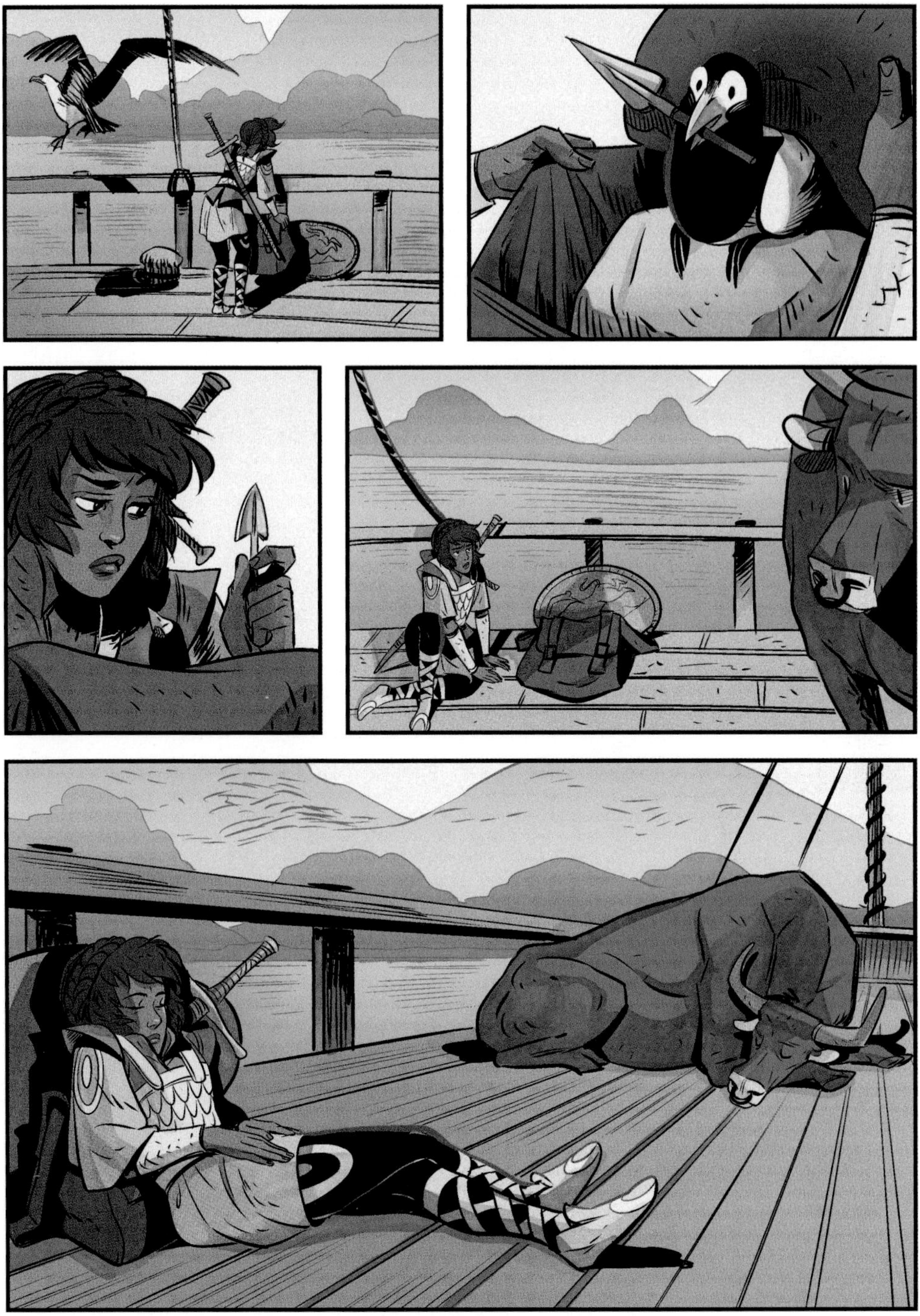

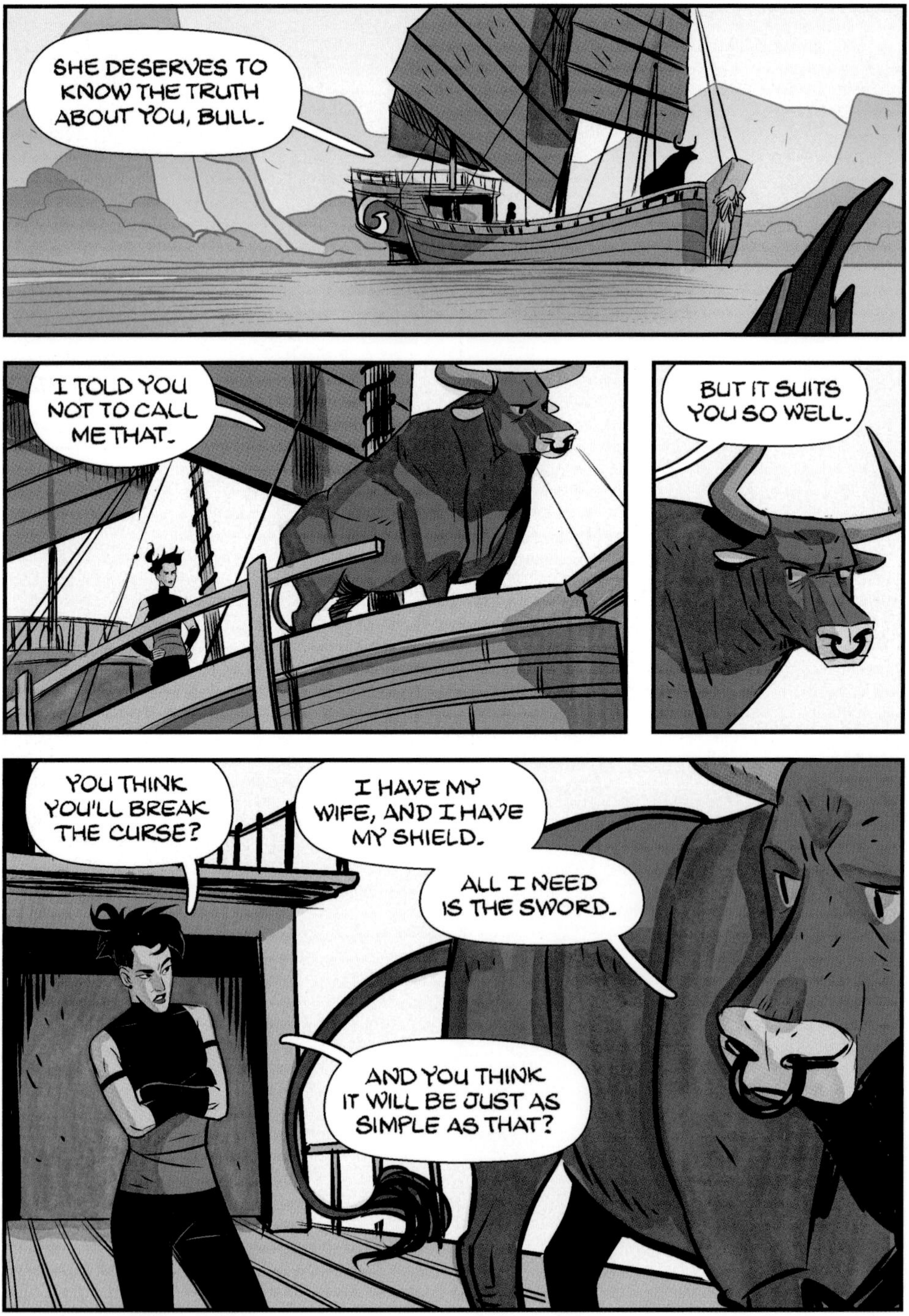
SHE DESERVES TO KNOW THE TRUTH ABOUT YOU, BULL.
I TOLD YOU NOT TO CALL ME THAT.
BUT IT SUITS YOU SO WELL.
YOU THINK YOU'LL BREAK THE CURSE?
I HAVE MY WIFE, AND I HAVE MY SHIELD.
ALL I NEED IS THE SWORD.
AND YOU THINK IT WILL BE JUST AS SIMPLE AS THAT?

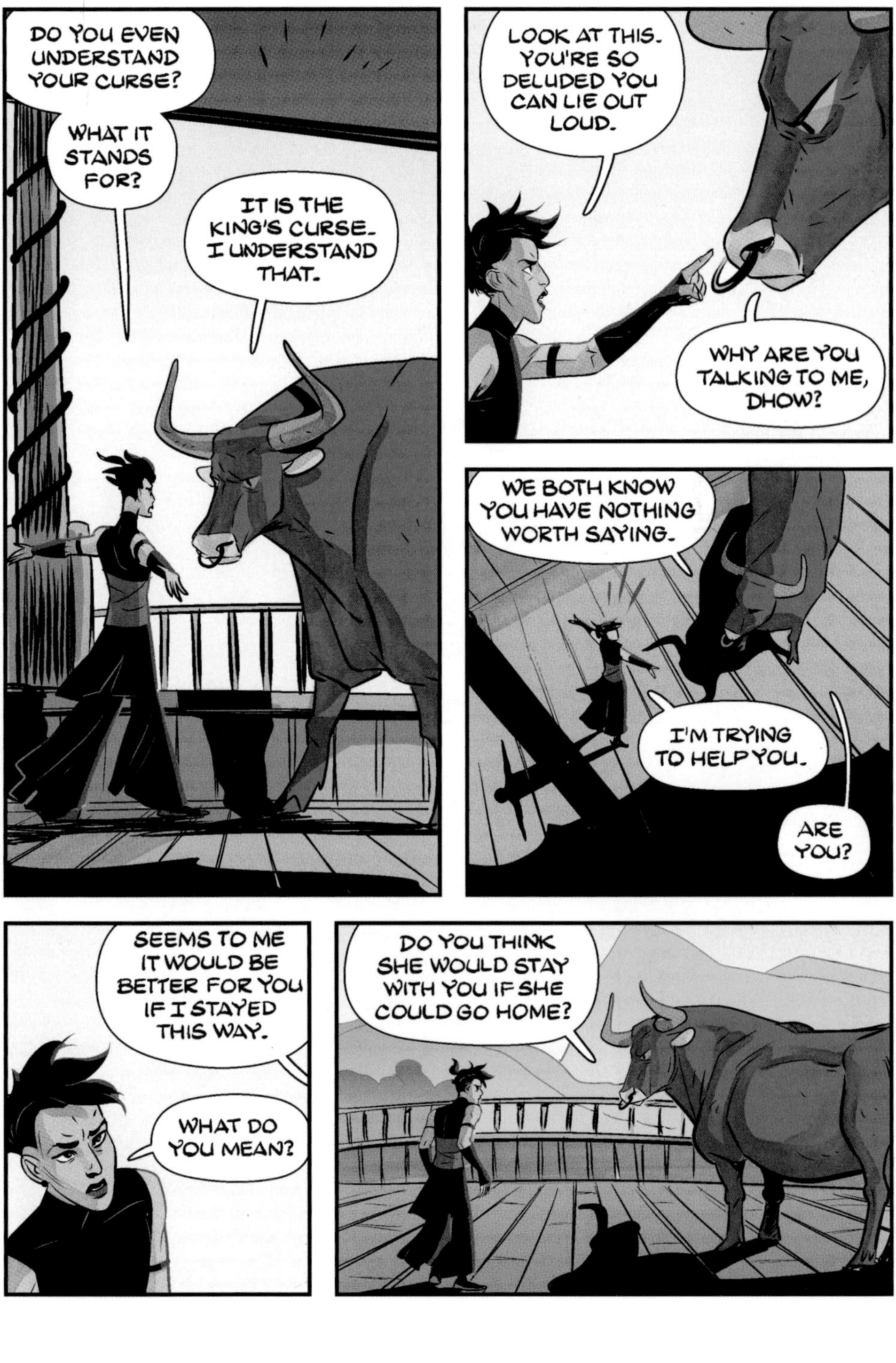
DO YOU EVEN UNDERSTAND YOUR CURSE?
WHAT IT STANDS FOR?
IT IS THE KING'S CURSE. I UNDERSTAND THAT.
LOOK AT THIS. YOU'RE SO DELUDED YOU CAN LIE OUT LOUD.
WHY ARE YOU TALKING TO ME, DHOW?
WE BOTH KNOW YOU HAVE NOTHING WORTH SAYING.
I'M TRYING TO HELP YOU.
ARE YOU?
SEEMS TO ME IT WOULD BE BETTER FOR YOU IF I STAYED THIS WAY.
WHAT DO YOU MEAN?
DO YOU THINK SHE WOULD STAY WITH YOU IF SHE COULD GO HOME?

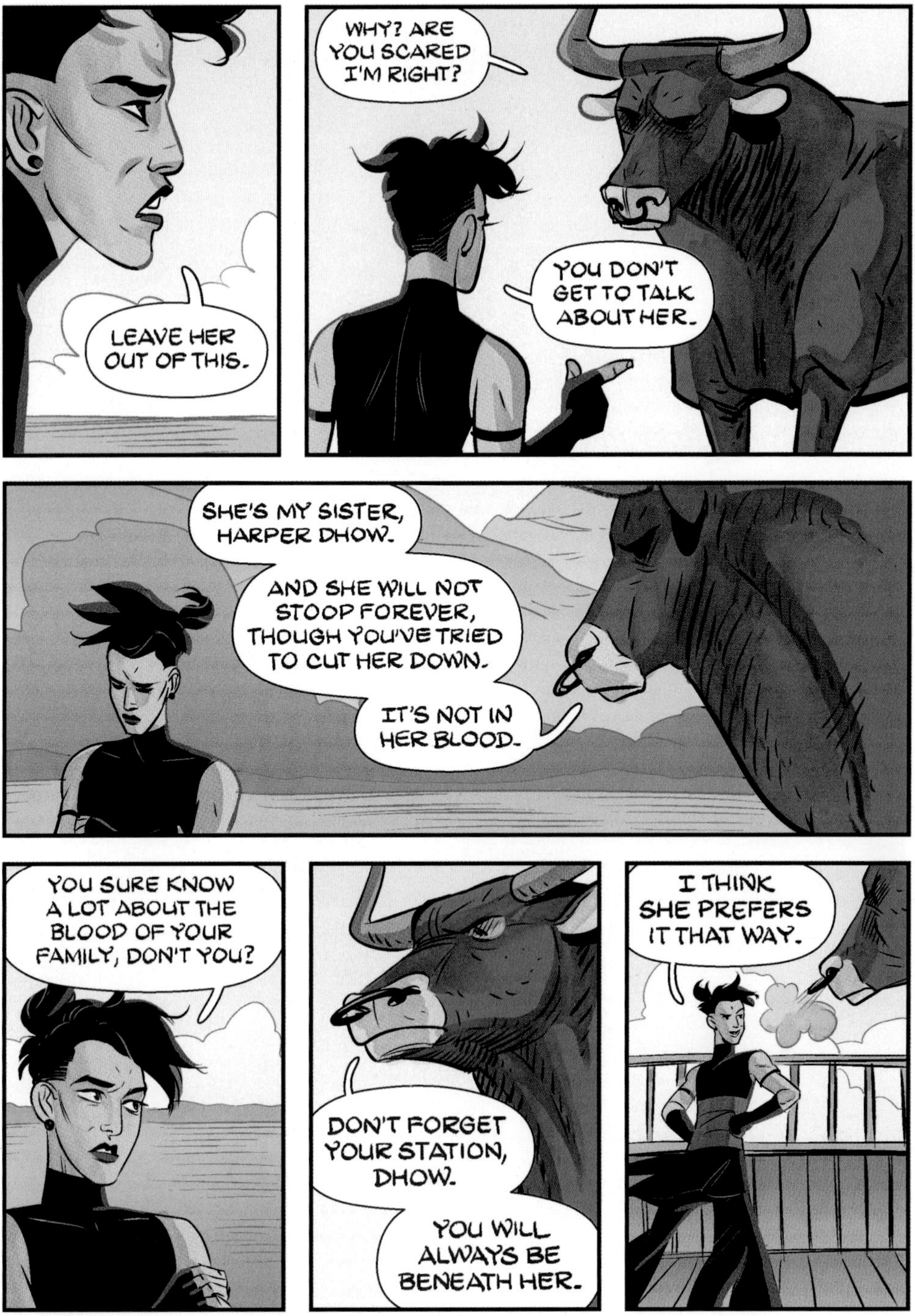
LEAVE HER OUT OF THIS.
WHY? ARE YOU SCARED I'M RIGHT?
YOU DON'T GET TO TALK ABOUT HER.
SHE'S MY SISTER, HARPER DHOW.
AND SHE WILL NOT STOOP FOREVER, THOUGH YOU'VE TRIED TO CUT HER DOWN.
IT'S NOT IN HER BLOOD.
YOU SURE KNOW A LOT ABOUT THE BLOOD OF YOUR FAMILY, DON'T YOU?
DON'T FORGET YOUR STATION, DHOW.
YOU WILL ALWAYS BE BENEATH HER.
I THINK SHE PREFERS IT THAT WAY.

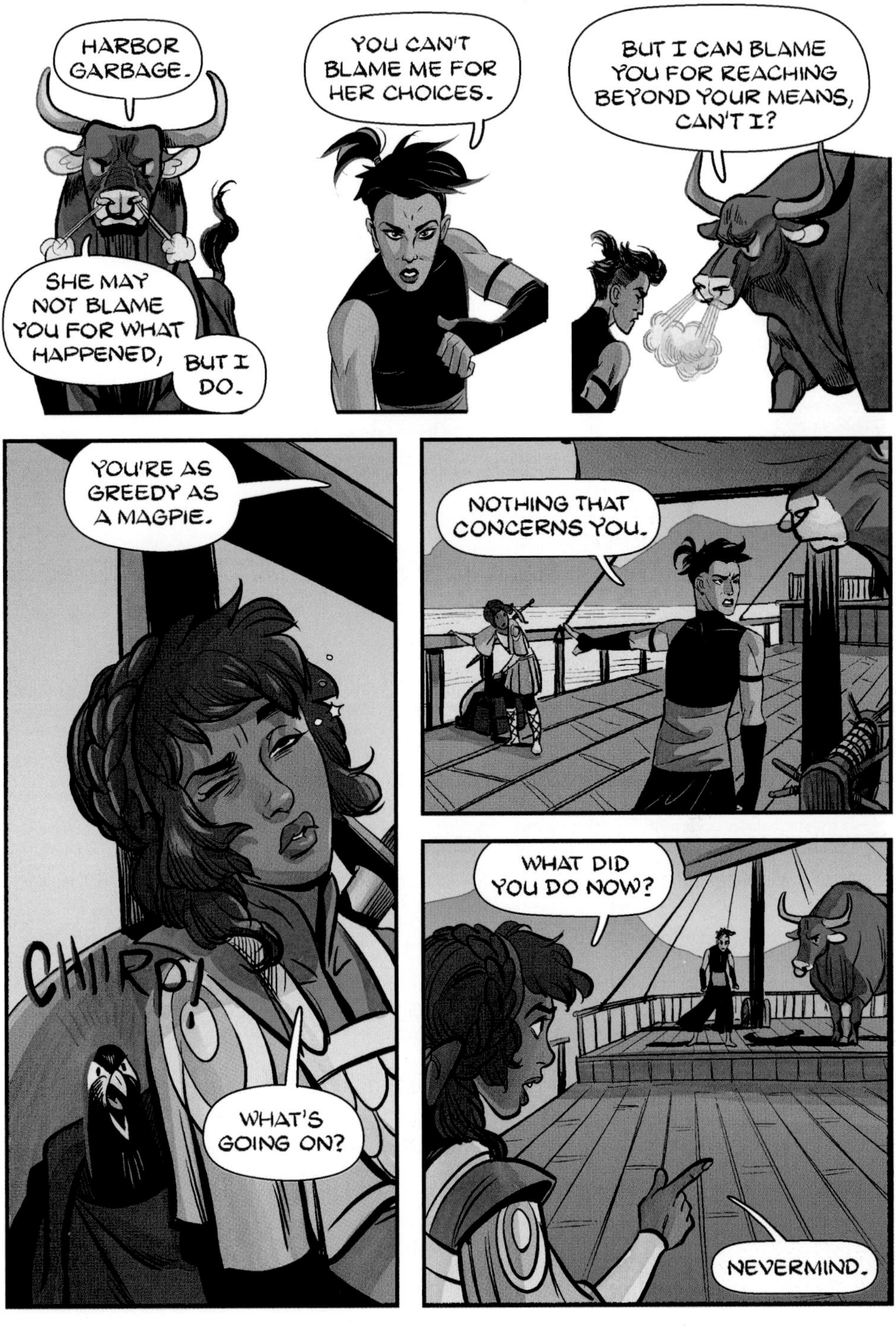
HARBOR GARBAGE.
SHE MAY NOT BLAME YOU FOR WHAT HAPPENED,
BUT I DO.
YOU CAN'T BLAME ME FOR HER CHOICES.
BUT I CAN BLAME YOU FOR REACHING BEYOND YOUR MEANS, CAN'T I?
YOU'RE AS GREEDY AS A MAGPIE.
CHIRP!
WHAT'S GOING ON?
NOTHING THAT CONCERNS YOU.
WHAT DID YOU DO NOW?
NEVERMIND.

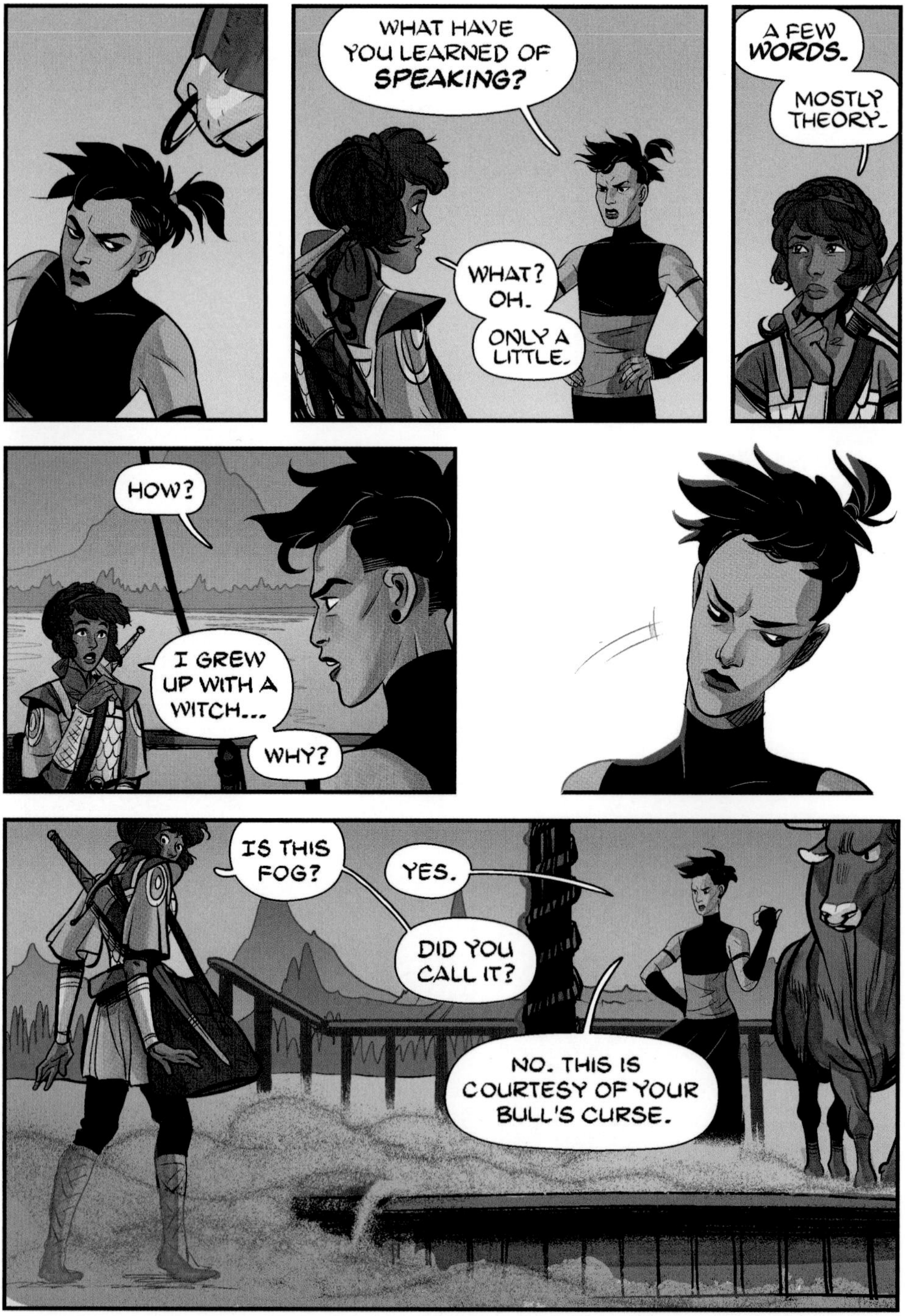
WHAT HAVE YOU LEARNED OF **SPEAKING?**
WHAT? OH.
ONLY A LITTLE.
A FEW **WORDS.**
MOSTLY THEORY.
HOW?
I GREW UP WITH A WITCH...
WHY?
IS THIS FOG?
YES.
DID YOU CALL IT?
NO. THIS IS COURTESY OF YOUR BULL'S CURSE.

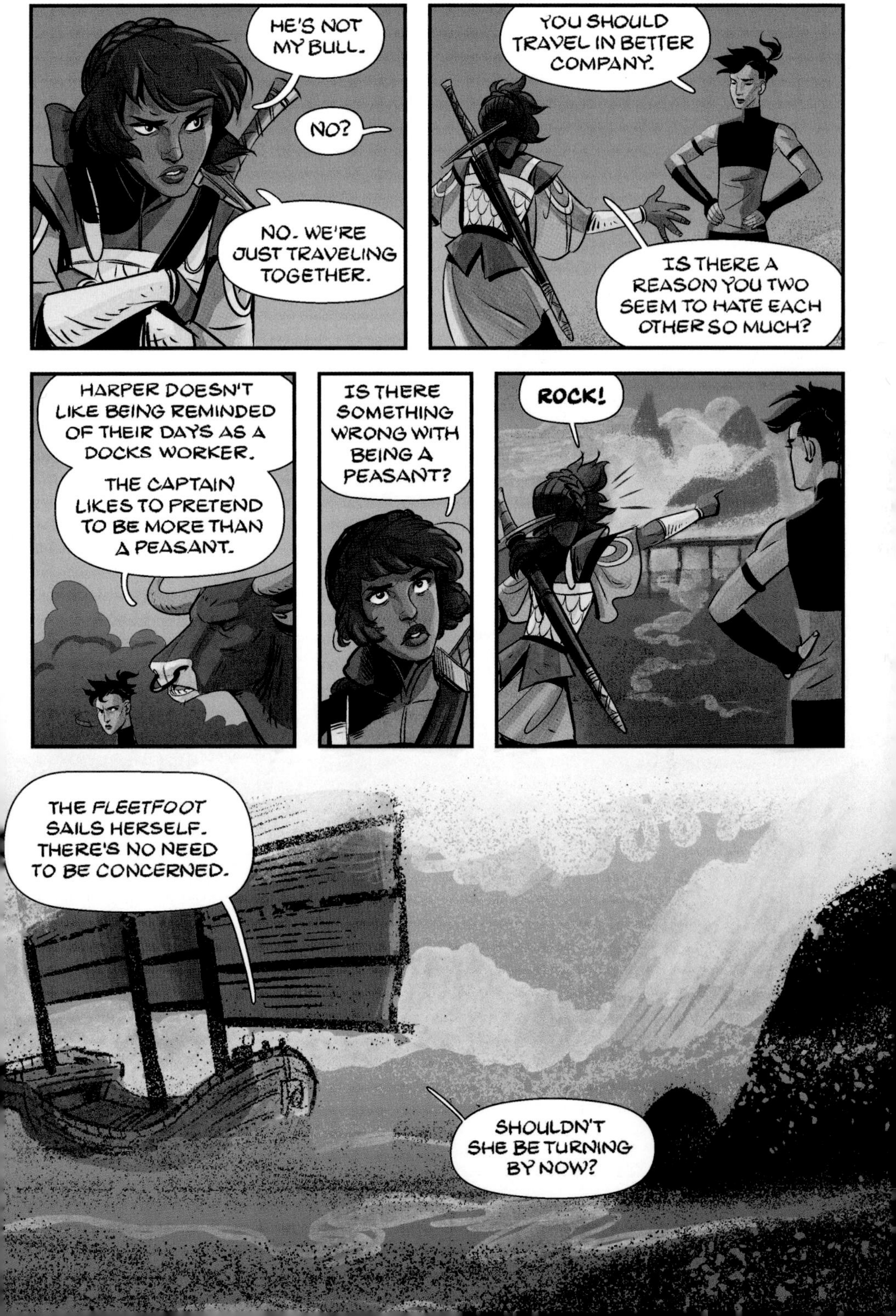
HE'S NOT MY BULL.
NO?
NO. WE'RE JUST TRAVELING TOGETHER.
YOU SHOULD TRAVEL IN BETTER COMPANY.
IS THERE A REASON YOU TWO SEEM TO HATE EACH OTHER SO MUCH?
HARPER DOESN'T LIKE BEING REMINDED OF THEIR DAYS AS A DOCKS WORKER.
THE CAPTAIN LIKES TO PRETEND TO BE MORE THAN A PEASANT.
IS THERE SOMETHING WRONG WITH BEING A PEASANT?
ROCK!
THE *FLEETFOOT* SAILS HERSELF. THERE'S NO NEED TO BE CONCERNED.
SHOULDN'T SHE BE TURNING BY NOW?

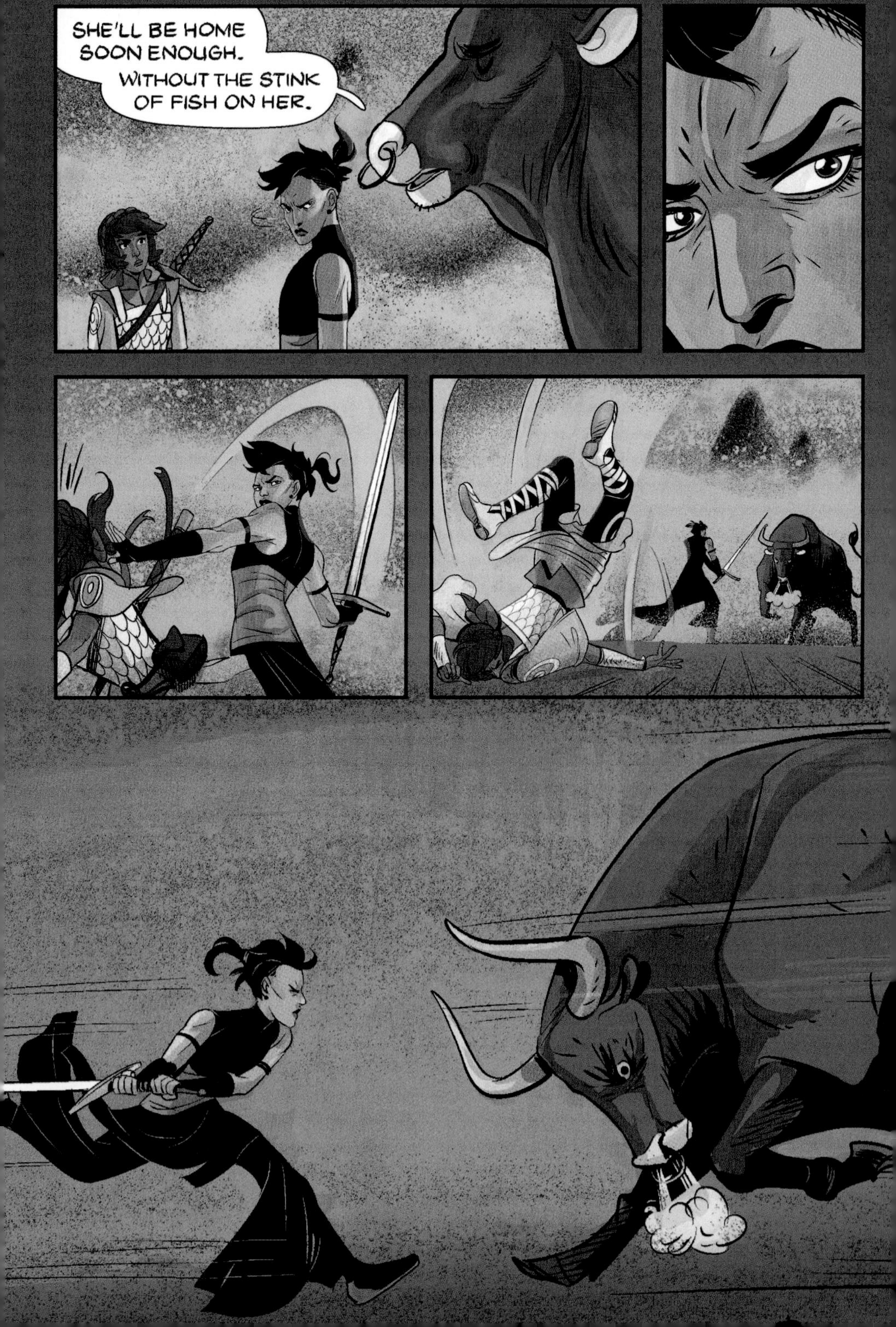
SHE'LL BE HOME SOON ENOUGH.
WITHOUT THE STINK OF FISH ON HER.

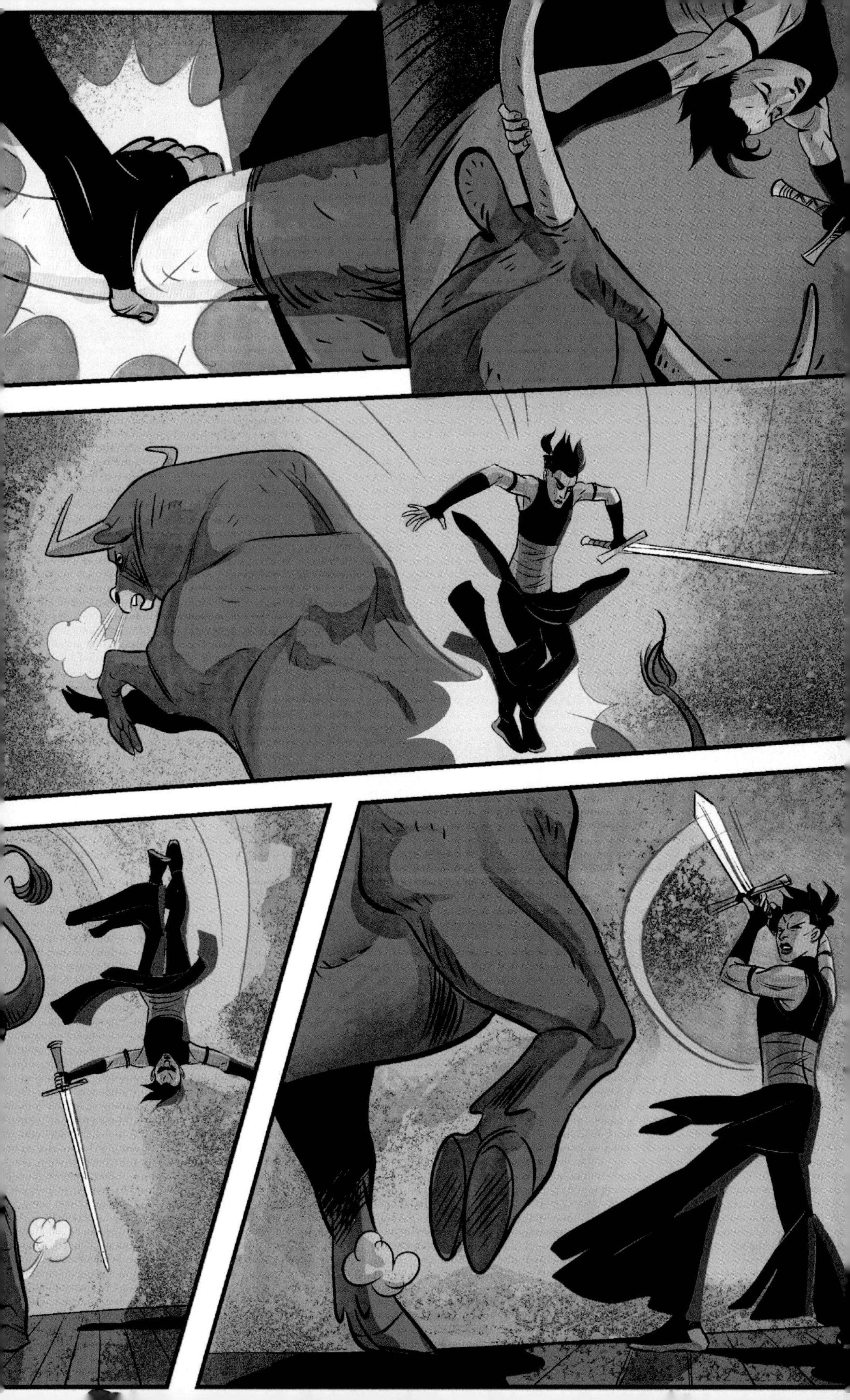

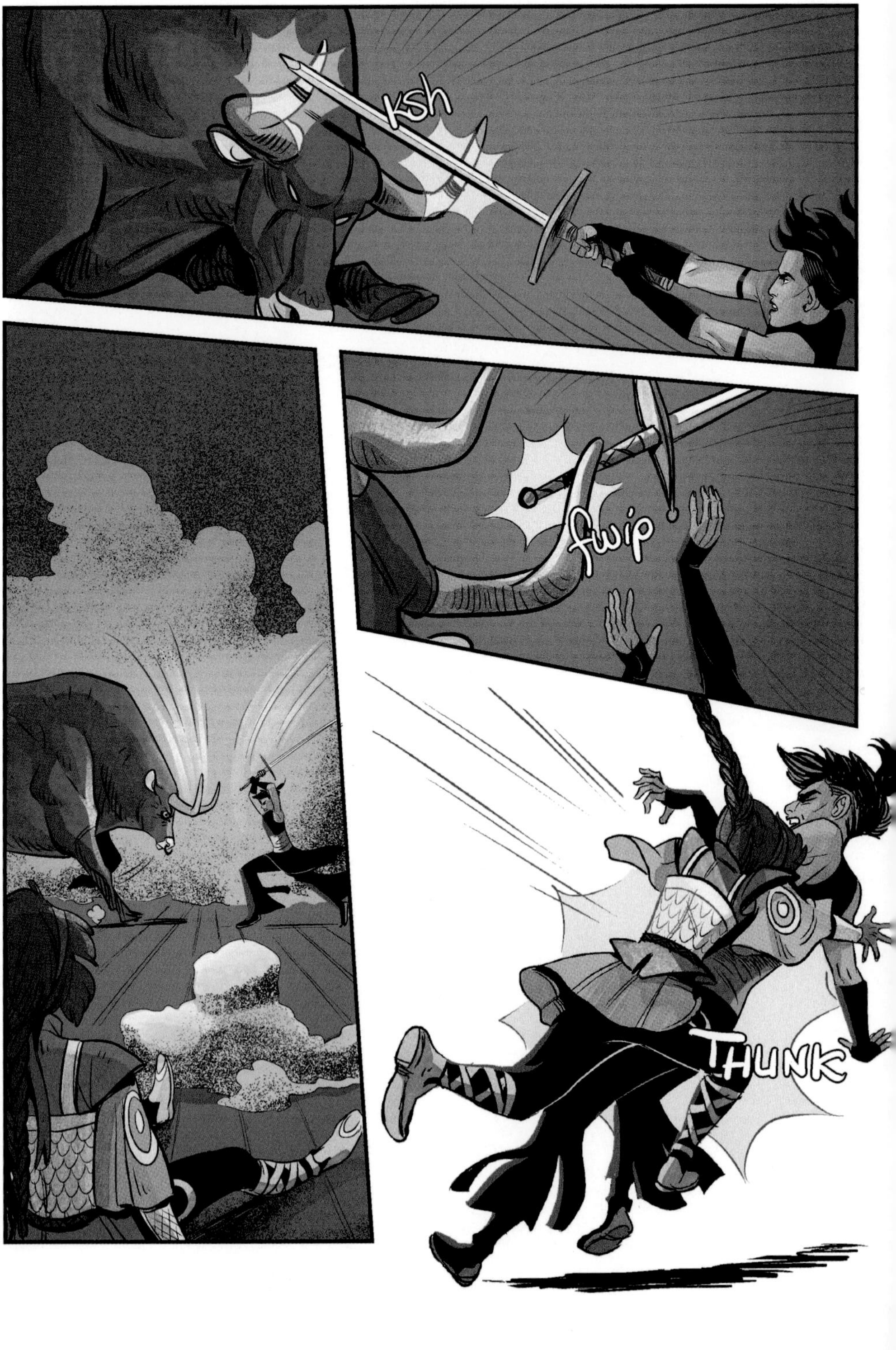
KSH
fwip
THUNK

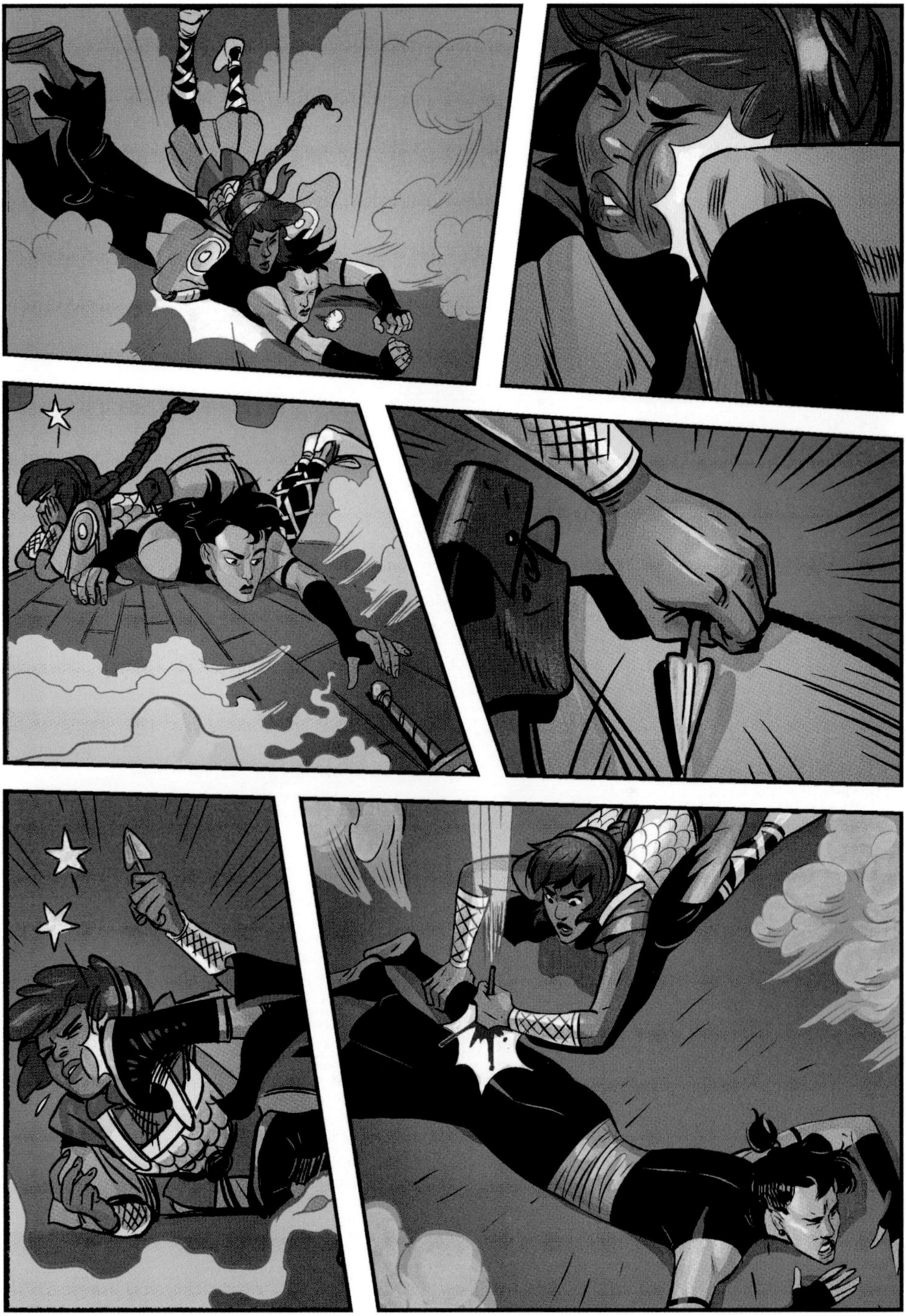

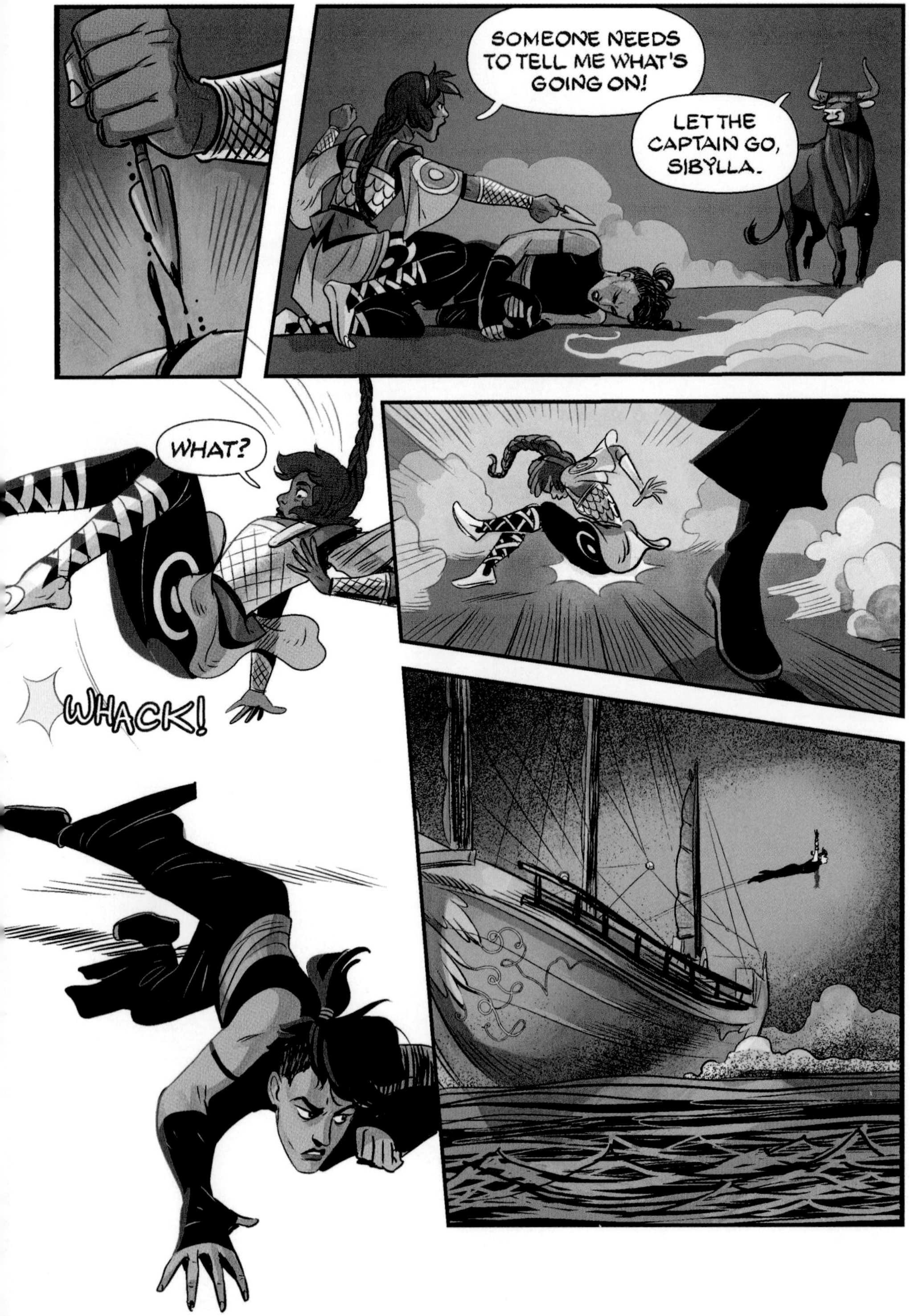
SOMEONE NEEDS TO TELL ME WHAT'S GOING ON!
LET THE CAPTAIN GO, SIBYLLA.
WHAT?
WHACK!

SPLASH!

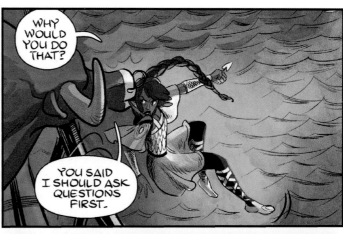

WHY WOULD YOU DO THAT?

YOU SAID I SHOULD ASK QUESTIONS FIRST.

YOU'RE TRYING TO HIDE SOMETHING FROM ME, AREN'T YOU?

SPEAK, SIBYLLA!

I CAN'T!

TRY!

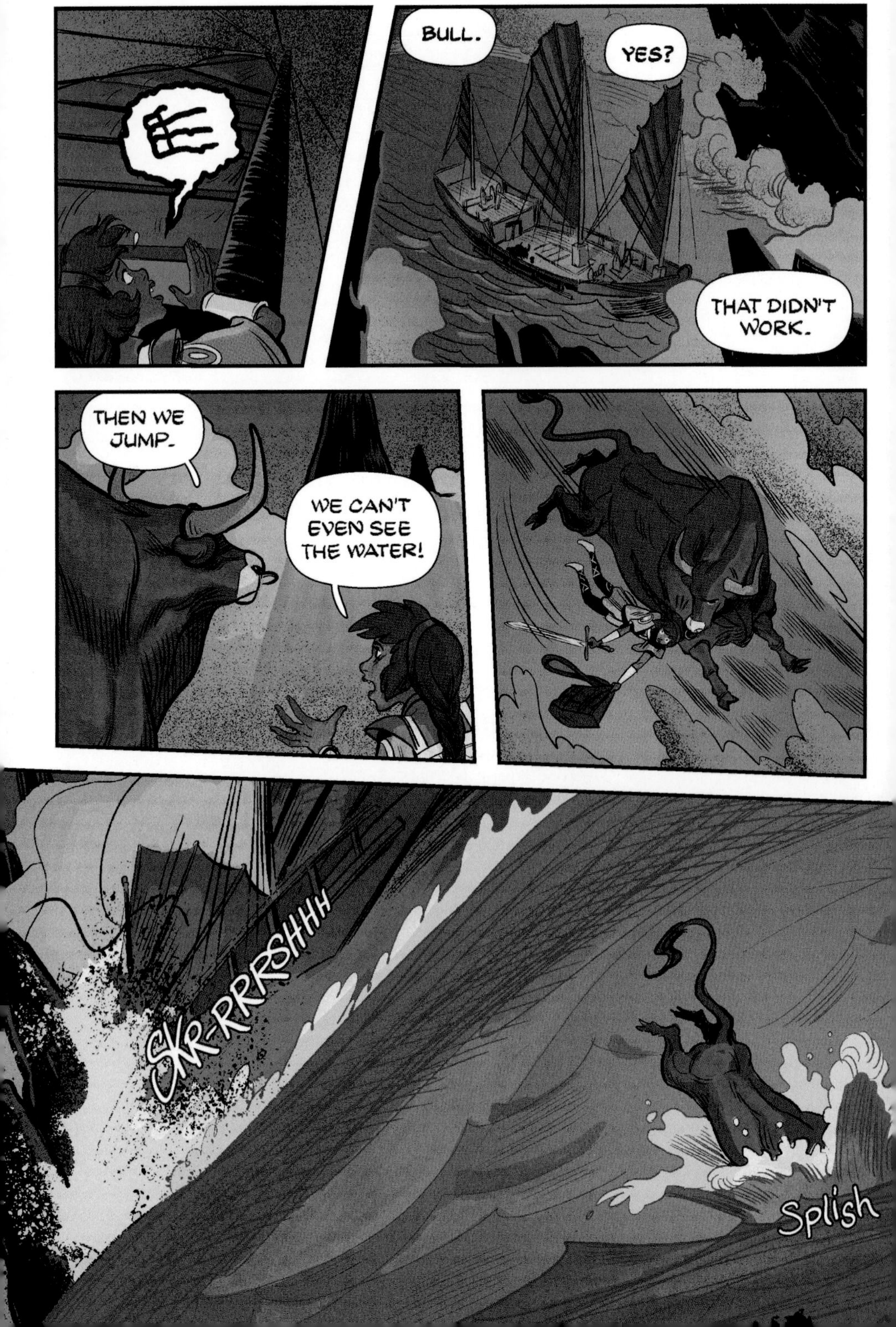

BULL.
YES?
THAT DIDN'T WORK.
THEN WE JUMP.
WE CAN'T EVEN SEE THE WATER!
SKR-RRRSHHH
Splish

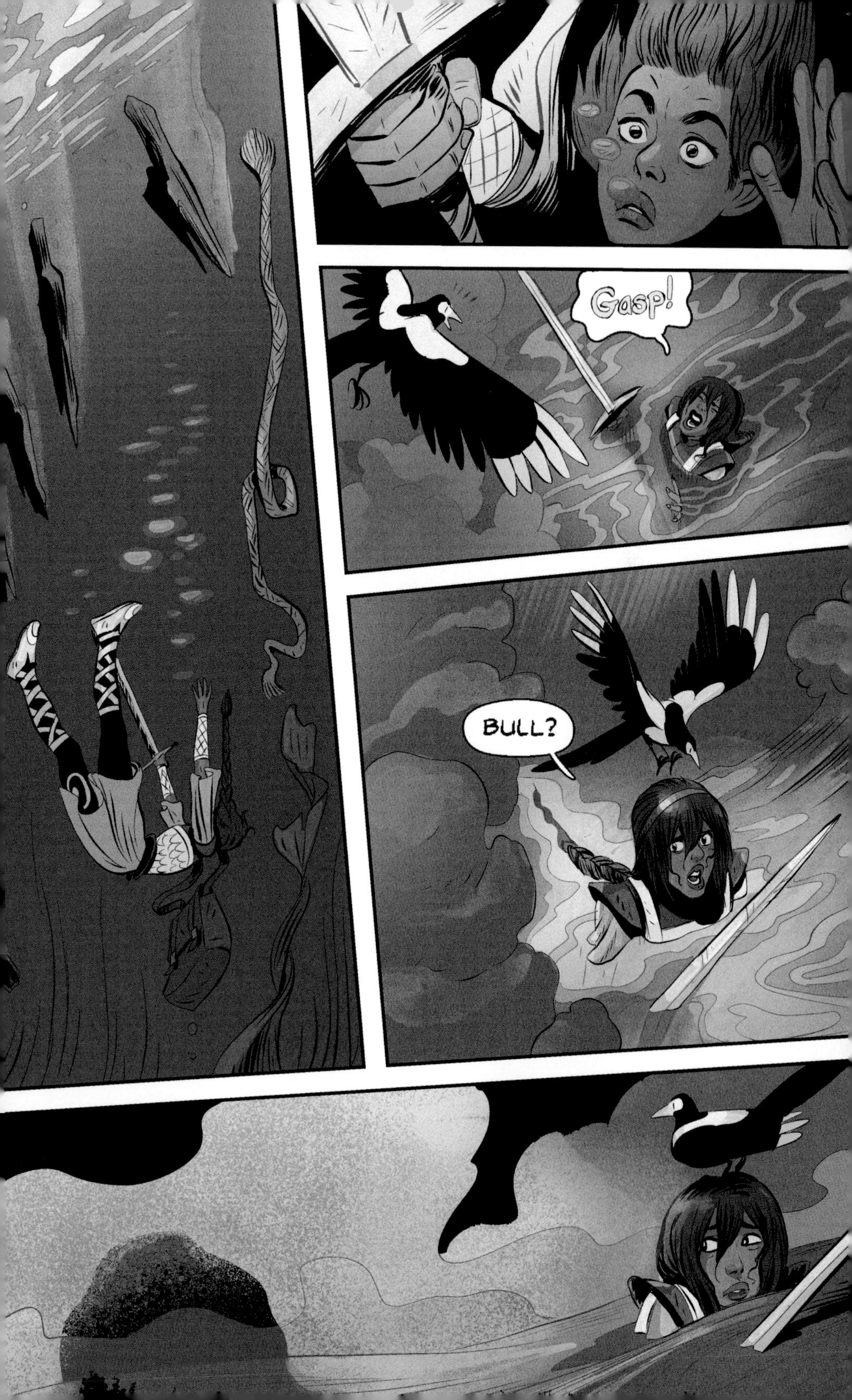
Gasp!
BULL?

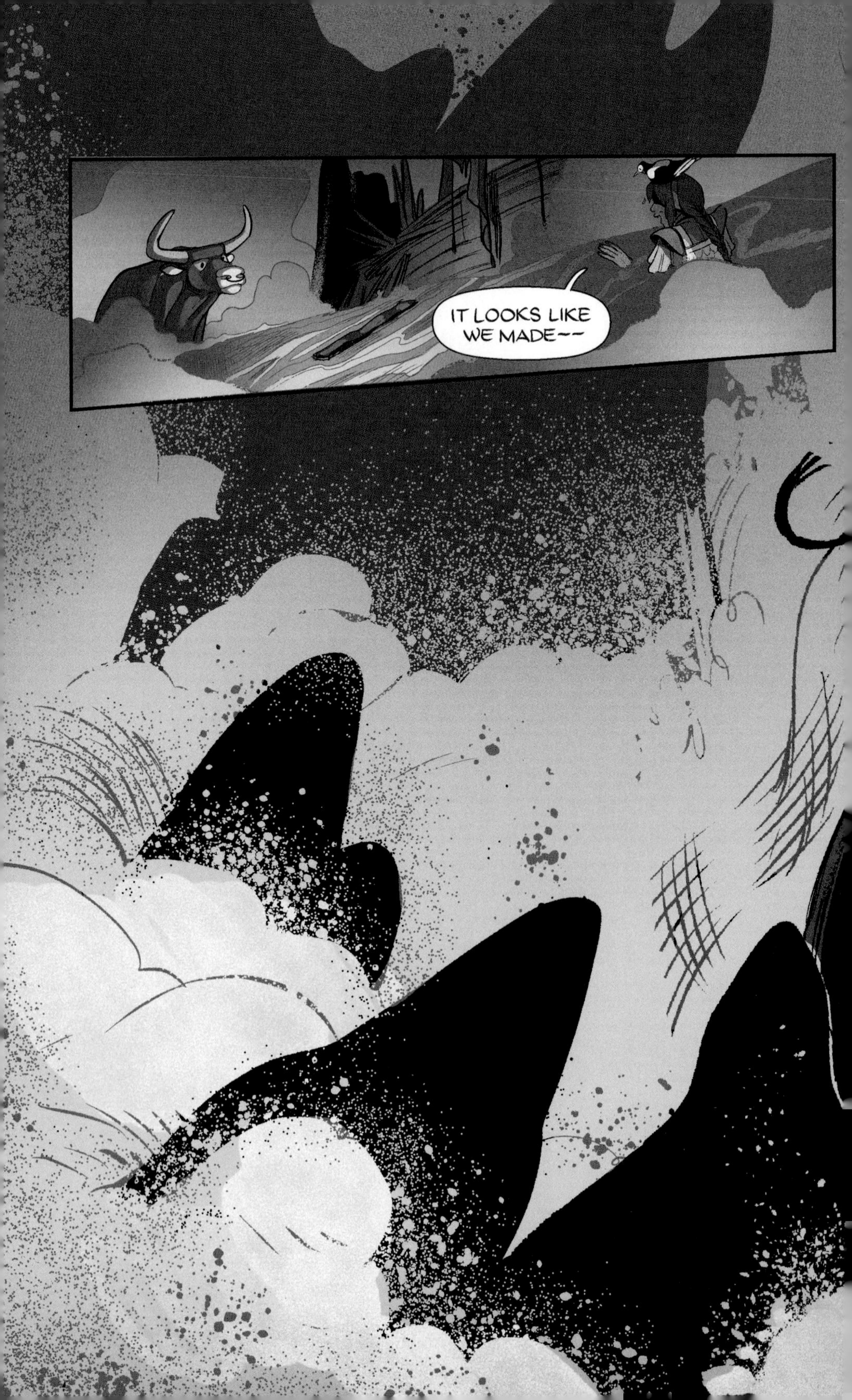
IT LOOKS LIKE WE MADE--

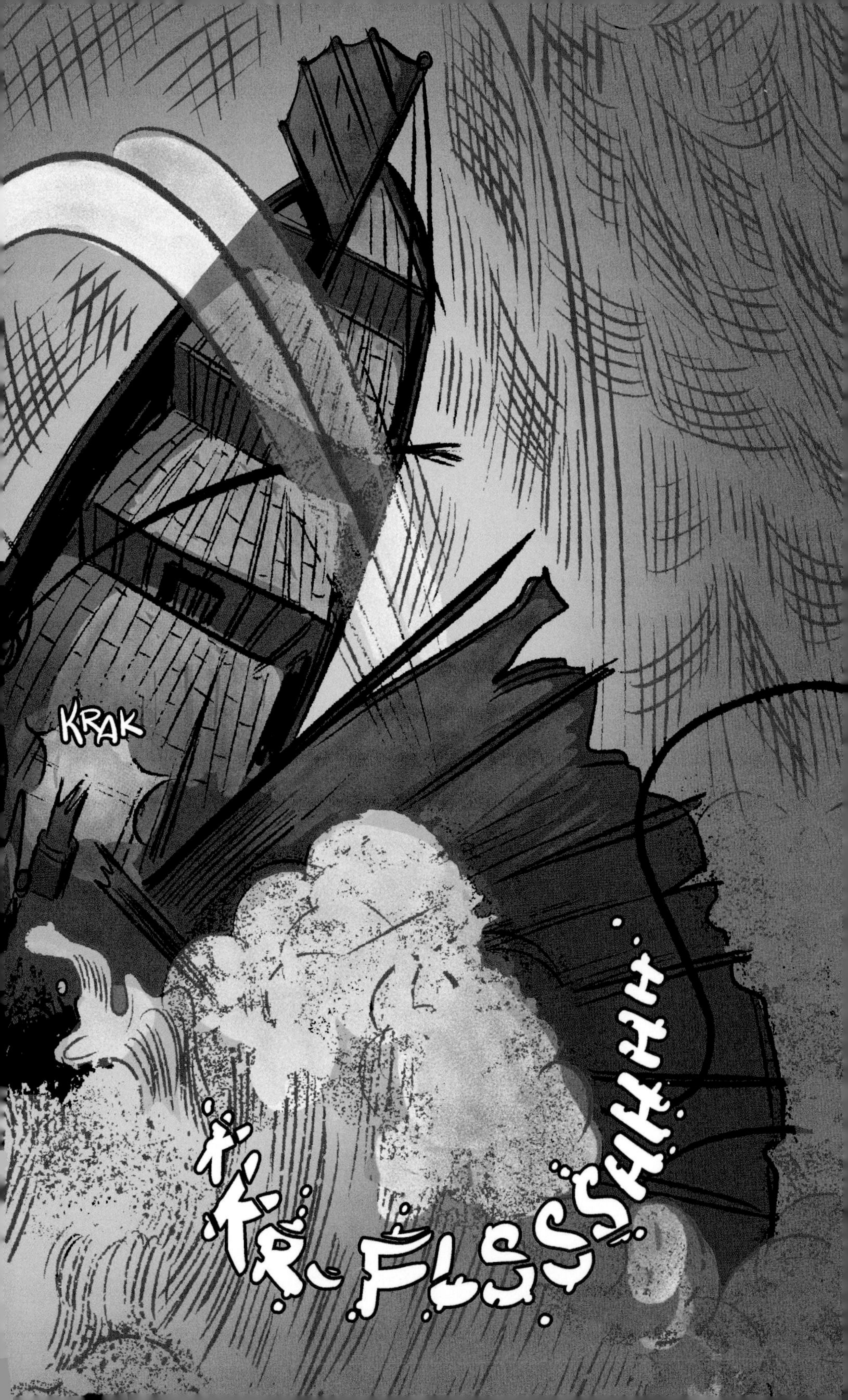
KRAK
KR-FLSSSHHH...

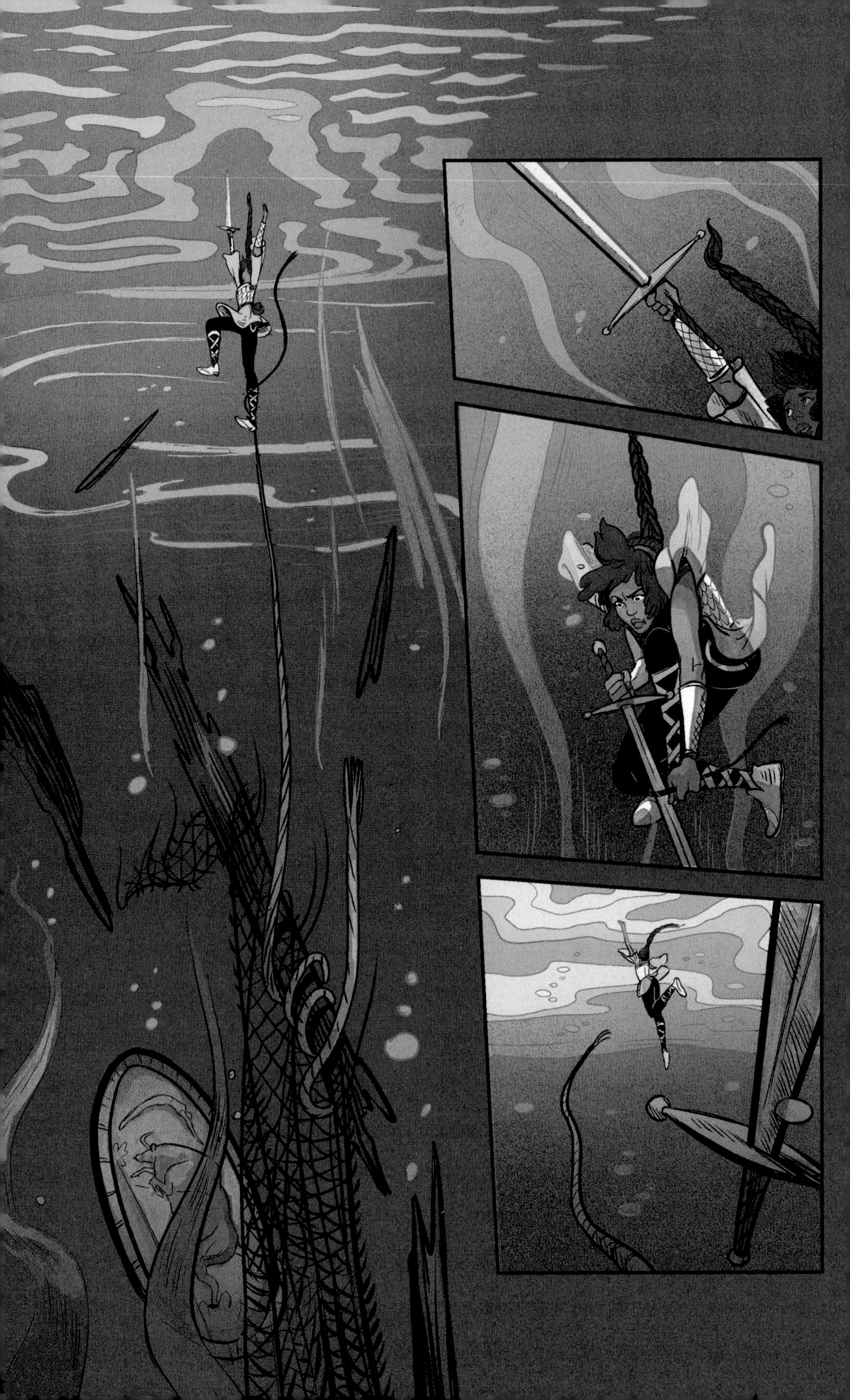

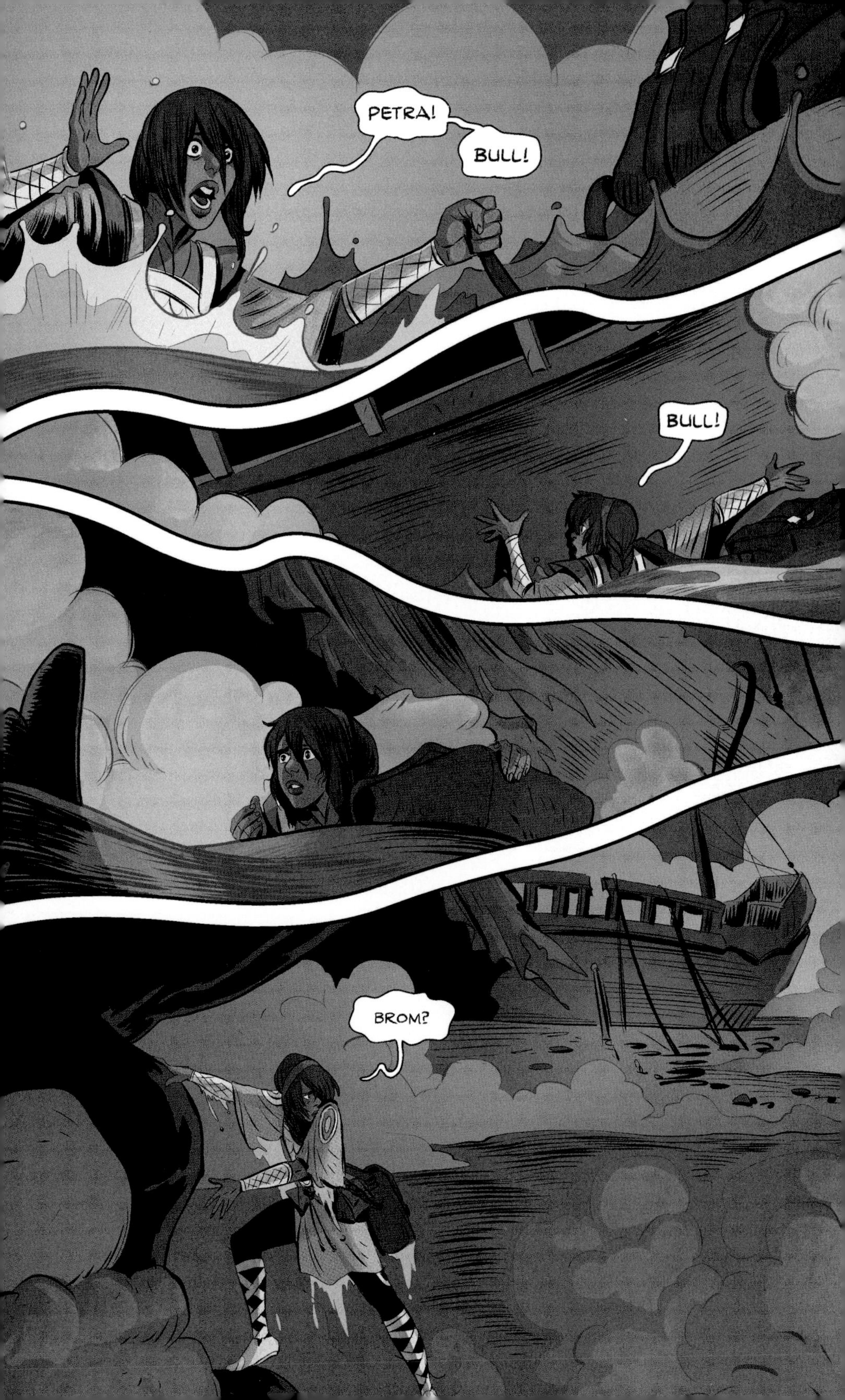
PETRA!
BULL!
BULL!
BROM?

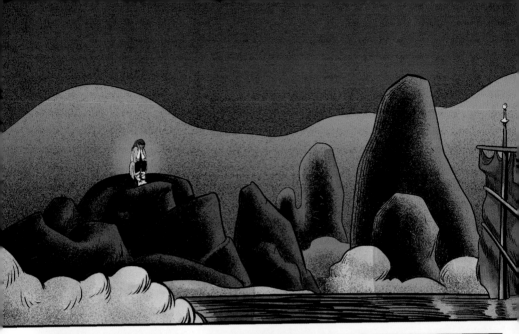

SPLORCH!

PT-TOO!

SQUAWK!

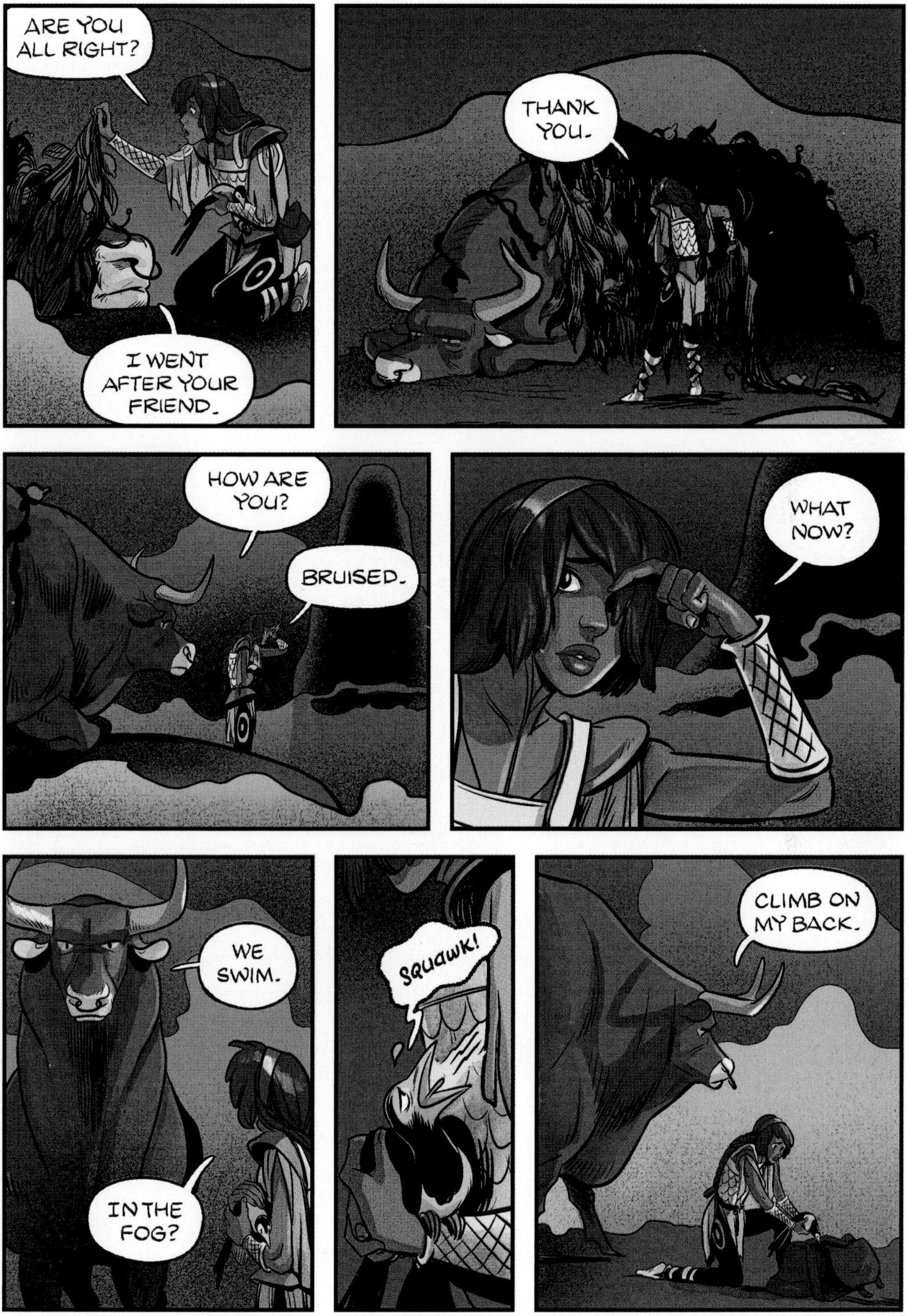
ARE YOU ALL RIGHT?
I WENT AFTER YOUR FRIEND.
THANK YOU.
HOW ARE YOU?
BRUISED.
WHAT NOW?
WE SWIM.
IN THE FOG?
SQUAWK!
CLIMB ON MY BACK.

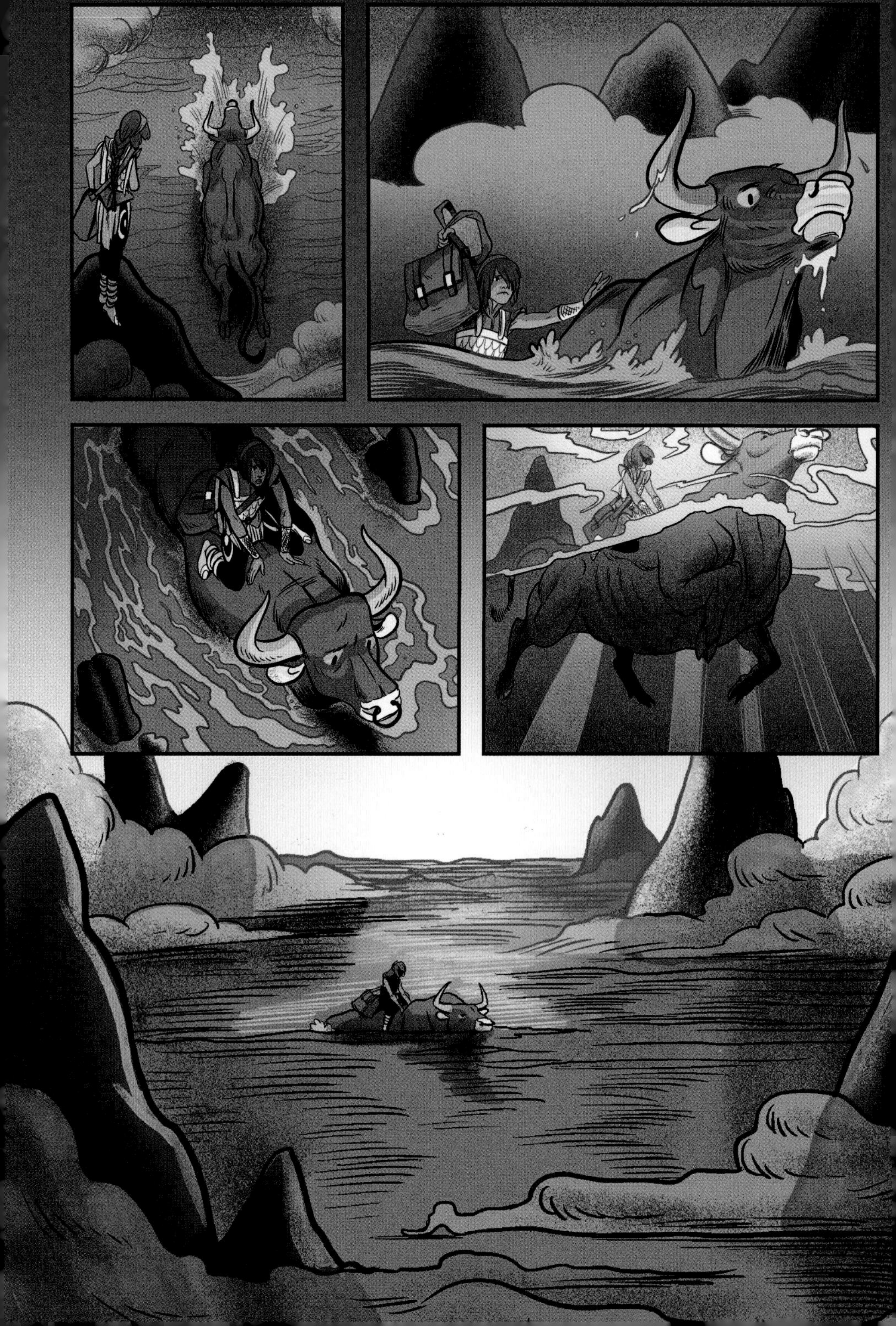

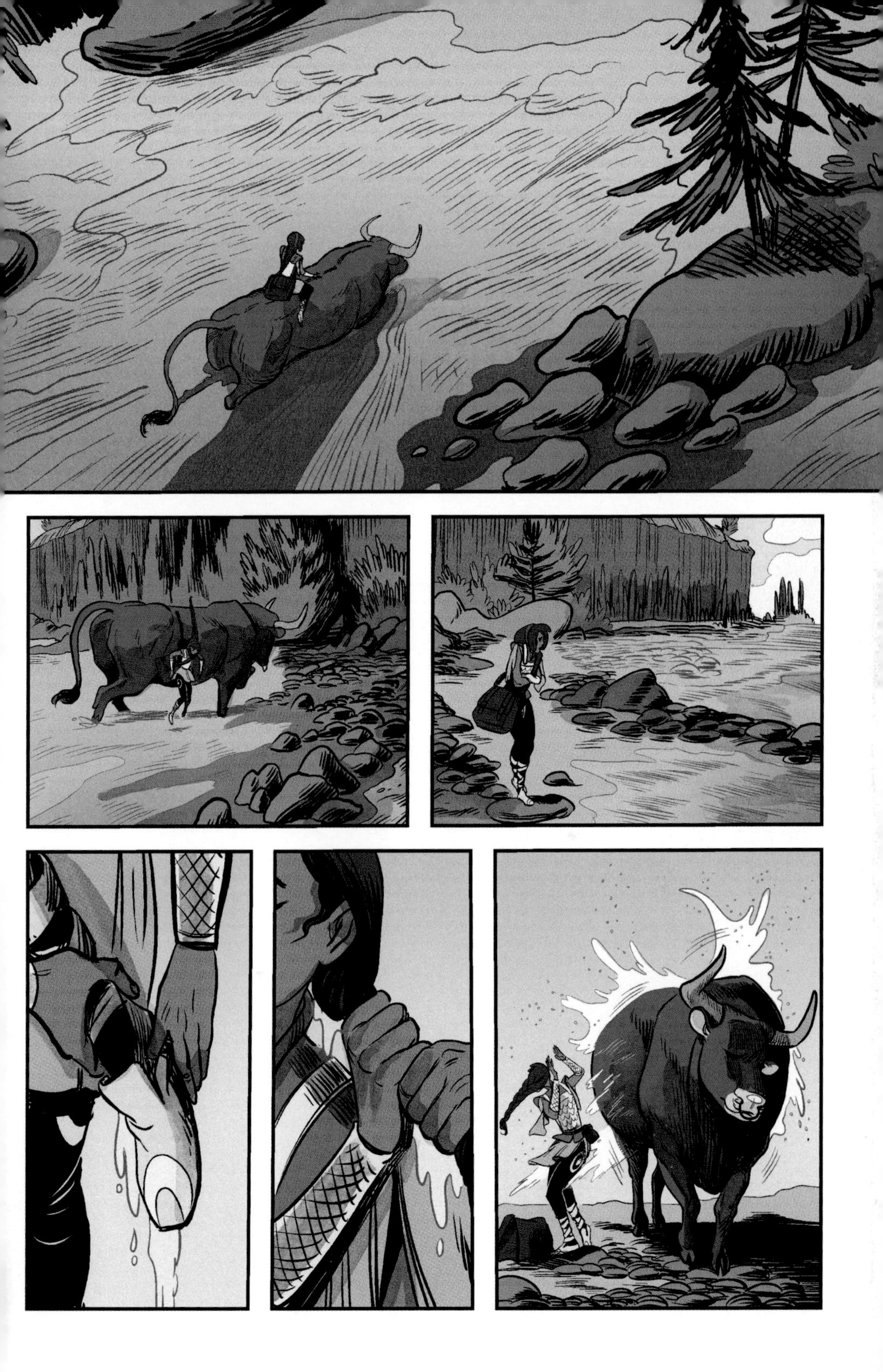

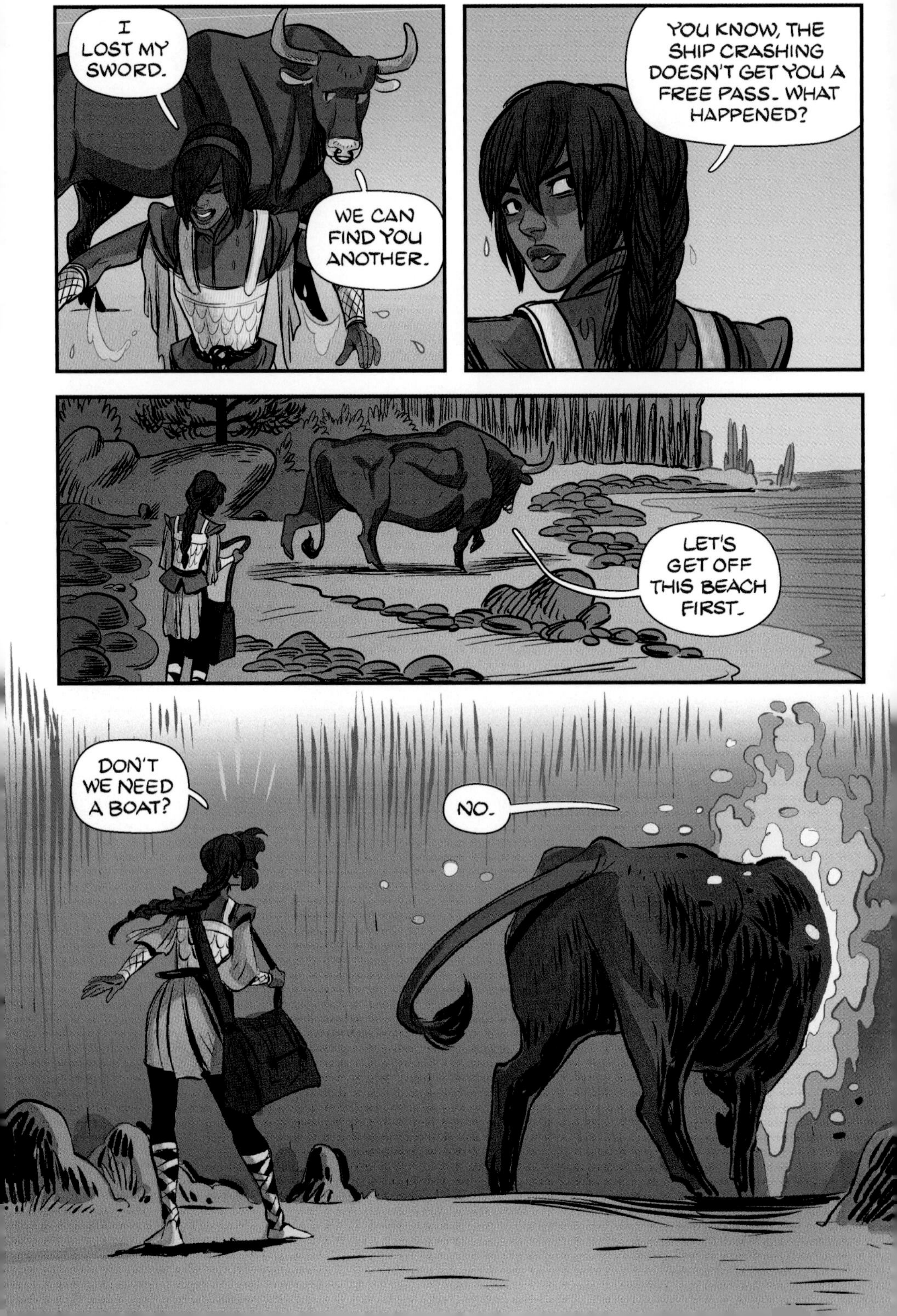
I LOST MY SWORD.
WE CAN FIND YOU ANOTHER.
YOU KNOW, THE SHIP CRASHING DOESN'T GET YOU A FREE PASS. WHAT HAPPENED?
LET'S GET OFF THIS BEACH FIRST.
DON'T WE NEED A BOAT?
NO.

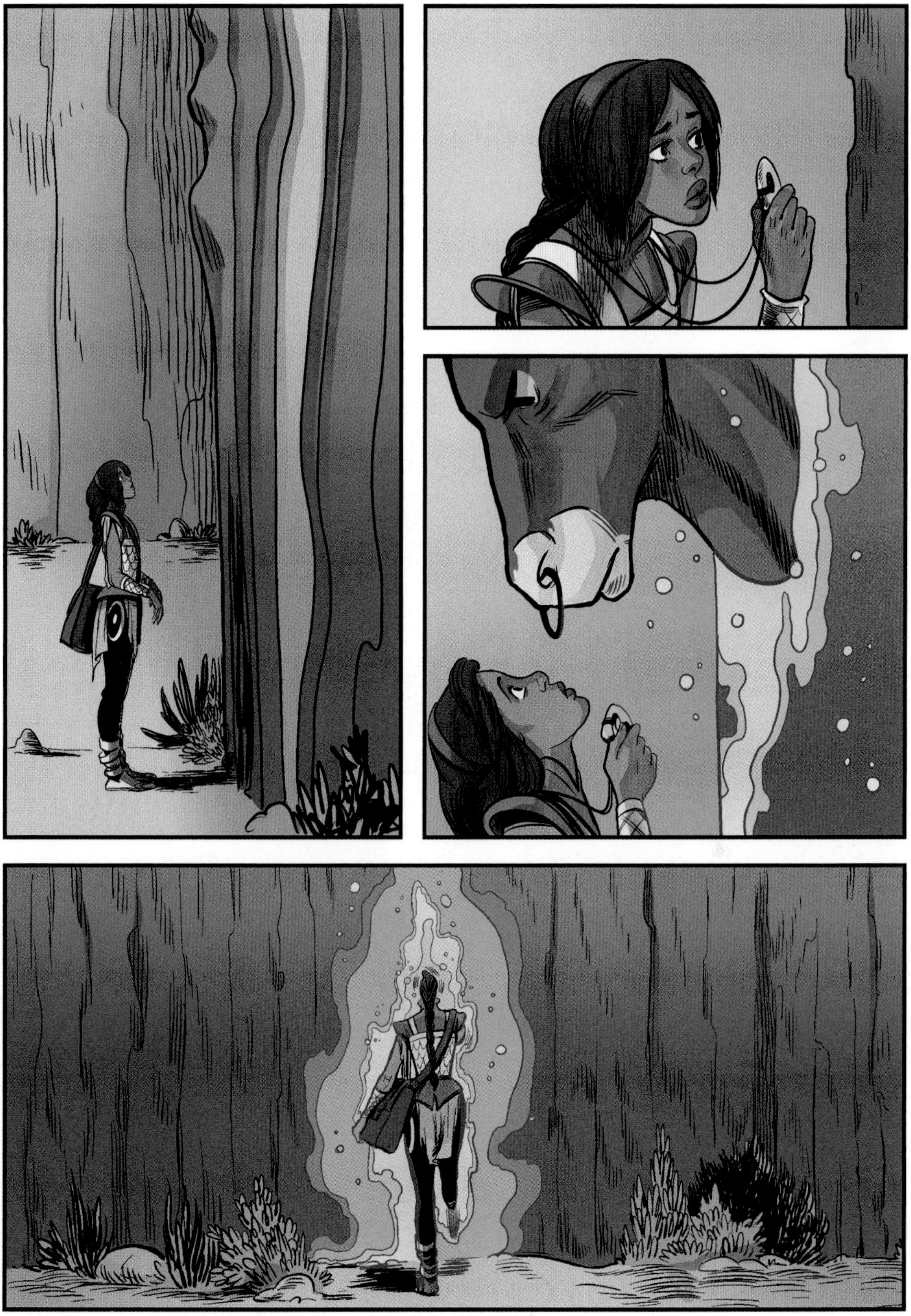

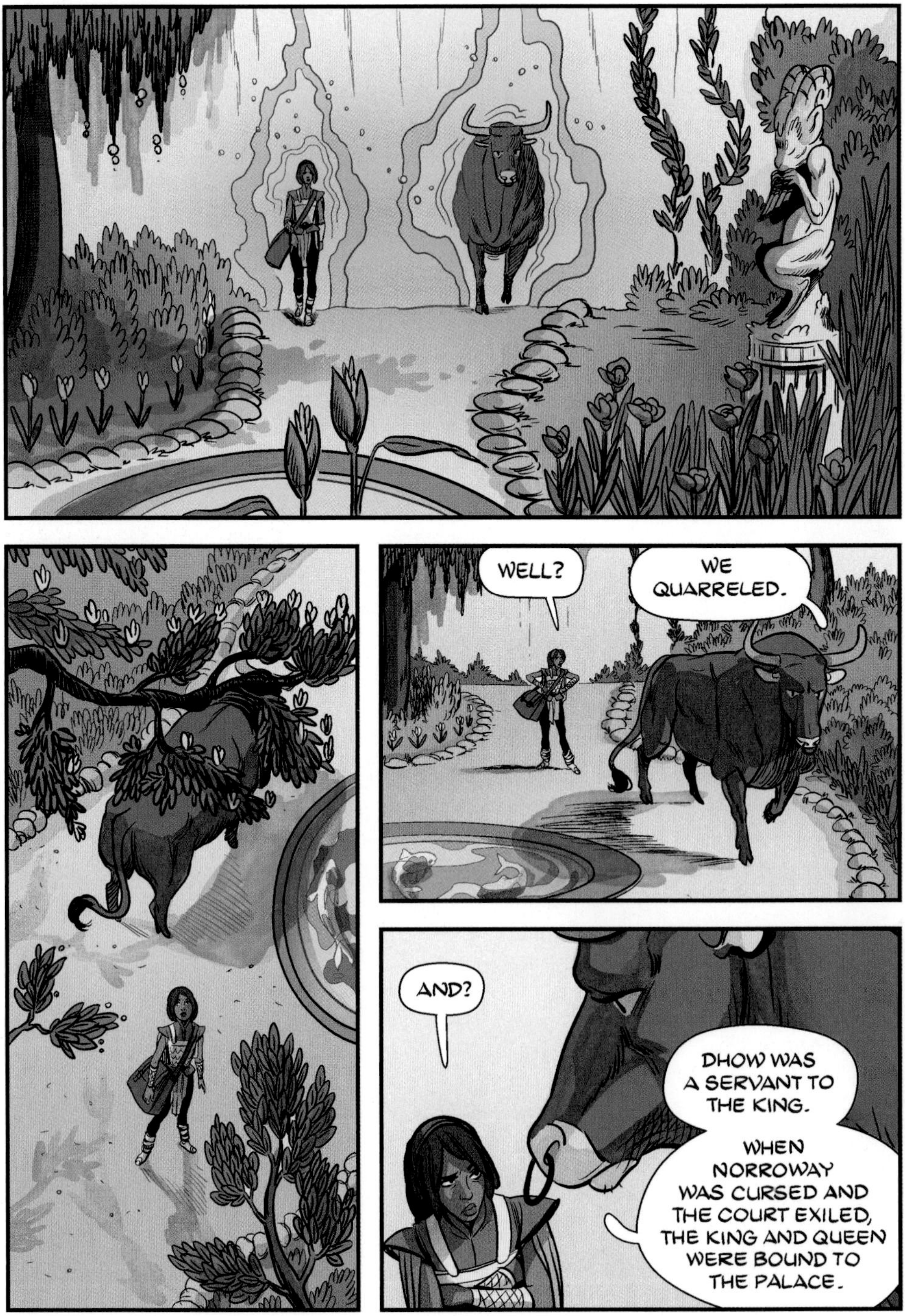
WELL?
WE QUARRELED.
AND?
DHOW WAS A SERVANT TO THE KING.
WHEN NORROWAY WAS CURSED AND THE COURT EXILED, THE KING AND QUEEN WERE BOUND TO THE PALACE.

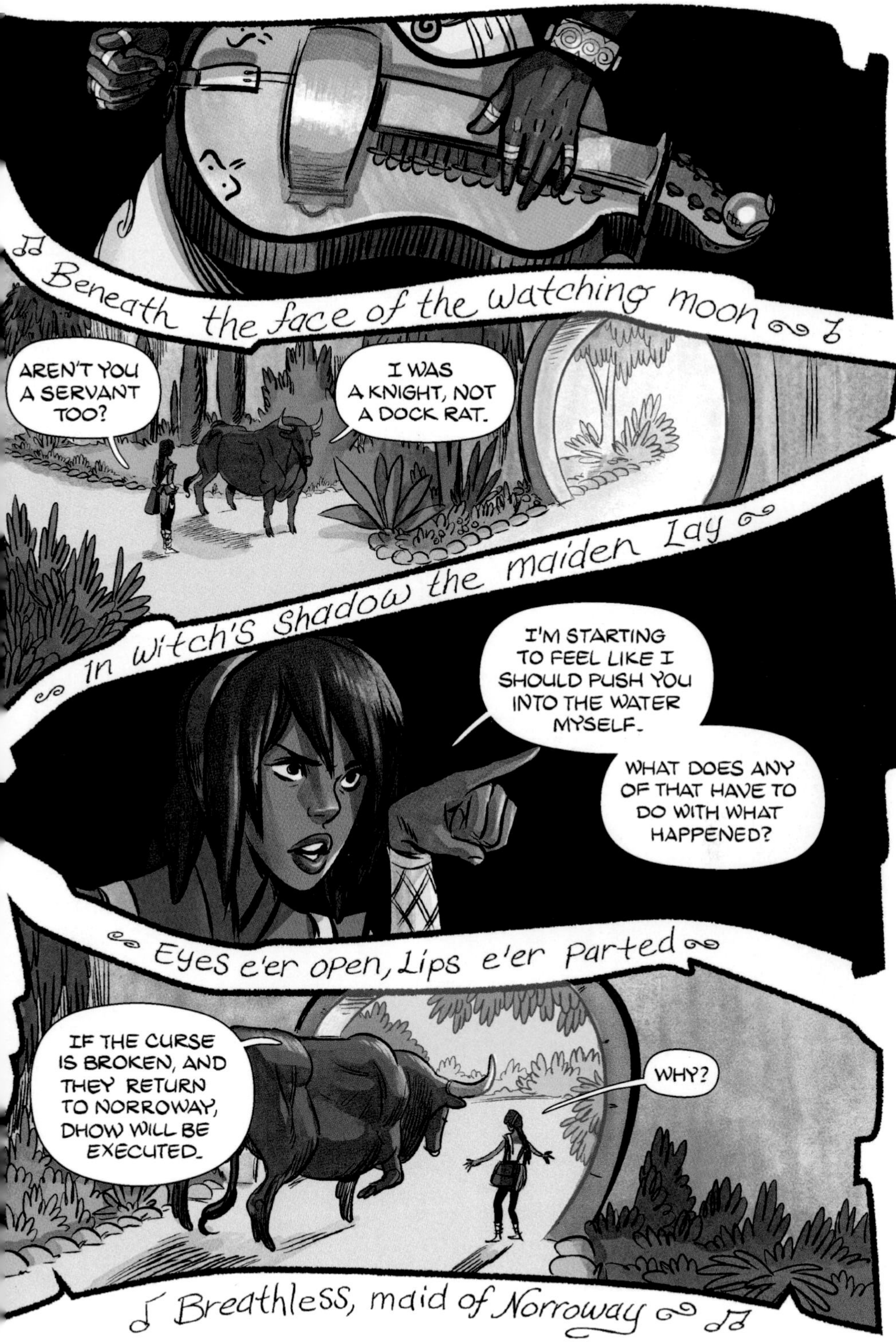
Beneath the face of the watching moon
AREN'T YOU A SERVANT TOO?
I WAS A KNIGHT, NOT A DOCK RAT.
In witch's shadow the maiden lay
I'M STARTING TO FEEL LIKE I SHOULD PUSH YOU INTO THE WATER MYSELF.
WHAT DOES ANY OF THAT HAVE TO DO WITH WHAT HAPPENED?
Eyes e'er open, lips e'er parted
IF THE CURSE IS BROKEN, AND THEY RETURN TO NORROWAY, DHOW WILL BE EXECUTED.
WHY?
Breathless, maid of Norroway

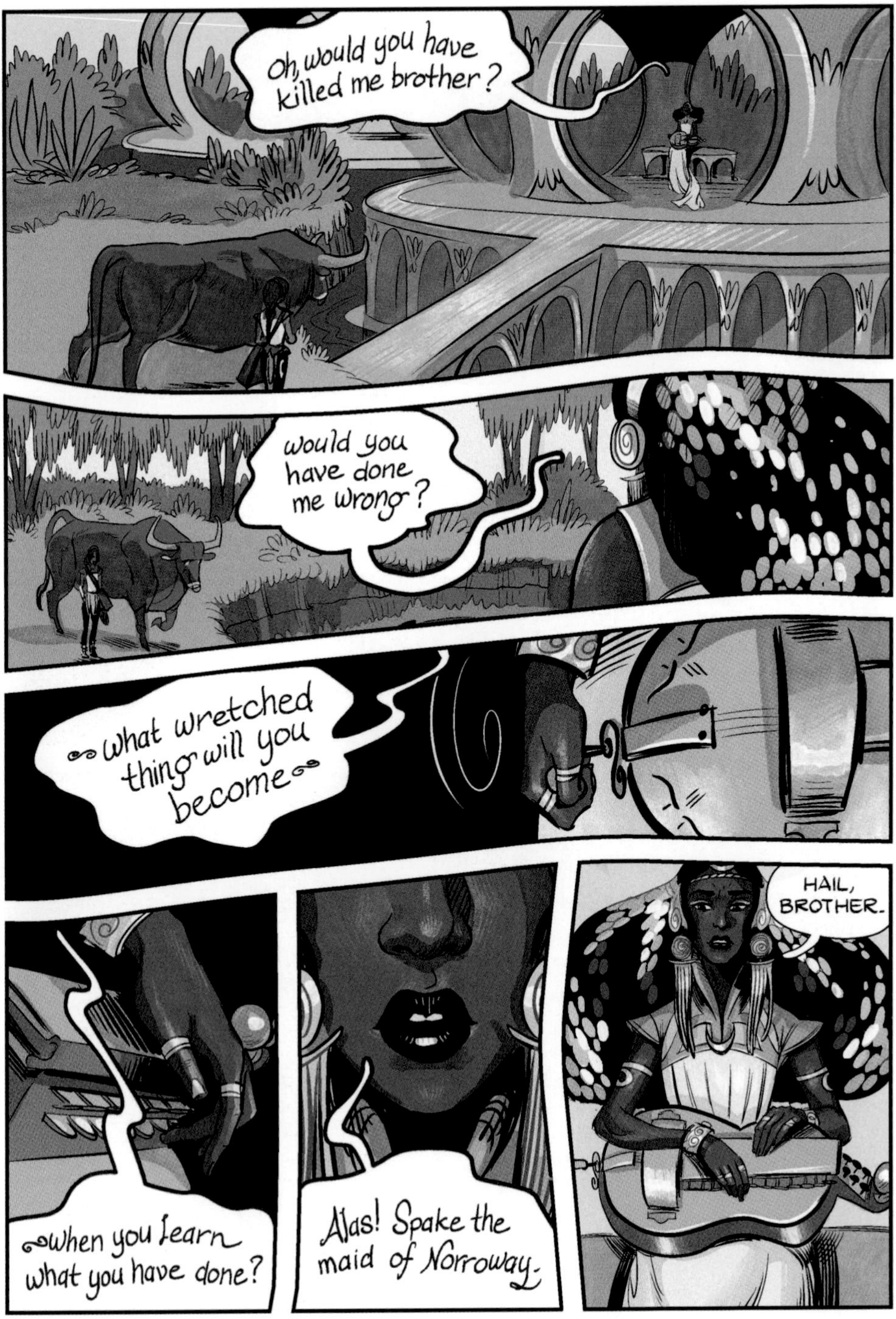
Oh, would you have killed me brother?
would you have done me wrong?
what wretched thing will you become
when you learn what you have done?
Alas! Spake the maid of Norroway.
HAIL, BROTHER.

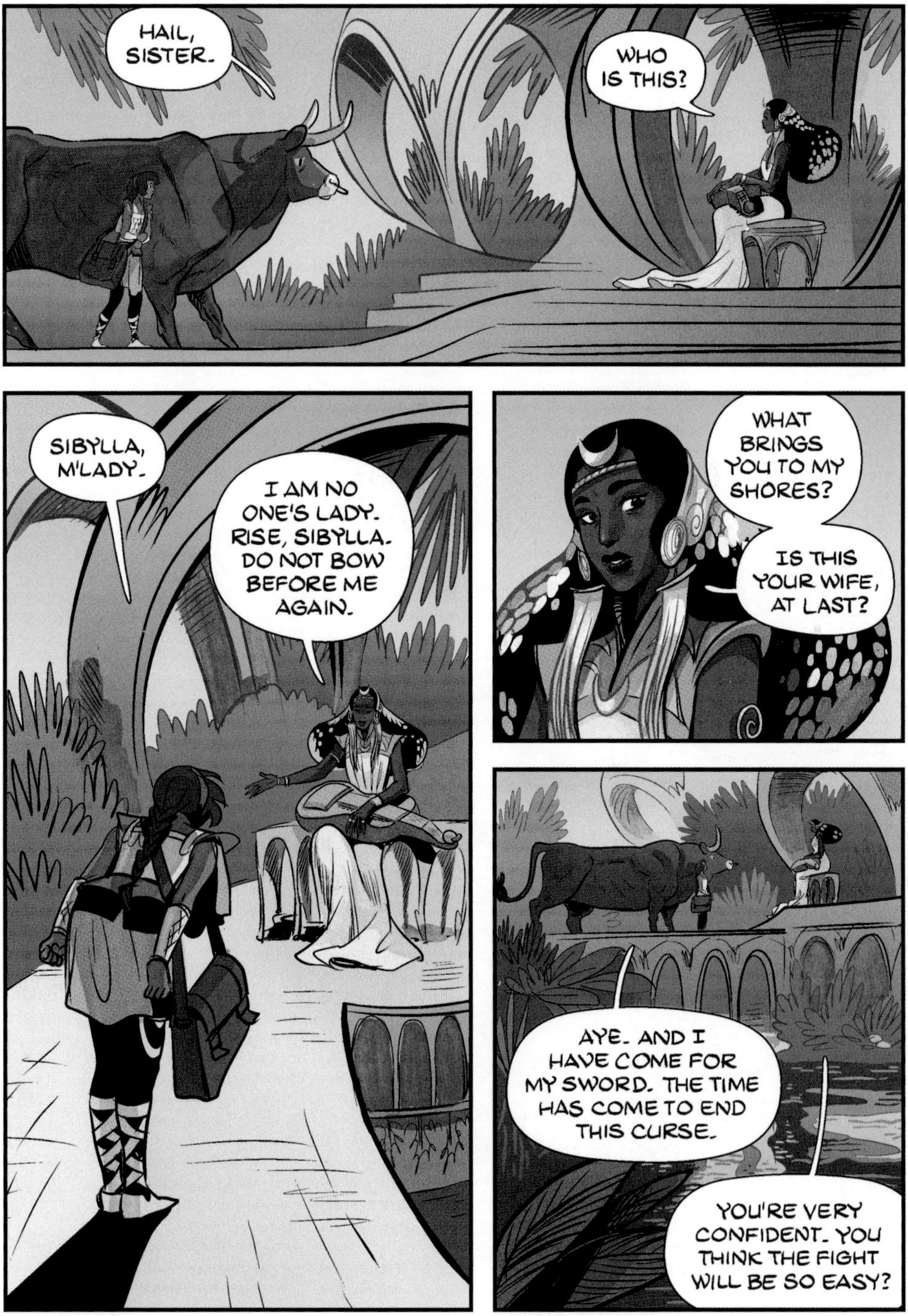
HAIL, SISTER.
WHO IS THIS?
SIBYLLA, M'LADY.
I AM NO ONE'S LADY. RISE, SIBYLLA. DO NOT BOW BEFORE ME AGAIN.
WHAT BRINGS YOU TO MY SHORES?
IS THIS YOUR WIFE, AT LAST?
AYE. AND I HAVE COME FOR MY SWORD. THE TIME HAS COME TO END THIS CURSE.
YOU'RE VERY CONFIDENT. YOU THINK THE FIGHT WILL BE SO EASY?

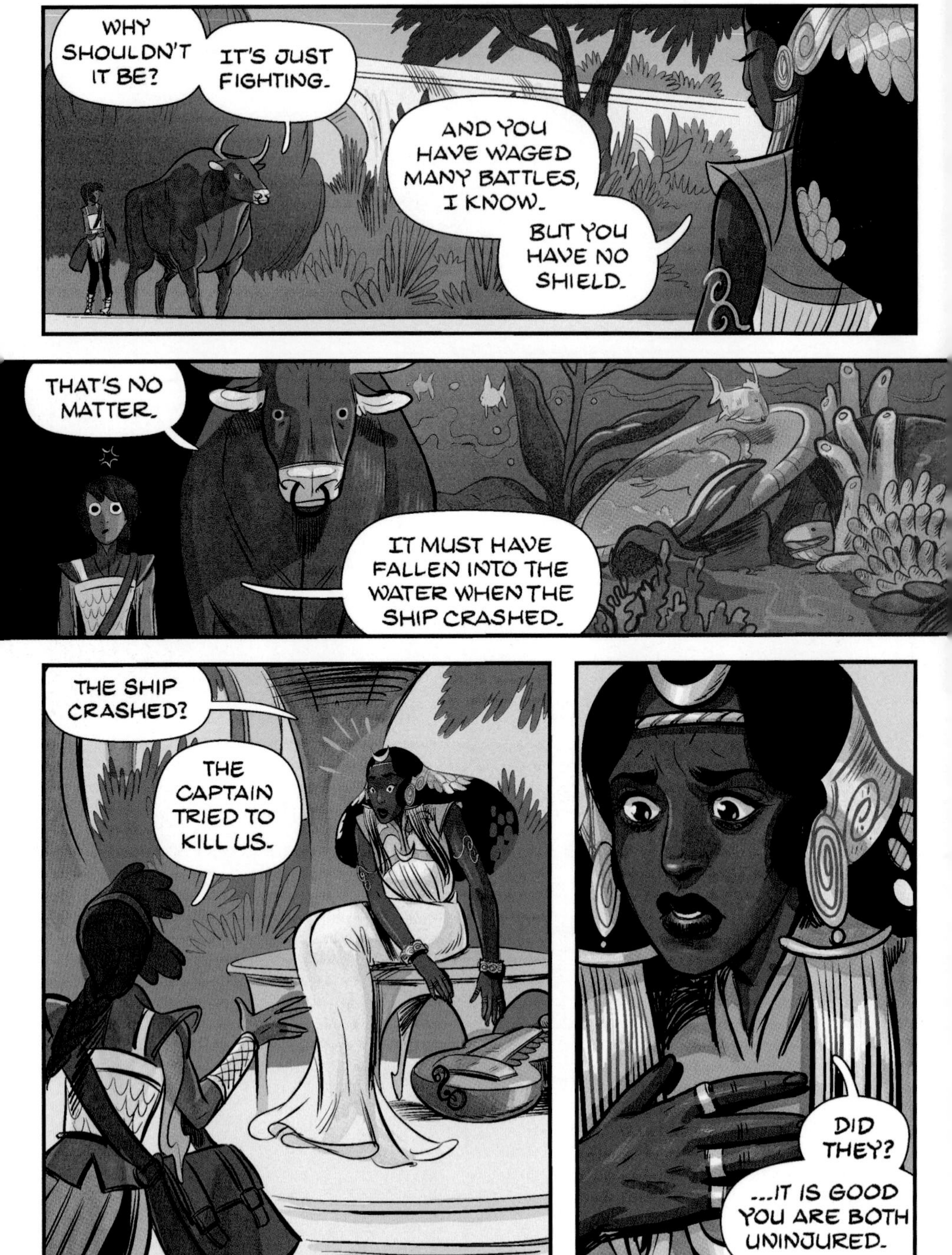
WHY SHOULDN'T IT BE?
IT'S JUST FIGHTING.
AND YOU HAVE WAGED MANY BATTLES, I KNOW.
BUT YOU HAVE NO SHIELD.
THAT'S NO MATTER.
IT MUST HAVE FALLEN INTO THE WATER WHEN THE SHIP CRASHED.
THE SHIP CRASHED?
THE CAPTAIN TRIED TO KILL US.
DID THEY?
...IT IS GOOD YOU ARE BOTH UNINJURED.

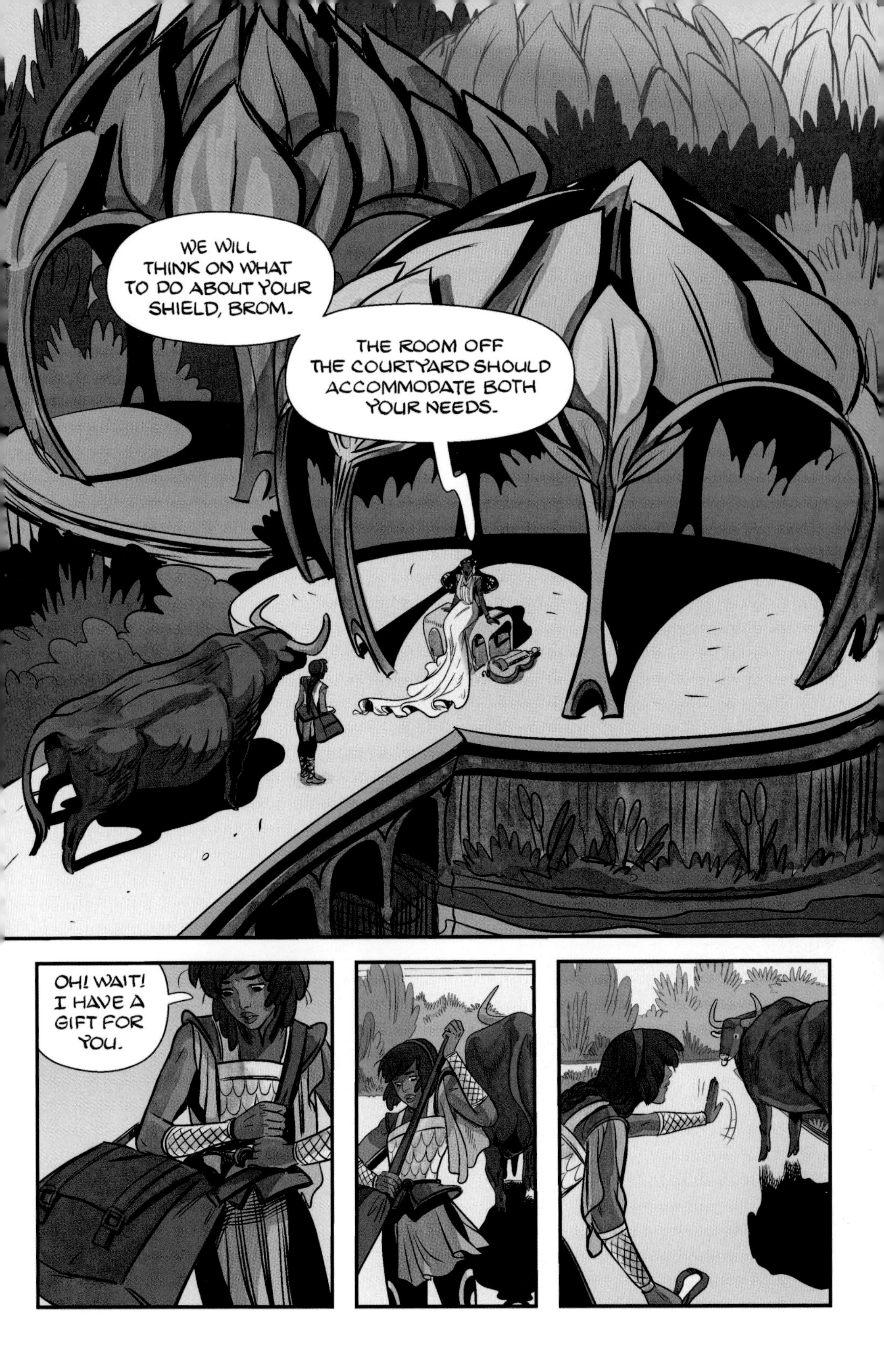
WE WILL THINK ON WHAT TO DO ABOUT YOUR SHIELD, BROM.
THE ROOM OFF THE COURTYARD SHOULD ACCOMMODATE BOTH YOUR NEEDS.
OH! WAIT! I HAVE A GIFT FOR YOU.

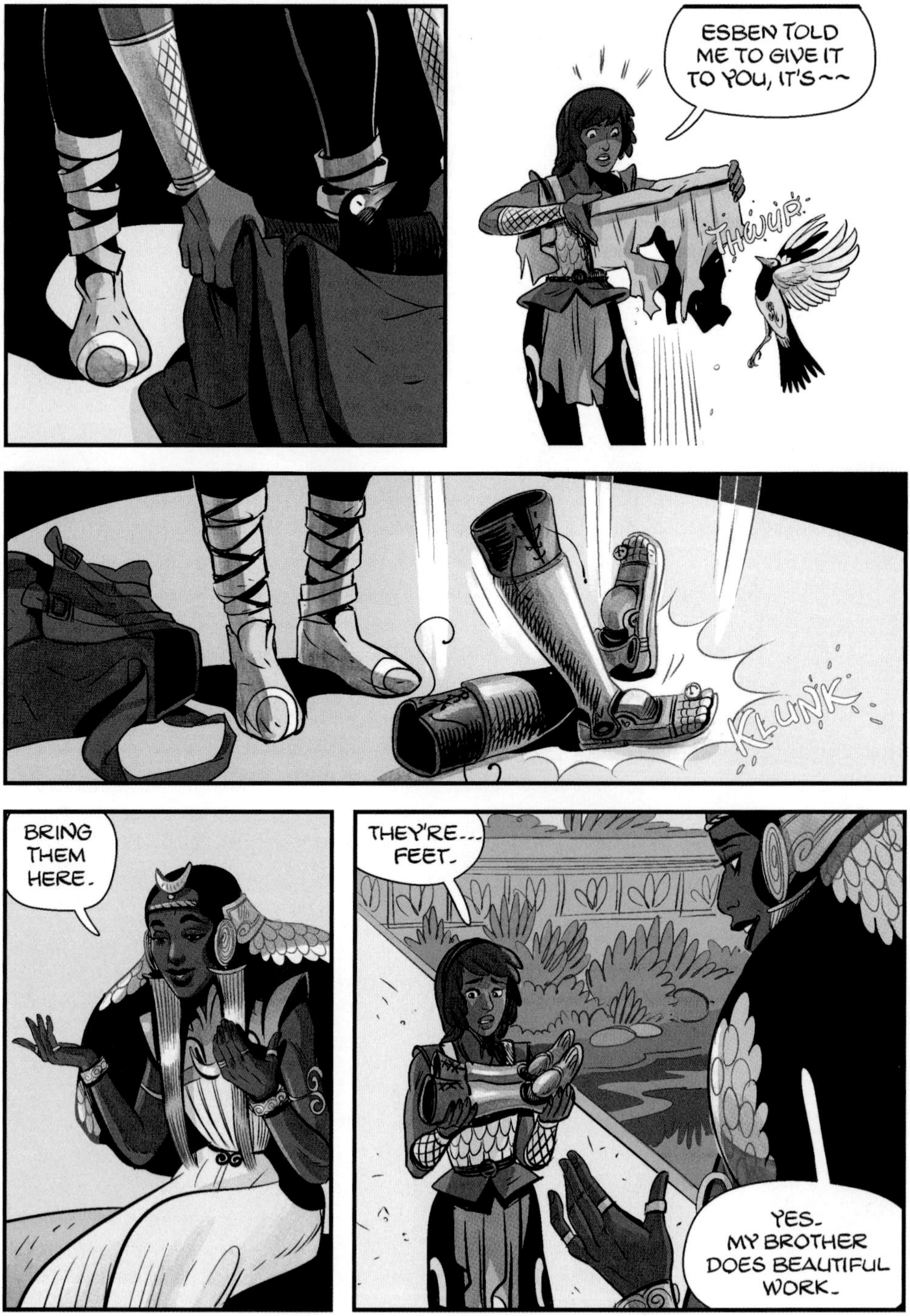
ESBEN TOLD ME TO GIVE IT TO YOU, IT'S~~
THWUP
KLUNK
BRING THEM HERE.
THEY'RE... FEET.
YES. MY BROTHER DOES BEAUTIFUL WORK.

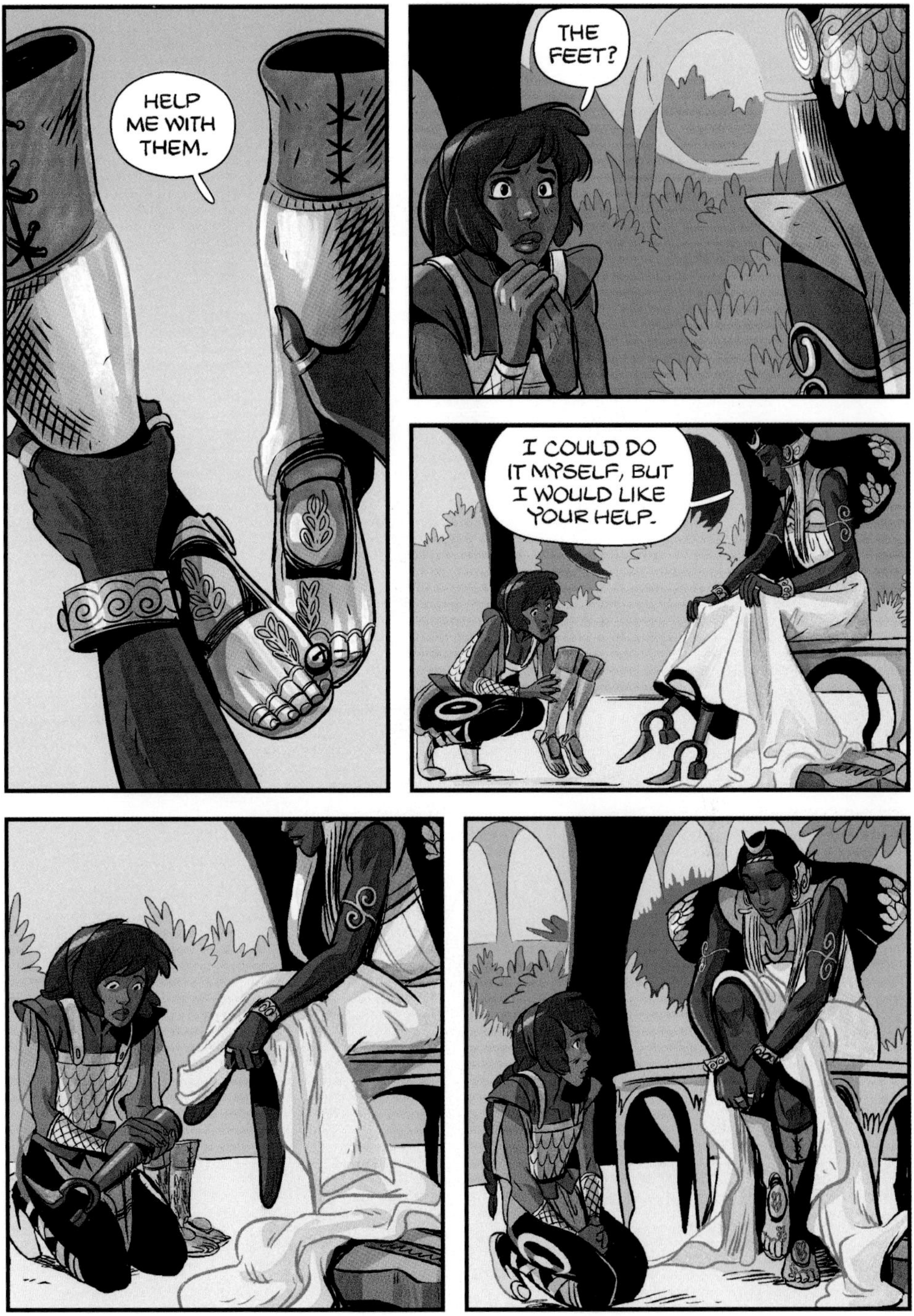
HELP ME WITH THEM.
THE FEET?
I COULD DO IT MYSELF, BUT I WOULD LIKE YOUR HELP.

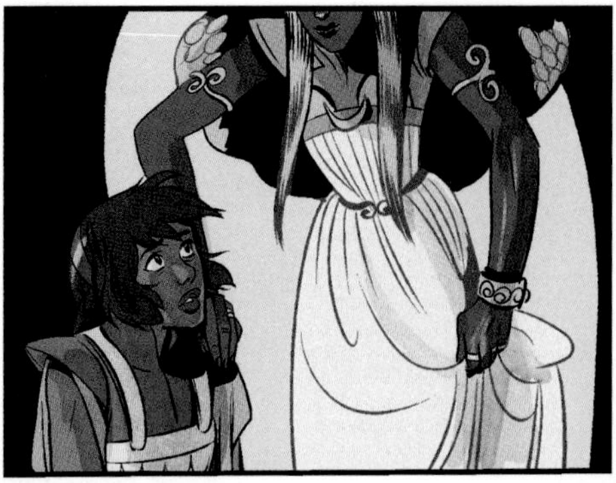
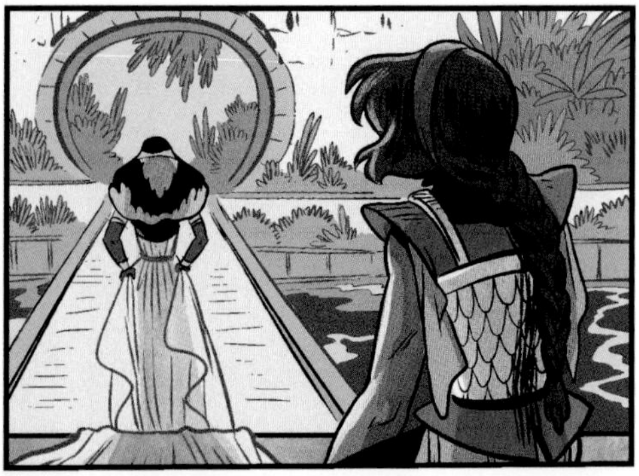
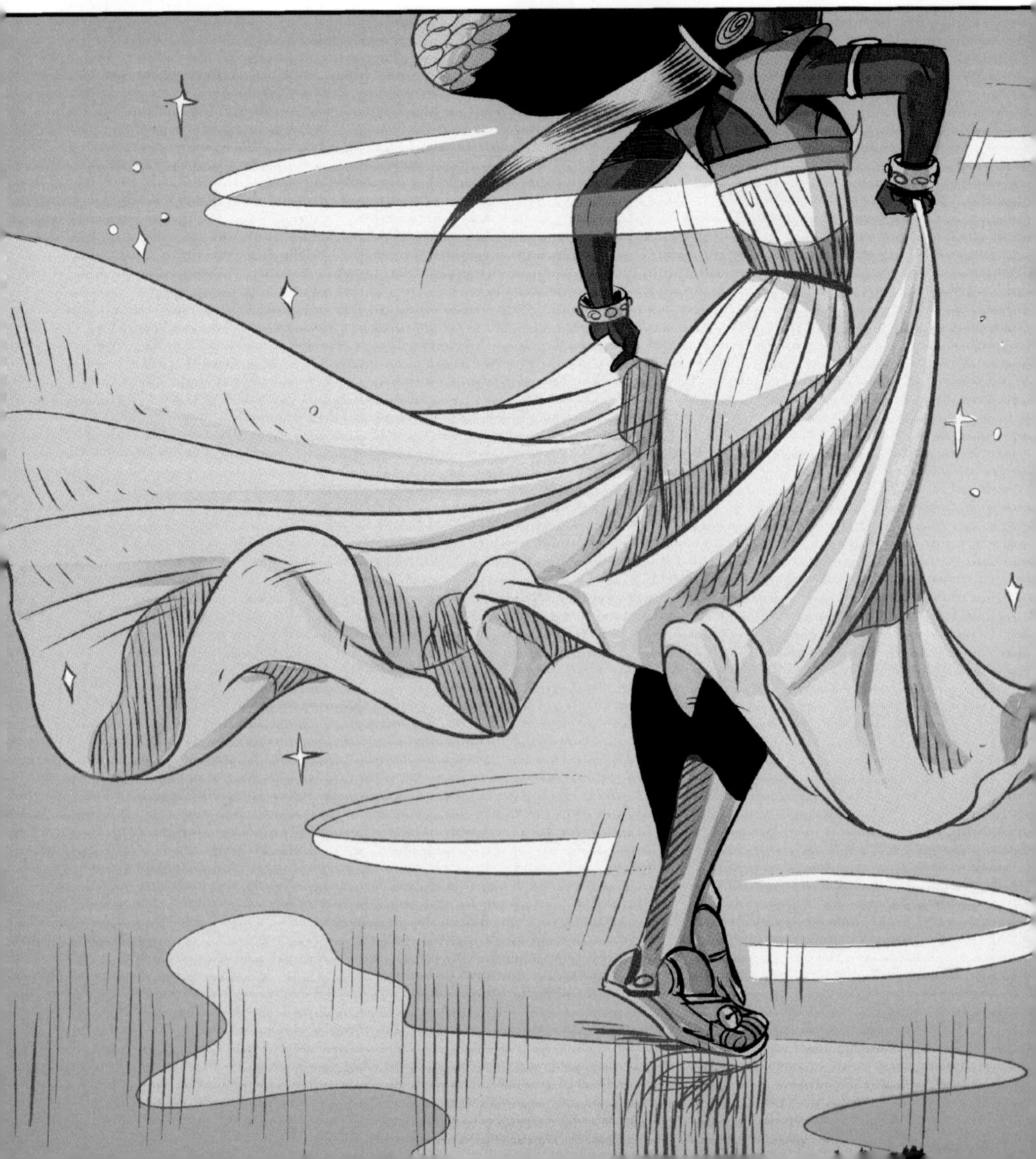

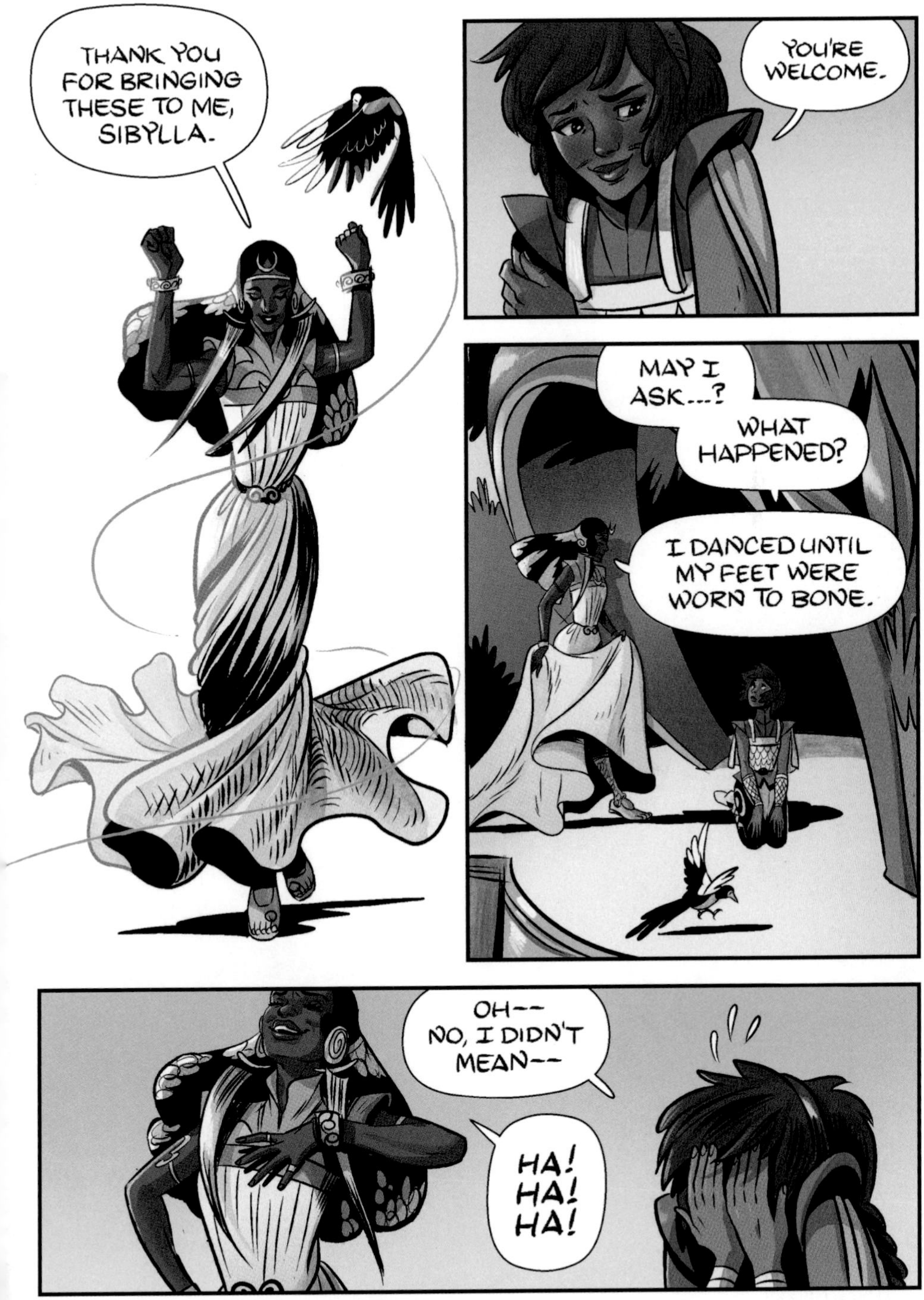
THANK YOU FOR BRINGING THESE TO ME, SIBYLLA.
YOU'RE WELCOME.
MAY I ASK...?
WHAT HAPPENED?
I DANCED UNTIL MY FEET WERE WORN TO BONE.
OH-- NO, I DIDN'T MEAN--
HA! HA! HA!

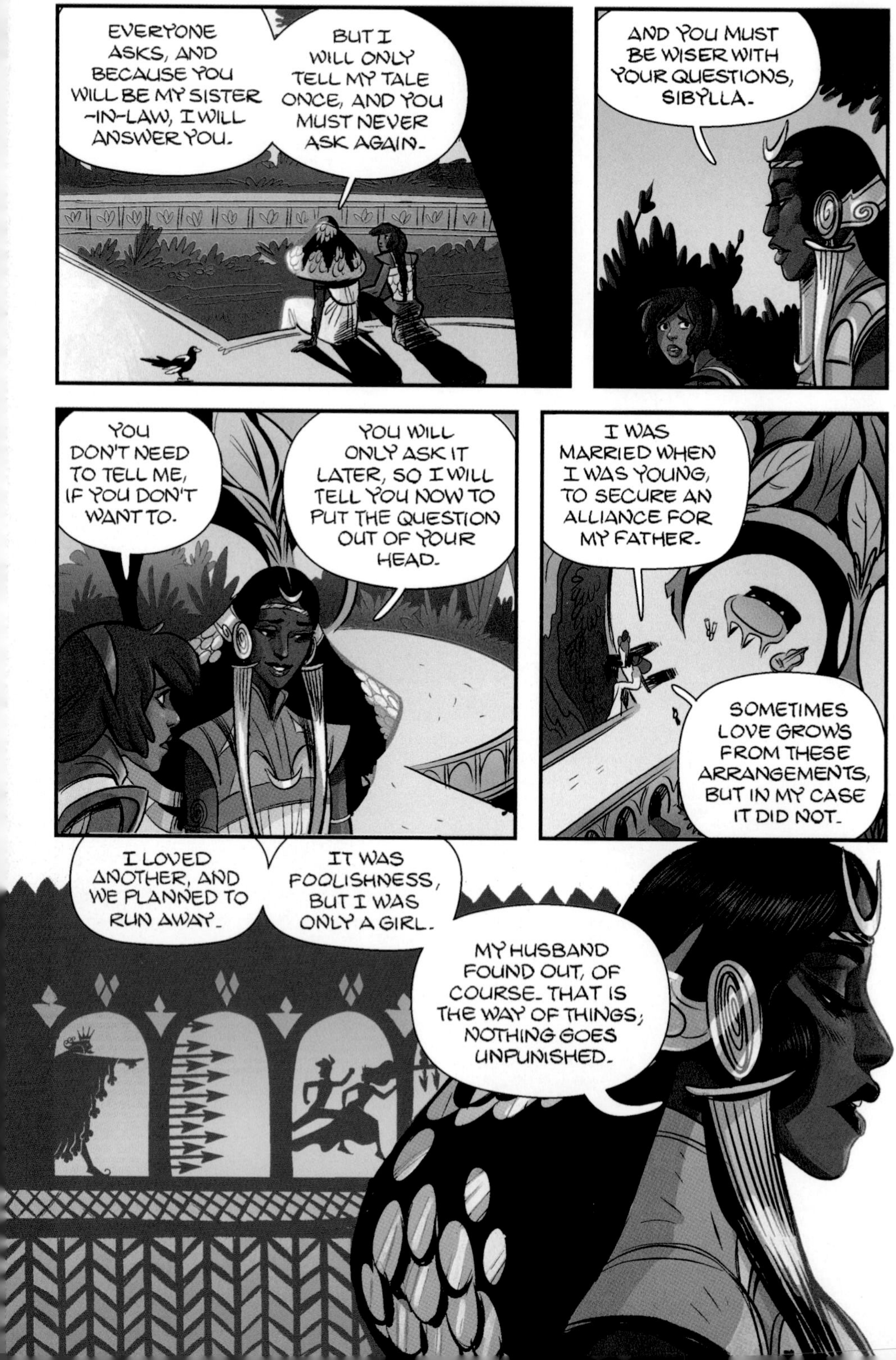
EVERYONE ASKS, AND BECAUSE YOU WILL BE MY SISTER-IN-LAW, I WILL ANSWER YOU.
BUT I WILL ONLY TELL MY TALE ONCE, AND YOU MUST NEVER ASK AGAIN.
AND YOU MUST BE WISER WITH YOUR QUESTIONS, SIBYLLA.
YOU DON'T NEED TO TELL ME, IF YOU DON'T WANT TO.
YOU WILL ONLY ASK IT LATER, SO I WILL TELL YOU NOW TO PUT THE QUESTION OUT OF YOUR HEAD.
I WAS MARRIED WHEN I WAS YOUNG, TO SECURE AN ALLIANCE FOR MY FATHER.
SOMETIMES LOVE GROWS FROM THESE ARRANGEMENTS, BUT IN MY CASE IT DID NOT.
I LOVED ANOTHER, AND WE PLANNED TO RUN AWAY.
IT WAS FOOLISHNESS, BUT I WAS ONLY A GIRL.
MY HUSBAND FOUND OUT, OF COURSE. THAT IS THE WAY OF THINGS; NOTHING GOES UNPUNISHED.

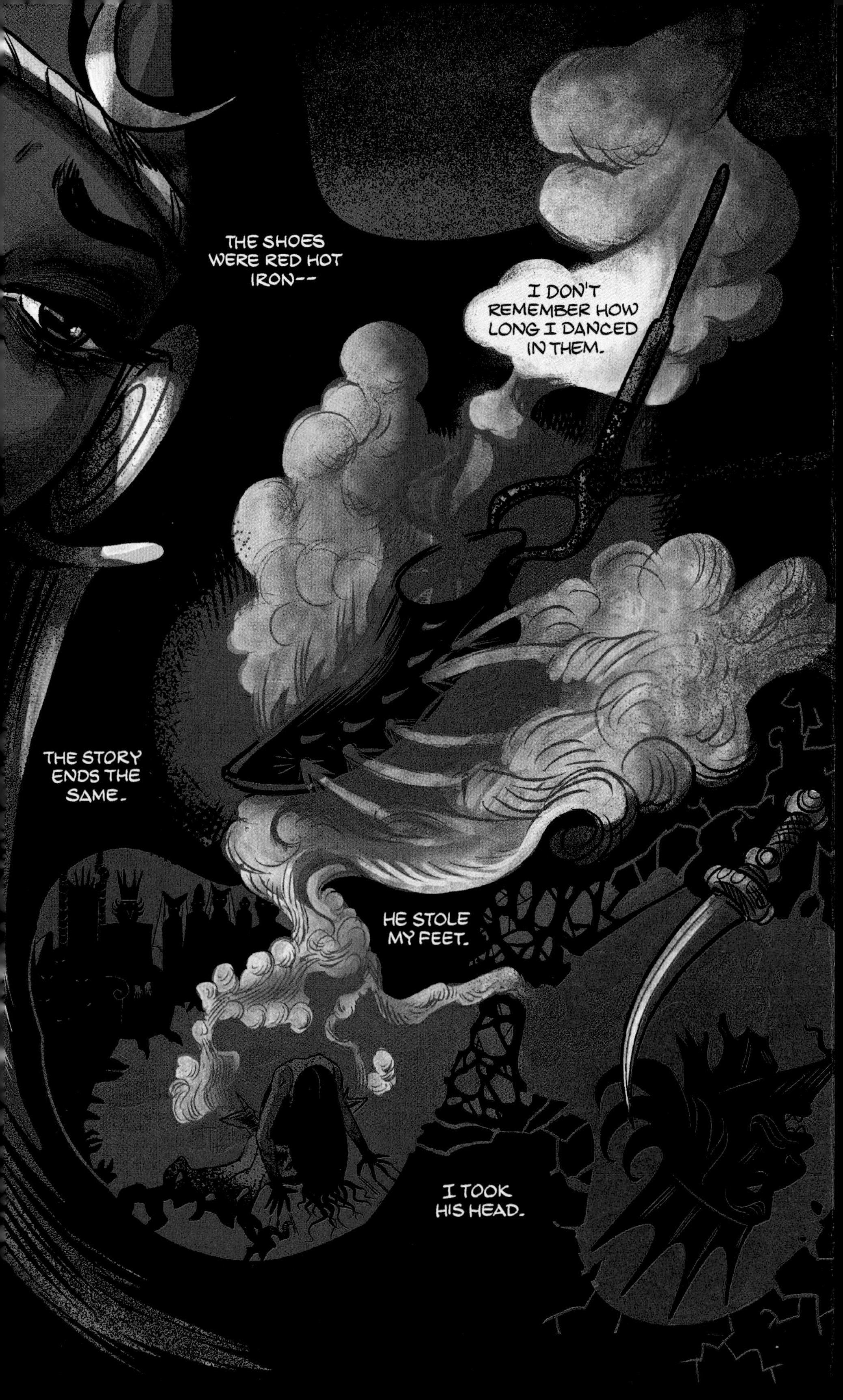
THE SHOES WERE RED HOT IRON--
I DON'T REMEMBER HOW LONG I DANCED IN THEM.
THE STORY ENDS THE SAME.
HE STOLE MY FEET.
I TOOK HIS HEAD.

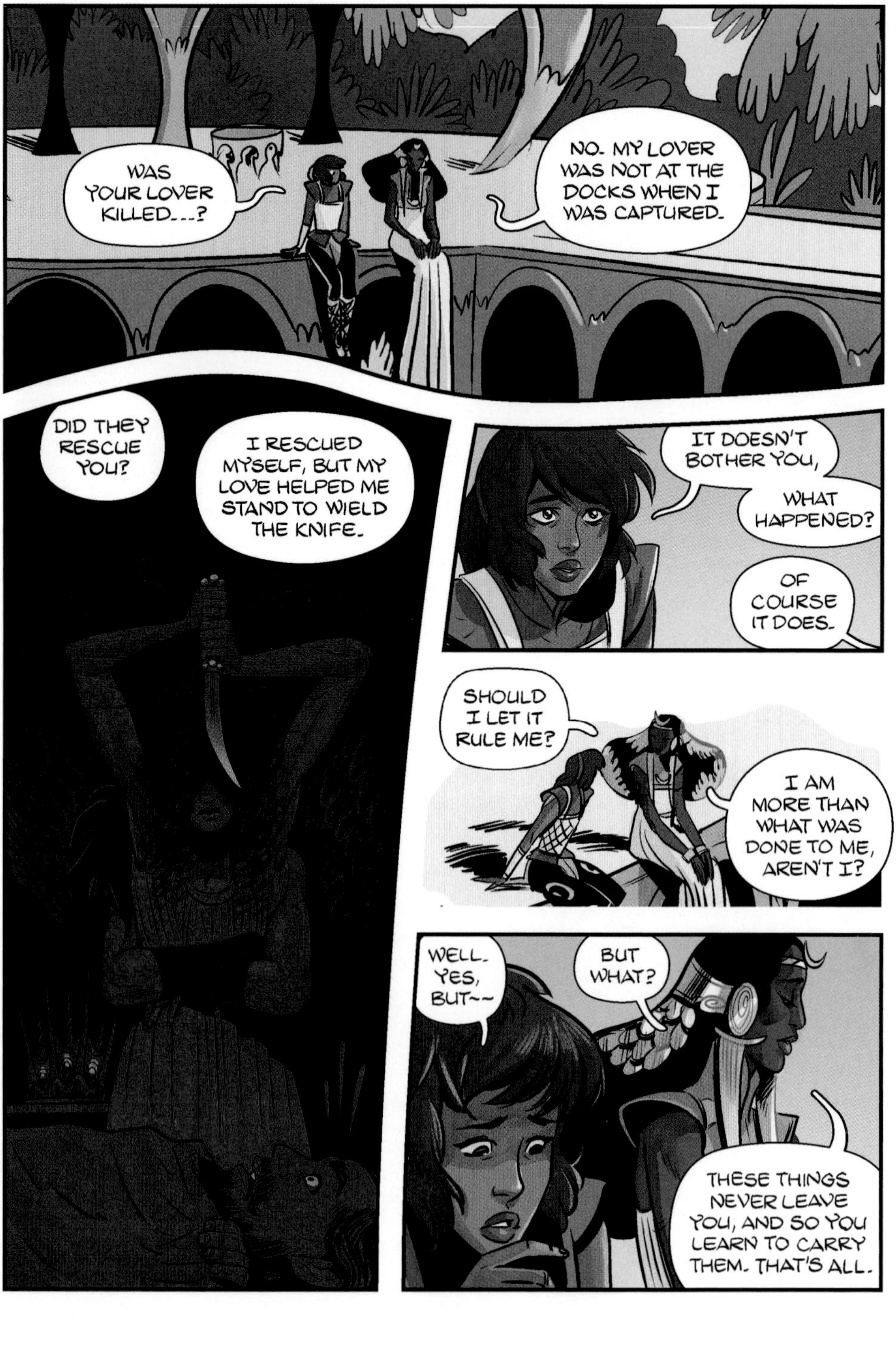
WAS YOUR LOVER KILLED...?
NO. MY LOVER WAS NOT AT THE DOCKS WHEN I WAS CAPTURED.
DID THEY RESCUE YOU?
I RESCUED MYSELF, BUT MY LOVE HELPED ME STAND TO WIELD THE KNIFE.
IT DOESN'T BOTHER YOU,
WHAT HAPPENED?
OF COURSE IT DOES.
SHOULD I LET IT RULE ME?
I AM MORE THAN WHAT WAS DONE TO ME, AREN'T I?
WELL. YES, BUT--
BUT WHAT?
THESE THINGS NEVER LEAVE YOU, AND SO YOU LEARN TO CARRY THEM. THAT'S ALL.

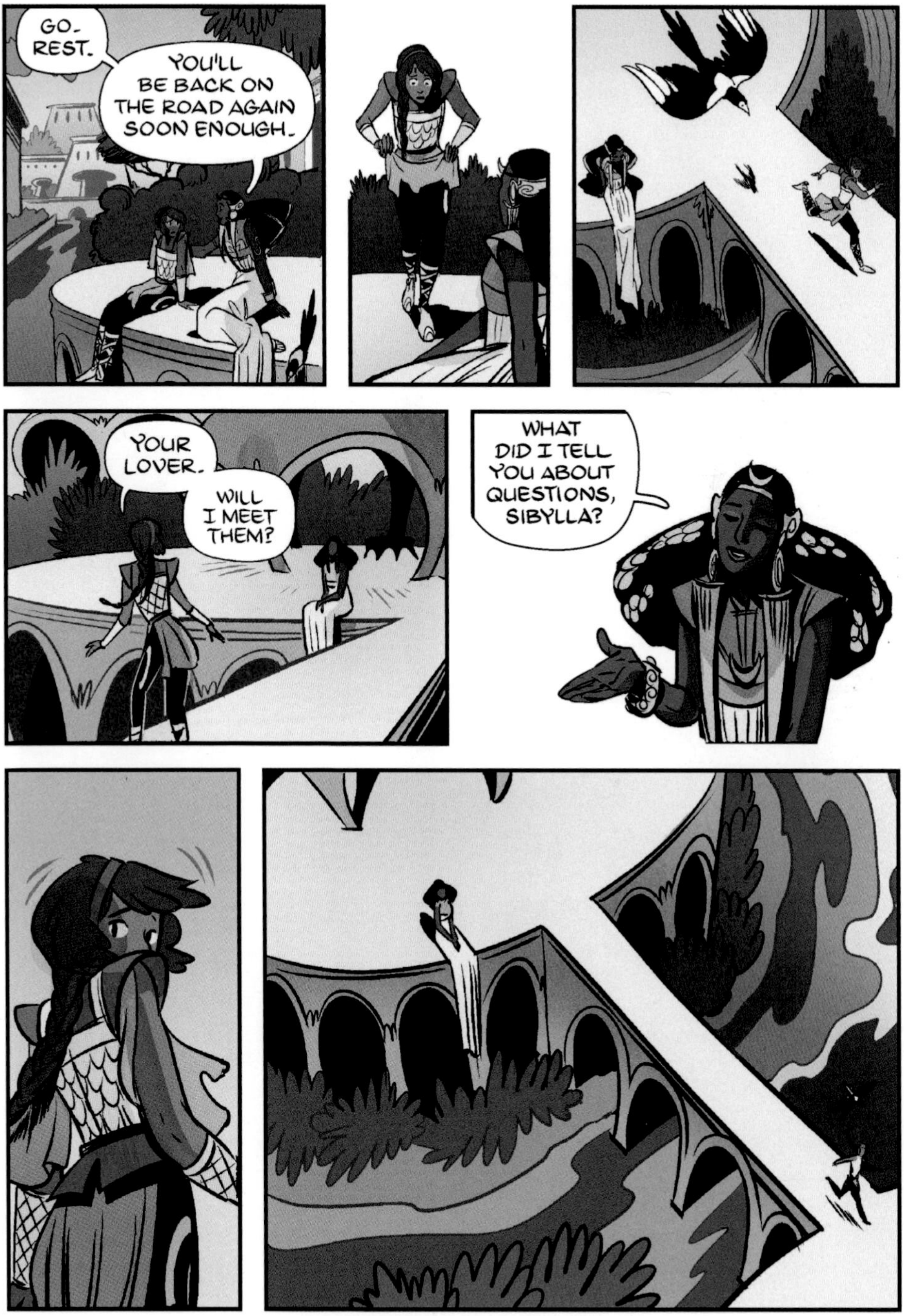
GO. REST.
YOU'LL BE BACK ON THE ROAD AGAIN SOON ENOUGH.
YOUR LOVER.
WILL I MEET THEM?
WHAT DID I TELL YOU ABOUT QUESTIONS, SIBYLLA?

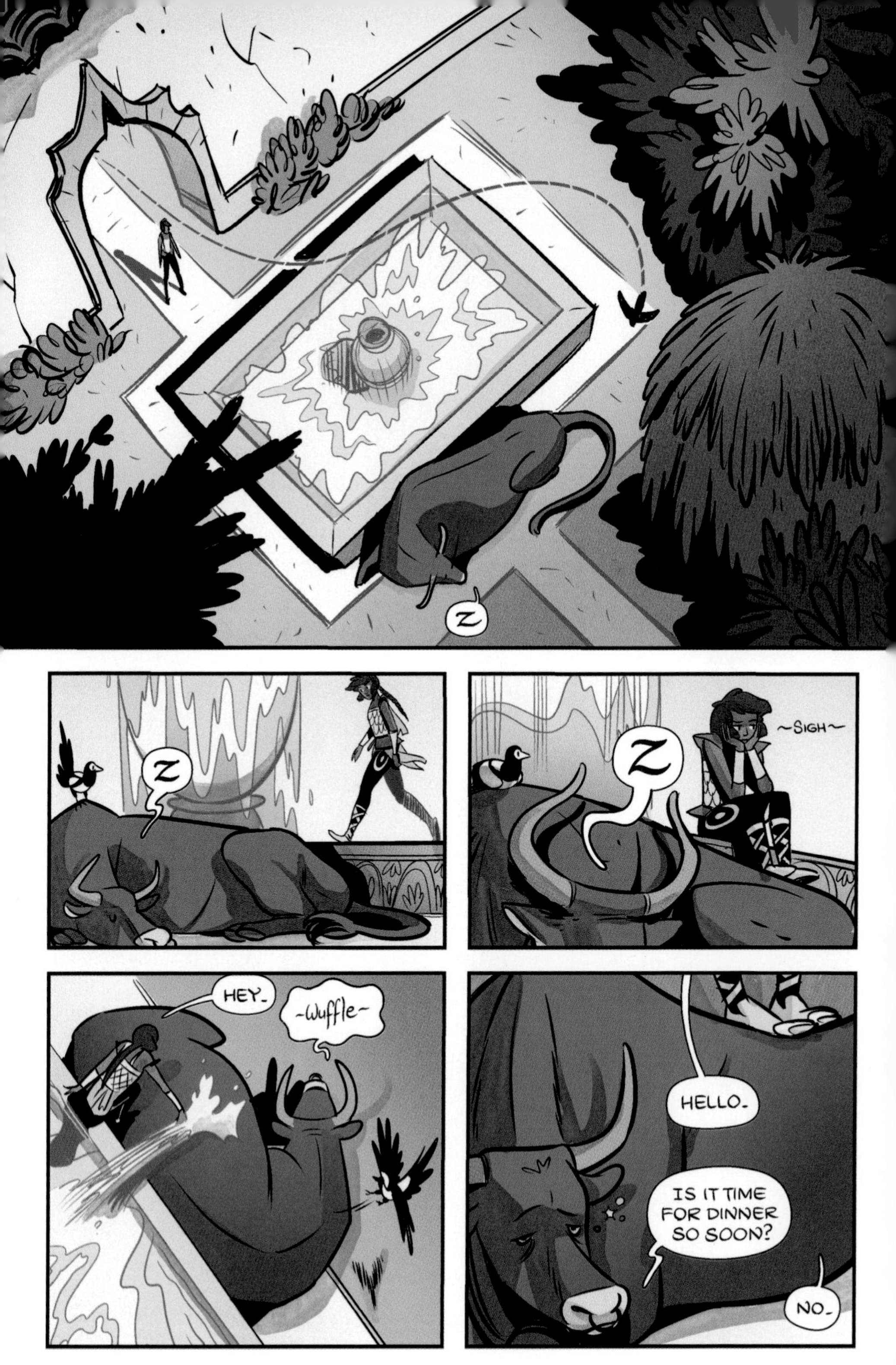
Z
Z
Z
~SIGH~
HEY.
-Wuffle-
HELLO.
IS IT TIME FOR DINNER SO SOON?
NO.

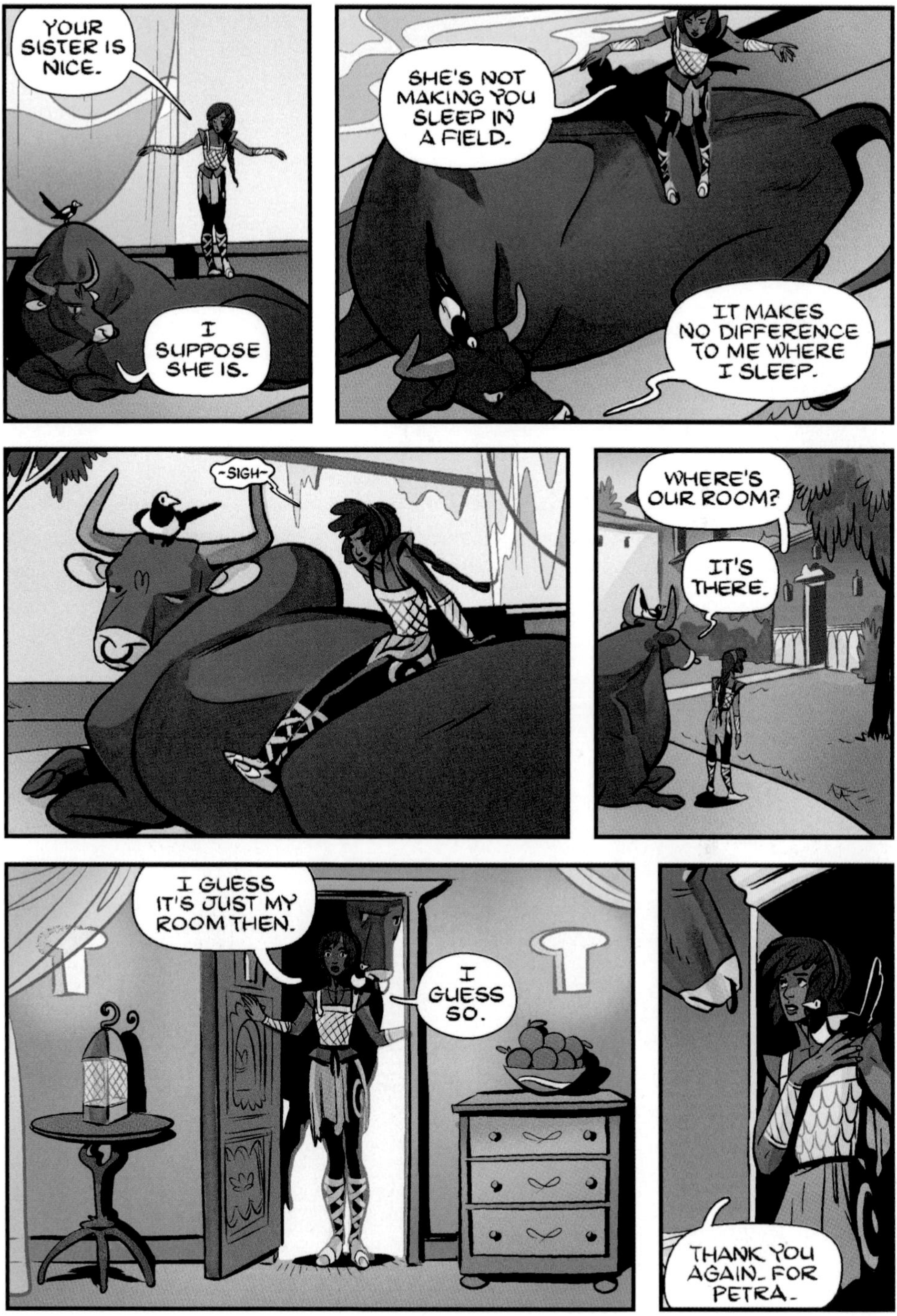
YOUR SISTER IS NICE.
I SUPPOSE SHE IS.
SHE'S NOT MAKING YOU SLEEP IN A FIELD.
IT MAKES NO DIFFERENCE TO ME WHERE I SLEEP.
~SIGH~
WHERE'S OUR ROOM?
IT'S THERE.
I GUESS IT'S JUST MY ROOM THEN.
I GUESS SO.
THANK YOU AGAIN. FOR PETRA.

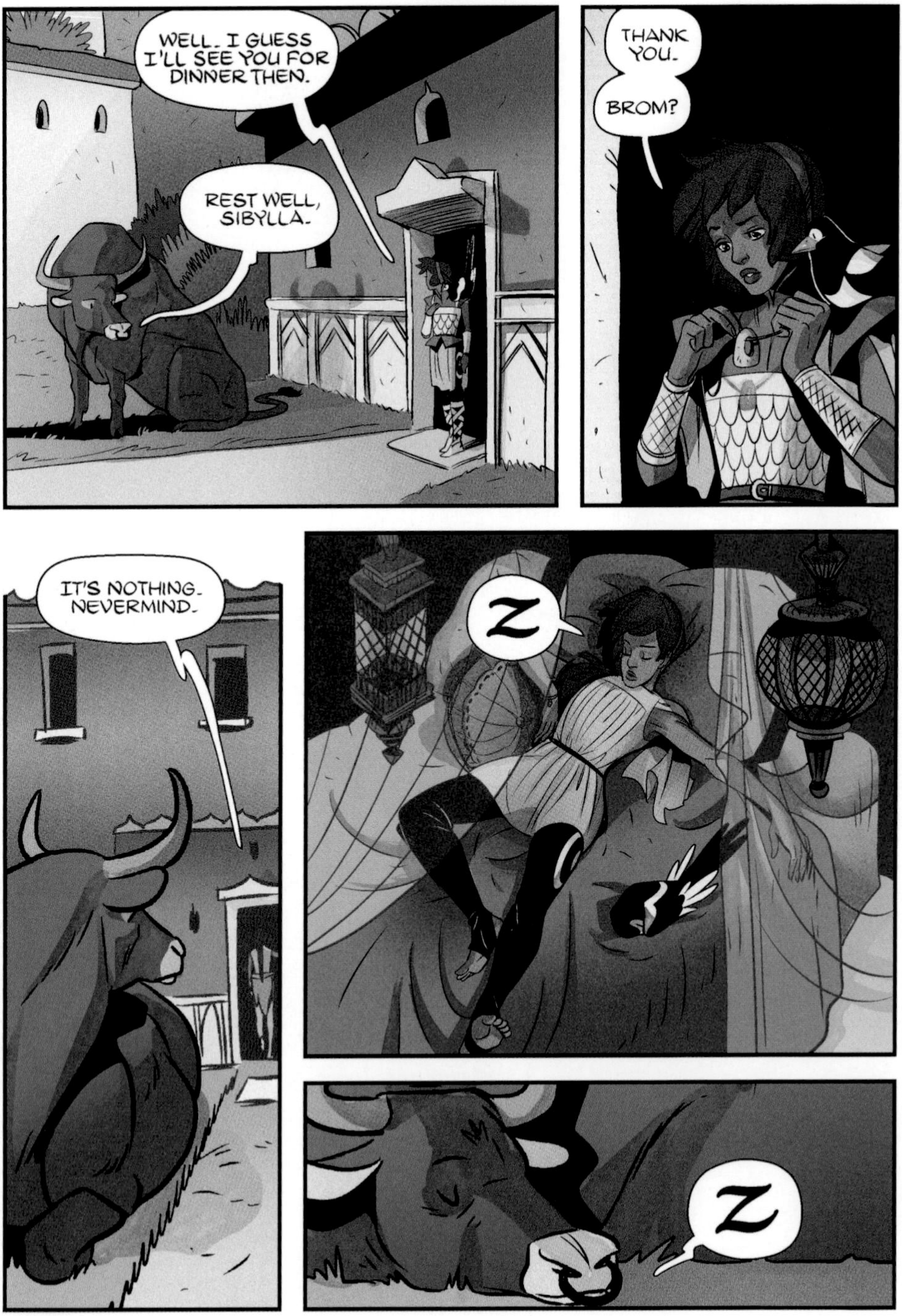
WELL. I GUESS I'LL SEE YOU FOR DINNER THEN.
REST WELL, SIBYLLA.
THANK YOU.
BROM?
IT'S NOTHING. NEVERMIND.
Z
Z

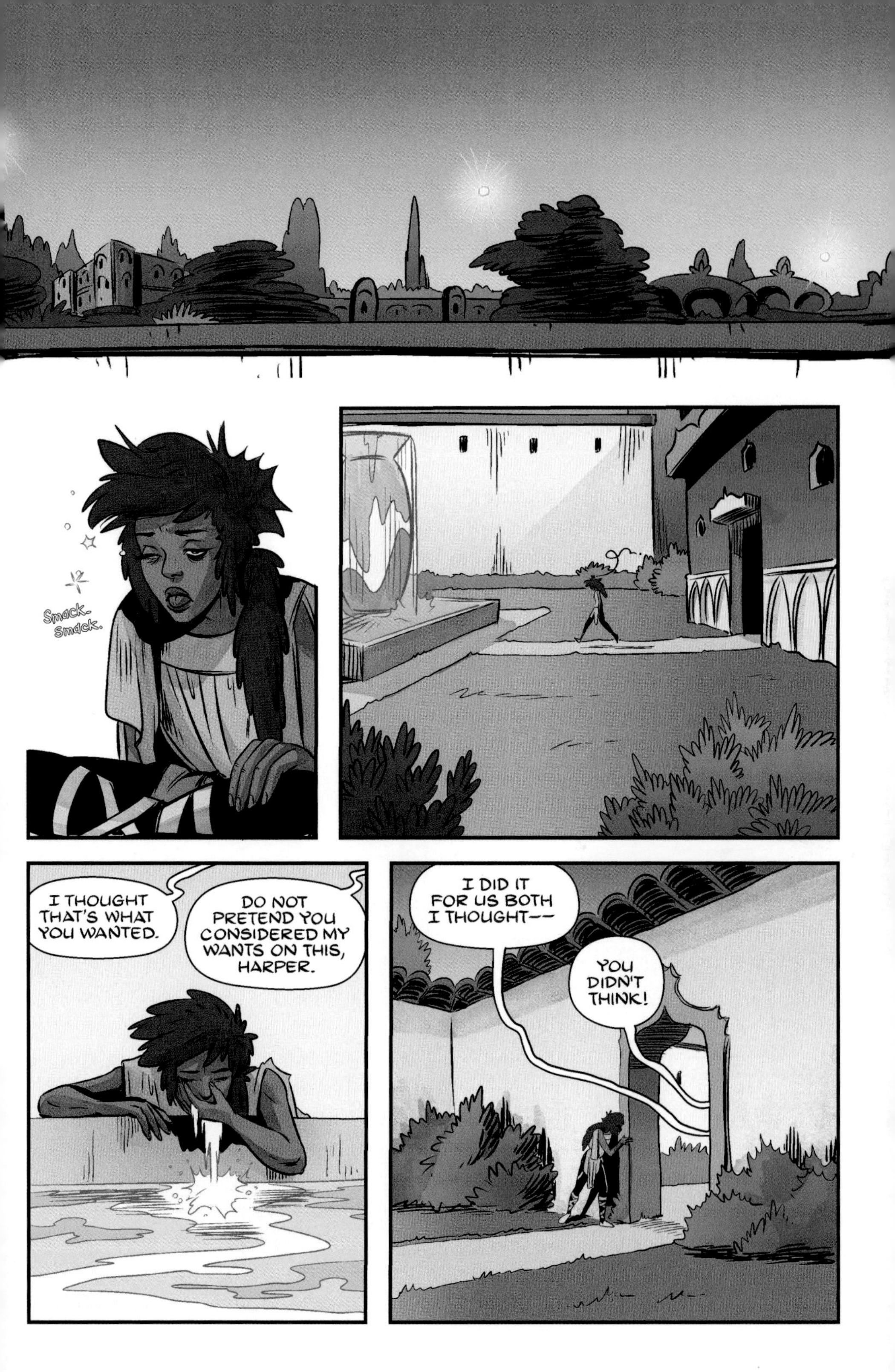
Smack. Smack.
I THOUGHT THAT'S WHAT YOU WANTED.
DO NOT PRETEND YOU CONSIDERED MY WANTS ON THIS, HARPER.
I DID IT FOR US BOTH I THOUGHT--
YOU DIDN'T THINK!

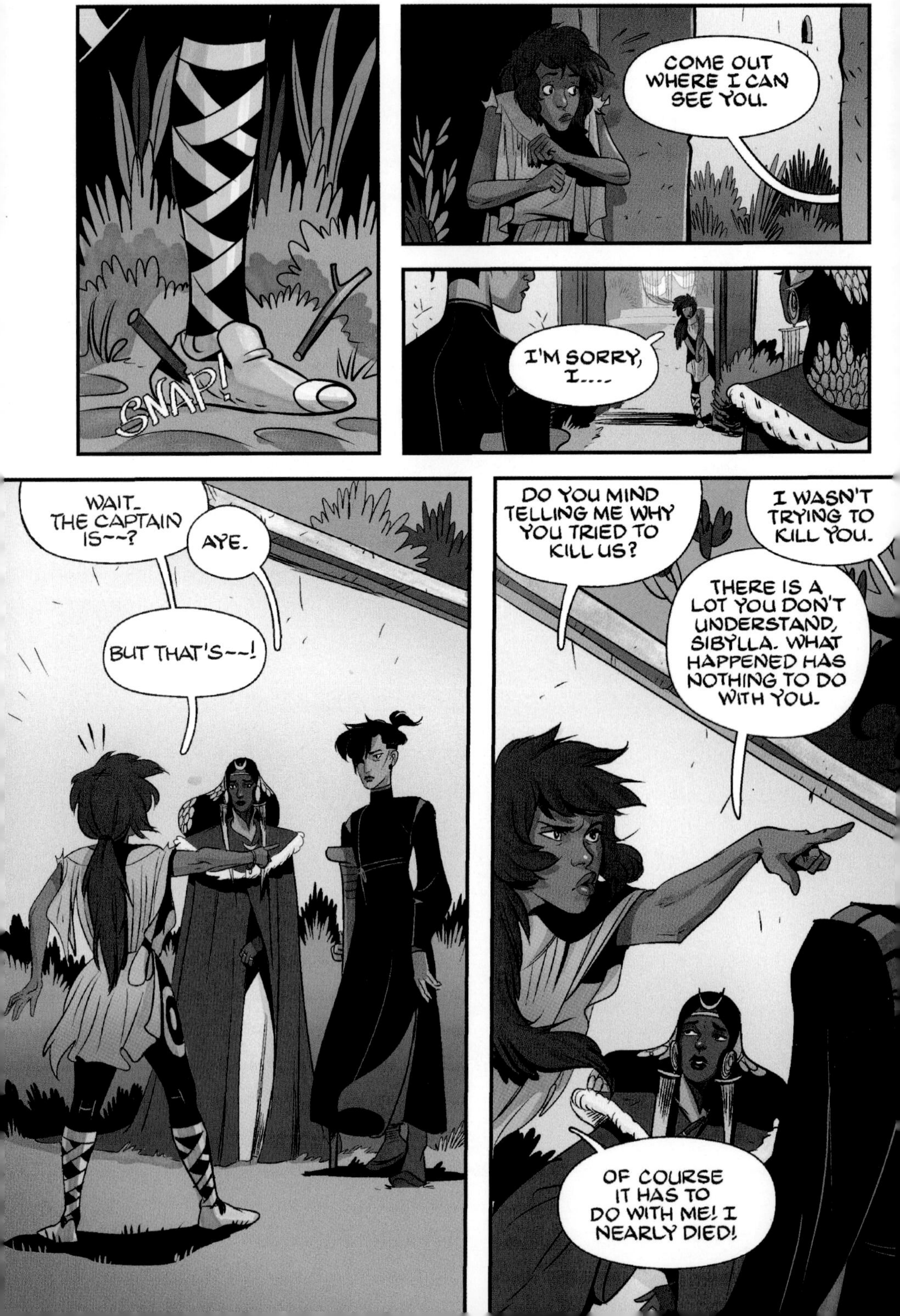
SNAP!
COME OUT WHERE I CAN SEE YOU.
I'M SORRY, I....
WAIT. THE CAPTAIN IS--?
AYE.
BUT THAT'S--!
DO YOU MIND TELLING ME WHY YOU TRIED TO KILL US?
I WASN'T TRYING TO KILL YOU.
THERE IS A LOT YOU DON'T UNDERSTAND, SIBYLLA. WHAT HAPPENED HAS NOTHING TO DO WITH YOU.
OF COURSE IT HAS TO DO WITH ME! I NEARLY DIED!

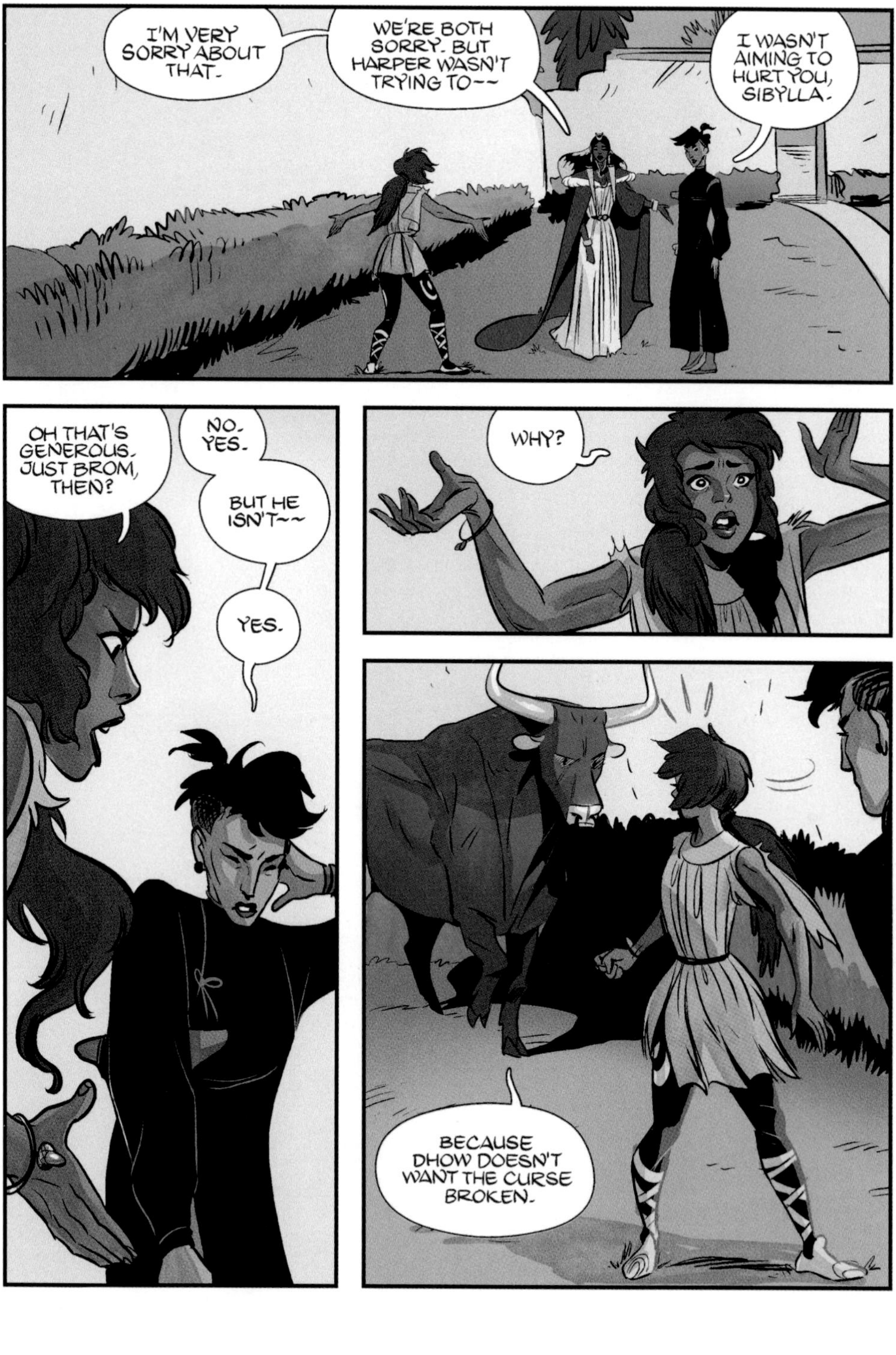
I'M VERY SORRY ABOUT THAT.
WE'RE BOTH SORRY. BUT HARPER WASN'T TRYING TO~~
I WASN'T AIMING TO HURT YOU, SIBYLLA.
OH THAT'S GENEROUS. JUST BROM, THEN?
NO. YES.
BUT HE ISN'T~~
YES.
WHY?
BECAUSE DHOW DOESN'T WANT THE CURSE BROKEN.

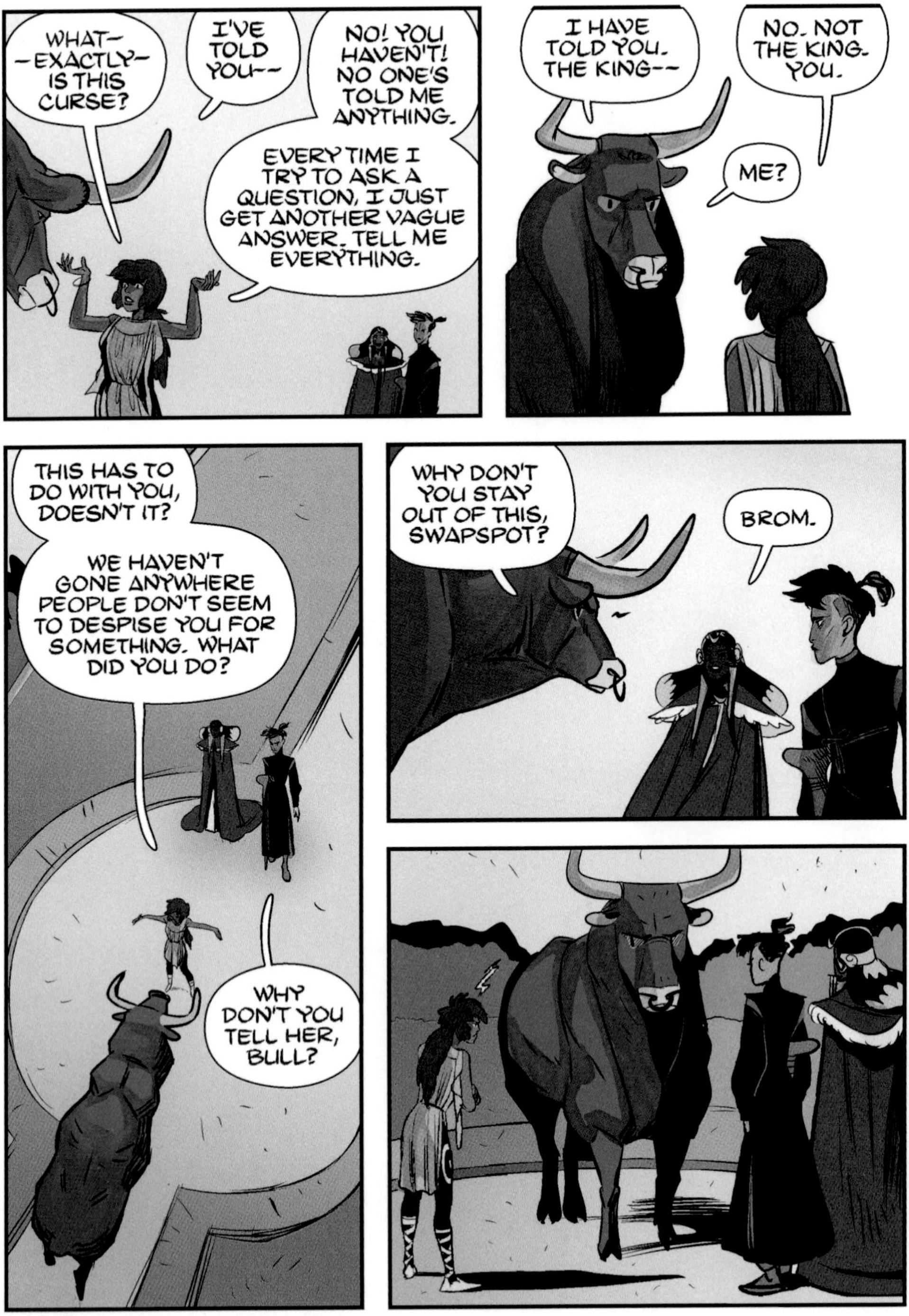
WHAT— —EXACTLY— IS THIS CURSE?
I'VE TOLD YOU--
NO! YOU HAVEN'T! NO ONE'S TOLD ME ANYTHING.
EVERY TIME I TRY TO ASK A QUESTION, I JUST GET ANOTHER VAGUE ANSWER. TELL ME EVERYTHING.
I HAVE TOLD YOU. THE KING--
NO. NOT THE KING. YOU.
ME?
THIS HAS TO DO WITH YOU, DOESN'T IT?
WE HAVEN'T GONE ANYWHERE PEOPLE DON'T SEEM TO DESPISE YOU FOR SOMETHING. WHAT DID YOU DO?
WHY DON'T YOU TELL HER, BULL?
WHY DON'T YOU STAY OUT OF THIS, SWAPSPOT?
BROM.

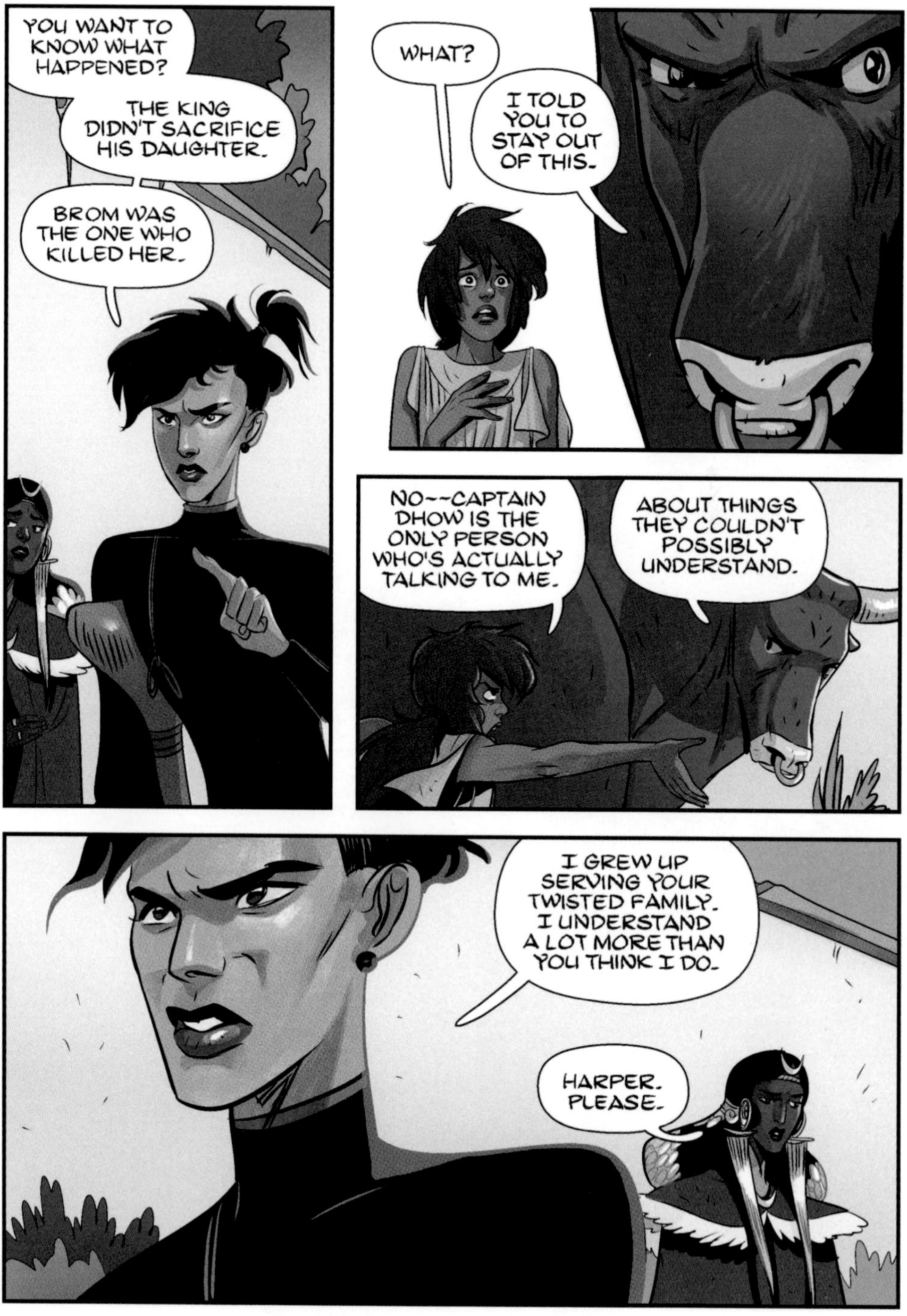
YOU WANT TO KNOW WHAT HAPPENED?
THE KING DIDN'T SACRIFICE HIS DAUGHTER.
BROM WAS THE ONE WHO KILLED HER.
WHAT?
I TOLD YOU TO STAY OUT OF THIS.
NO--CAPTAIN DHOW IS THE ONLY PERSON WHO'S ACTUALLY TALKING TO ME.
ABOUT THINGS THEY COULDN'T POSSIBLY UNDERSTAND.
I GREW UP SERVING YOUR TWISTED FAMILY. I UNDERSTAND A LOT MORE THAN YOU THINK I DO.
HARPER. PLEASE.

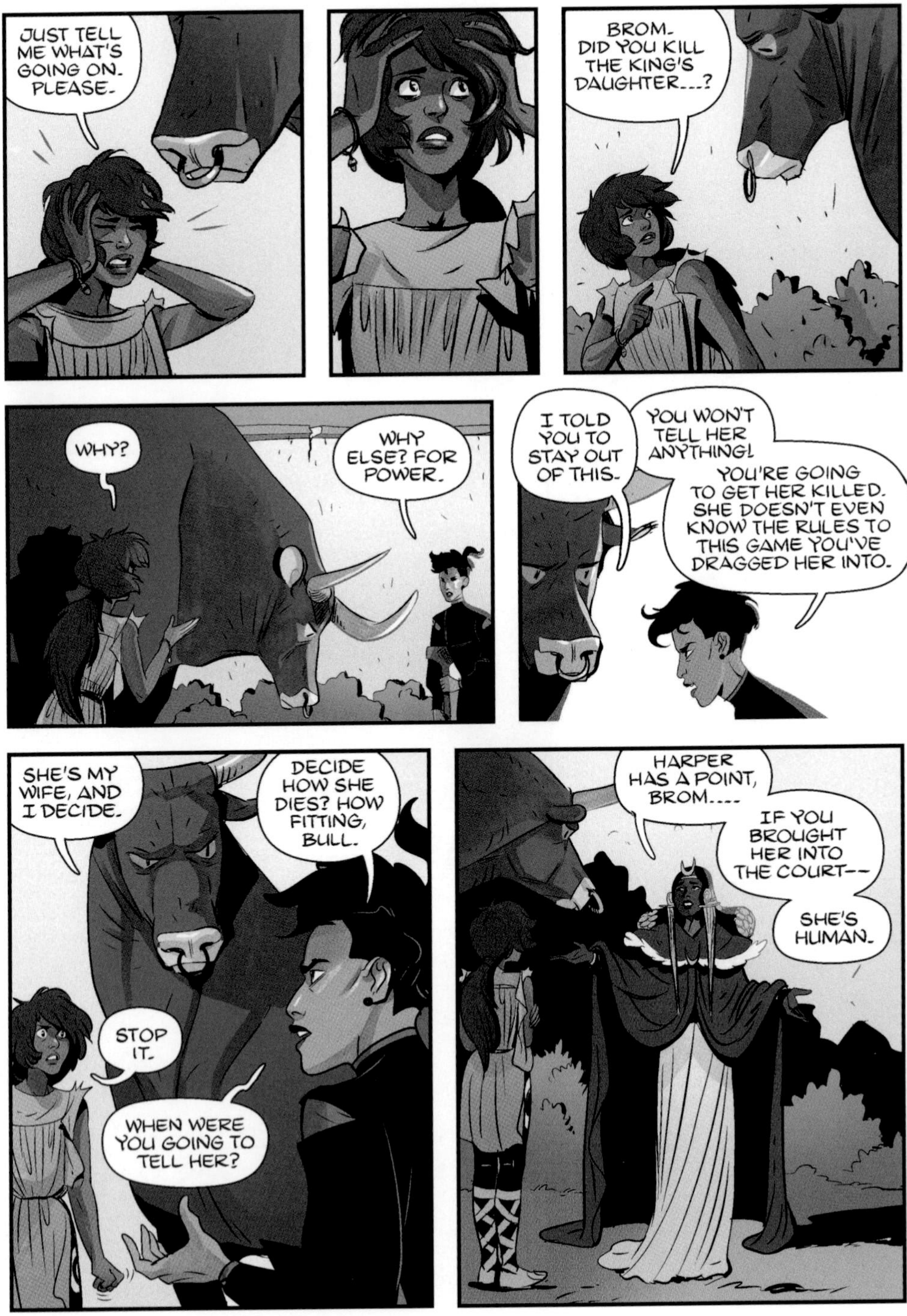
JUST TELL ME WHAT'S GOING ON. PLEASE.
BROM. DID YOU KILL THE KING'S DAUGHTER...?
WHY?
WHY ELSE? FOR POWER.
I TOLD YOU TO STAY OUT OF THIS.
YOU WON'T TELL HER ANYTHING!
YOU'RE GOING TO GET HER KILLED. SHE DOESN'T EVEN KNOW THE RULES TO THIS GAME YOU'VE DRAGGED HER INTO.
SHE'S MY WIFE, AND I DECIDE.
DECIDE HOW SHE DIES? HOW FITTING, BULL.
STOP IT.
WHEN WERE YOU GOING TO TELL HER?
HARPER HAS A POINT, BROM....
IF YOU BROUGHT HER INTO THE COURT--
SHE'S HUMAN.

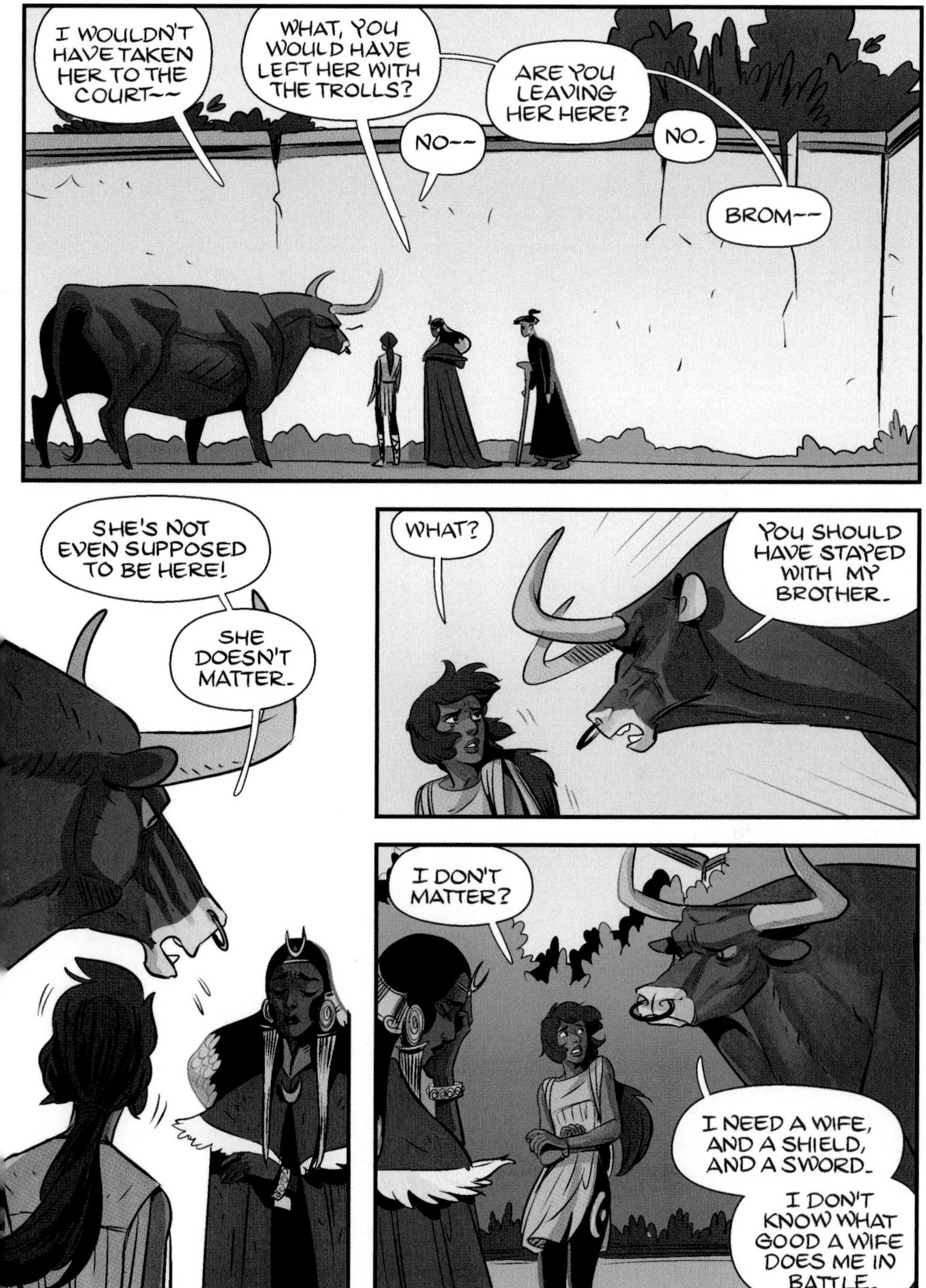
I WOULDN'T HAVE TAKEN HER TO THE COURT--
WHAT, YOU WOULD HAVE LEFT HER WITH THE TROLLS?
NO--
ARE YOU LEAVING HER HERE?
NO.
BROM--
SHE'S NOT EVEN SUPPOSED TO BE HERE!
SHE DOESN'T MATTER.
WHAT?
YOU SHOULD HAVE STAYED WITH MY BROTHER.
I DON'T MATTER?
I NEED A WIFE, AND A SHIELD, AND A SWORD.
I DON'T KNOW WHAT GOOD A WIFE DOES ME IN BATTLE.

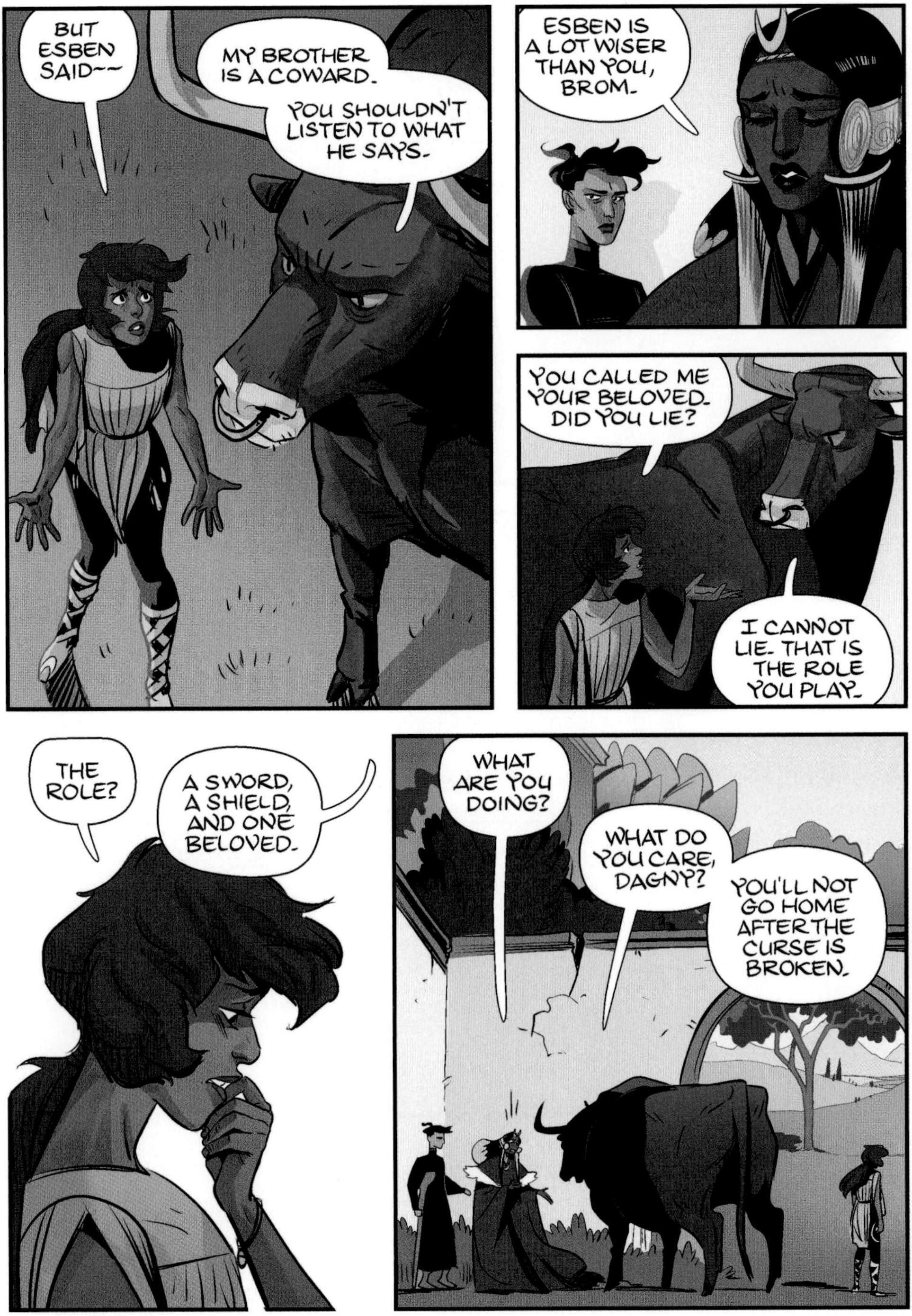
BUT ESBEN SAID--
MY BROTHER IS A COWARD.
YOU SHOULDN'T LISTEN TO WHAT HE SAYS.
ESBEN IS A LOT WISER THAN YOU, BROM.
YOU CALLED ME YOUR BELOVED. DID YOU LIE?
I CANNOT LIE. THAT IS THE ROLE YOU PLAY.
THE ROLE?
A SWORD, A SHIELD, AND ONE BELOVED.
WHAT ARE YOU DOING?
WHAT DO YOU CARE, DAGNY?
YOU'LL NOT GO HOME AFTER THE CURSE IS BROKEN.

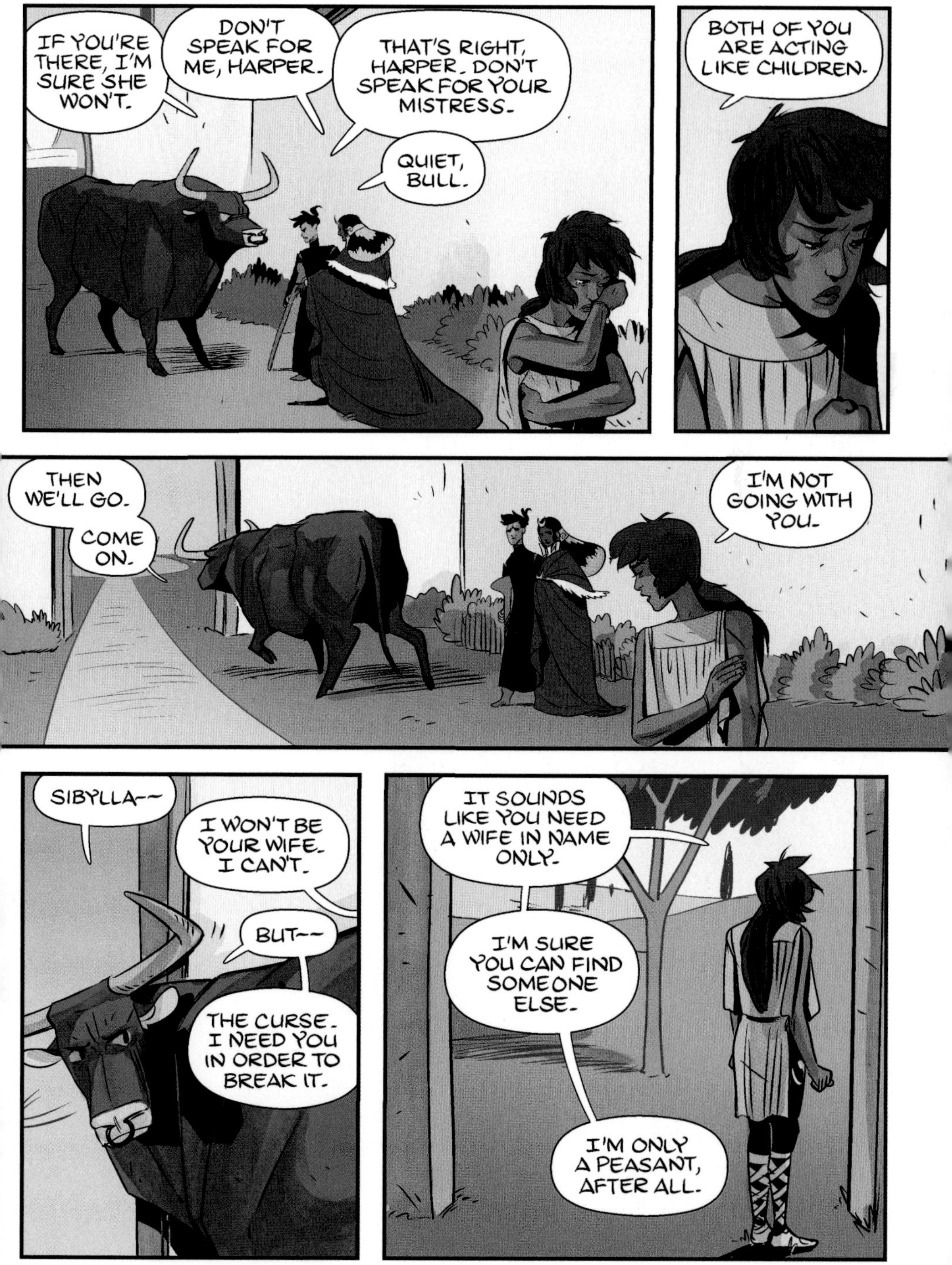
IF YOU'RE THERE, I'M SURE SHE WON'T.
DON'T SPEAK FOR ME, HARPER.
THAT'S RIGHT, HARPER. DON'T SPEAK FOR YOUR MISTRESS.
QUIET, BULL.
BOTH OF YOU ARE ACTING LIKE CHILDREN.
THEN WE'LL GO.
COME ON.
I'M NOT GOING WITH YOU.
SIBYLLA--
I WON'T BE YOUR WIFE. I CAN'T.
BUT--
THE CURSE. I NEED YOU IN ORDER TO BREAK IT.
IT SOUNDS LIKE YOU NEED A WIFE IN NAME ONLY.
I'M SURE YOU CAN FIND SOMEONE ELSE.
I'M ONLY A PEASANT, AFTER ALL.

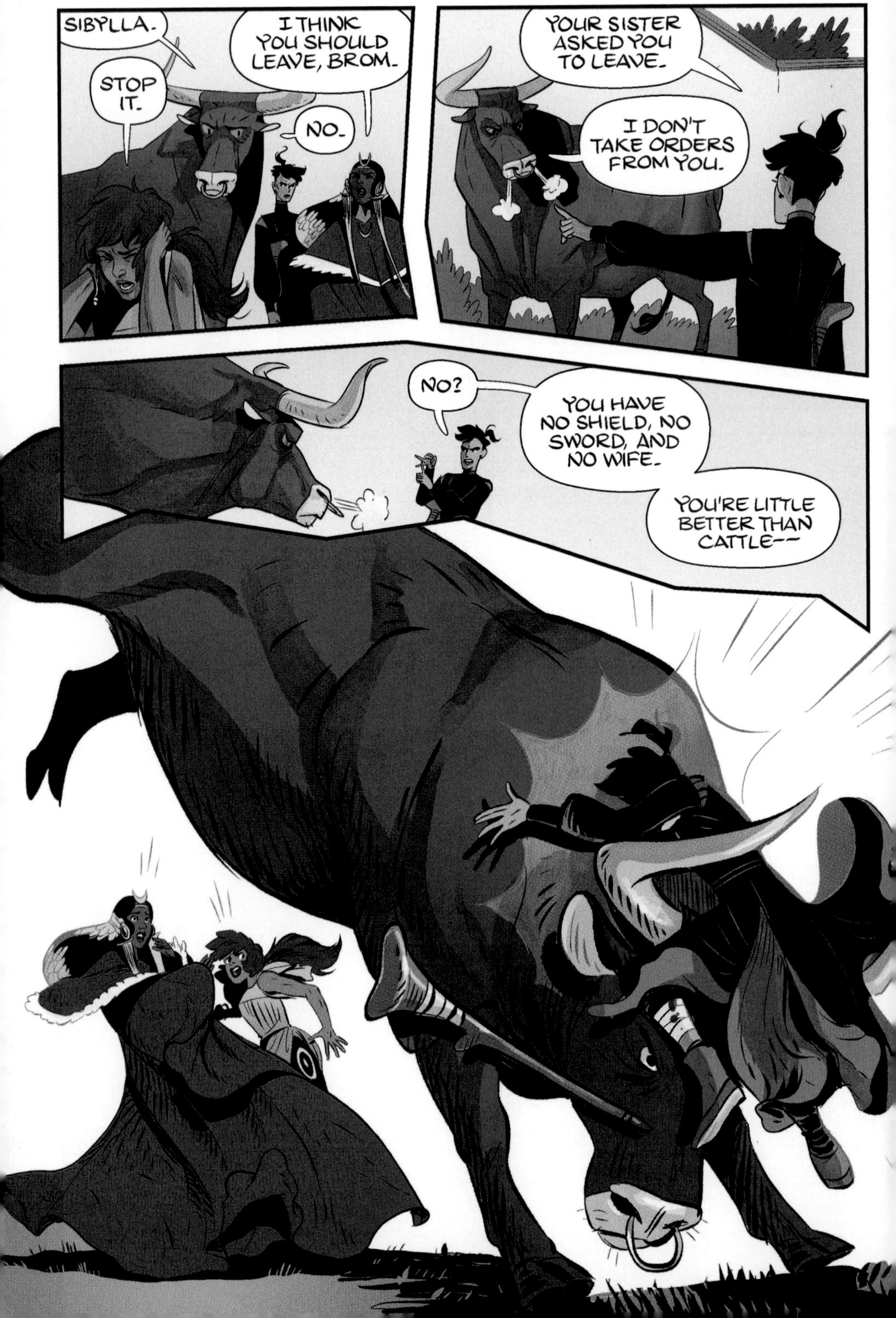
SIBYLLA.
STOP IT.
I THINK YOU SHOULD LEAVE, BROM.
NO.
YOUR SISTER ASKED YOU TO LEAVE.
I DON'T TAKE ORDERS FROM YOU.
NO?
YOU HAVE NO SHIELD, NO SWORD, AND NO WIFE.
YOU'RE LITTLE BETTER THAN CATTLE--

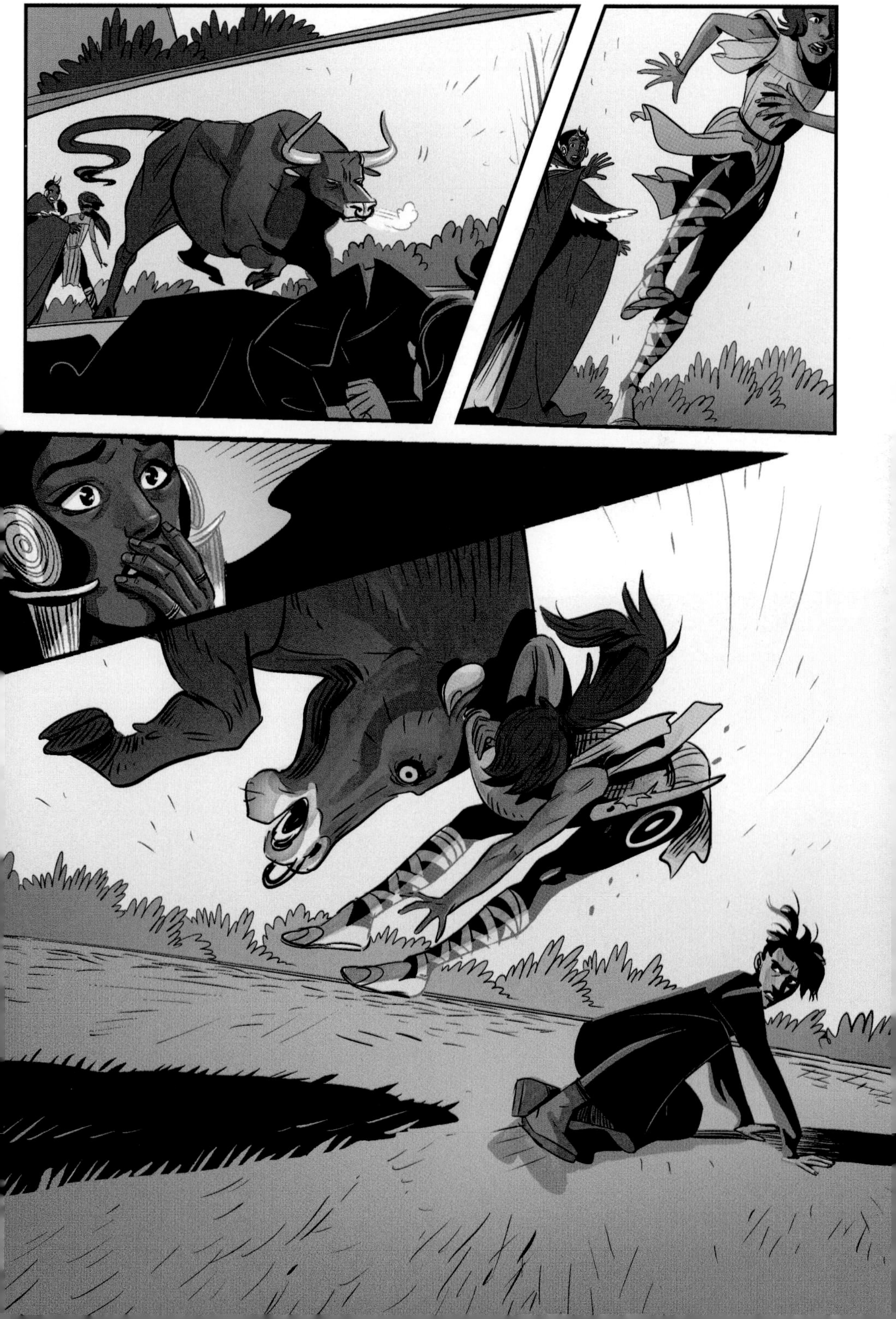

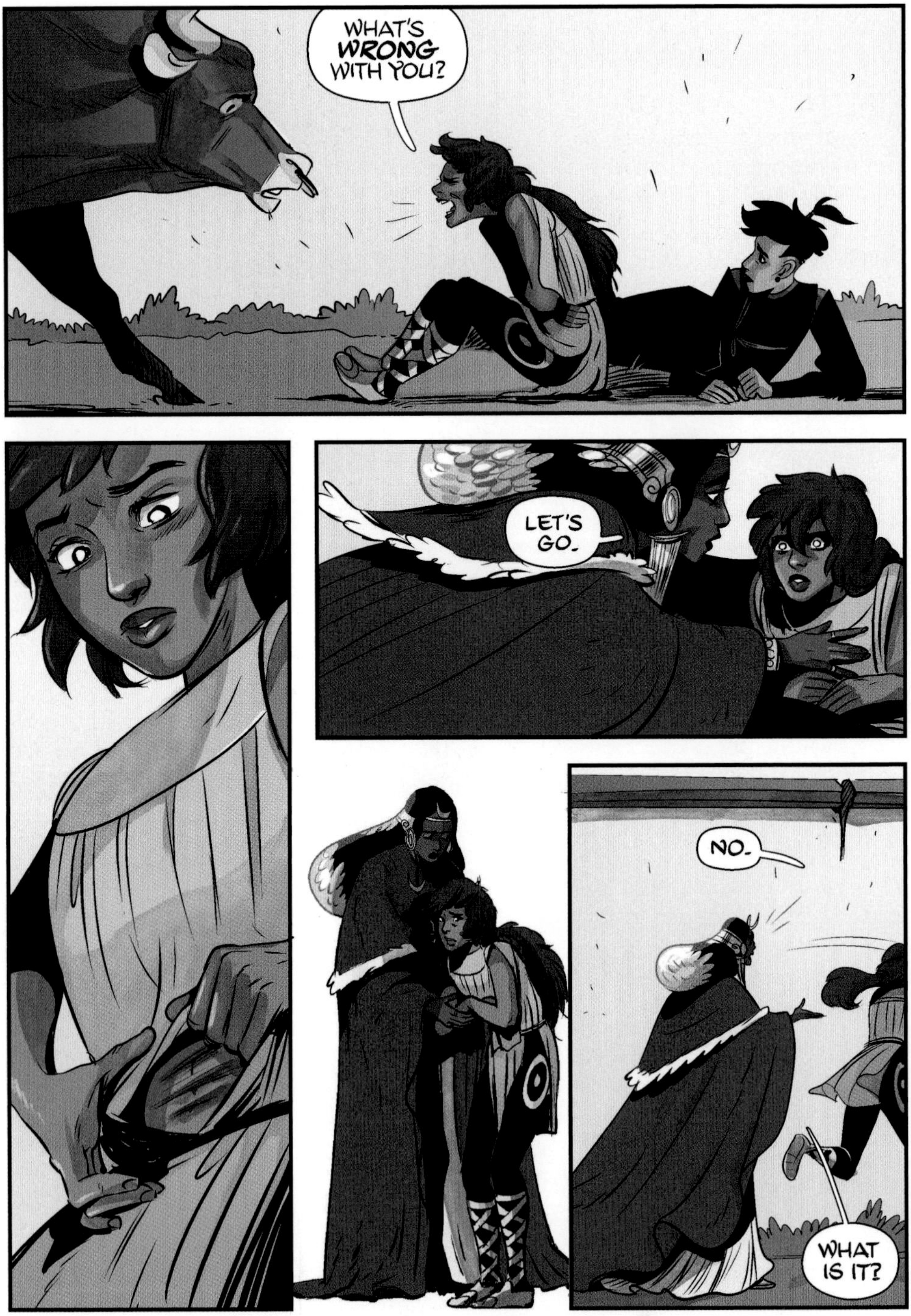
WHAT'S **WRONG** WITH YOU?
LET'S GO.
NO.
WHAT IS IT?

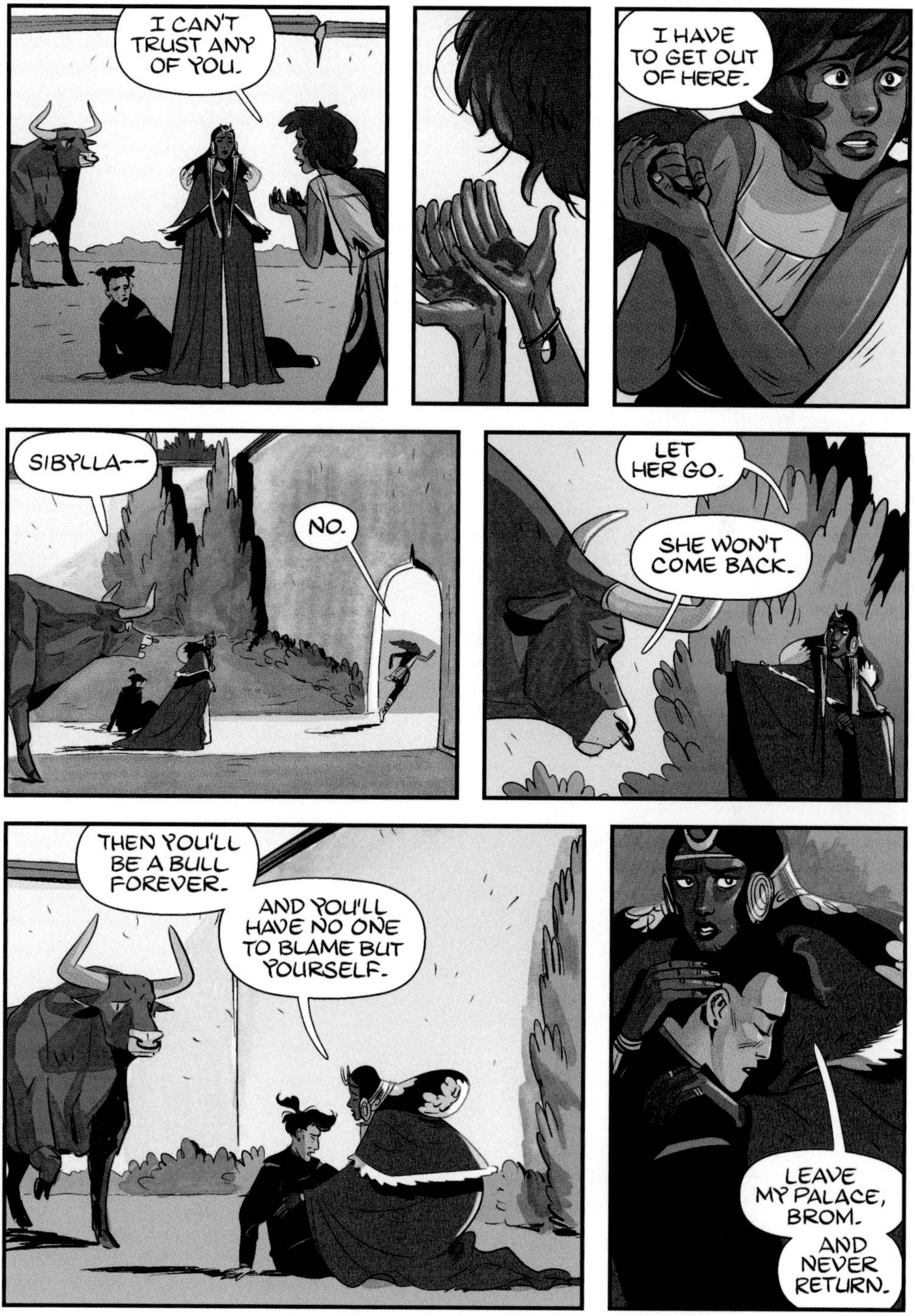
I CAN'T TRUST ANY OF YOU.
I HAVE TO GET OUT OF HERE.
SIBYLLA--
NO.
LET HER GO.
SHE WON'T COME BACK.
THEN YOU'LL BE A BULL FOREVER.
AND YOU'LL HAVE NO ONE TO BLAME BUT YOURSELF.
LEAVE MY PALACE, BROM.
AND NEVER RETURN.

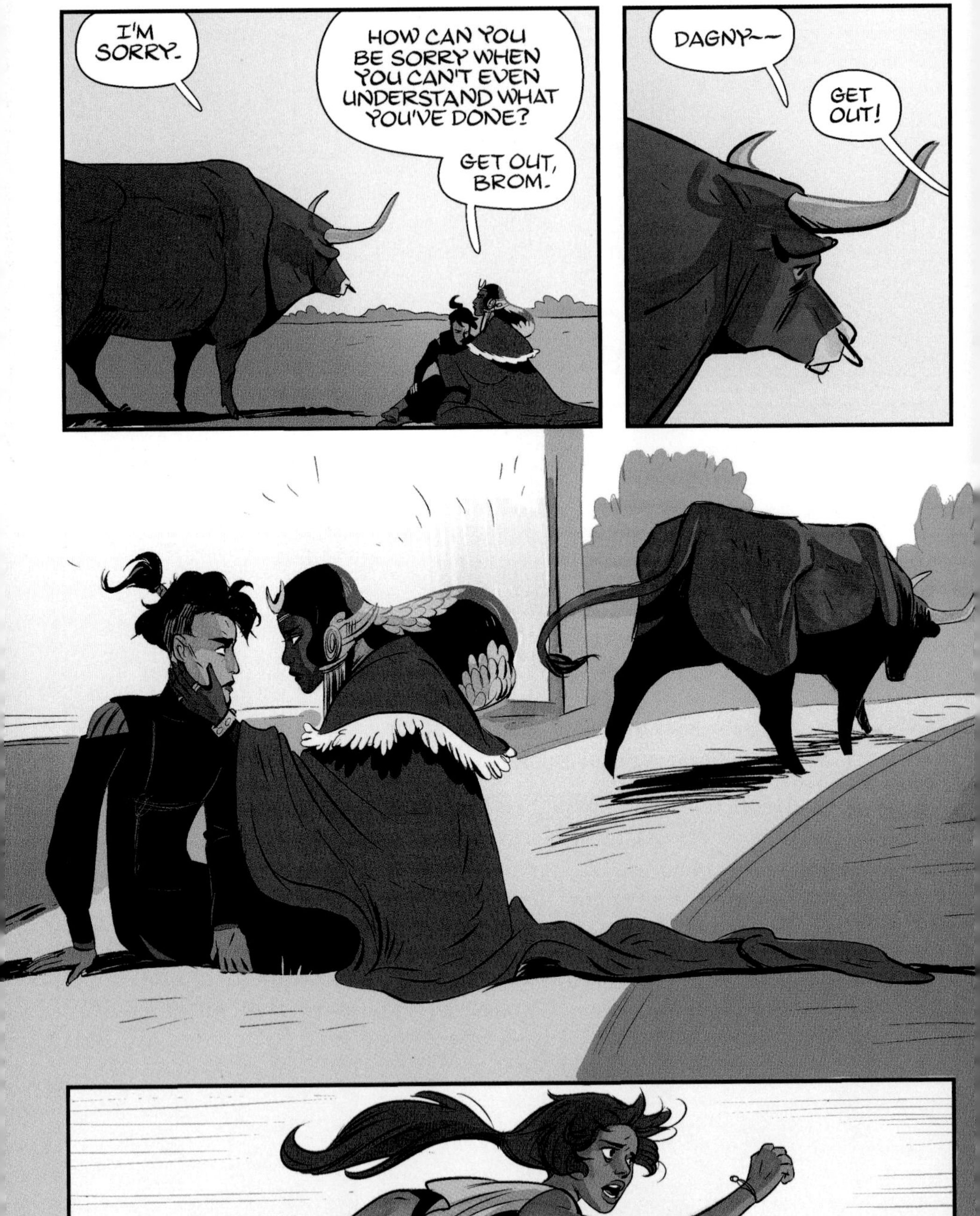
I'M SORRY.
HOW CAN YOU BE SORRY WHEN YOU CAN'T EVEN UNDERSTAND WHAT YOU'VE DONE?
GET OUT, BROM.
DAGNY--
GET OUT!

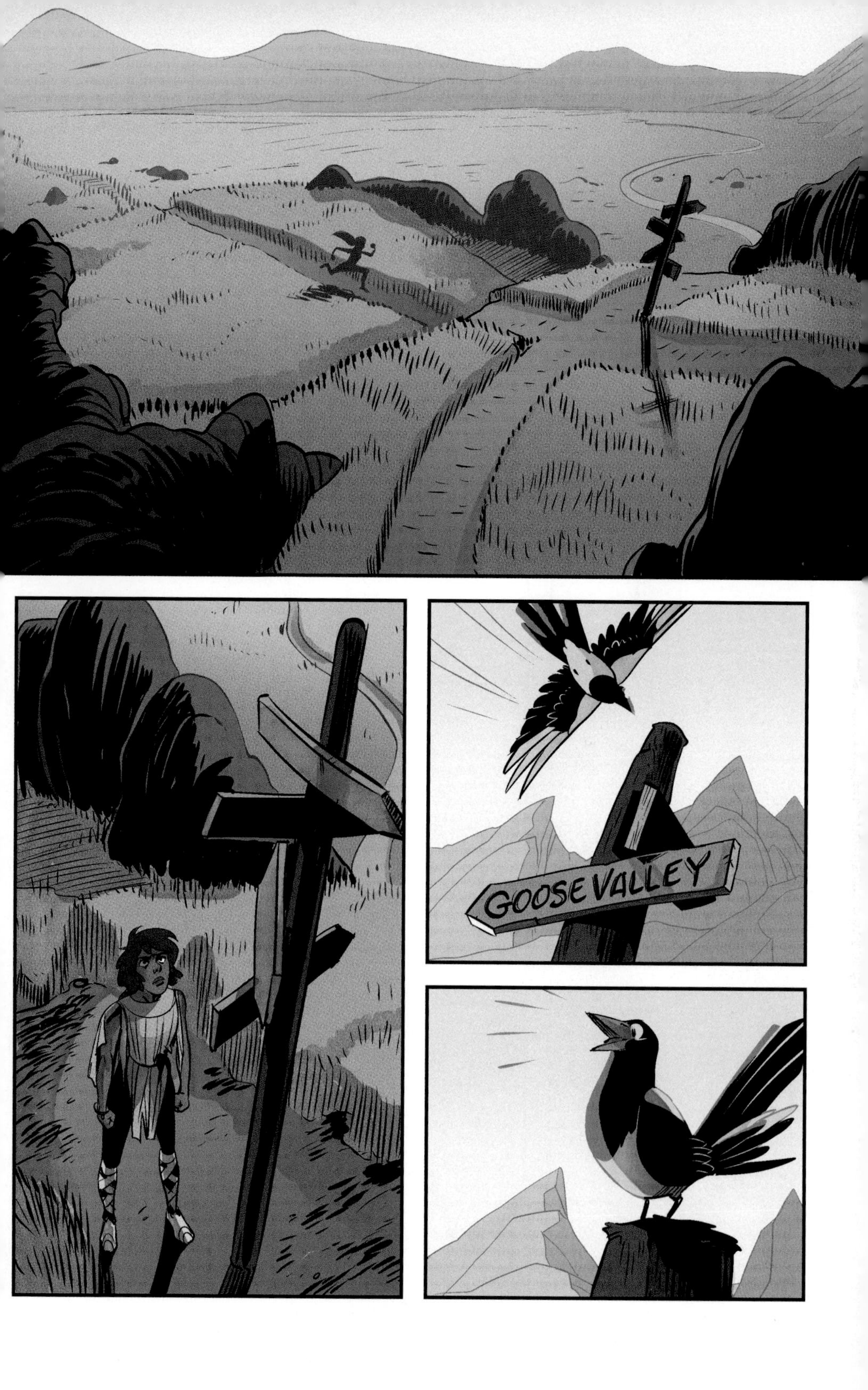
GOOSE VALLEY

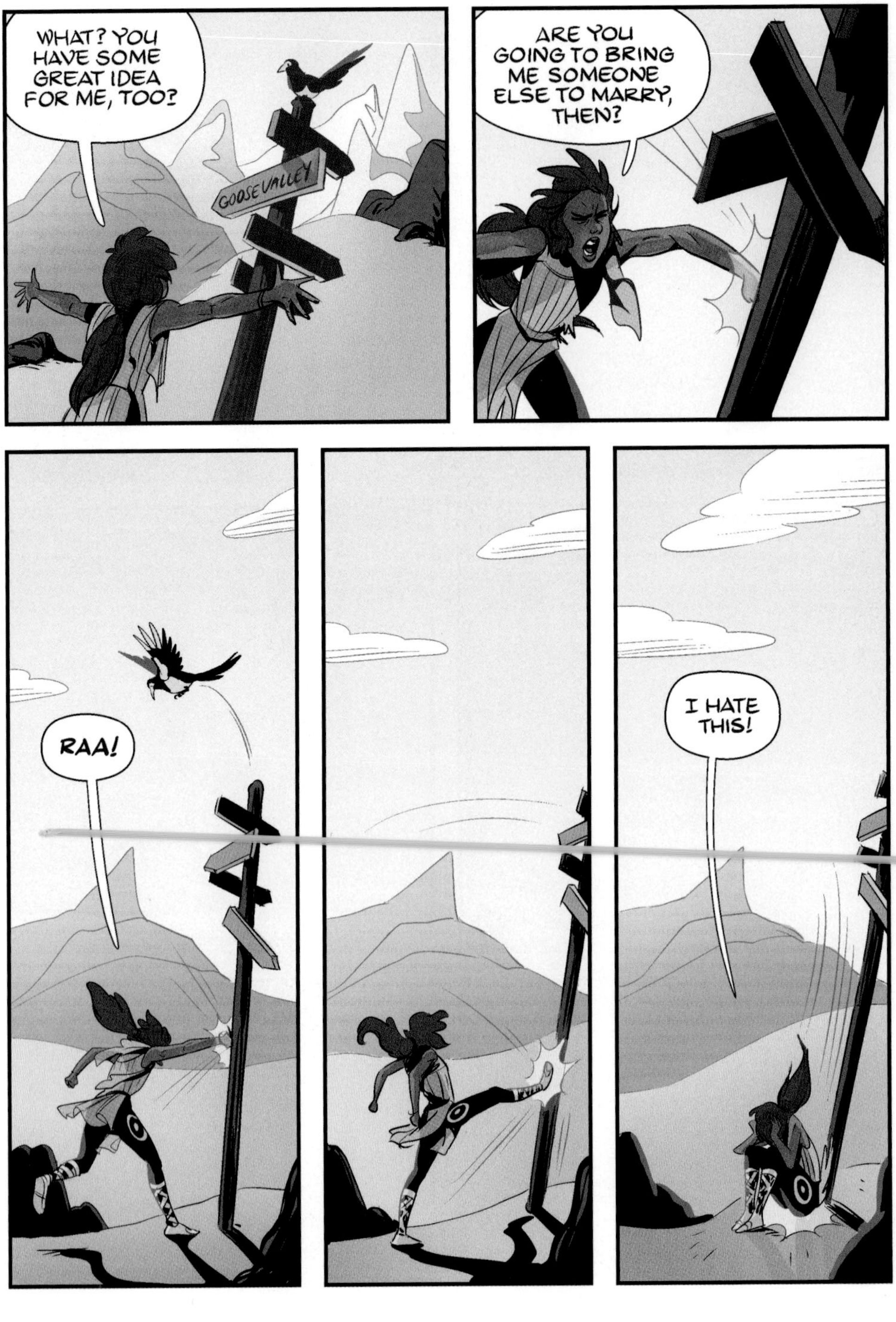
WHAT? YOU HAVE SOME GREAT IDEA FOR ME, TOO?
GOOSEVALLEY
ARE YOU GOING TO BRING ME SOMEONE ELSE TO MARRY, THEN?
RAA!
I HATE THIS!

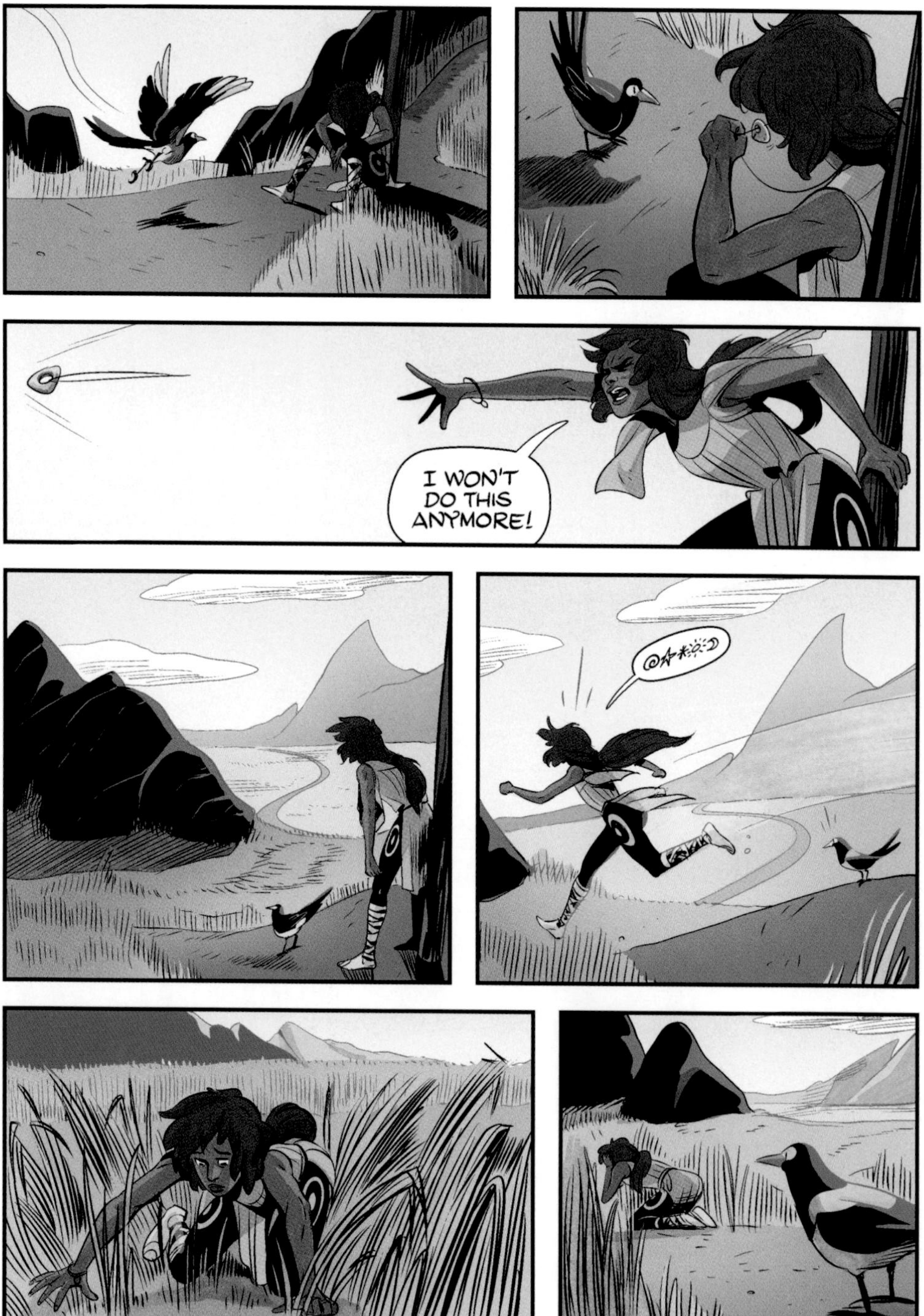
I WON'T DO THIS ANYMORE!

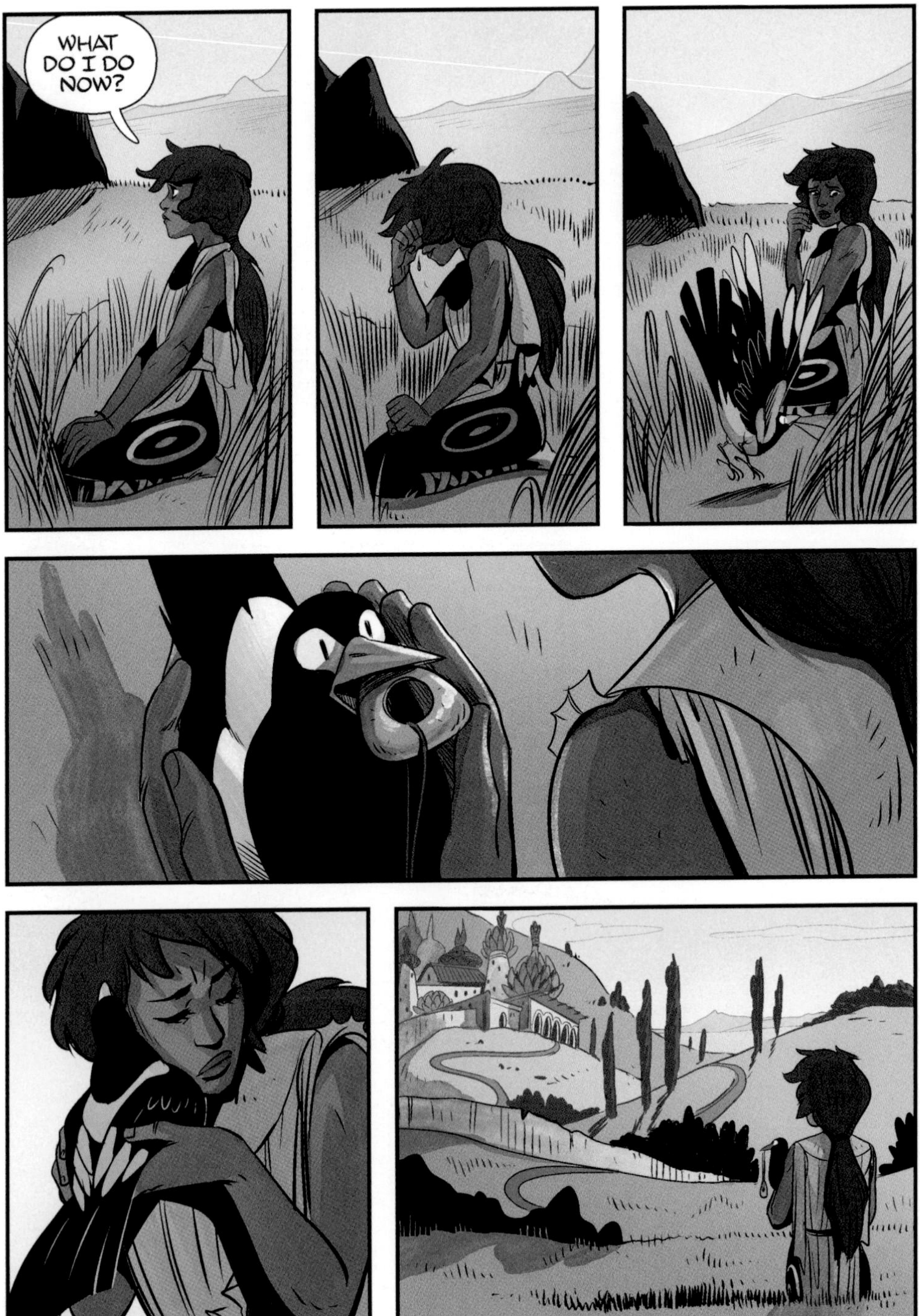
WHAT DO I DO NOW?

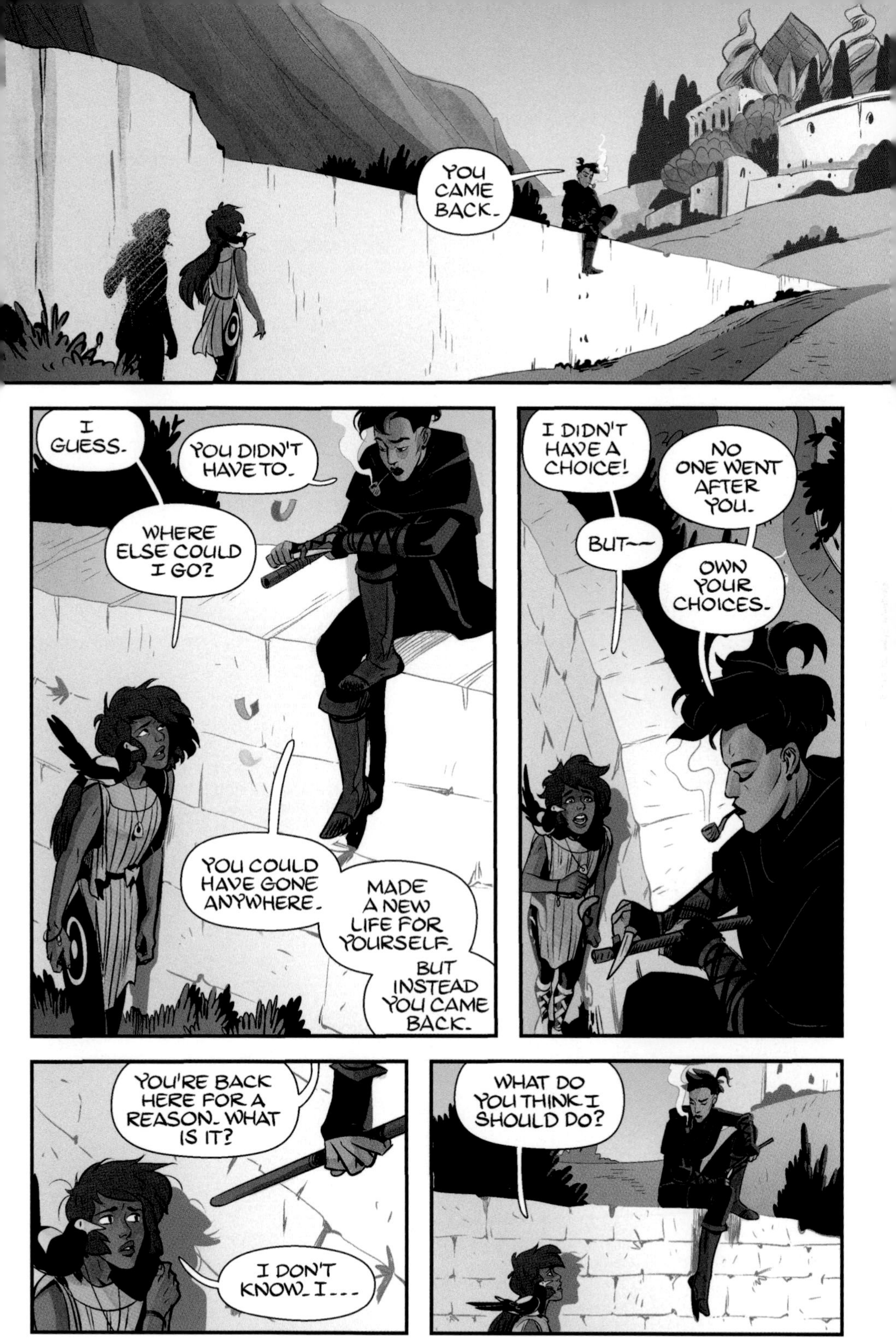
YOU CAME BACK.
I GUESS.
YOU DIDN'T HAVE TO.
WHERE ELSE COULD I GO?
YOU COULD HAVE GONE ANYWHERE.
MADE A NEW LIFE FOR YOURSELF.
BUT INSTEAD YOU CAME BACK.
I DIDN'T HAVE A CHOICE!
NO ONE WENT AFTER YOU.
BUT--
OWN YOUR CHOICES.
YOU'RE BACK HERE FOR A REASON. WHAT IS IT?
I DON'T KNOW. I...
WHAT DO YOU THINK I SHOULD DO?

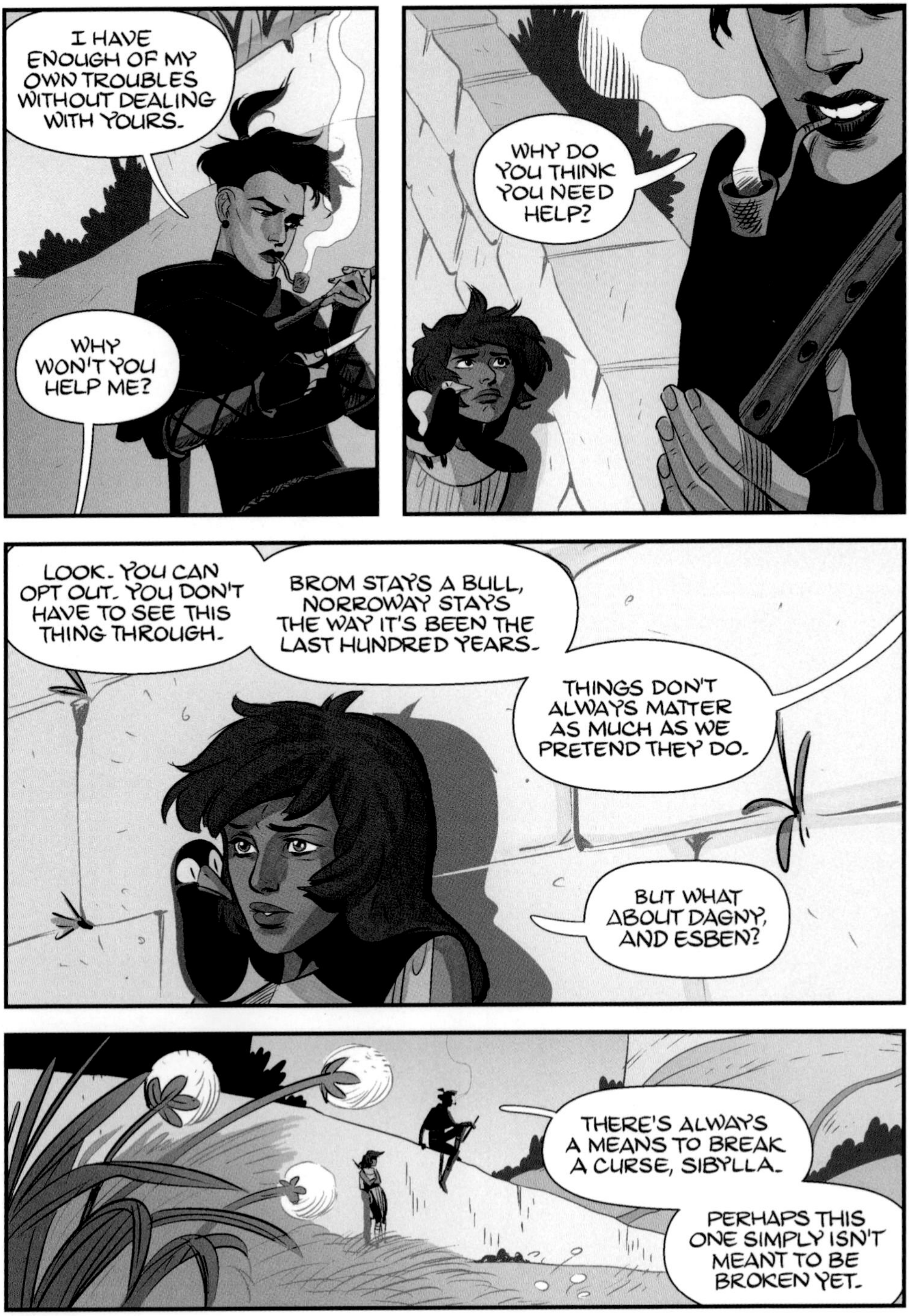
I HAVE ENOUGH OF MY OWN TROUBLES WITHOUT DEALING WITH YOURS.
WHY WON'T YOU HELP ME?
WHY DO YOU THINK YOU NEED HELP?
LOOK. YOU CAN OPT OUT. YOU DON'T HAVE TO SEE THIS THING THROUGH.
BROM STAYS A BULL, NORROWAY STAYS THE WAY IT'S BEEN THE LAST HUNDRED YEARS.
THINGS DON'T ALWAYS MATTER AS MUCH AS WE PRETEND THEY DO.
BUT WHAT ABOUT DAGNY, AND ESBEN?
THERE'S ALWAYS A MEANS TO BREAK A CURSE, SIBYLLA.
PERHAPS THIS ONE SIMPLY ISN'T MEANT TO BE BROKEN YET.

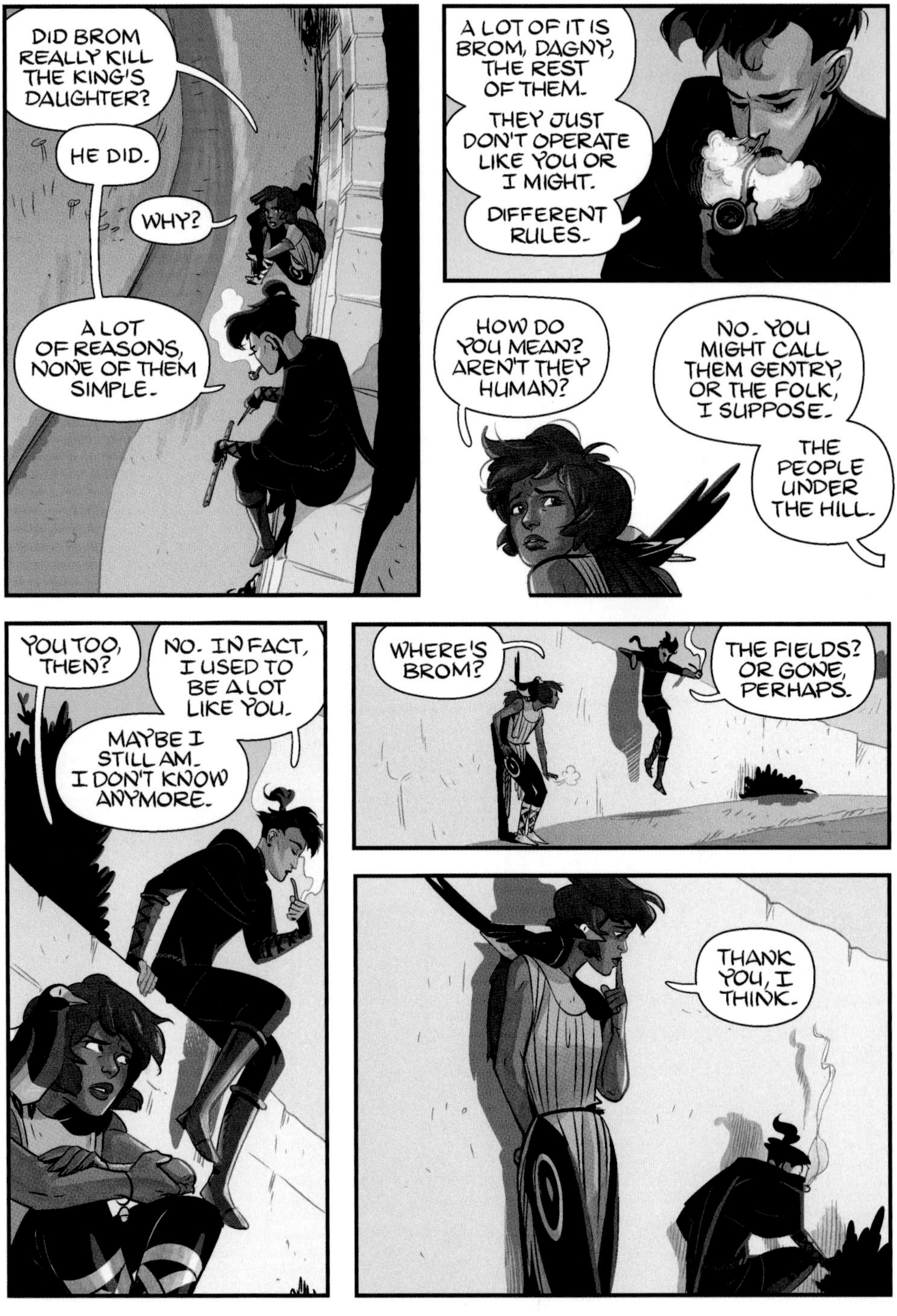
DID BROM REALLY KILL THE KING'S DAUGHTER?
HE DID.
WHY?
A LOT OF REASONS, NONE OF THEM SIMPLE.
A LOT OF IT IS BROM, DAGNY, THE REST OF THEM.
THEY JUST DON'T OPERATE LIKE YOU OR I MIGHT.
DIFFERENT RULES.
HOW DO YOU MEAN? AREN'T THEY HUMAN?
NO. YOU MIGHT CALL THEM GENTRY, OR THE FOLK, I SUPPOSE.
THE PEOPLE UNDER THE HILL.
YOU TOO, THEN?
NO. IN FACT, I USED TO BE A LOT LIKE YOU.
MAYBE I STILL AM. I DON'T KNOW ANYMORE.
WHERE'S BROM?
THE FIELDS? OR GONE, PERHAPS.
THANK YOU, I THINK.

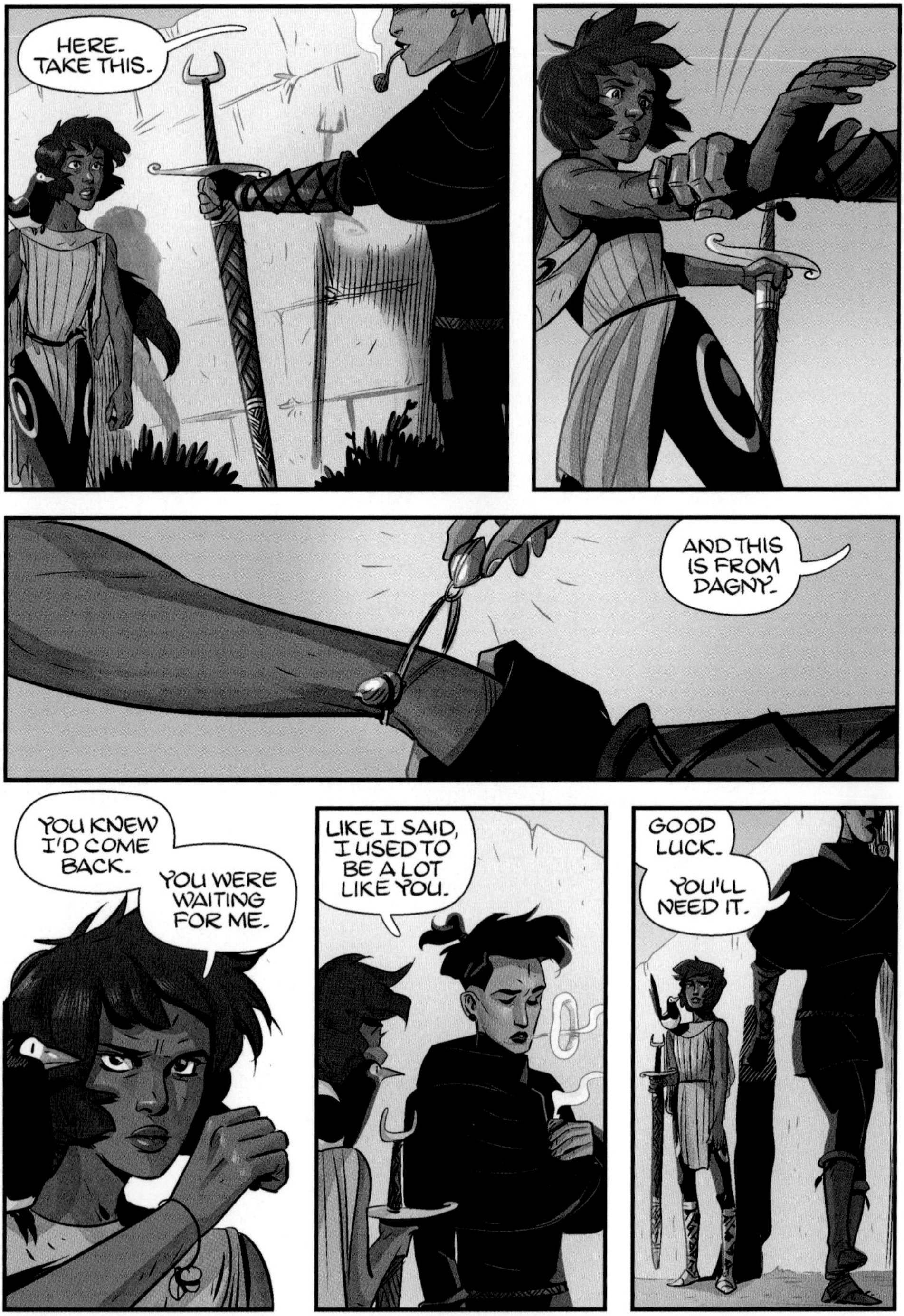
HERE. TAKE THIS.
AND THIS IS FROM DAGNY.
YOU KNEW I'D COME BACK.
YOU WERE WAITING FOR ME.
LIKE I SAID, I USED TO BE A LOT LIKE YOU.
GOOD LUCK.
YOU'LL NEED IT.

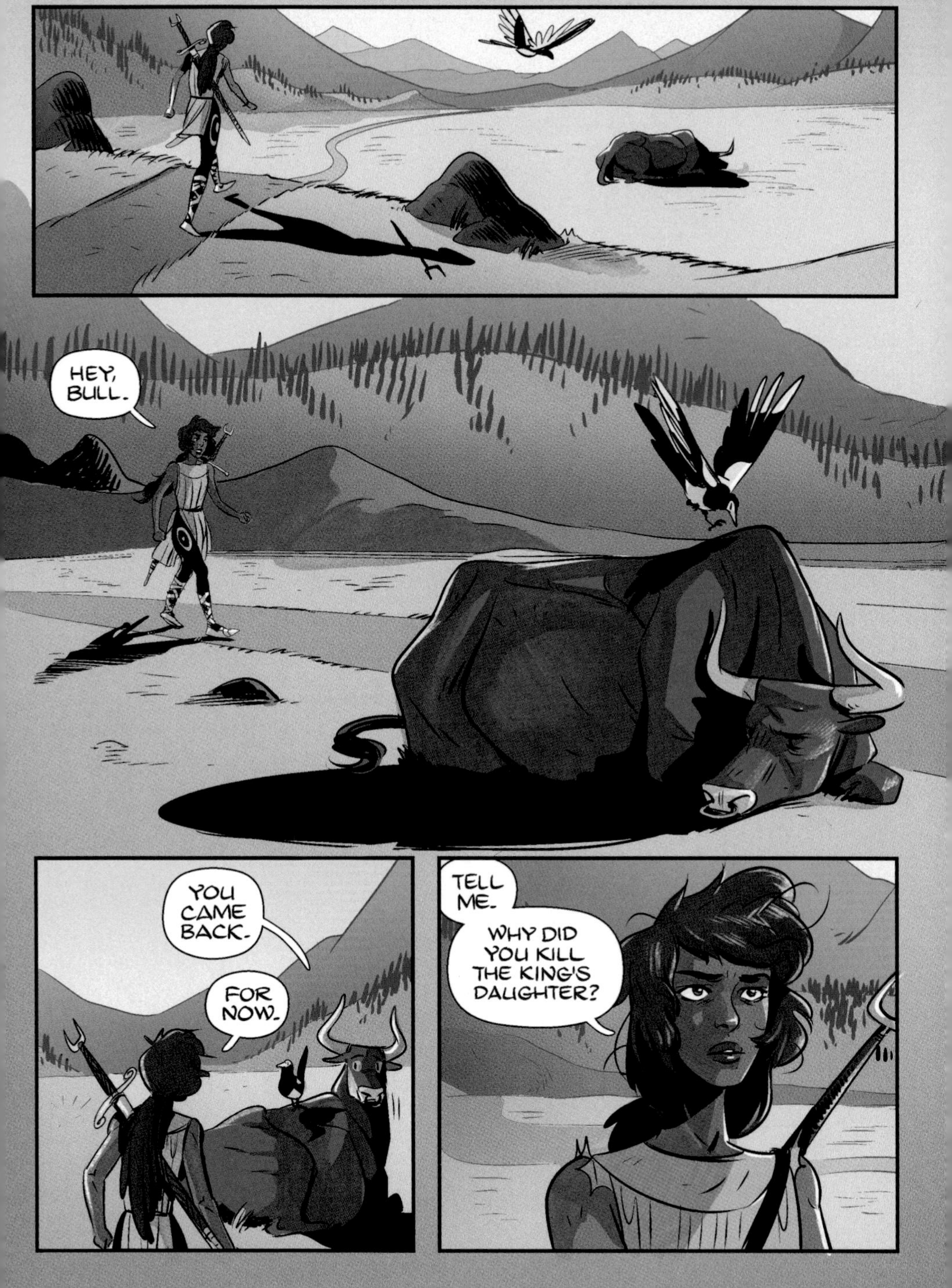
HEY, BULL.
YOU CAME BACK.
FOR NOW.
TELL ME.
WHY DID YOU KILL THE KING'S DAUGHTER?

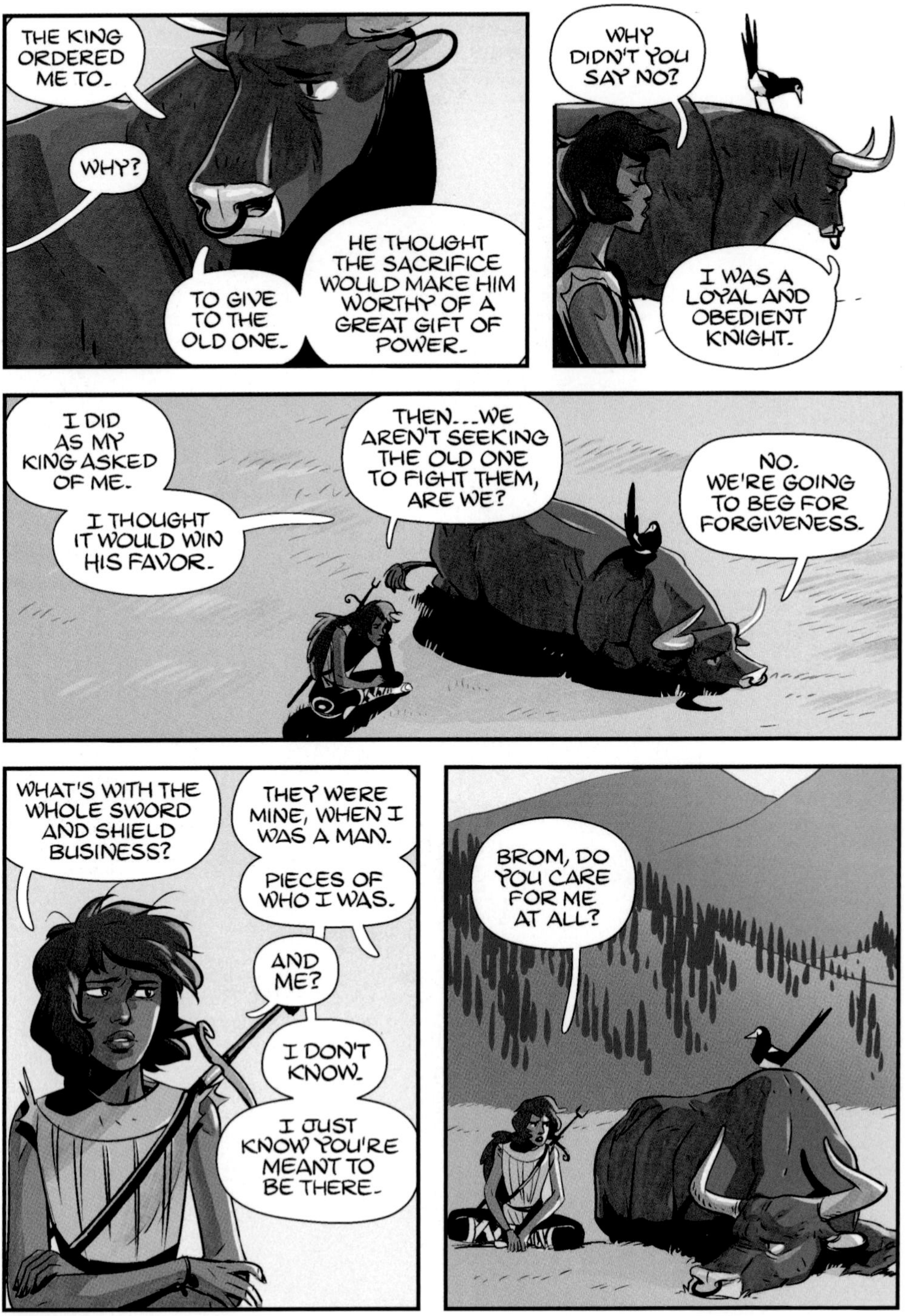
THE KING ORDERED ME TO.
WHY?
TO GIVE TO THE OLD ONE.
HE THOUGHT THE SACRIFICE WOULD MAKE HIM WORTHY OF A GREAT GIFT OF POWER.
WHY DIDN'T YOU SAY NO?
I WAS A LOYAL AND OBEDIENT KNIGHT.
I DID AS MY KING ASKED OF ME.
I THOUGHT IT WOULD WIN HIS FAVOR.
THEN...WE AREN'T SEEKING THE OLD ONE TO FIGHT THEM, ARE WE?
NO. WE'RE GOING TO BEG FOR FORGIVENESS.
WHAT'S WITH THE WHOLE SWORD AND SHIELD BUSINESS?
THEY WERE MINE, WHEN I WAS A MAN.
PIECES OF WHO I WAS.
AND ME?
I DON'T KNOW.
I JUST KNOW YOU'RE MEANT TO BE THERE.
BROM, DO YOU CARE FOR ME AT ALL?

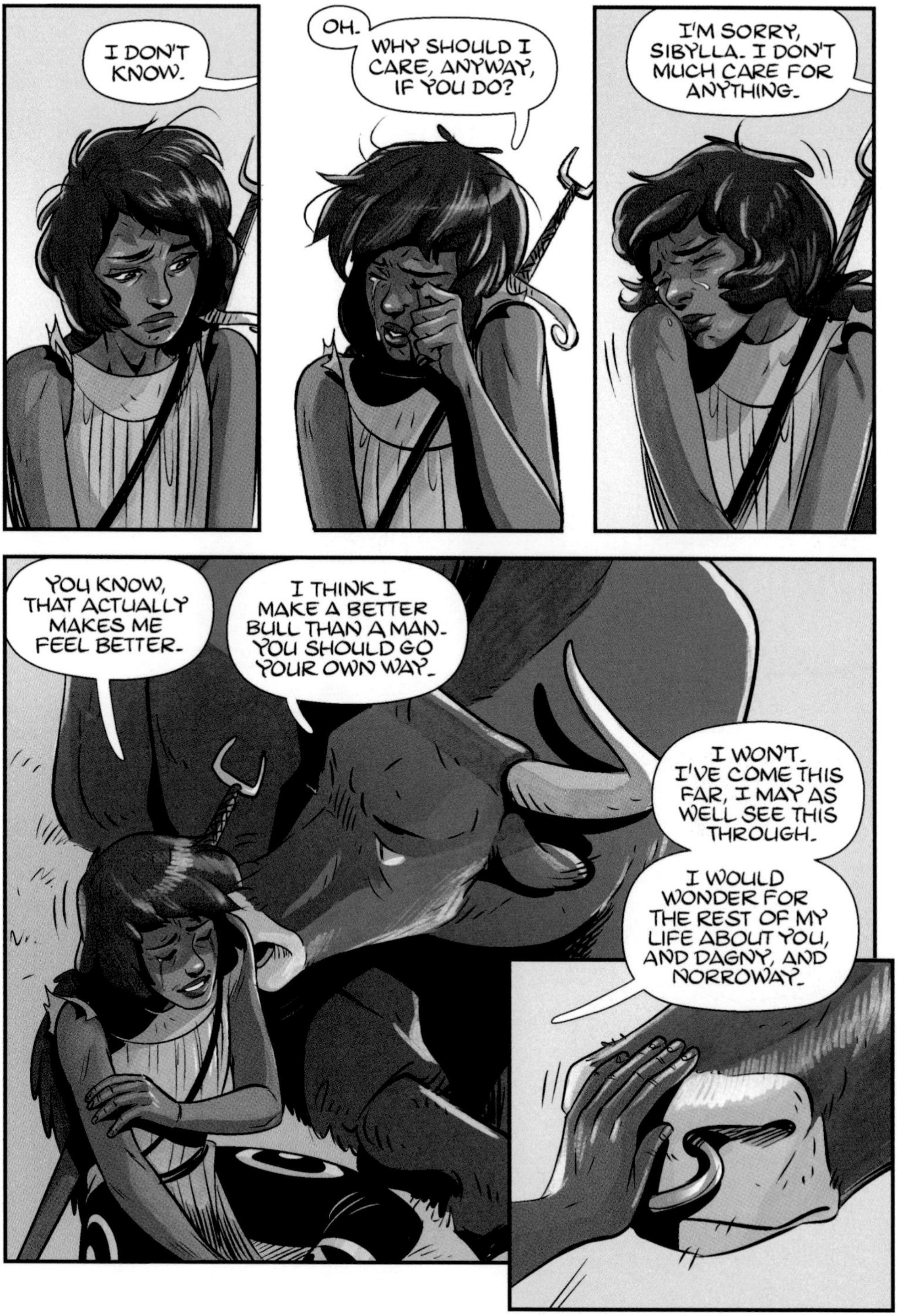
I DON'T KNOW.
OH.
WHY SHOULD I CARE, ANYWAY, IF YOU DO?
I'M SORRY, SIBYLLA. I DON'T MUCH CARE FOR ANYTHING.
YOU KNOW, THAT ACTUALLY MAKES ME FEEL BETTER.
I THINK I MAKE A BETTER BULL THAN A MAN. YOU SHOULD GO YOUR OWN WAY.
I WON'T. I'VE COME THIS FAR, I MAY AS WELL SEE THIS THROUGH.
I WOULD WONDER FOR THE REST OF MY LIFE ABOUT YOU, AND DAGNY, AND NORROWAY.

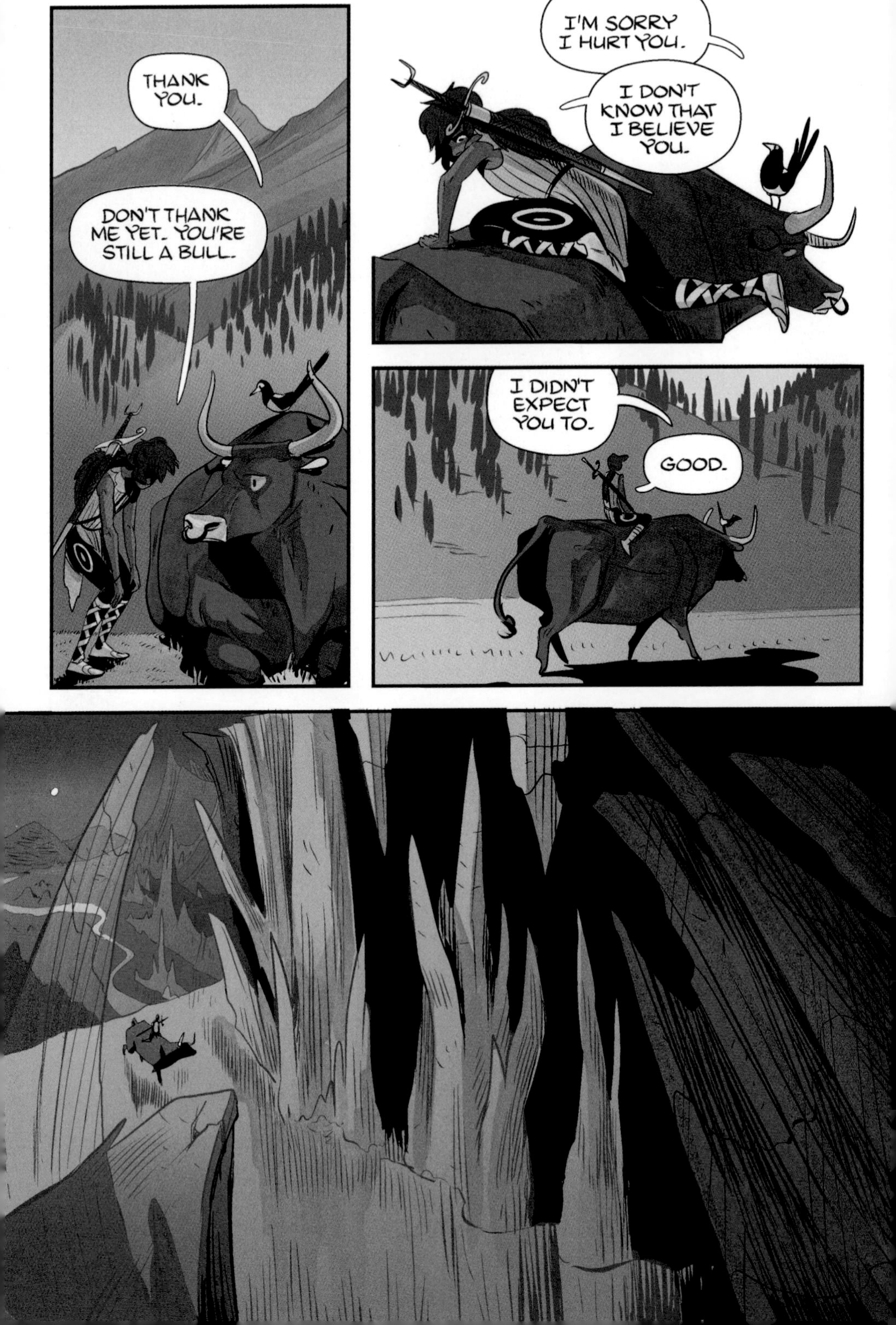
THANK YOU.
DON'T THANK ME YET. YOU'RE STILL A BULL.
I'M SORRY I HURT YOU.
I DON'T KNOW THAT I BELIEVE YOU.
I DIDN'T EXPECT YOU TO.
GOOD.

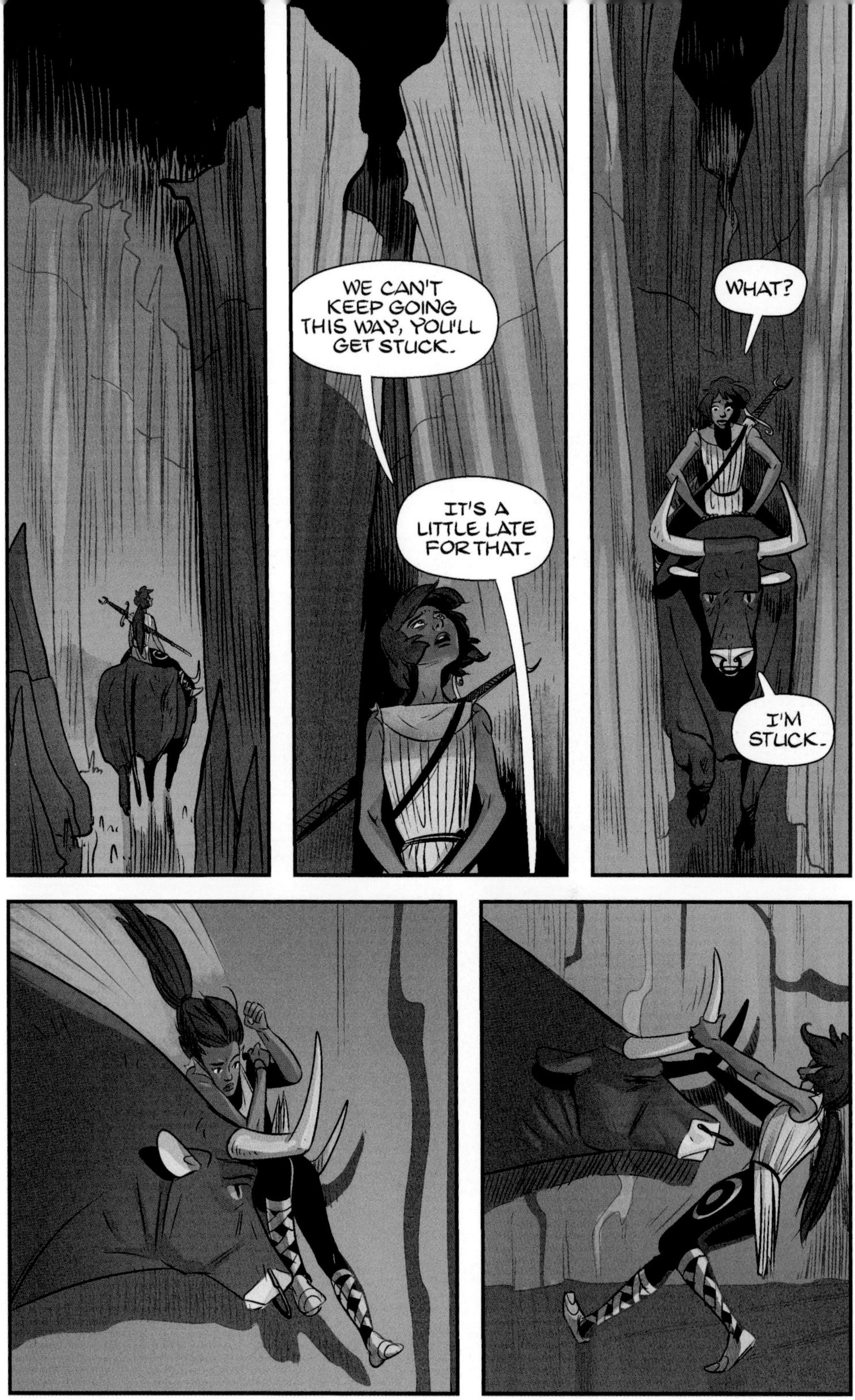
WE CAN'T KEEP GOING THIS WAY, YOU'LL GET STUCK.
IT'S A LITTLE LATE FOR THAT.
WHAT?
I'M STUCK.

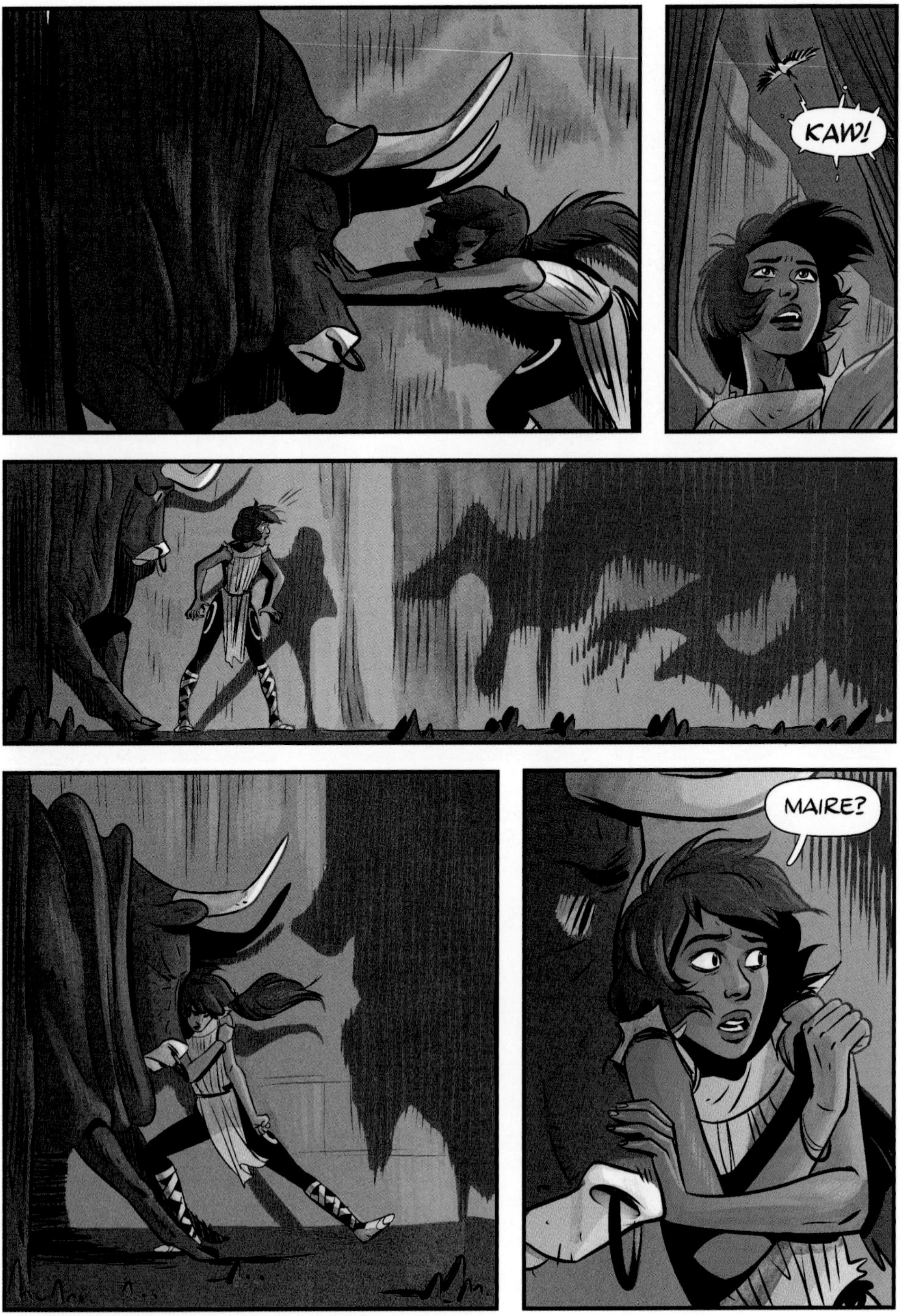
KAW!
MAIRE?

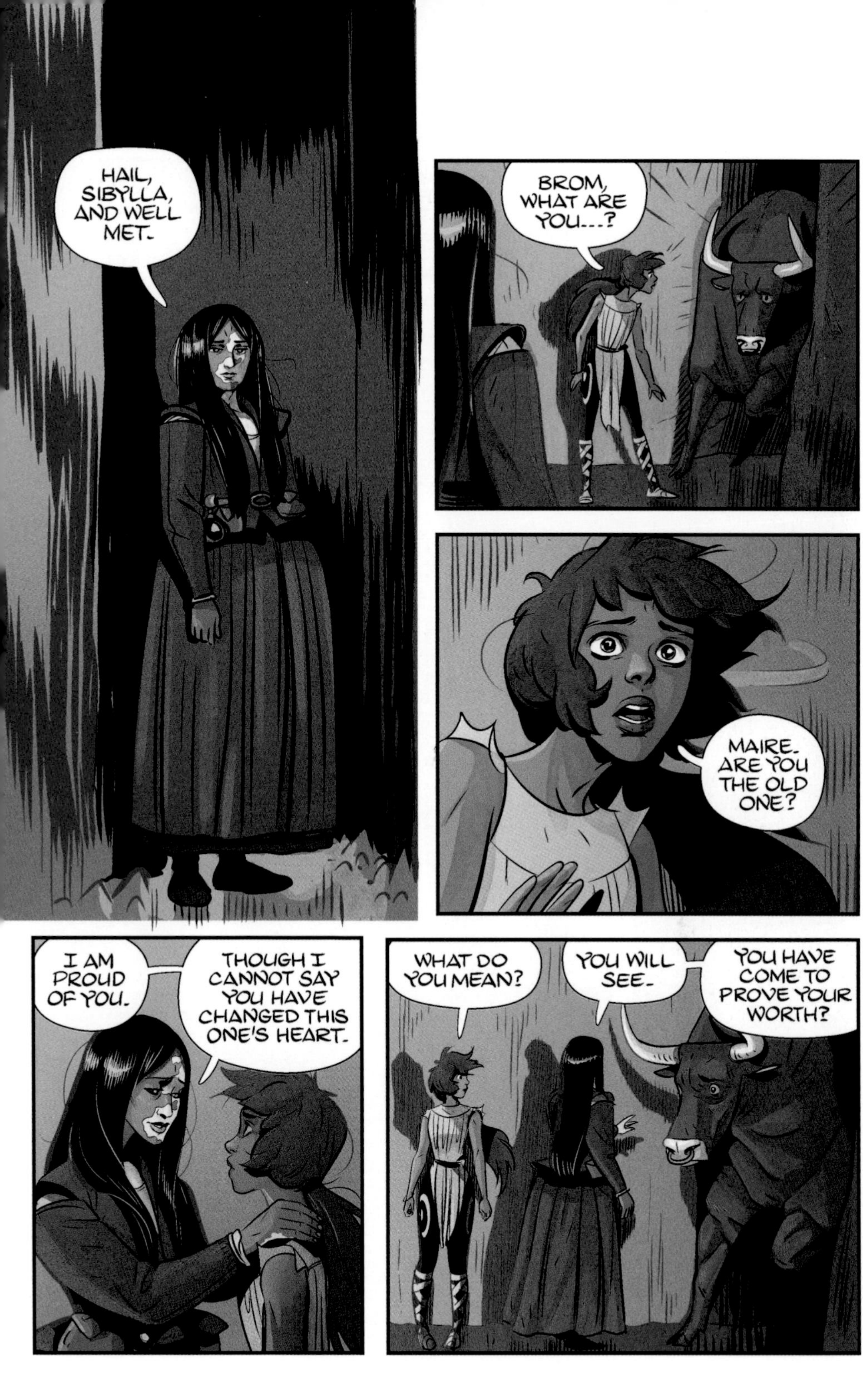
HAIL, SIBYLLA, AND WELL MET.
BROM, WHAT ARE YOU...?
MAIRE. ARE YOU THE OLD ONE?
I AM PROUD OF YOU.
THOUGH I CANNOT SAY YOU HAVE CHANGED THIS ONE'S HEART.
WHAT DO YOU MEAN?
YOU WILL SEE.
YOU HAVE COME TO PROVE YOUR WORTH?

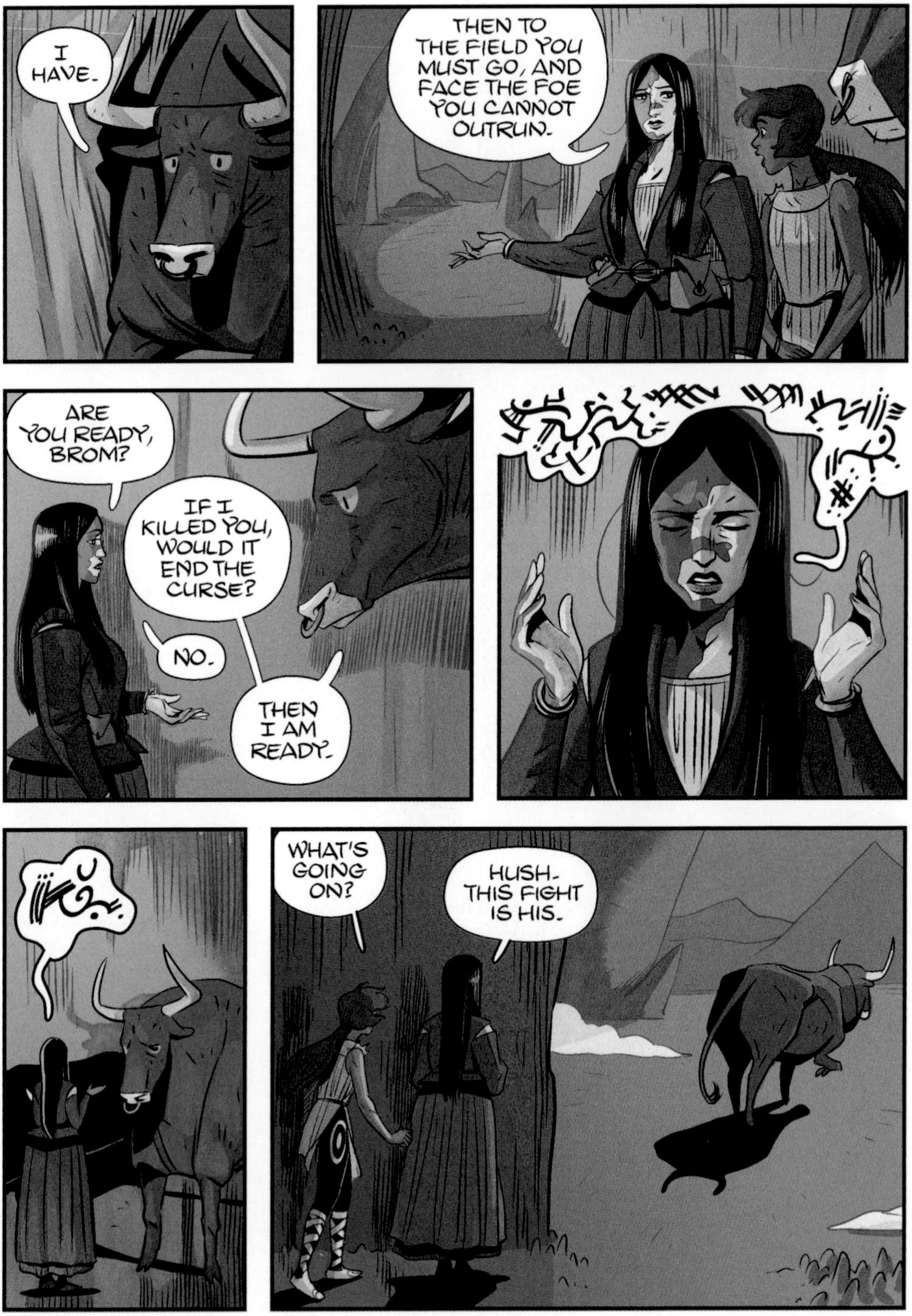
I HAVE.
THEN TO THE FIELD YOU MUST GO, AND FACE THE FOE YOU CANNOT OUTRUN.
ARE YOU READY, BROM?
IF I KILLED YOU, WOULD IT END THE CURSE?
NO.
THEN I AM READY.
WHAT'S GOING ON?
HUSH. THIS FIGHT IS HIS.

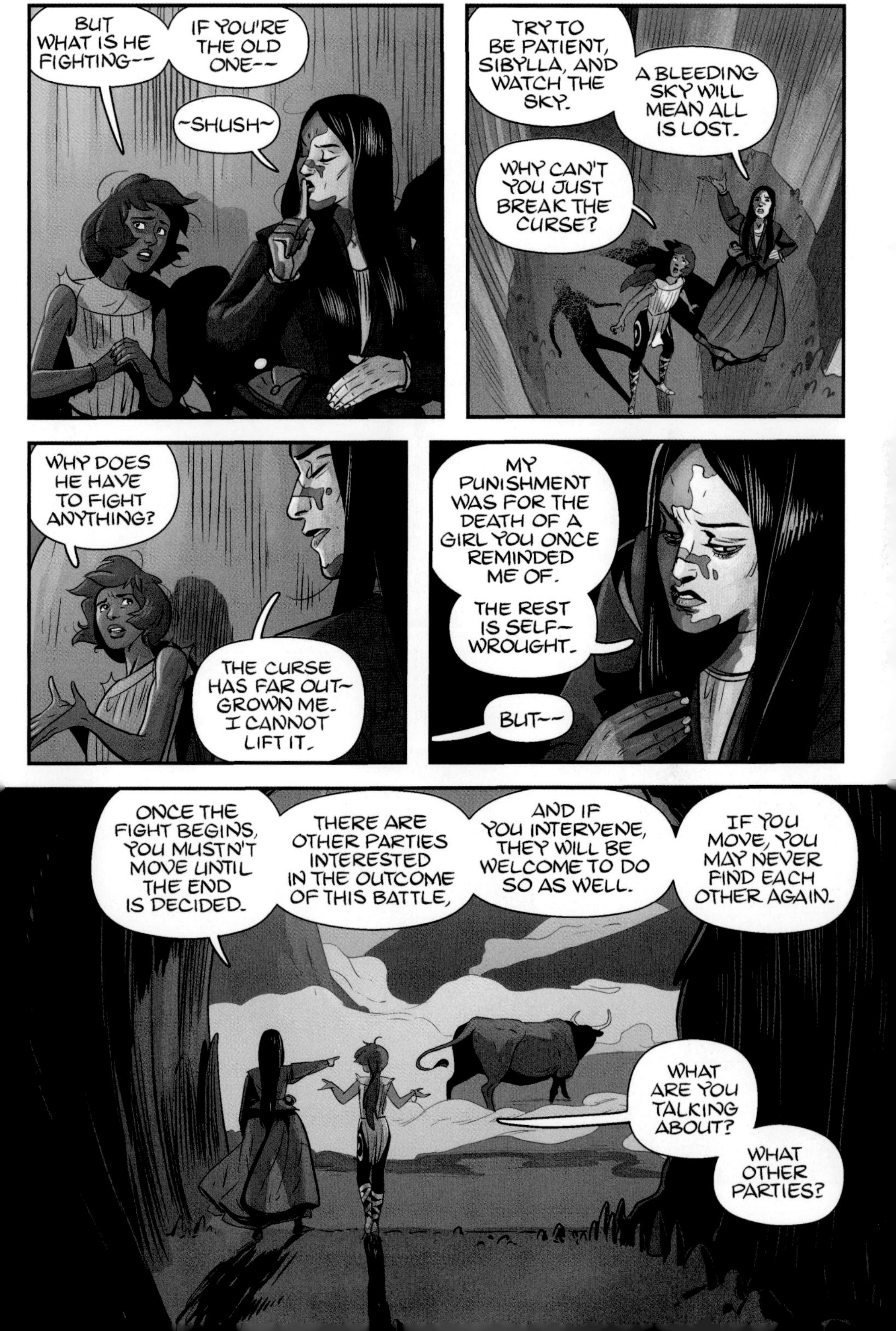
BUT WHAT IS HE FIGHTING--
IF YOU'RE THE OLD ONE--
~SHUSH~
TRY TO BE PATIENT, SIBYLLA, AND WATCH THE SKY.
A BLEEDING SKY WILL MEAN ALL IS LOST.
WHY CAN'T YOU JUST BREAK THE CURSE?
WHY DOES HE HAVE TO FIGHT ANYTHING?
THE CURSE HAS FAR OUT-GROWN ME. I CANNOT LIFT IT.
MY PUNISHMENT WAS FOR THE DEATH OF A GIRL YOU ONCE REMINDED ME OF.
THE REST IS SELF-WROUGHT.
BUT--
ONCE THE FIGHT BEGINS, YOU MUSTN'T MOVE UNTIL THE END IS DECIDED.
THERE ARE OTHER PARTIES INTERESTED IN THE OUTCOME OF THIS BATTLE,
AND IF YOU INTERVENE, THEY WILL BE WELCOME TO DO SO AS WELL.
IF YOU MOVE, YOU MAY NEVER FIND EACH OTHER AGAIN.
WHAT ARE YOU TALKING ABOUT?
WHAT OTHER PARTIES?

JUST STAY ON THIS SIDE OF THE BARRIER, SIBYLLA.

WAIT! WHAT GAVE YOU THE RIGHT?

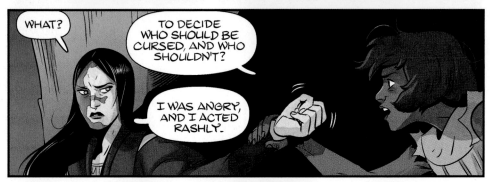

WHAT?

TO DECIDE WHO SHOULD BE CURSED, AND WHO SHOULDN'T?

I WAS ANGRY, AND I ACTED RASHLY.

HOW COME YOU DECIDED THEIR PUNISHMENT?

OR MADE THEM INTO MONSTERS?

OR MADE THEM FIGHT?

HOW COULD YOU?

MAIRE, YOU TAUGHT ME THE ONLY PERSON I SHOULD STRIVE TO CONTROL IS MYSELF.

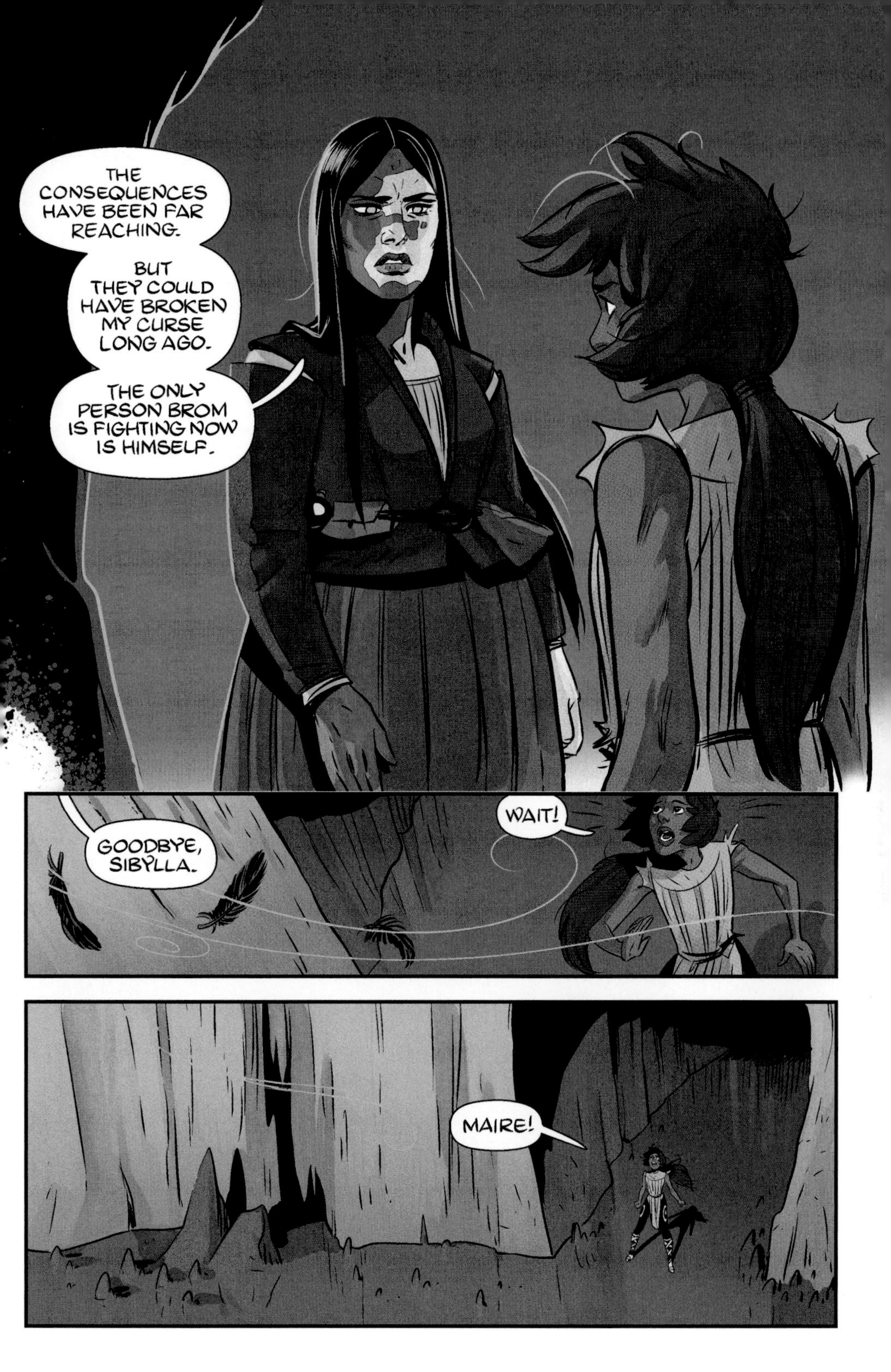
THE CONSEQUENCES HAVE BEEN FAR REACHING.
BUT THEY COULD HAVE BROKEN MY CURSE LONG AGO.
THE ONLY PERSON BROM IS FIGHTING NOW IS HIMSELF.
GOODBYE, SIBYLLA.
WAIT!
MAIRE!

WITCHES! NO STRAIGHT ANSWERS. SHE'S WORSE THAN~~

BROM!

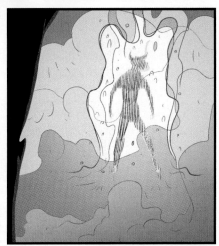

BROM, YOUR SWORD!

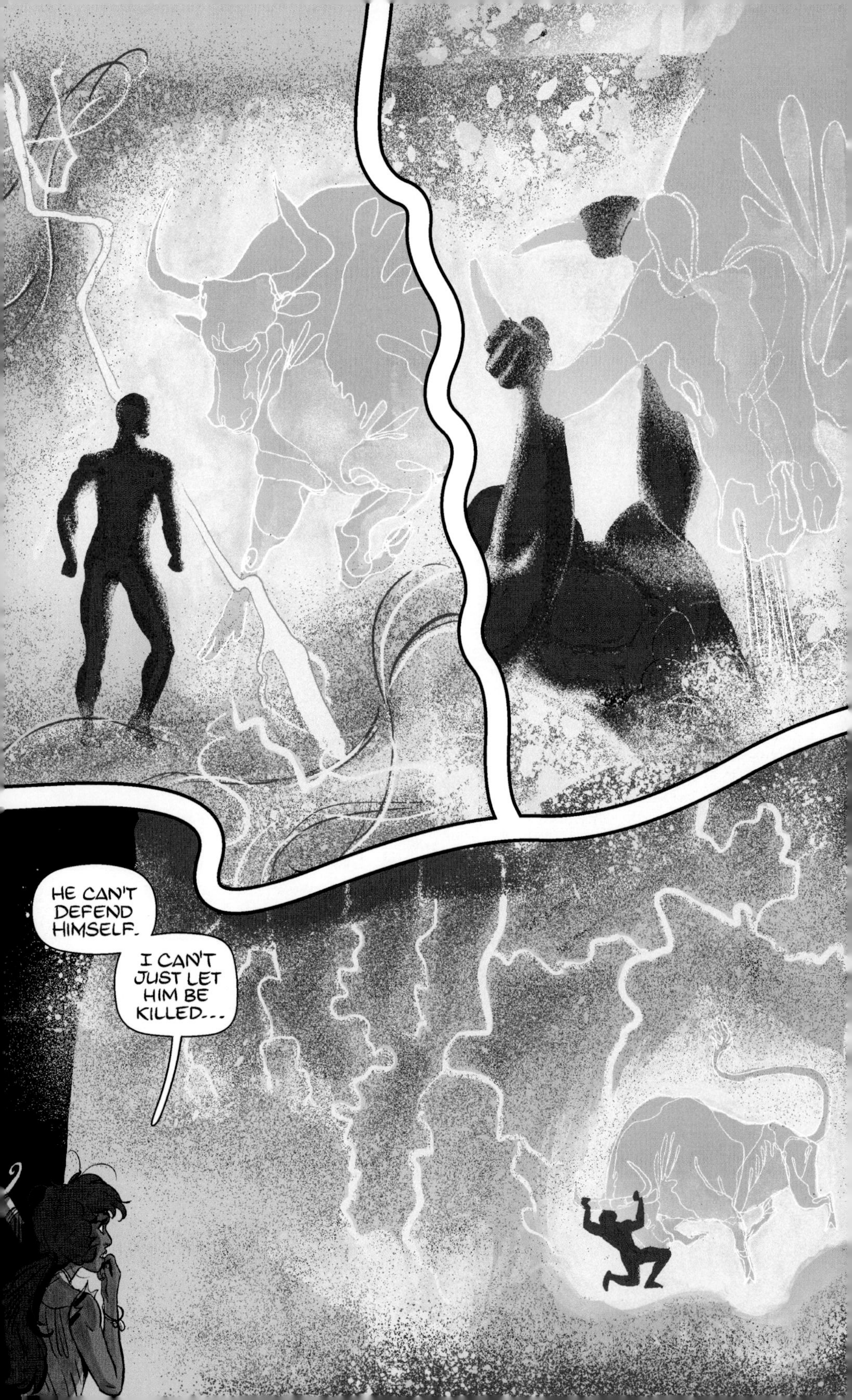
HE CAN'T DEFEND HIMSELF.
I CAN'T JUST LET HIM BE KILLED...

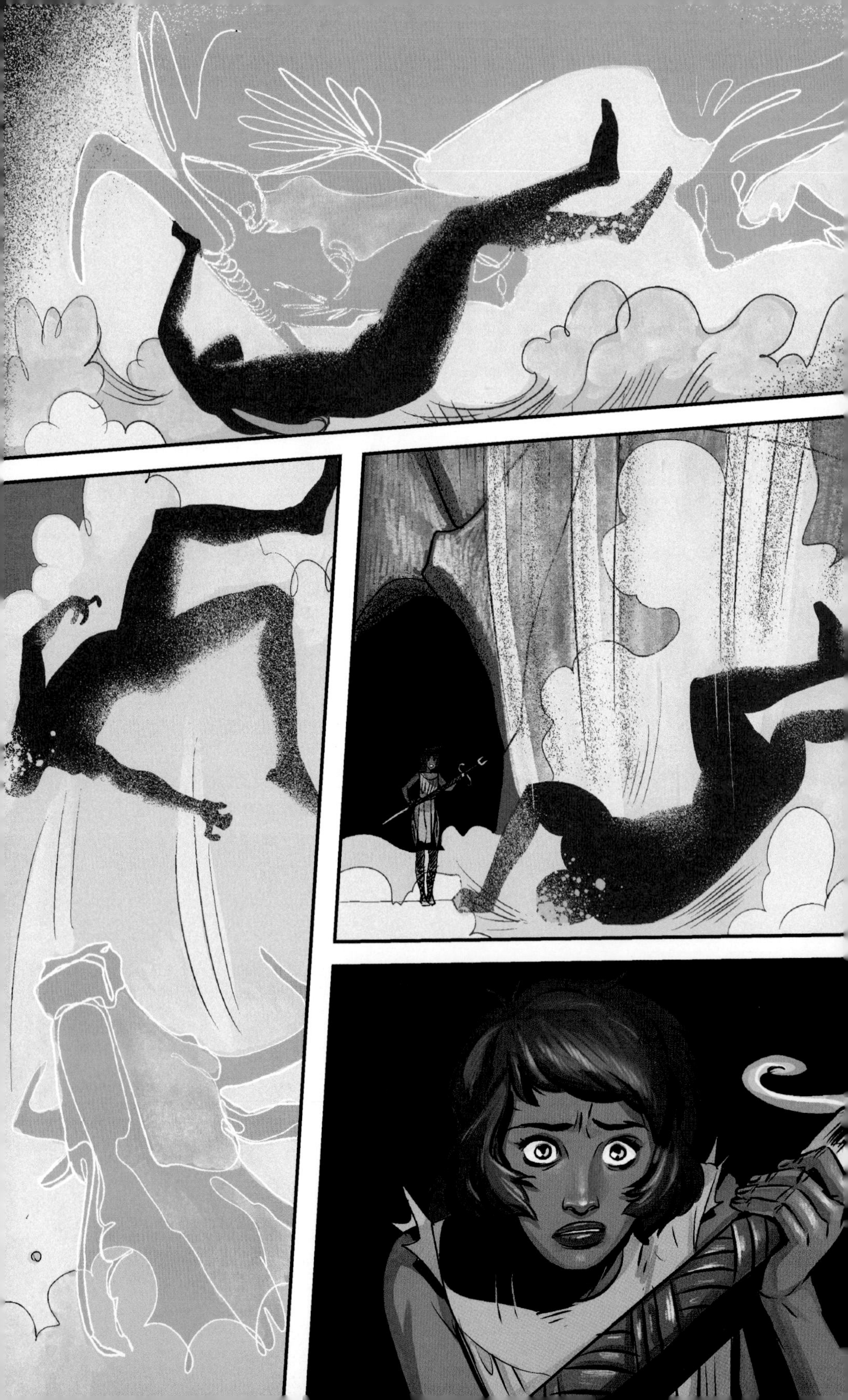

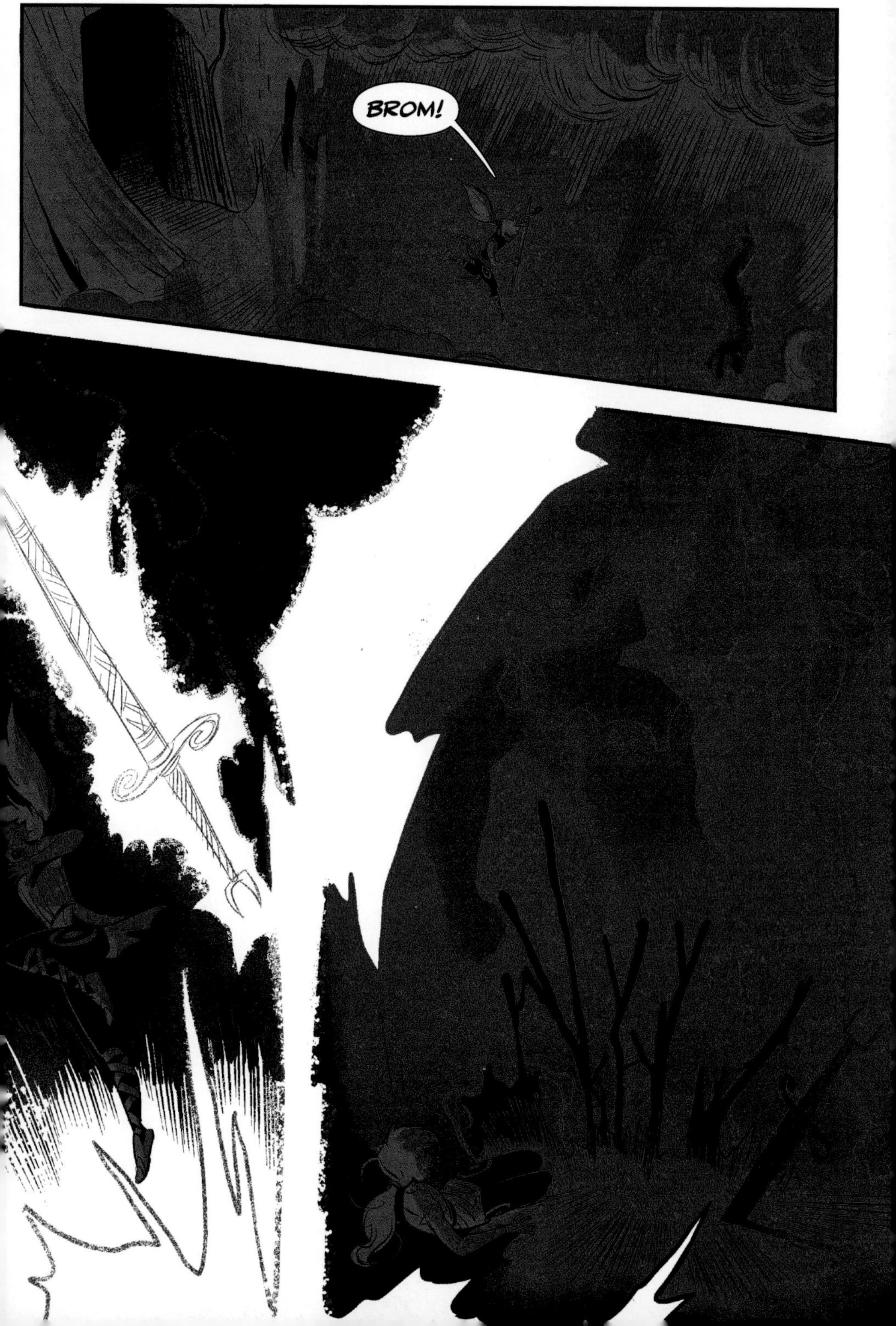
BROM!

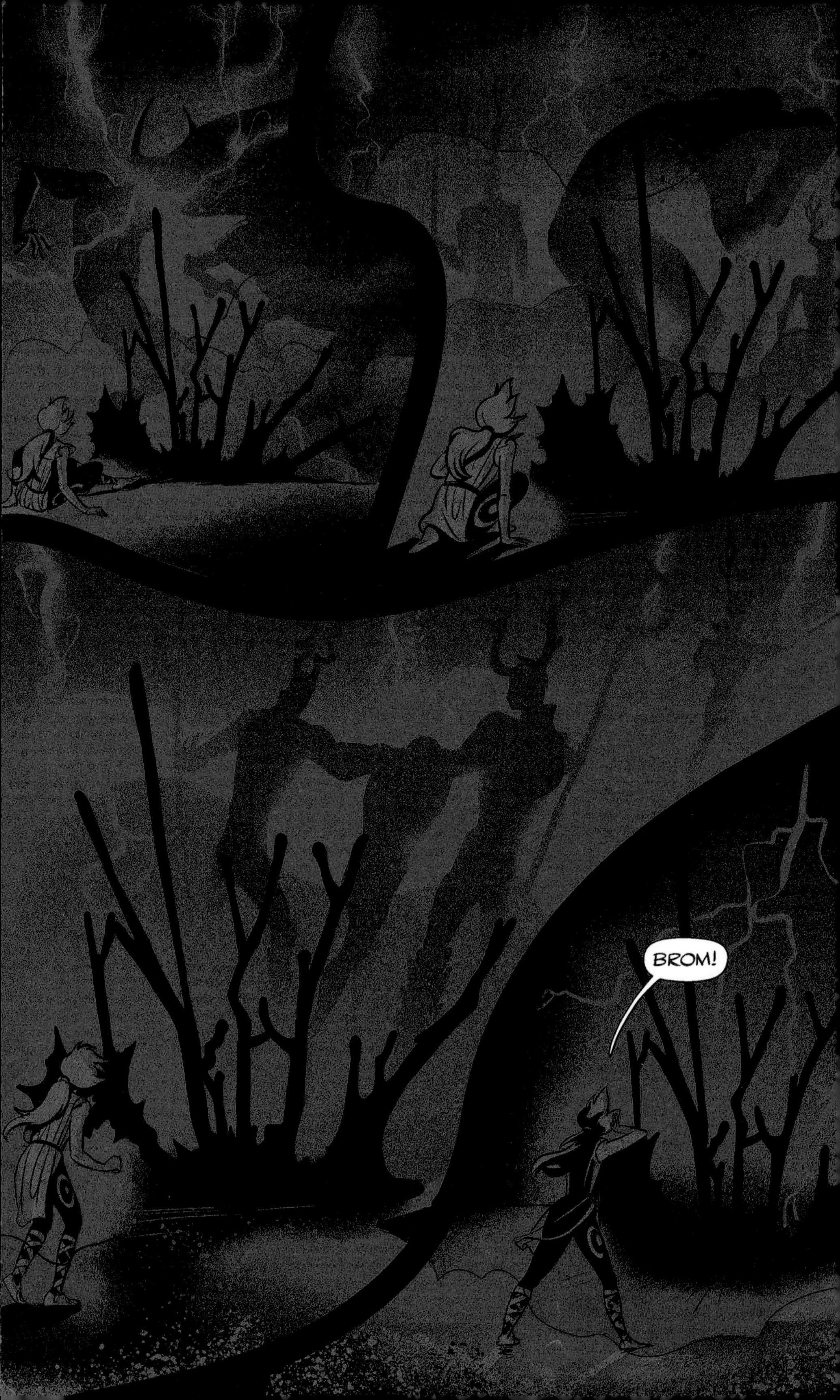
BROM!

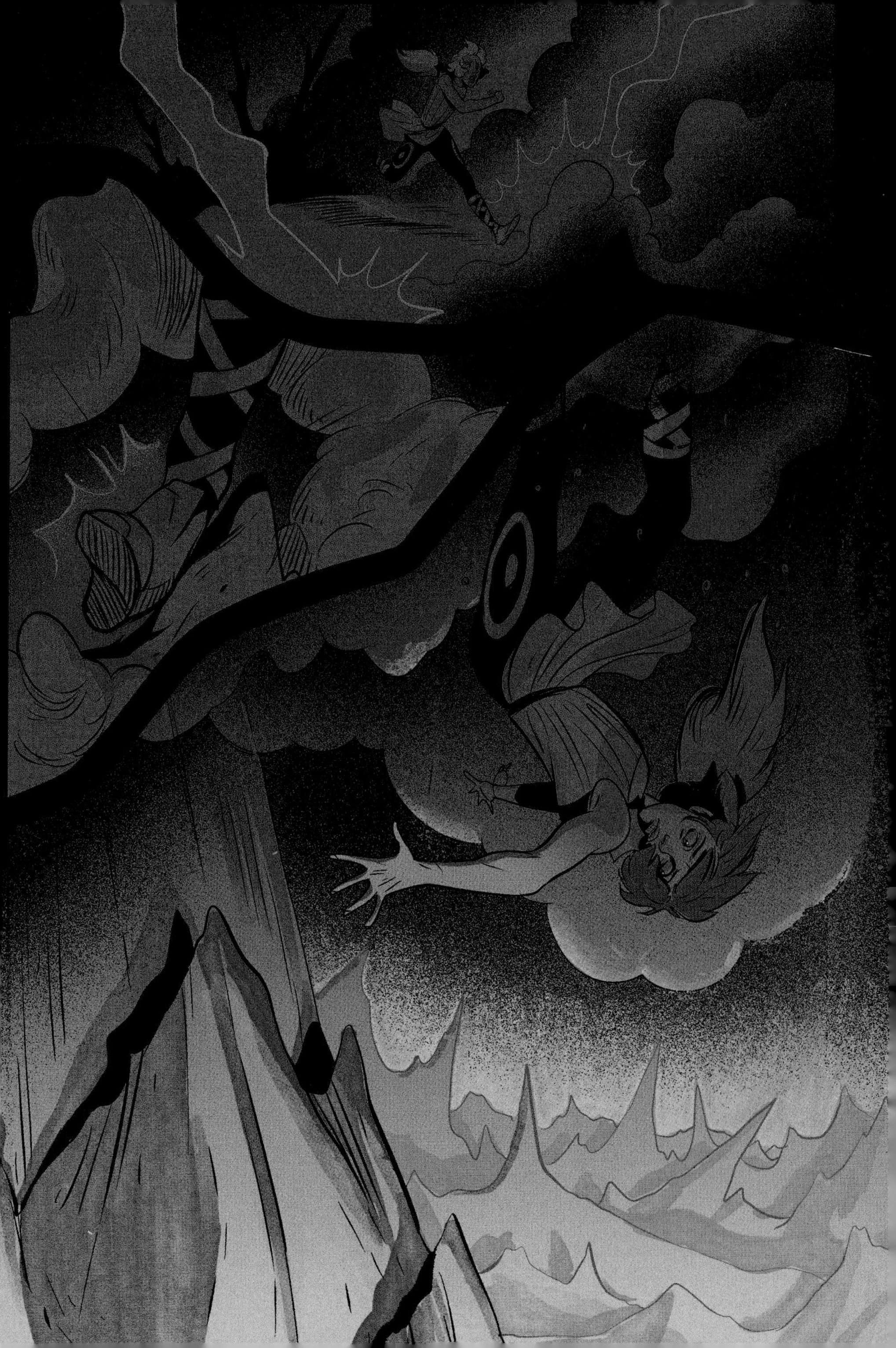

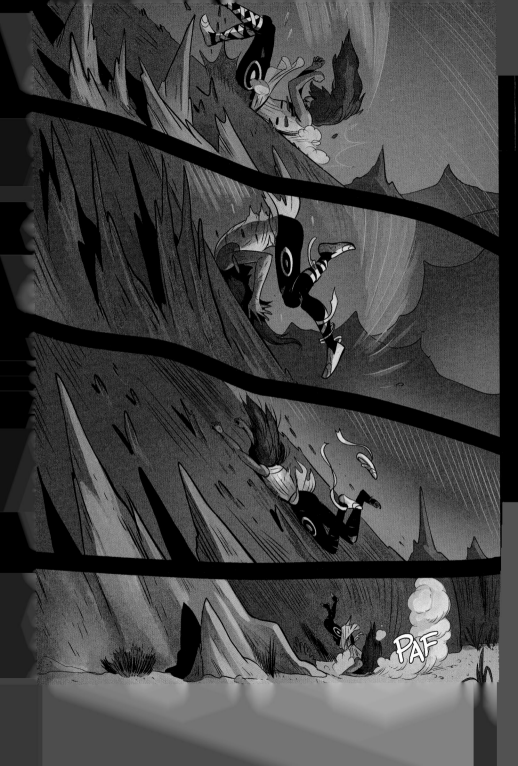

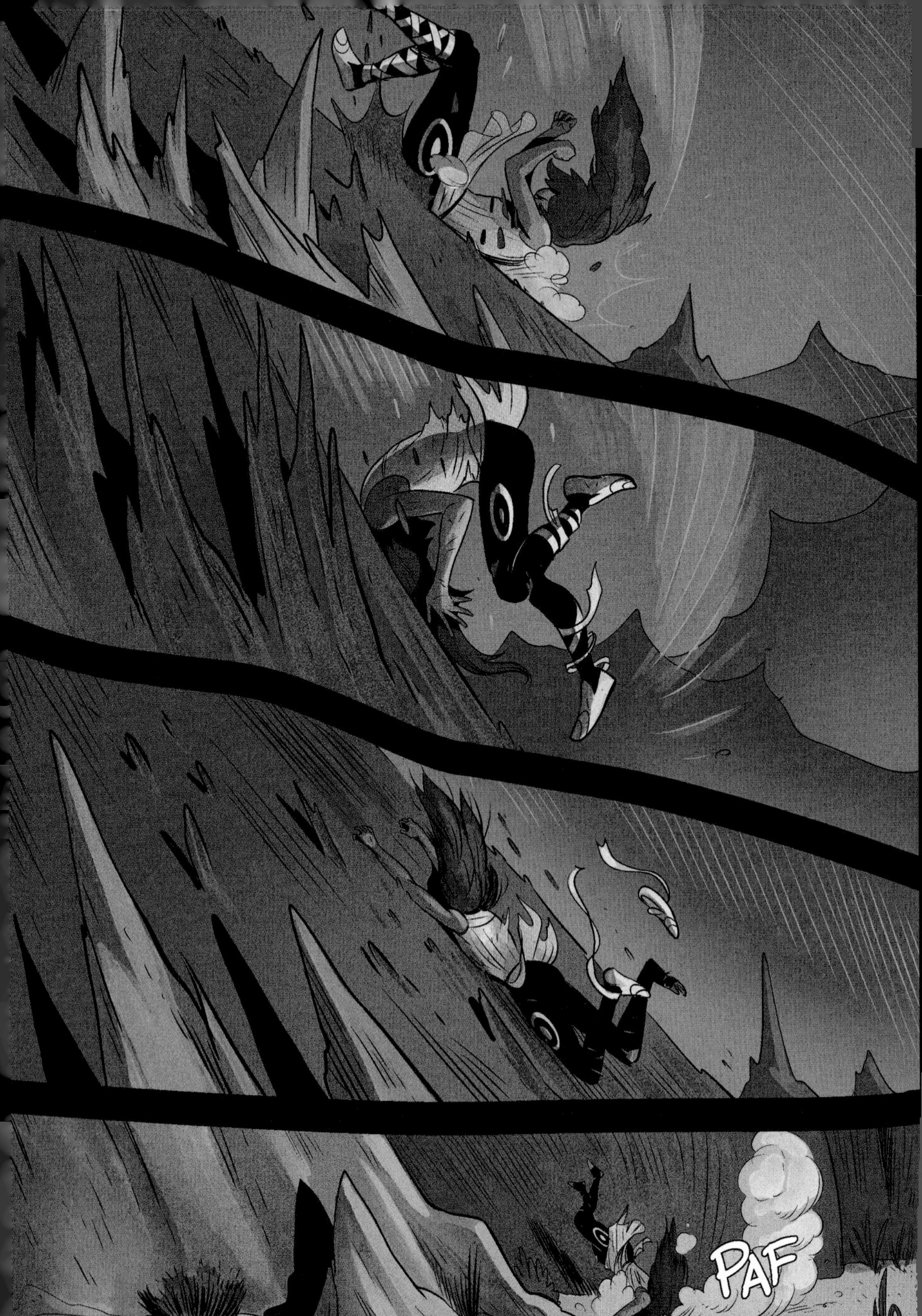
PAF

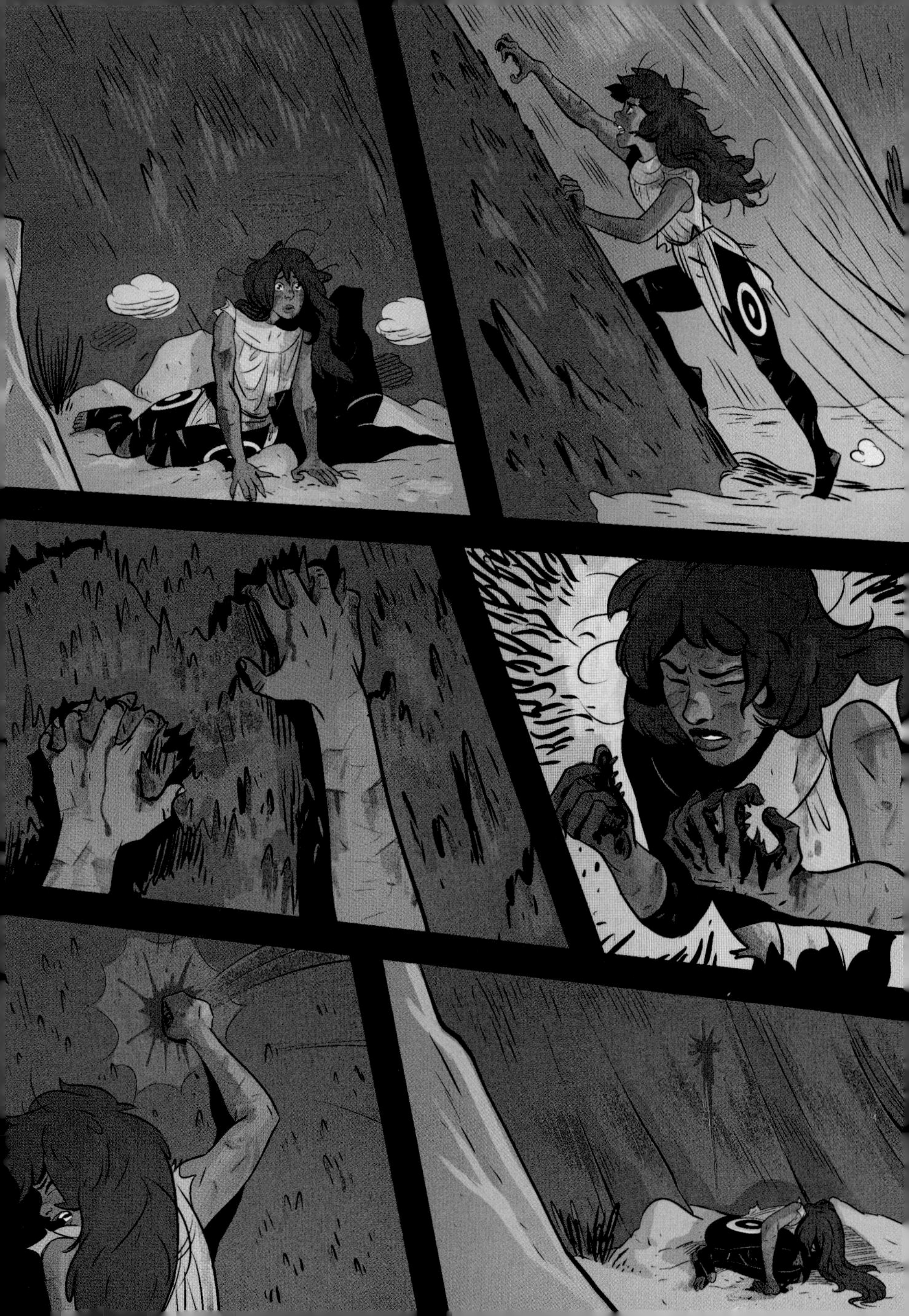

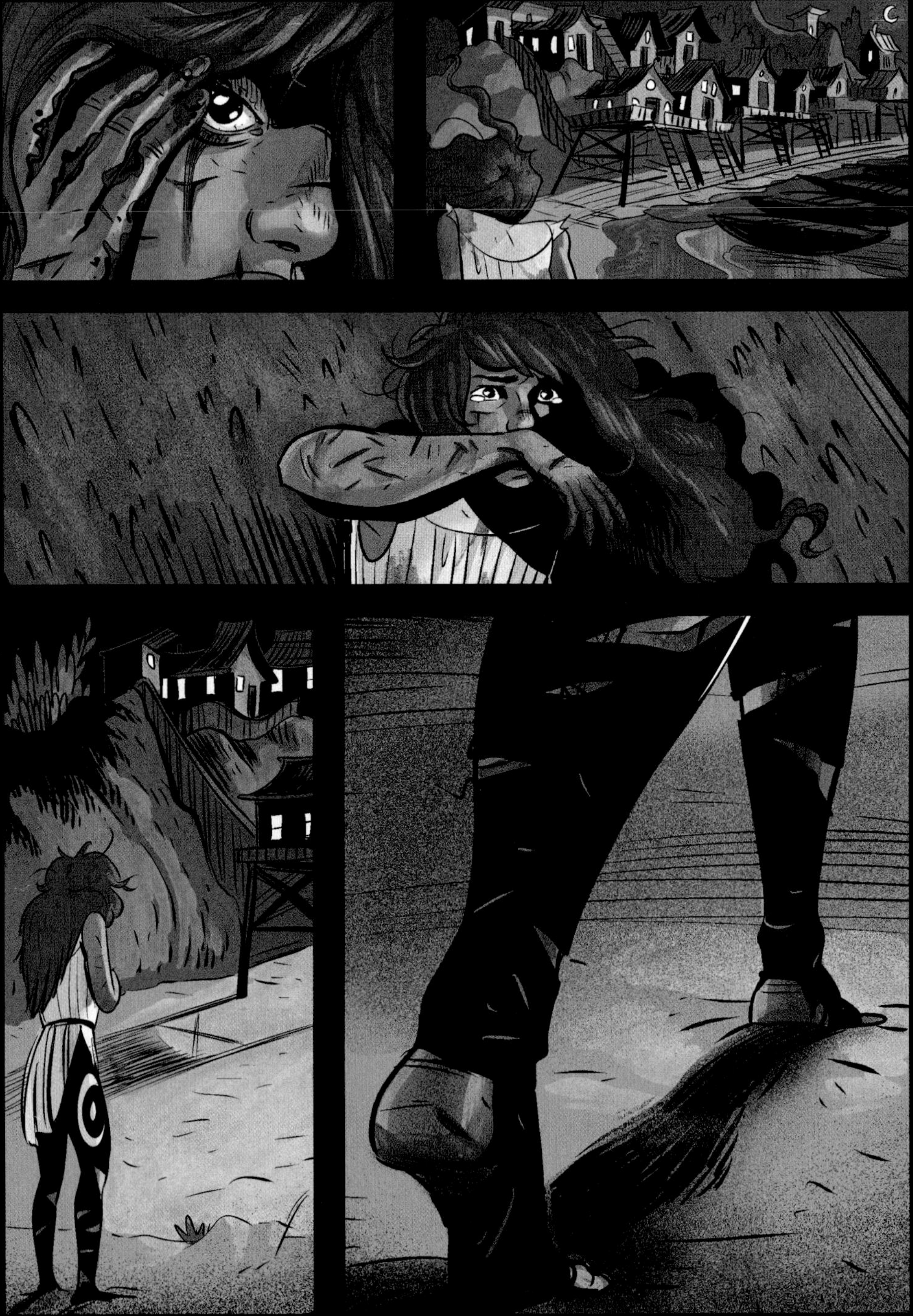

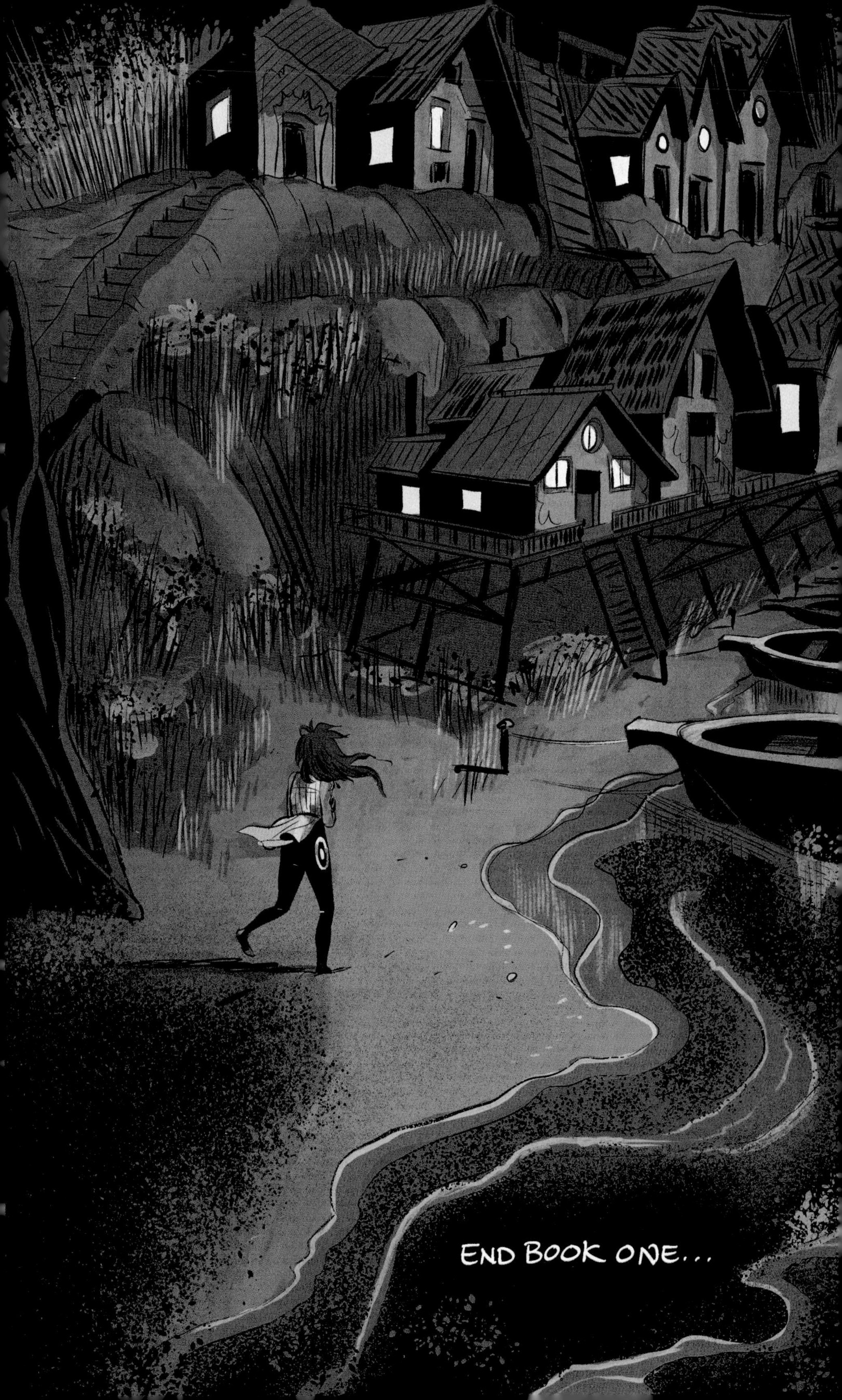
END BOOK ONE...

THE BLACK BULL OF NORROWAY IS THE MOST MONSTROUS CREATURE EVER TO WALK THE LAND...

They say he was once a man, a knight so merciless in battle that even his own king came to fear him. The king paid the Old One his very own daughter to transform the knight into a monster...

...AND SO THE OLD ONE DID.

Sibylla always knew she was fated for adventure—the forest witch told her when she was just a girl. But when destiny comes knocking, she'll learn that some curses are more literal than others.

From small-minded Goose Valley to the edge of the Glass Mountain itself, Sibylla's journey will force her to decide: will she play along in someone else's game, or are some curses better left unbroken?

BE BRAVE. YOU HAVE MANY TRIALS TO COME.

Based on the classic Scottish tale of the same name, THE BLACK BULL OF NORROWAY is the first in an ongoing series of graphic novels brought to you by creative sibling team, Kit & Cat Seaton. An epic adventure story, NORROWAY is an exploration of undesired destinies, failed expectations, and what it means to grow up in a world where the line between human and monster isn't as clear as the fairy tales promised us.

CAT SEATON grew up in the Inland Northwest where she never learned to swim. Born to a family of theatrical types, she's prone to errant whimsy and reckless symbolism. As a child, she was an avid devourer of fairy tales, poetry, and horror flicks. Now, she wants to create works that mix elements of all three. Her goal is to create stories that illuminate, challenge, and amuse. Her preferred habitats include coffee shops and unpopulated forest trails.

KIT SEATON is a comics artist, illustrator, and educator based in Southern California. She dabbled in theatrical costume design and a bit of directing, before deciding that she was more suited to drawing characters than cajoling actors, and that a blank page can pose as many interesting challenges as an empty stage. When not in the classroom, you can find Kit haunting local cafes, museums, and comic book shops like a fantod. She is also the artist and co-creator of the original graphic novel AFAR, also from Image Comics, with Leila del Duca.